# WHEN EVERYTHING WAS FRESH & GREEN

## THE HOUSE COVEN CHRONICLES

BOOK 1

BETHANY TAP

QUILLS & COSMOS PRESS

ISBN (paperback): 978-1-965790-07-6

ISBN (ebook): 978-1-965790-08-3

ISBN (hardback): 978-1-965790-09-0

Library of Congress Control Number: 2026931319

**Human Authored™, Reg #: 1942057,** https://authorsguild.org/human

"Such Silence" by Mary Oliver
Reprinted by the permission of The Charlotte Sheedy Literary Agency as agent for the author.
Copyright © 2014 by Mary Oliver with permission of Bill Reichblum

**CONTENT WARNINGS IN BACK.**

*For Clarissa, my favorite witch, and our brood,
Xander, Rory, Cole, and Liam*

# CONTENTS


| | |
|---|---|
| Chapter 1 | 1 |
| Chapter 2 | 15 |
| Chapter 3 | 33 |
| Chapter 4 | 45 |
| Chapter 5 | 57 |
| Chapter 6 | 71 |
| Chapter 7 | 79 |
| Chapter 8 | 87 |
| Chapter 9 | 93 |
| Chapter 10 | 105 |
| Chapter 11 | 113 |
| Chapter 12 | 121 |
| Chapter 13 | 137 |
| Chapter 14 | 147 |
| Chapter 15 | 159 |
| Chapter 16 | 171 |
| Chapter 17 | 185 |
| Chapter 18 | 201 |
| Chapter 19 | 213 |
| Chapter 20 | 223 |
| Chapter 21 | 237 |
| Chapter 22 | 245 |
| Chapter 23 | 257 |
| Chapter 24 | 265 |
| Chapter 25 | 273 |
| Chapter 26 | 281 |
| Chapter 27 | 295 |
| Chapter 28 | 307 |
| Chapter 29 | 319 |
| Chapter 30 | 329 |
| Chapter 31 | 337 |
| Chapter 32 | 347 |
| Epilogue | 359 |

Acknowledgments 367
About the Author 369
Content Warnings 371

*Sometimes there's only a hint, a possibility.*
*What's magical, sometimes, has deeper roots*
*than reason.*
*I hope everyone knows that.*

"Such Silence" by Mary Oliver

# CHAPTER
## ONE

All day, Tessa Andrews' chest felt heavy, like her childhood plague of asthma was back with the ferocity of a dog kept too long in a hot yard. That morning, her phone gave an air quality alert and when she opened the window, the air smelled of sulfur and felt coarse, like it was made of sand. She coughed. It hurt to breathe.

As she closed the window, her phone chimed. The text from her mom read: *The news says Grand Rapids has the worst air quality in the country. Those Canada fires. Stay inside! Stay safe.* Rather than reply, Tessa gave it an "emphasis" reaction. She knew she should be a better daughter, but she'd struggled to be good, let alone better, at much of anything for the last year.

All day, Tessa thought of Theo, wondered what they were doing, and if they were happy doing it. Had they made plans for their eleventh birthday yet? What were they reading? Had they finished the Percy Jackson series? Were they still obsessed with Greek mythology?

This was nothing special. She'd thought of Theo every day since they'd first entered her life as her foster kid more than three years earlier. She continued to think of them even after they'd left it again last summer, and still… still.

Did they still love indie rock? Could they still recite the names of the fifty state capitals, or had that knowledge been buried by time and neglect?

Were they happy? Did they think about Tessa? Did they miss her?

Were they angry? Did they resent her?

Would she ever see them again? Was there any way to get them back?

All day, Tessa tried to scratch an itch between her shoulder blades to no avail. She cringed at the irritation and tried to set her mind on other things: her work, the loom of climate change, Theo, what she should make for dinner, things she needed to do around the house, Theo, the texts and emails waiting for her reply, Theo. For hours and hours, the itch remained, a ghost haunting the corners of her mind, until, eventually, she forgot it and it, in turn, disappeared.

The day stretched on, as short and endless as every other day.

She ate lunch at her desk, which was also her dining room table. She worked late because what else was there to do?

Dinner was a frozen vegan pizza in front of a rerun of *Ghosts*, which she remembered first watching with Theo and if she closed her eyes, she could listen to the words and her own laughter and pretend they were there. Of course, it wasn't the same.

In bed, she picked up the book on her nightstand, *The Left Hand of Darkness*, and managed to read one sentence before sighing and closing the book. She picked up her phone to scroll through updates on the war in Ukraine, cat videos, Strange Planet memes, and plant-based recipes.

Finally, she opened up her old photos to find Theo, smiling at her. She smiled back.

She was on edge of sleep, phone still in hand, when Sanjay called.

"Got a placement for you, Tessa," he said, not even bothering with hello. "Astrid Laveau. She's fifteen. I just texted you a photo."

*The name "Astrid" did not fit the girl's picture*, Tessa thought. The girl had curly blonde hair, tawny-brown skin, a smattering of freckles, a deep frown, and green eyes. Tessa pushed up her glasses and squinted at her phone. Those eyes were eerily bright green; that had to be a filter. They gave Tessa an unsettled feeling, like they were watching her, Mona Lisa-esque.

"Can I drop her tonight?"

"Yeah, sure," Tessa immediately replied. She tried to keep her voice calm, but her heart was racing. It had been almost a year since her last placement. While she had kept up on her certifications and trainings and never explicitly told Sanjay not to place a child with her, it had been an unspoken acknowledgment that Tessa needed time and space after what had happened with Theo.

"Really?" Sanjay exclaimed, genuine surprise in his voice. "It's just —I don't have anyone else with the experience you have, or I wouldn't—"

Tessa cut him off. "It's fine, Sanjay."

"T…" She could hear the smile in his voice. "You are truly the best."

A thin smile flickered across Tessa's lips but she kept her voice steady and ignored the compliment. "What's the situation?"

He wouldn't give any information over the phone, other than the girl's name and age. "She's here with me," he said. "I just sent you an email with details. We're finishing up at the precinct. It'll probably be another hour."

Tessa glanced at her watch. It was already half past ten. "So midnight?"

"Ish," Sanjay replied. "Sorry."

"Don't be. I'll make her bed now. Has she eaten?"

"No, and she probably won't. I brought her some food, but she won't eat. Check your email. It's… a lot. I'll see you soon. And thank you, Tessa."

"Yeah, Sanjay. Of course. Bye."

Tessa got up and went to her computer. The email was just Sanjay's typed up case notes.

*Neighbors heard gunshots, called police. She was found alone in the home in her bedroom. Covered in blood, but unhurt. No parents, alive or dead. Just blood everywhere.*

*Talked to police; they can't find a weapon. All neighbors say she's a good kid. They were a quiet family. No issues at school. No close friends. No idea where the parents are, but they're presumed dead. Police believe the blood is theirs. She's not a suspect. For now. No bodies... No other family from what I can tell.*

*She's not talking to me.*

Tessa sighed deeply and pulled off her glasses, massaging her temples. This was going to be rough. Nothing she couldn't handle, of course. Or at least, nothing she couldn't have handled before...

*Theo. Theo. Theo.* The name pulsed through her brain.

She stood up from her computer desk. It was now after eleven.

*You can do this, Tessa,* she told herself, as she walked around the house, straightening up. *You're Tessa Andrews, foster mama-bear extraordinaire. You made a mistake, getting too close to Theo like that.* She was using her mother's verbiage, her mother's scolding tone of voice in her own head as she pulled fresh linens out of the closet and set about making the bed in the kids' room. Theo's old bed. She forced her thoughts to be "less Kathy, more Tessa," as her adolescent-era therapist would have said. *You broke Rule #1. Instead of putting the kid's needs first, you prioritized yourself over what was best for them. But everything worked out in the end, right? Theo's with their bio mom, so that's that. Your job, right now, is to love this kid, Astrid, and to help her. For now. Temporarily.*

This was only ever meant to be temporary.

She vacuumed the bedroom and then moved on to the bathroom, wiping down the toilet and sink and putting out fresh towels. Despite their sometimes contentious relationship, Tessa's mother was reason she'd become a foster parent. Kathy, who had adopted Tessa, always talked about the importance of time and love over blood and DNA and Tessa grew up understanding that the only family worth having was one built on love.

Placing the hand towel on the hook, she caught a glimpse of herself in the mirror and sighed. Sometimes she forgot how old she had started to look. When did she get all these gray hairs? Her hair was thinner now, too, than it had been in her twenties. At least her glasses covered the bags under her eyes. If she held her face perfectly serene, there were only a couple wrinkles still visible on her forehead.

She even dressed in what she was sure would be considered a "frumpy" way to teens these days. Before Theo, her last long-term placement had been a fifteen-year-old queer boy named Jacob who would do her hair and makeup while giggling and calling her style "fun?" with a drawn-out question mark. But that was over six years ago, she realized. She was mostly dressed in baggy sweatshirts and leggings these days, now that she worked from home. And on the days when she had a video conference call, she usually put on a scarf over her sweatshirt and a pair of earrings and called it good.

She splashed some water on her face and put on lip balm glancing down at her checkered pajama pants and hoodie and decided that this was good enough for a midnight greeting. *Rule #3: Never set an expectation that you can't meet.*

While she was washing the last of the dishes, the doorbell rang. *Perfect timing,* she thought, going to the door. She counted to three in her head before opening it wide to the torrid night air. It was hotter and drier than most June nights were in Michigan; the air had the acrid stench of burning from those Canada fires. The light across the street buzzed and went out, then blinked on again and again. The street wavered in and out of hazy darkness. Despite the heat and humidity, Sanjay wore a fully buttoned collared shirt, his black hair slicked back, a glimmer of sweat along the hairline and his upper lip. Tucked slightly behind him, Astrid studied her feet.

"Hi Tess," Sanjay said, stepping to the side so that Astrid was fully visible. "This is Astrid. Astrid, meet Tessa. She's going to take care of you."

Astrid looked up and Tessa nearly gasped. It wasn't a filter. Her eyes were unnaturally green.

*Those have got to be contacts,* Tessa decided, composing herself and reaching out a hand to Astrid, who did not take it. "Hi there, Astrid. I'm so sorry about your parents."

Astrid's eyes narrowed. Hostility was normal, Tessa knew, as was misplaced anger. Trust is something you earn and it can take a long time. *Rule #4: Trust the kid.* They'll never trust you if you don't trust them. But something about Astrid reminded Tessa less of a scared kitten with its hackles raised and more of a tiger, ready to attack.

"What do you know about it?" Her voice was even, low, and venomous.

Now it was Sanjay's turn to look surprised. He glanced between Astrid and Tessa. "I told her—"

Astrid cut him off with a flap of her hand. "No. She knows something. Do you know where they are?"

"What?" Sanjay started, but Tessa shook her head.

"Do you, Astrid?" She took a step toward the girl, her hand still outstretched.

"If I did, do you think I'd be here?" She stepped up to Tessa, bumping a flowerpot with her toe. It shifted precariously close to the edge of the porch.

"No, I don't," Tessa answered. "And I don't know where they are, either. What I said upset you."

"They *aren't* dead. You're acting like they are dead, but they're not." Astrid's breath was coming in fast and heavy. Panic radiated off her.

Tessa took her hand, which was warm—hot, even—to the touch, but Tessa was determined not to flinch. *Rule #2: Keep your cool.* She held Astrid's weird green gaze and breathed in deeply, willing the girl to be calm, to absorb Tessa's projected serenity.

She thought of Theo, then. How their shoulders would tense up, their little body shaking until—

"They're not dead," Astrid cried, but the frenetic edge was gone. "I know they aren't. I can still *feel* them."

Tessa's head snapped up. Her eyes met Sanjay's gaze. He shrugged slightly and Tessa took this as an acknowledgment, on his part, for what this was, why he had reached out to her—Tessa—specifically with this child: this was Theo all over again.

But what could she say, with the kid right here in front of her? She couldn't say *no*. All she could do was glare at Sanjay.

"I believe you," she told Astrid. "I really, truly do. Let's go inside now, ok? Get some rest. We'll talk about it in the morning, figure out what to do."

"How do you know there's time?" Astrid asked, even as she let Tessa lead her into the house.

Sanjay moved to follow, but Tessa blocked the door and took the bag from his hand. She shut the door on him without a look or a word. She'd give him an earful in the morning.

"I don't," Tessa answered. "But I do know that nothing good ever comes of sleep deprivation. We'll both be better in the morning. Come on, your bedroom is upstairs."

Glancing behind her, she could see Sanjay's shadow through curtains.

* * *

When she came back downstairs after helping Astrid to bed, he was still there.

She sighed and opened the door.

"Tess," he started.

"That was shitty, Sanjay Veda Lahiri."

"Don't full-name me!"

"Sanju!"

"You sound like my moth—"

"Get inside," Tessa interrupted. "The air quality's god-awful."

"I know. I *know*," he said, stepping just inside the door and shutting it behind him. "But it's not the same. We *know* her parents are dead."

Tessa folded her arms across her chest. "We 'knew' Theo's were dead, too. Until *she* wasn't."

Sanjay sighed, rubbing his hand over his face. "You still don't have AC?" He was sweating through his shirt.

He unbuttoned his top button and Tessa caught a glimpse of why he was covering up. It looked like he had a bite or possibly a rash, some kind of mark right where his neck and shoulder joined. It made Tessa itchy just to look at it, so she averted her eyes.

"I have window units in the bedrooms for emergencies," Tessa replied. "And fans," she added, gesturing to three different fans within range of the front door.

"It's like ninety degrees, Tessa."

"Yeah, climate change sucks. Unbridled usage of fossil fuels won't fix it."

Sanjay rolled his eyes. "You and your idealism."

Now, Tessa rolled her eyes. She and Sanjay had played through variations on this argument many times. Once, Tessa had even attempted to explain to Sanjay why she couldn't rightly be called an "activist" because nothing she did felt inconvenient or like any kind of hardship, really. Air conditioning made her itch; eating animal products hurt her stomach. Driving anywhere when she could walk or bike made her chest hurt. Car fumes made her hack and sometimes break out in hives. She'd been an early EV user; her 2013 Nissan Leaf was still alive and kicking.

Sanjay would say, "It's all in your head." Maybe it was.

"I turned the window unit on for Astrid." Tessa sighed, absently scratching her neck. "Anyway, you can't pretend the similarities between her and Theo aren't glaring," she went on. "Presumed-to-be orphans who are convinced their parents aren't dead, just missing? That they can *feel* them alive somewhere." Tessa kept the other similarities to herself: the heat of Astrid's hand and her weird green eyes reminded Tessa of Theo, too, somehow. She couldn't quite figure out why. It was like her memories of early childhood, all sensory details and feelings, but nothing concrete that she could hold, let alone describe. In her head, Theo and Astrid were the same kind of kid, not just because of their shared circumstances but because they shared something ineffable. *Something like the scent of yarrow, sage, and cinnamon*, Tessa thought, *or that feeling like a storm is coming, a sudden change in air pressure, the scent and color of the world shifting.* "They are both different—extraordinarily so. You see that, right?"

"I barely know Astrid," Sanjay started, but a quick glance into

Tessa's eyes caused him to pause. "But Theo was. They were extraordinary, Tessa. I'm sorry things didn't work out the way we had hoped."

It was a little word—*we*—but it was enough to dull Tessa's anger. She shook her head. "This will have the same ending," she said.

"Then this time, let's hope for that ending."

Tessa nodded.

"I should go," Sanjay said. "Joss and Billie were asking about you, by the way. Dinner next week like old times?"

"Old times" being the time before Theo. Tessa hadn't hung out with their old crew much since Theo left. All of her friends except for Sanjay were coupled with children. Permanent children. And they just didn't get it.

"Save me from seventh wheeling every single social event, please?" Sanjay asked, pressing his hands together in front of him and continuing to walk backward toward the car.

Tessa sighed, then nodded.

Sanjay fist bumped the air as Tessa waved. She moved to shut the door, but a thought occurred to her and she paused. "Were they good people, Sanjay? Astrid's parents?"

"As far as I can tell, yes," he replied.

"So that's a big difference then," Tessa said, "between them."

Sanjay winced, then nodded. "The biggest difference you could imagine. Night, T."

* * *

**NOV 1966**   The smog that morning was like a glaze over New York City, thick and cloying. Val could feel it, could roll it between her fingers like a cigarette, breathe it in, and then choke on it. She stayed inside, staring out the condensation-covered window of her apartment. She drew a picture on the windowpane as she waited for Tish. It was rudimentary, the stick figures of childhood, her and Tish, her coven-sister, holding hands. She drew Tish's long white-blonde hair and included the constellation of freckles just below her left eye. Val drew herself as she wanted to be, her olive wings fully unfurled, wrapping around her and Tish, closing them into a secure cocoon.

"Safe," Val whispered. "No monsters."

Below their feet, she sketched the salt marshes, the sea couch grass lilting on a breeze. As she drew, Val closed her eyes and remembered the coastal coven of her youth: that little, unnamed, largely unknown island among the Outer Banks. She could feel the breeze kiss her cheeks and tousle her hair. She could smell the air, the sting of salt that tasted like days spent with the sun on her skin. She felt the call of the Carolina wren overhead, the notes etching a wavelike pattern across her vision.

Tish's voice was a warm caress: *I love you, Val. I hope we stay like this forever.* Her hand in Val's as they lay on their backs, the tall grass hiding them from the world, hiding the world from them, so that all they could see was the wide blue sky.

Then the air around Val began to tighten. The sky began to yellow, like the drying pages of a wet book. She tasted sulfur. Her lungs clenched. She felt her throat begin to swell up. The air, that clean, salty air, was now thick and black. The island was gone. Taken from them. *By the sea*, the coven leaders had said, contempt and blame and even hatred in their voices. As if the sea had a choice in the matter. As if it could do anything more than just be.

Val's finger continued to move frantically against the windowpane, turning and turning into a terrible cyclone. She pulled her finger away, opening her eyes. She'd smudged out the picture of her and Tish.

Val shook her head and drew a third figure above the tumult: a man with fangs and an aquiline nose.

It was Andor Chernoff. Or rather, it was a grotesque caricature of the man who was, that very day, going to marry her best friend, the love of her life. An easier enemy than the chaos, this flesh and bone man. Val tried to inhale a deep breath, but even inside, she struggled to breathe.

Still, the smog over New York City wasn't nearly as thick as the smog clogging Val's lungs and heart. This city… God, the air was putrid. How could she ever have thought she could survive in a place like this?

*Come on, Val!* Tish had a voice like the wind chimes on Val's mawmaw's porch. *It'll be fun. A big city! There's nothing left for us here anyway. Think of it! We'll have so much fun together.*

*Together.*

*Together.*

What a lie that had been.

There was a knock on Val's apartment door and then a voice. "Valerie! You in there?"

*Of course I am,* Val thought. *Where else would I be? Where else could I even go?* She couldn't go out with the air like this; she'd suffocate.

"It's not as bad out as it looks," the peppy voice continued. "I promise! Come out, please? We'll have so much fun together!"

*Together? Hmph.*

"Yes, together! Open the door, you doof."

Val went to the door and stood with her palm against it. She could feel the heat radiating off Tish on the other side, could feel the light and warmth of her. She was so bright. A force to be reckoned with. A person with a planetary presence. She pulled you to her. The strongest person Val had ever known.

"Valerieeee!"

Val opened the door and gasped.

"Oh, Morticia," she breathed. "You look like something out of a fairy tale."

"You like it!" Tish giggled, twirling so that her white gown spun out around her and sparkled in the fluorescents of the hall, catching and refracting so that the light seemed to radiate from the dress itself.

"I love it," Val murmured. She meant, of course, I love *you.*

Tish reached for Val then, taking both her hands into her own.

"It will all be fine," she said. "Nothing's going to change with *us,* got it? It'll always be us, me and you. Andor is… a stepping stone. A convenience. See?"

"He's a monster," Val said.

Tish rolled her eyes and her face shifted into Andor's. "Don't be prejudiced!" she chided in his booming voice. "Just because you grew up among Southern, Sea-Magix, doesn't mean our Northern kind are bad."

"I'm not talking about vampires in general," Val hissed. "Just. Him."

Tish changed back, pressing a cold finger against Val's lips. She held it there for several seconds as they looked into one another's eyes. Tish's eyes were the steel blue-gray of skyscrapers and fog. Val's eyes were the deep brown of the marsh waters, magnified by her round, emerald-rimmed glasses.

"You and I," Tish said. "We are destined for greatness. Andor… he's our ticket."

"Ticket to what? To money?"

Tish shrugged. "Of course. And so much more! To change! To freedom! We're going to save the world, you and I."

Val snorted. "From what?"

Tish took her hand and pulled her to the window. "From this!" she exclaimed, gesturing past Val's drawing to the gray world beyond.

"The city?"

"Have you ever seen smog like this? We've lived here for more than two years now and each year, it gets a little worse."

Val harrumphed.

"You know it does."

Val glared at Tish. Of course she knew. She could hardly breathe with all the knowing.

"There's a name for it," Tish continued. She pointed at the sky. "This. And what happened back home. The sea level rise, the hotter air, the storms, the smog, all of it. It's called the Greenhouse Effect."

Val narrowed her eyes, but the fight was leaving her. She could visualize the truth of this phrase, could look up at the sky and feel the particulates in the air churning, closer and thicker, like a ceiling. Like a mirror, reflecting the sun back down again, the heat rising and sinking and growing and growing and growing.

"The Greenhouse Effect," she repeated. "I've heard of it."

"They say," Tish continued. "Scientists say, that is."

"Scientists?" Val repeated skeptically.

"Of *every* background," Tish added. "Magix, too. They say that if we don't do something to stop it, the planet will warm, the polar ice caps will melt, and we could… the whole of humanity, life itself, could become…" She snapped her fingers. "Extinct."

Val wanted to roll her eyes at Tish, at her dramatic tendencies and her air of gravitas. But all she could do was wince. Because hadn't she known this—this "Greenhouse Effect" was happening all along? As an air fairy hadn't she felt it in the sticking of her lungs, in the cramping of her heart? The air itself was changing. She knew this. Her kind had evolved to know these things as intimately as they understood their own bodies. Her people had an old saying, "As the air, so the body." She could hear her mother's voice whispering it, over and over, like an incantation, gripping Val's shoulder as they stood on the mainland shore, in the shallows, looking out at the waves and what had once been their home, what the sea had taken back, only rooftops and tree-tops. Her father waded back to them with her baby sister's body in his arms. *As the air, so the body.* Tish, on the shore, soaked head to toe, crying. The only time Val had ever seen her weep. But they'd all been weeping, hadn't they?

*As the air, so the body.*

"A stepping stone, you said?"

Tish grinned, hugging Val and kissing her cheek. "I *knew* you'd understand. Hurry and get dressed now! Andor's waiting with his coven leader in their meeting house."

Val rolled her eyes and dragged her feet as Tish tugged her toward the bedroom. She flopped onto the bed while Tish pulled out dress after dress and flung them away with a "No no no!" or a "Hmph" or an "Honestly, Val!"

"I *hate* the Odessa Coven's meeting house, you know?"

Tish pulled out a drab mustard yellow dress and held it out in front of her, head cocked to one side. She swirled it around in her hand and the dress began to glow, turning golden and shimmering in the gray filtered light. She held it in front of Val and nodded. "That'll do."

"I hate Brighton Beach," Val said. "I hate Brooklyn."

"Oh hush," Tish chided. "You hate New York City."

"I hate New York City."

"But you love our world."

"I love our world." And when she said it, she was thinking only of Tish.

Tish pressed the dress into Val's hands and stood back. "Oh, I love way the glitter and gold looks against your skin, your hair."

She curled a finger through a lock of Val's umber hair. Drawing back, her fingertips brushed the edge of Val's mossy green wings. Val held her breath.

"Perfect," Tish declared, stepping back. "Oh, Val. We're going to save the world, you and I!"

# CHAPTER
## TWO

Too exhausted to go upstairs, Tessa lay down on the couch. Sleep reached out like a claw, dragging her down into a heavy dream in which someone was knocking at the door. A small knock, like a thin branch tapping against a window, but it was too steady, too persistent to be a trick of wind and trees. Tessa found herself standing at the front door, listening to the knocking and watching the spectral outline of a human through the curtains for several seconds before she opened the door a crack.

It was *her*, standing there with her long white-blonde hair, toothy grin, silver-blue beady eyes, and that gaudy silver cross necklace. Tessa wasn't surprised. She'd known it would be her. She always came to her like this, in dreams.

"Morana," Tessa said. "Where's Theo?"

"At home," Morana replied, turning her smile up a saccharine notch.

"Are they ok?"

Morana shrugged, eyes rolling up, still smiling. Her skin was almost as white as her hair, blueish in the LED light. "I'm not here about Theo," she said, licking her lips. "May I come in?" She stepped closer, her toes at the edge of the threshold, her face less than a foot from Tessa's. Her breath smelled metallic and woody, like an old piano after days of sitting out in the rain. Or an old, unearthed and emptied coffin.

Tessa stepped back. She remembered the last time they'd stood here like this, toe-to-toe, with Theo cowering behind Tessa and Sanjay in front of her, shoulder to shoulder with this woman: the enemy. "No, you may not."

A momentary rage filled Morana's eyes and wiped away her smile, but she composed herself quickly, rearranging her face with a deep sigh and wide grin. It was mechanical, a learned—or remembered—response rather than a natural one.

"May I come in, *please*?" she repeated, her lips curling around the minor civility as it left her mouth like she was chewing on a clove of garlic.

"No," Tessa repeated. "You may not."

This time, the anger did not dissipate. Her eyes narrowed and blackened and she seemed to grow, standing there on the porch, her legs, arms, and torso lengthening until she towered over Tessa, monstrous and pale. She bared her sharp, bloody teeth in a sardonic grin.

"You think you're so powerful? That you can keep me out forever."

"I'm not powerful," Tessa replied. "It's just that you—all this?—it's a dream."

Morana scowled. "I'll break you. Someday. This isn't over." Her voice was the low groan of settling houses, echoing and empty.

Tessa shivered and opened her eyes. She lay on the couch, covered in a thin blanket. She shook her head to dispel the dream. Her hands were shaking.

Outside, the wind was blowing a twig against the front window. Tap. Tap. Tap

"It's ok," she told herself. "You're safe. She can't get in and she can't hurt you."

By default, she pulled out her phone to search for Morana Aronov, remembering how she used to type in this same name, every night after

Theo was in bed, to see if there was any news of their vanished mother. Always, the same handful of articles would pop up:

*Abandoned Child Found in Apartment on Fourth*

*Police Search Continues for Morana Aronov*

*Vanished Mom Presumed Dead*

And then later:

*Like Magic: Mother and Son Aronov Reunited*

Memorized headlines, burned onto her retina.

Now, her finger hovered over enter. She wondered if there would be updates, if she'd see Theo's sweet face again, their off-kilter smile and too-big glasses over wise brown eyes. She wondered what color Theo had dyed their hair now. It was purple last year when they left. She wondered if they'd hit puberty yet; they'd be ten, almost eleven now. Would Morana have helped them get on hormone blockers, like they'd wanted? Would she let Theo wear those ridiculous, power-clashing outfits that they wore with such fierce pride?

Tessa grimaced and deleted the search entry. She'd promised Sanjay and herself that she wasn't going to keep going down this rabbit hole that inevitably led to long sob sessions while she blasted every album by Florence and the Machine on repeat because Theo had been obsessed with the band (well, mostly Florence Welch—"Gawd, she's *fabulous*," Theo would whisper) right before Morana came back into their lives.

"Don't let her take me, Mom," Theo had begged.

What was she supposed to say? Should she have reminded Theo that she, Tessa, wasn't their mom, and Morana was? Or should she have fought for parental rights, sued for custody? Should she have run away with Theo?

"Theo, I love you," she said. "But my hands are tied."

Their face had contorted and become a thing unreadable, just like the day she'd first met them. Theo was a changeling, no longer her soft, sweet kiddo, but hard and unfeeling as the garden gnomes peppering the yard across the street.

"If you loved me, you'd fight for me." Their voice was flat.

Then they'd walked out the door, head down. They never looked back and she never saw them again, although Morana still visited her dreams regularly.

Tessa went upstairs to check on Astrid. She was asleep in the bed, on top of the comforter with a flimsy throw over her torso and legs, her coat and shoes still on. *Ready to run,* Tessa thought. Or perhaps—*very likely*—she was just *that* exhausted.

On Theo's first night, they'd burrowed under the blankets, tucked into a ball like an armadillo. That'd been Tessa's nickname for them: Theo the Armadillo. Theo had been so terrified when she first met them, Tessa recalled. She could still see their unblinking brown eyes staring at her through fogged up glasses and a too-big medical grade mask. It was easy to forget all the fear, both Theo's and the terror of those early pandemic days. Those months of isolation, of dance parties and no-contact food delivery and board games, had been the petri dish in which Theo and Tessa's relationship had grown and thrived. Theo had quickly opened up, unfurling into a magnificent and astonishingly well-adjusted kid.

"How'd you get so amazing?" Tessa would ask.

"Magic!" They'd grin.

Her chest hurt from thinking about them.

*Were they good people, Astrid's parents?*

*As far as I can tell, yes.*

There was nothing good about Morana. She was neglectful and abusive, and Theo was terrified of her. But when she mysteriously came back after more than two years away, after being presumed murdered by Theo's still-unaccounted-for father, the courts handed Theo back to her without batting an eye.

"She's bewitched them," Sanjay had shrugged. He'd squeezed Tessa's hand. "Our hands are tied."

That same stupid platitude that she'd repeated back to Theo.

*This will be different,* Tessa thought. It had to be.

* * *

The next morning, Astrid didn't wake until nearly noon. More than halfway through her workday, Tessa hopped off the computer to fix them both some lunch.

"So like, what do you do?" Astrid asked, after a few bites of her PB&J.

"I'm a contractor. I do payroll administration for a handful of small firms."

"Sounds boring."

"Absolutely. It's dull as shit."

Astrid lips curled upward, and Tessa had to work hard to keep her own glee at this development to herself.

They ate in silence for a couple more minutes. Tessa wanted to let Astrid guide the conversation, hoping she would voluntarily turn it inward and open up. She knew this usually took time. Sanjay had sent her more information on Astrid, including her school, hobbies, and general academic performance information. She was a bright kid at the best public school in the area, who liked to swim and sing. She'd also just lost her parents. While she'd been vocal about it last night, that could have been adrenaline. Every person handles trauma differently, Tessa reminded herself. She might not talk about it again for days, weeks, even months.

"You wanna know what happened?" Astrid asked, not looking up from her empty plate.

Tessa stopped chewing, her mouth slightly ajar. She swallowed her partially chewed bite so it stuck in her throat and she coughed twice before taking a large gulp of water. "Y-yeah," she finally answered, her voice a croak.

Astrid smirked. "You're a weird lady," she said.

"Ok," Tessa shrugged. "You don't have to tell me anything you don't want to," she added.

"I know. If I did, I wouldn't tell you shit. Like that dude last night."

"Sanjay?"

"Him, and the cops." She was tracing the granite lines in the countertop with her fingernail. They were long and painted the same bright green as her eyes.

The color reminded Tessa of her summer trips up north. There were places where Lake Michigan's waters were that same stunning mélange of seafoam, shifting to emerald or kelly green in the sunlight. Though a staunch atheist to her mother's chagrin, Tessa had always felt there was something holy and otherworldly about the lakeshore in these kaleidoscopic moments.

"I like your nails," she commented.

Astrid smiled. "Thanks. Green is my color, my mom always said."

"Because of your eyes?"

Astrid gave a half shrug, half nod, a wincing movement. "They're not dead," she said. "My mom and dad. They're hiding; I know it. I was supposed to be with them, but something went wrong. There were…" She trailed off, looking out the kitchen window into the backyard.

Tessa turned her head to follow her gaze. There was a deer standing in the backyard, not an impossible thing in the small city. The deer approached the house, and Tessa's breath caught in her throat as it came within feet of the window. Its face was ghostly white and it had a pattern on its neck, almost like a cross. It stood there, watching them. Tessa took a step toward the window. The deer didn't move.

Astrid murmured, "They've found me."

Tessa turned to see the color drained from Astrid's face, her hands clenching the edge of the counter, knuckles white with force of her grip. Her lower lip trembled in what appeared to be abject terror.

"It's just a deer," Tessa murmured, reaching for Astrid, who pulled back her hand, jumping up from the counter and scuttling backward, nearly tripping over her stool.

"It's not," Astrid whimpered, tears forming in her eyes. She'd backed up against the kitchen wall, curling in on herself. "It's never *just* anything. You're not like us; you're just… just a *common*."

She spat it like a curse word and Tessa, confused, instinctively smiled, the way she would at a four-year-old calling her *silly* as an insult.

Astrid sneered. "So common, you don't even realize."

"No, I realize you're *trying* to insult me," Tessa replied. Instead of stepping toward Astrid, she moved toward the window and opened it. Behind her, Astrid whimpered.

"Shoo," Tessa said to the deer.

In response, the deer bowed its head, abruptly turning, and running off, leaping over the fence in a graceful bound.

Tessa turned back to Astrid, who sat open-mouthed on the ground. "See, just a deer?"

Astrid shook her head. "It wasn't. It really wasn't. But you—*you* sent it away. That was… amazing."

Tessa smiled. "Call me the deer whisperer."

And to her delight, Astrid smiled back.

* * *

The next day passed without event. They ate lunch together in the kitchen and after work, Tessa found Astrid curled up with a copy of *Howl's Moving Castle*.

"My mom read me the whole series," she said.

"Mine, too," Tessa told her and they exchanged stories of their favorite parts and memories.

After dinner, they streamed the movie. Astrid fell asleep on the couch and Tessa tucked a blanket over her. Then, still haunted by the dream from two nights before, by the fear that Morana would come and take away another child, Tessa made a pile of blankets and slept on the floor.

The next day was Friday, a light workday for Tessa, and she decided to stop at noon.

The air was slightly better and Tessa suggested they walk for ice cream.

"Thought you were a vegan?"

"This place has oat-based ice cream. It's delicious."

Astrid wrinkled her nose, then shrugged. Later, she would acknowledge the fact that the dairy-free ice cream was *almost* as good as the real thing.

"So why are you a vegan?" Astrid asked as they walked back. "Animal rights?"

Tessa shook her head. "I just don't like animal products. They make me sick."

"Like an allergy?"

"More like a sensitivity."

Astrid turned her face to stare hard at Tessa. There was something almost robotic about her green eyes, not inhuman, but beyond human. After staring at her for a while, Astrid asked, "So what's for dinner tonight?"

On their fourth day together, they drove out to the Lake and Astrid whooped and squealed at how cold the water was, even on the first of July.

On Sunday, the fifth day, the deer came back.

Tessa came downstairs to find it staring in through the dining window, Astrid hiding in the kitchen under the island.

Like before, Tessa shooed it and the deer acquiesced, although this time it did stomp its foot twice before retreating.

"I might need to call animal control," Tessa said, offering Astrid a hand. When she didn't take it, Tessa sighed and sat down beside her.

"My parents are hiding," Astrid whispered. Her hands shook. "There are people, *dangerous* people, after them." She folded her arms, tucking her hands inside her elbows to hold them still, but the shaking moved up to her trembling jaw. "After me."

Tessa wanted to ask what this had to do with the deer, but instead she kept it simple: "Why?" She wanted to grab a blanket for the girl, as she shivered there, hugging her knees to her chest. "Why would someone want to hurt you or your parents?"

"We're different," Astrid said.

"Oh shit. Is it like a white supremacist cult?"

"No, not that. I mean, they're probably all tied up in *common* hate groups, too." That word again and strange venom that went with it. "But we are more different than that. Different like…" Her eyes roamed around the room and landed on the refrigerator, which was still papered with pictures of Theo. Astrid's eyes narrowed and she stood up. "Different like him."

"Them," Tessa automatically corrected, but Astrid had walked over to the fridge and pulled down a picture of Theo.

"He's—*they* are like me," she said, holding out the picture.

Tessa frowned. "Like you… how?"

Astrid stared at her, wide-eyed. "This was one of your other fosters, right? How long were they with you?"

"Two years, three months," Tessa replied, not liking the incredulity in Astrid's question.

As if Astrid through Tessa didn't really know Theo at all, when Tessa knew everything about Theo: their favorite color (purple or rainbow), their favorite food (vegan chicken nuggets), which board games they liked (Monopoly, Life) and which were "boring" (chess), who they got along with at school (Avery, Kim, mostly the other queer kids), what they liked to read (fantasy and anything about dinosaurs), what music they liked (Florence and the Machine, duh), how they liked to be tucked in at night (no socks, blankets to the chin). For more than two years, Theo had been Tessa's everything. *Still is,* Tessa thought and then tried to push the notion away, tried to be present. With Astrid.

"And they never told you what they really were?"

Tessa blinked. "What?"

Astrid said something else, but there was a sudden throbbing in Tessa's head and a ringing in her ears. She closed her eyes against the pain, pressing her fingers to her temples.

"Are you ok?" Astrid asked.

Tessa nodded, now hearing Astrid just fine. "Sorry, headache." Already, the pain was fading. When Tessa managed to open her eyes, Astrid was watching with worry. "I'm ok," Tessa assured her.

Astrid glanced nervously over at the fridge and the picture of Theo, opened her mouth and then closed it.

That evening, after Tessa hollered up twice for Astrid to come to dinner, she went looking for her and found her glued to the old laptop Tessa had let her borrow.

"What are you doing?" Tessa asked.

Astrid looked up, green eyes sparkling. Already, Tessa was used to them and she smiled at Astrid, at the look of fervor on her face.

"What rabbit hole did you go down?"

Astrid tilted her head to one side and spoke a phrase in Latin.

Tessa blinked. "Excuse me?"

Astrid said something else and again, there was a ringing in Tessa's ears and she missed it. This time, no headache accompanied the ringing, but still Tessa screwed up her face in discomfort.

"What did you say?"

"I said, Theo is a—"

Tessa gasped as the ringing roared back.

Astrid frowned and tapped her chin, before closing the computer and roping her arm through Tessa's. "You said dinner's ready?"

Tessa shook her head to clear it. "Yeah. Yes, um, pesto spaghetti with leeks, sundried tomatoes, and cashew cream."

"Yum!"

At the dining room table, Tessa tried to press Astrid for more information about her parents. "You said you think they're hiding?"

"I don't *think* they're hiding."

"Sorry. You said your parents are hiding."

Astrid nodded.

"Because they are different? Like… Theo?"

Astrid's lips curled into a half smile. "This must be very odd for you."

Tessa shrugged, not quite sure what Astrid meant. "I'm enjoying having you with me."

Astrid smiled, a wide open expression that Tessa hadn't yet seen. "You're not so bad yourself."

Later, as they were clearing the dishes, Tessa asked, "Where do you think they're hiding?"

Astrid stiffened, nearly dropping the plate she was loading into the dishwasher. "If I knew, I wouldn't be here. I'd be looking for them."

Tessa winced. "Fair enough." She handed Astrid another rinsed plate. "I could help you. Find them. If you… I don't know… have an epiphany or something."

Keeping her eyes locked on Tessa's, Astrid lowered the plate into the dishwasher, bending slightly at the waist. Tessa held her breath. Had she gone too far? She should've left it alone. She was dangerously close to breaking Rule #3 and setting an impossible expectation for herself. But as Astrid raised up, she cocked her head to one side and smirked.

"Mom would like you," she said. "Dad, too. You're good people."

* * *

**JULY 2023** The next morning, Tessa woke and got to work long before Astrid got up. Breaking for lunch, Tessa found the girl in the kitchen, staring at the picture of Theo.

"Morning," Tessa said and Astrid jumped.

"Shit! You scared me."

Tessa walked over to the fridge, too, smiling back at Theo's sweet face.

"You really loved them, huh?"

"*Love* them. The love doesn't go away, no matter where they are."

Astrid was watching her carefully. "How's your head?"

Tessa shrugged. "Oh fine. It's been coming and going."

Astrid nodded sagely. "Yeah. I think I figured it out though. Look. You're not gonna like this. But I have to do it, ok? It's gonna hurt, but you have to try and hear me."

Tessa frowned, but nodded. "O-ok."

"I'm a w—," Astrid said.

Tessa's head exploded in pain.

"Fight it!" Astrid said. "It'll get easier. I'm a witch!"

Tessa gasped as the pain surged around the word, but she'd heard it. "A-a what?"

"A witch, the green eyes, you know?"

Tessa shook her head. The pain was sharp, the ringing insistent, but it seemed to be fading. Slowly.

"They're a shapeshifter." Astrid pointed to Theo's school picture, taken days before Morana had reclaimed them. "See, they've got the marking?" Astrid took it off the fridge, moving her finger over the cluster of freckles on their cheek.

Tessa moaned.

"Breathe," Astrid instructed. "I know this is hard to hear. It must be hard for Nons to process."

"N-nons?"

"Non-magical people. Listen, stay with me. Every shifter has a distinctive birthmark, so you can recognize them, right? This kid though… their teeth are sharp, not quite like a vampires but almost. Maybe one of their parents is a vampire? I don't think the sharp teeth are typical for shifters."

The pain was definitely fading. Tessa sucked in a deep breath, felt her stomach unclench, felt her cognition start to come back. What was happening here? Clearly, this was a child's delusion. A trauma-induced psychosis, maybe? Tessa wasn't a doctor. She'd call Sanjay as soon as she could get away.

Her phone rang. It was nearly 1:30 p.m. Somehow, she'd blasted past her lunch hour though it had felt like only a few minutes passed.

"I have to get back to work," she told Astrid.

Astrid looked at her blankly. "I know you can hear me now. So why aren't you listening?"

"If you want to come into my office w—"

"No! Listen to me!" Astrid flung the picture of Theo to the floor.

"I don't think now is the best time—"

But Astrid was spiraling. "If you're not gonna listen, then I'll have to show you." She ran past the dining room and into the living room, where she stopped in front of the row of plants sitting on the bay window ledge. She closed her eyes.

A sudden hum filled the air, subtle at first, then louder. Tessa followed her into the room. Was the buzzing just in her ears? Did the room feel warmer? Was this some other manifestation of her sudden, bizarre bouts of pain? Tessa glanced at the thermostat. It was rising rapidly: 76. 80. 83.

"What the hell?" Tessa covered her ears as the buzzing grew

louder, throbbing. The room seemed to vibrate, then shake. She fell to her knees, looking toward Astrid to find her standing there, facing the plants, hands raised like she was readying to conduct an orchestra.

In front of her, the plants were growing.

The spider plant's spindly leaves were extending, baby ones popping up on them within seconds. The oleander Tessa had been meticulously attending to was blooming giant pink flowers that opened and grew, faded and fell, while the plant kept growing, new buds forming. The monstera plants cracked open their pots, their roots winding along the window ledge, their leaves widening, thickening. The dragon toes agave thrust its orange talons toward Tessa and the plump echeveria varieties swelled, inflating like living green balloons. The two cacti were now taller than Tessa, with spikes several inches long, red blooms filling their many arms.

As the plants grew, they tilted away from the window and toward Astrid, as if she were now their sun. They wrapped themselves around her ankles, brushed blossoms against her cheeks. As she moved her hands, they came to her, servants in the thrall of a tender master.

New plants burst up from the carpet, pink azalea bushes and purple hydrangeas, marsh marigolds, Queen Anne's lace, crepe myrtle and magnolia trees popping up next to red pine and sugar maples, combinations that would never exist in nature. Morning glory vines snaked around the walls. Spanish moss dripped from the ceiling.

The humming lessened, faded, and stopped. The room remained warm; the thermometer stopped at 85 degrees. The heat in the room was radiating off Astrid's body.

Slowly, Tessa dropped her hands from her ears and stood. Her living room had transformed into a strange forest, with tiny blue tears sedum succulents turned bulbous, dwarfing miniature oaks and aspens. The humid air smelled like sage and mint and... green? Everything smelled green: pistachio, laurel, juniper, fern, jade, shamrock, chartreuse, and olive. It smelled like spring and reminded Tessa of running down the overgrown alley behind her house as a child, barefoot, the feel of grass and clover between her toes.

Tessa breathed in. The air—when was the last time she'd breathed in air this clean? She reached out and touched a coral-colored rose.

"How?" she murmured, looking at Astrid, who still had her arms out, like some benevolent goddess of nature and fertility. Tessa fought the urge to bow.

Astrid smiled. "Do you believe me now?"

"I—" Tessa couldn't get the words out. Her jaw worked up and down, as she touched the various flowers and leaves in disbelief and awe. "Will they stay like this?"

"It'll fade in a couple hours, back to normal," Astrid answered.

"Even the pots?" Tessa asked, picking up a couple pieces of Theo's favorite pot, panda-shaped, that had held a tiny—now behemoth—pothos.

Astrid nodded. "They'll fix themselves. Although, I *could* make it permanent, if you like it. And the pots, I could make them bigger." She snapped her fingers and the pothos was back in its panda pot, which was now the size of a caldron.

Tessa liked it. She *loved* it. But the words caught in her throat.

Astrid sighed. "I know it's a lot. But you've been a Familiar for so long. Theo should've told you what they were."

"A Familiar?"

"A non-magical human bound to a Magick."

"A Magick?"

"A magical human. A Familiar is a Magick's guardian in the non-magical world, their advocate. And vice versa. The Magick is bound to the Non, too. The Familiar helps their Magick navigate the non-magical world, like a link between the two worlds, magical and non-magical, right?"

"I didn't… I don't…" Tessa stammered. Her hands flapped around like tiny, useless wings. This was too much. Clearly, she'd lost her grip on reality. "This can't be real," she murmured, throwing a wide gesture around the room.

Astrid reached out and took Tessa's hands. Astrid held them firmly and stared straight into Tessa's eyes. Tessa wanted to look away but found she couldn't. Astrid's eyes were hypnotic. The irises flickered with static electric sparks. Her pupils were too ovular, almost catlike. Tessa could feel the weight of Astrid's gaze, pressing against her face and chest, holding her head in place, slowing her pulse, deepening her breathing, until she felt suddenly, strangely serene.

"It's ok," Astrid said. "This is a lot to take in. I've never had a Familiar before, so I'm sorry if... if I didn't do a good job of explaining it all."

"I'm very confused," Tessa whispered.

Astrid squeezed Tessa's hands and she remembered the feeling of her mother's arms around her, the sensation of being lifted up. It was a safe, weightless feeling.

"Magic is real," Astrid said. Her hands were so warm. "There are Magix everywhere: witches, vampires, werewolves, sirens, shapeshifters, fairies, even some ogres still, though they're mostly extinct. Some of us live among you Nons. Non-magical humans, that is. Most of us hide. There's a coven north of here. You'd never know about it unless you were initiated. That's where we were supposed to be, but..."

Astrid's gaze fell. Tessa felt panic grip her again. Astrid began to cry, dropping Tessa's hands to rub at her eyes.

*This is insane,* Tessa thought. *I'm going crazy.*

"There's a war going on," Astrid continued over sniffles. "Among the Magix, those of us that want to just live our lives among the Nons, and others that want to rule over them, over everyone. We've always hidden away; almost no one wants to keep doing that. But how do we come out in this world that's always, always hated us? In a world full of *DOMS*?"

"DOMS?"

"Destroyers of Magic. They're, like, the opposite of Magix."

"Like... witch hunters?"

"Worse. They're *anti*-Magic. They can take magic and destroy it." Astrid had tears in her eyes, but she held them back, her jaw clenching and unclenching. "I don't want to be afraid anymore."

"Who are you afraid of?" Tessa asked. She was definitely losing her grip on reality.

And yet.

Astrid was a child in mourning, in need. No matter what chaos surrounded her, Tessa was, first and foremost, a caregiver, a protector and defender of children.

She reached for Astrid's hand, squeezed it. "I'm not going to pretend everything is ok because *clearly* it's not." Tessa gave a vague flick of the wrist to the room. "And I'm… concerned? About this magic and… anti-magic stuff. But. I'm ok with being your… *Familiar.*" The word was honey in her mouth, sweet with promise. "I can help you navigate the world. But you have to tell me *everything.* Ok?"

Astrid nodded and then threw her arms around Tessa, hugging her tightly. In turn, Tessa wrapped her arms around Astrid and they stood there for several seconds past Tessa's comfort level, before Astrid let go and stepped back.

"We have to seal it," Astrid said.

"Wait, what?"

"The agreement," Astrid continued. "That you'll be my Familiar. It has to be… oh, it'll only hurt for a moment. May I?"

Tessa blinked. "Is this like a blood oath or something?"

Astrid shook her head. "Not exactly. Just… hold still." She closed her eyes and inhaled deeply.

At that same moment, Tessa felt a singeing sting on her left forearm and swatted at it, thinking there was bee or something on her. There was nothing but a red mark, slightly raised and puffy.

Astrid sucked in through her teeth when she caught sight of the wound. "I'm sorry," she whispered. "Ice will help it."

She snapped her fingers and held out a cube of ice, which Tessa mutely took and pressed against the welt.

"I probably did it badly," Astrid said, her face scrunched up as though she were the one who'd been bitten and was in pain.

Tessa's thoughts were racing. "This mark. I remember…"

"Theo gave you the Familiar Mark, too?"

Tessa nodded. "A couple weeks after Theo came, I was out in the garden and they were sitting by the door and they… they asked me if I wanted to take care of them forever. Forever. Such a weird way to phrase it. And so obviously not what I was meant to do. Fostering is… well…" Tessa knew she was babbling, but she just kept talking, processing what had happened, what was happening, as she spoke. "It's not forever, right? But I… I told them *yes*. It wasn't a lie. I *wanted* to. I said *yes*. And then, like some sort of fated chide from the universe, a bee stung me. Or, that's what I thought—assumed—at the time. It was here." Tessa rolled up the sleeve of her right arm to show the white crater of an old scar near her shoulder. She hadn't thought of it in months, at least. She was surprised at how much it had faded. For a while, she'd been convinced she would always have a slightly pink divot on her bicep, a tiny imprint that would forever remind her of Theo.

Astrid placed a tender finger on the mark as if she were caressing the cheek of a newborn. "You must miss them," she said.

Tessa nodded. A long quiet curled between them, seeming to pull them together in the warm embrace of the room until Astrid physically stepped back and shattered the silence and its hypnotic hold.

One thought swooped in where the silence had been: *Everything is going to change.*

As if conjured, there came a sharp knock on the door. Astrid and Tessa both jumped.

"It's probably Sanjay," Tessa said, noticing she'd missed a call from him and her boss. She went to the door and moved to unlock it.

*It's not Sanjay.* It was Astrid's voice in Tessa's head, stopping Tessa's hand midair as she reached for the knob.

Startled, Tessa looked up and Astrid and mouthed, *Who is it then?*

Astrid shrugged. Then added, again, somehow *inside* of Tessa's brain: *Someone magical. But they're… good.*

Tessa raised her eyebrows.

*They're good. I can tell. You can open it.*

*Rule #4*, Tessa thought. *Trust the kid.* She opened the door.

* * *

**APRIL 1977**

## April 6, 1977

*My dearest Valerie,*

*It was wonderful to see you the other day, as always. I'm so happy you got to meet our little Ana (Andor insists on using her full name, Morana, but I think Ana is sweet and perfect as is).*

*And, well, you were right. Of course you were right. It's not post-partum depression, although I suppose that could be aggravating things. No, I have been desperately unsatisfied for years, Val.*

*Andor has no idea. He is too caught up in his work and success to notice.*

*I want to do something. To be someone. Not just a mother. I've never really wanted to be a mother, but here we are. I love her, Valerie, I do. Sometimes, when I look at her sleeping face I can hardly bear the love, hardly bear the idea that already she is so far away from me. When I was pregnant, all I thought about was the birth and now… there are times when all I want to do is put her back inside of me, so that she will be with me always, safe and contained and known.*

*And yet. If I imagine my future revolving around her and only her, I want to scream. But I can't! It feels as though a vise grip has already encircled my throat, cutting off my airway, killing me slowly and softly.*

*This is not the life I want. It's not the life I was supposed to have. This isn't the life we promised each other.*

*I don't know what to do to change that.*

*Your friend,*

*Tish*

CHAPTER
# THREE

**JULY 2023** The woman at the door was gorgeous. Beautiful. Stunning. Breathtaking. She was all of the adjectives and none of them were quite enough to capture her. Her skin was smooth and flawless, the perfect, warm umber shade of a sunflower's center through which her smile shown. She was dressed like a 1950s movie star, an entirely yellow ensemble complete with pencil skirt accentuating an impossibly thin waist. Her hair was pulled up in two afro puffs full of glittering prism beads, which sent rainbows dancing every which way. She wore large, black sunglasses.

"Hi, I'm Cece," she said, holding out an elegant hand.

Tessa took it, blushing and worrying over her sweaty palms. "Heeeyy," she replied, drawing it out awkwardly and kicking herself for being so weird at the same time. "I'm Tessa." She kept holding Cece's hand, shaking it up and down while Cece just smiled. "I... um... I…" *Let go of her hand! What's wrong with you?!* "I love your ring!" she shouted, before dropping Cece's hand with too much force.

She didn't seem to mind or notice. "Thank you," she said, holding up her ring to the light. "It's peridot. My birthstone. Bringer of peace and good health." She grinned widely, looking up toward Tessa. It was hard to tell if she was looking directly at her because of the dark sunglasses.

"Emerald," Tessa blurted. "My birthstone's an emerald. Also… green."

Cece tilted her head to one side, her lips curling into a thin, amused smile. "Green is a magic color, isn't it? And emeralds are the symbol of true love. May I come in?"

Without hesitating, Tessa stepped aside to let her in, closing the door behind her.

Tessa turned around to find Cece and Astrid staring at each other, unsmiling. Slowly, Cece removed her sunglasses to reveal… *oh shit*, Tessa thought, remembering Astrid's offhand comment about witches and green eyes. Cece's eyes were even more vibrant than Astrid's, shifting between saffron yellow and key lime, standing out in dynamic, dazzling contrast to Cece's dark skin.

There was an electric tension in the air. The hairs on Tessa's arms stood on end and she worried that if she moved, she'd be zapped by an invisible electrical current that buzzed, suddenly everywhere.

But then, Astrid spoke, haltingly, "Auntie?"

In response, Cece held out her arms. "It's been a while, Sassy."

Astrid grinned then and rolled her eyes. "No one calls me that anymore," she said, walking toward Cece and falling into her embrace.

Cece squeezed her tight, whispering something that Tessa couldn't quite make out into her ear, then adding, louder, "I'll take you somewhere safe now."

Astrid pushed herself out of the embrace, frowning. "Where?"

Cece glanced over her shoulder at Tessa before shaking her head.

"You can't just tak—" Tessa started at the same time as Astrid shook her head right back at Cece.

"I'm not leaving without my Familiar."

From behind, Tessa noticed Cece's posture stiffen at the word. It was the bristling movement of an adult who'd been called out, beaten at their own game by a child. While Tessa didn't understand what code or rule Astrid was throwing in Cece's face, Tessa could tell that Cece was reluctant to break it, even though she clearly didn't want Tessa involved any more than she already was.

Cece looked at Tessa then, really looked at her, squinting as she looked Tessa up and down, arms folded across her chest, clearly bemused. Tessa was suddenly aware that she wearing sweatpants with a hole in the one thigh and a raggedy T-shirt that read, "Be Mine, Vegan-tine." But what caught Cece's eye was the red welt on Tessa's arm. Cece stared at it for a second before turning her eyes back to Astrid with a wince and a head shake.

Tessa considered throwing her a lifeline. If she actually was Astrid's aunt, it would be easy enough for her to get temporary custody of the child. She could give her Sanjay's number, offer to help with any paperwork. Kids should be with their families, after all. She *should* say something. Before Theo, she would certainly have. But now, there was this nagging thought in her head, ever since Astrid had told her that Theo was *also* magic, that maybe, with Astrid's help, Tessa could find Theo again.

It was the first hope she'd had in such a long time. She wasn't going to let that go, not for rules or policies or a beautiful woman. Plus, Astrid clearly wanted Tessa to come. And she would get to keep covertly looking at Cece, maybe get to know her better, or…

Tessa was looking at Cece's breasts, the curve of them showing where the v-neckline of her blouse dipped. She hadn't meant to be looking there. She shifted her gaze away quickly.

*Why are you blushing?* It was Astrid's voice in Tessa's head again. Tessa jerked her head up and glared at Astrid, but said nothing, feeling her face grow even warmer.

*You look like a beet.*

"That's enough!" Tessa said aloud.

Cece turned around. "Enough?"

"Enough… chitchat," Tessa said, forcing a wide smile. "I'll just go pack a bag and we can get out of here."

"There's no time," Cece said, turning back to Astrid. "We need to go now, Sass."

"Not without my Fam—"

Cece held up a silencing hand and turned back to Tessa. "You're going to have to come as you are or not come at all."

Tessa didn't hesitate. "I'm coming."

Cece smiled at her, and Tessa warmed, then blushed, before Cece said, "Get ready for a road trip! Have you gone to the bathroom recently?"

"Um, no. Should I?"

She smiled, her nose wrinkling. "It's a joke. You'll see." Then she took Tessa and Astrid each by the hand, murmuring nonsense syllables that sounded at first like Latin mixed with clicks and hisses, but then grew louder, droning, gong-clangs, inhuman and mechanical, before morphing into a rhythmic, yet melodic humming in parallel octaves, that thrummed with the weight and speed of cascading water.

Tessa didn't remember closing her eyes, but even before she opened them, she knew she was no longer standing in the entryway of her house; she was somewhere else entirely.

But where? It was dripping hot and there were the sounds of traffic, loud voices, and underneath it all, the buzzing of hungry mosquitoes. The ground beneath her shoes felt rough and uneven. She opened one eye, looking down at her feet to see she was standing on gravel. She opened the other eye and looked around her. There were people everywhere and… tombs? They were standing in a cemetery, but it was unlike any of the rolling green Midwestern grave sites peppered with square stone grave markers that Tessa was used to. These were all aboveground tombs and mausoleums, a patchwork of mini-houses in a city of the dead.

"Welcome to St. Louis Cemetery Number One," Cece whispered.

"Is that…?" Tessa whispered.

"The Voodoo Queen herself," Cece smiled. "This is the tomb of Marie Laveau."

"My great-great-great grandma," Astrid added, stepping toward the tomb.

There were people—tourists—everywhere, their bodies sweaty and slick, smelling of sunscreen, body odor, and cigarettes. They wore big black sunglasses and baseball caps for every possible team and T-shirts of every color with shoulders bare and reddening, dark midriffs swaying with sparkling belly button rings, exposed arms covered in black and gray tattoos. They were all there, right next to Astrid, Cece, and Tessa as they stood in front of the tomb of Marie Laveau, but no one made eye contact with the three of them or even seemed to see them. No one had noticed when they arrived. *We must have appeared out of nowhere,* Tessa thought. How had no one noticed?

Tessa reached out her hand to try and touch a woman who was standing next to the tomb with her hand against it, rubbing her foot along the bottom. Tessa tapped the woman's shoulder, and she stepped back. As she did so, the woman removed her hand from the tomb to reveal an "X" scratched into the stone. She held a cup in her hand and put a couple of quarters in it, then closed her eyes, and set the cup down like an offering.

"What are you doing?" Tessa asked, but the woman had already turned away and vanished into the crowd.

"They can't see, hear, or feel us," Cece answered. "We aren't really here. This is just a quick detour, if you will."

Tessa just gaped at her in response, so Cece continued.

"Transportation magic, going from here to there, leaves a sort of… footprint. And footprints…"

"… can be followed," Tessa murmured.

"Exactly. So we take detours to particularly potent, high-trafficked areas…"

"Like the tomb of a voodoo priestess?"

"… to muck things up a bit and ensure that no one can easily track us. And for other reasons, too." Cece nodded her chin toward Astrid, who was standing next to the tomb, her hands and forehead pressed against it. "It's a silly superstition, but the tourists, these Nons, they draw the 'Xs' on the tomb and leave offerings to the Voodoo Queen, so she'll grant their wishes." Cece chuckled. "You Nons make up such silly things; if only it were that simple to commune with what is lost."

She smiled, and while Tessa couldn't see her eyes through the sunglasses, she imagined the smile stopped at her mouth, imagined sad eyes beneath the dark shades. While it was impossible to tell what

Cece was looking at, Tessa assumed from the direction that her face was inclined that she was watching Astrid, so she chanced a long side-glance at Cece. Her skin was absolutely flawless. Her right ear was pierced about ten times, with a tiny jewel of every color tracing the lobe. She smelled coconut oil, juniper, and amber.

"What is the other reason we're here?" Tessa asked.

Cece inclined her head slightly toward Tessa. "Memory is a strange thing, don't you think? Supposedly, it's something that occurs in our brains. Synapses formed and all that." She waved a dismissive hand. "But I think memory lives well beyond our brains. It's in our bones, so it will outlast our consciousness, our flesh. It takes a long, long time to decay."

Tessa was frowning. "That's cryptic as hell."

Cece smiled. "Witches tend to be cryptic. It's kind of our thing. I brought us here for Astrid. The living still long for answers from the dead."

"You think they're dead, then? Her parents?"

Cece shook her head, then turned to face Tessa. Removing the sunglasses to reveal those enchantingly weird eyes, Cece leaned in so that her lips were almost touching Tessa's ear, sending shivers up and down her body.

"When we are in a safe place, we will talk more." Cece pulled back, taking Tessa's hand. "We all want to believe in life after death, in something beyond ourselves. All of us." Cece squeezed Tessa's hand before turning to Astrid and saying, quietly, "Any luck?"

Astrid jerked her head around as if Cece had shouted. Astrid shook her head as she walked back "They didn't pass through here," she replied, taking Cece's other hand.

Cece sighed. "Worth a try."

"Wait, what were you doing?" Tessa asked.

"Checking to see if my parents passed through here," Astrid answered. "This is a favorite thoroughfare of theirs because of the family connection, you know?"

Tessa looked from Astrid to Cece and back to Astrid. "So you weren't communing with the dead?"

Astrid wrinkled her nose. "Ew, no."

Cece laughed and smiled at Tessa. "Shall we?"

"Can we try another hub?" Astrid asked. "Maybe Salem? Or maybe Bethlehem?"

"I'm not going all the way to the Middle East today."

"Salem?"

Cece nodded and they were off again. This time, Tessa made a conscious effort to keep her eyes open as the hisses and clicks and pseudo-Latin words morphed into drumbeats, cymbal crashes, and the steady pounding like fast-moving water, but there was too much movement to take any of it in. It was like being in the eye of a storm and watching everything, the entire world, all that ever has been, is, or will be dance around. Her brain could not accept any of it, the colors and sounds and emotions, and so her vision darkened until she could see nothing.

She heard Astrid's voice saying, "Shoot, nothing here anyway" followed by "Ew!" because it was at this point that Tessa vomited.

Cece's arms entwined around Tessa, holding her up. "Come on. Let's get you back to The House."

* * *

**JULY 1977** The beautiful man sitting at the bar winked at Val. She ignored him and continued sketching in her notebook. A drink appeared beside her, the bartender disappearing back behind the bar with a nod toward the beautiful man. Val sniffed it. Not poisoned. She didn't drink it. The man continued to watch her. He had dark skin, thick, curly hair, and light brown, almost yellow eyes. She didn't think he was a Magick, but he was certainly not a Non.

*Maybe he's an ogre.* She started sketching him, unthinking, eyes closed, so she could feel the way the air moved in her pencil's wake, tiny vibrations.

It was hot, even in the air-conditioned bar. She felt a bead of sweat making its unhurried way down her nose, heard it land on the paper with ping. Val opened her eyes. The sweat had dripped into the man's penciled afro. She used her eraser to swirl and texture the hair.

"A fairy and an artist," said a voice above her.

Too close. She jumped. No one should have been able to get that close without her knowing. *Definitely not a Non*, she thought. And probably not an ogre.

"What are you?" Val asked the man.

The lights flickered. No one in the bar seemed to notice, but Val could taste nitrogen on the tip of her tongue. Another lightning strike.

The man sat down across from her at the booth. His fingers formed a steeple, his elbows, jutting out like the horizontal beams of a cross, perched on the table.

"My name—"

Before he could finish, the lights went out and the bar plunged into total darkness.

The occupants held a collective breath, everyone assuming the lights would come right back on. They did not.

"What the hell is going on here?"

The shout sounded like a trickle of water allowing a flood to crash through the dam. The room exploded in sound. Before, it had been hot and humid with the exhalations of intoxicated breaths and the pressing clutch of a summer storm. It had smelled rank, body odor and cigarette smoke in the air, the carpet and walls, sour exhales of beer breath and the stench of decades of beer spilled on the carpet and sticky on the tables. Now, everything was multiplied by the power of panic. Val felt the temperature rise several degrees in a matter of seconds as the void of the AC's silence was filled with angry shouts and smashing glass.

A hand grabbed hers. That voice was too close again. "My name's Gunner. We should get out of here."

"I'm not interested." Val pulled her hand from his.

He smiled. She couldn't *see* him smile, but she knew he was smiling. "You never know."

"I'm not interested in *you*."

"Fair enough."

Her eyes were adjusting to the dark. She could tell his teeth were bleached white. They seemed to glow.

"Are you interested in saving the world?" he asked.

Val frowned. "Who are you?"

"I told you. I'm Gunner. Gunner Engers."

"*What*. Are. You."

His smile never faltered. "I'm an AntiMage. And you're a Magick. A fairy, if I'm not mistaken."

Val shuddered. Wariness like a blast of icy air moved through her, brought her senses into a heightened state of alert. She realized she couldn't smell the man. Most people, she could smell across the room. Two tables away sat a man she'd smell before she'd even entered the building. "You're a DOM?" she hissed.

Even in the near-total dark and surrounded by chaos, Val saw and felt the man stiffen. The air in the room stilled and sounds slowed around them until it felt like it was only the two of them, the DOM and the Magick, in a room full of statues.

"I'd prefer to be called an AntiMage. Destroyer of Magic, well, that's not exactly what we *are*, is it?"

"It's not?" Val snapped. She was gripping the table. She could feel the stickiness of it beneath her fingertips. *Real,* she thought, inhaling the sweaty air. *Real.*

He was smiling again, his teeth an eerie beacon. "Of course not. We're not enemies, you and I. Not essentially. We're simply… opposites."

"Opposites." Val wondered how well he could see her in the darkness, if DOMs could see in the dark, like she'd always heard.

"Creatures of Darkness," Tish would say. "Half the myths about vampires actually lead straight back to DOMs, you know."

Val missed Tish. Tish would know what to say, what to do, how to get out of this dark hellhole.

"Opposites attract, as they say," Gunner said, smiling.

"What do you think is going on with the power?" Val asked through clenched teeth.

"Blackout."

"No shit."

"Let's go outside and see."

The streets were as black as inside. Looking up, Val could see the pinpricks of stars. So many stars! She nearly gasped as she looked up at them.

"Beautiful," Gunner whispered in her ear and she did not flinch.

"They remind me of home."

"Where's that?"

Val shook her head. "Gone."

"Gone?"

"The ocean took it."

Gunner nodded. "I'm sorry for your loss."

"Thank you." Val turned her head to look up at him. He was beautiful in the way untouchable things are. Forbidden fruit, a poison apple.

"I've been touched intimately by the effects of pollution and pollutants on our planet," Gunner said. The pupils of his eyes were too large, extending nearly to the whites, leaving only a thin golden outline.

"Can you see in the dark?" she asked.

He nodded.

"Thought so."

"Can I walk you home?"

"I told you; I'm not interested."

He shrugged. "Neither am I."

"Then, yes. Sure." She pointed left. "Ten blocks that way."

They started walking.

"What happened to you?" Val asked after a few minutes.

Their steps were quiet on the pavement, almost soundless, as though they didn't exist. Around them, people shouted and screamed. Val saw someone throw a chair at a bodega window. It bounced back at them. She almost laughed, but they'd pulled out a gun and were shooting at the window. She stopped walking.

Gunner took her arm and led her around. "You're safe with me."

Val was surprised to realize she believed him.

"I had a daughter," Gunner said. "She died of mercury poisoning from the fish we ate and from our water. We lived in Sarnia, Ontario at the time. Near the St. Clair River. My wife is Anishinaabe of the Aamjiwnaang First Nation."

"A Native DOM?"

"A First Nations *AntiMage*. My sons were older, but my daughter was a baby. We lived with my wife's family. This was in '64. You were probably still a child then."

1964. The year that had taken her home and her five-year-old sister. "I was seventeen," Val murmured.

"I wasn't there," Gunner continued. "I should've been, but I was away. On business."

"And what is that business?" Val wasn't sure why she was being so interrogative, so nasty when the man was telling her about his dead child. She thought of her sister, her tiny hands, swollen with water.

"It doesn't matter," Gunner replied. "I wasn't there when she moved on to the next world. I carry that with me. Now, I work elsewhere."

"And that matters?"

"Very much so," Gunner answered. "Have you heard of the Magix and AntiMagi Projected Amalgamation Confederation?"

# CHAPTER
## FOUR

"Is she dead?"

Tessa felt something press on her chest. A small finger poked her cheek.

"Luca, get off her."

"Is she dead?" The voice repeated, now close to Tessa's ear. It was a child's voice, gravelly and warm. Their breath smelled tangy and metallic.

"Don't bite her, Luca! I'll tell Mama Cece!" This voice was high-pitched, but clearly older. They spoke with scolding authority.

"She smells good." The child with the gravelly voice murmured, their breath against Tessa's neck.

"Mom! Luca's trying to bite the Familiar!"

The weight lifted from Tessa's chest and there was a scuffling sound beside her, followed by a slight kick to her side and a couple screams.

She opened her eyes to find she was lying on a large bed in a completely white room. Beside her, two small children were wrestling. The larger child had long, flowing brown hair and large, butterfly-like wings of the same brown hue, but slightly translucent, with patches of dazzling cerulean that flicked sparkles against the white walls. The smaller one had a mat of bright red hair that stood up on his head like actual flames. He was hissing as he tackled the older, larger child, showing off a pair of unsettlingly long fangs.

The older child managed to roll out of the younger's grasp and into the air, leaving the red-headed child leaping on the bed, trying to grab the flying child, who taunted him from above.

"Nanny nanny boo boo, you can't catch me!" The taunting was interspersed with squeals for help. "Mom! Mommy!"

Cece was in the doorway now with her hands on her hips. She clapped her hands twice and the children quieted for a moment before beginning to scream over one another.

"Luca was gonna bite her!"

"Mama Cece, I was *not*. Silas is lying."

"Were too! And I'm not lying!"

"Yes, you *are! Hssssssssssss!*"

Cece pressed two fingers into her temples. "Luca, please stop hissing. Silas, please stop flying around like that. This is no way to greet our guest."

"Our *common* guest," Luca said and Silas gasped.

"Bad word! Bad word alert. Wee-oo-wee-oo!"

Cece held up a finger to Silas as she addressed Luca. "Now, Luca," she said, sitting down on the edge of the bed between the two children. "That's not a nice word to call a non-magical person. Non is better. Besides, Tessa here…" She glanced over her shoulder at Tessa and mouthed "sorry," before continuing. "She's not just *any* Non. She's a Familiar. That's a very special kind of Non."

Luca raised his eyebrows, making his already large blue eyes practically pop out of his tiny face. "Why?" he whispered.

"Because Familiars are chosen by Magix to be their helpers, to navigate the non-magical world."

"Can I have a Familiar?" Silas asked.

"Me too!" Luca shrieked.

Cece shook her head. "What do you need a Familiar for?" she asked. "You live here among Magix and you have everything you need." She reached out to tousle Luca's hair and briefly cup Silas' chin in her hand. "A Familiar can only be called upon in times of need, when a Magick is struggling to navigate a piece of the Nons' world. And once called upon, a Familiar is bound to the Magick until death." She let the word hit with an ominous emphasis, before adding, "Or until the Magick releases them."

Tessa frowned. "Can a person be a Familiar for more than one Magick at a time?"

Cece shook her head. "Nope. It's a monogamous commitment."

Tessa's face must have given something away, opened a window or door or drilled a hole down to the core of herself, to the gaping wound of grief that she had kept wrapped up in minutia and tasks and routine. Cece reached out her hand and squeezed Tessa's, a gesture that should have thrilled Tessa, but all she could think about was Theo. Everything was breaking now. The hairline fractures that had always been there were widening. Tessa willed herself not to cry.

"How do you… how does a Magick… release a Familiar?" Tessa asked, already sensing the answer lay somewhere in the memory of Theo's back as they walked away, hoodie over their head so their purple hair was hidden, back and shoulders hunched as though they were pulling against some unseen rope that bound them to Tessa and her to them. Morana had slammed the car door and Tessa felt it like a punch in the gut. She'd doubled over in pain, unable to watch as Theo was taken away. After a moment, Sanjay had come and placed a hand on her shoulder, probably thinking she was only sad, not in physical pain. But with his touch, the pain had gone. It had been weird, the whole thing. But Tessa had been too buried by her grief to parse it.

Cece narrowed her eyes. "I don't know." Her gaze shifted away from Tessa as soon as she said it and Tessa was certain that she was lying, though she hadn't a clue as to why.

Tessa sat up. "So where am I exactly? Is Astrid ok? And I'm sorry I… was sick."

Cece smiled. "Astrid's fine. Oscar is showing her around. I've got her staying in the room across the hall. And don't apologize; it happens. I should've warned you. Sometimes it's better to close your eyes and pretend you aren't moving at all. If you try to take it all in…

it's too much, even for a lot of us Magix." She winked at Tessa and Tessa felt her cheeks redden and her pulse quicken. "And this is our house. *The* House, we call it."

"Like *The* Queen!" Silas said.

Cece nodded. "Silas has been watching *The Crown*."

"Did you know that Princess Diana *dies?* She is really, actually *deceased*."

"What!" Luca exclaimed, bouncing up and down. "She's *dead?*"

"*Really* dead."

Cece rolled her eyes. "Silas, please don't encourage his… proclivities." To Tessa, she continued, "When we came here, we couldn't agree on a name so… we didn't really give it one."

"What's a pwo-co-cookie?" Luca asked.

"Proclivity," Silas corrected.

"Who's we?" Tessa asked. "You three? Are you their…"

"Foster mom," Cece smiled. "Like you. Astrid explained it to me," she added.

"Proclivity?" Luca repeated.

"It means you like weird things, like dead stuff," Silas said.

"There's actually nine of us now, including you and Astrid, of course," Cece continued.

"I don't *like* dead stuff, Silas," Luca said, hands on his hips. "I *love* it! I love dead bugs and dead leaves." He ticked off the items on his fingers as he spoke. "And hair because that's just, you know, dead cells."

"So, it's you and six kids?" Tessa asked. "Or do you have a—?"

Cece raised her eyebrows, and opened her mouth to answer, but Silas was shouting: "You. Are. *Weird!*"

"Silas, that's not kind," Cece interjected.

"But Mama Cece, weird is *good*." Silas flopped backward on the bed, his wings folding up behind him and seeming to vanish into his skin.

"Dead branches… that's sticks," Luca continued.

"Weird is good," Cece nodded. "It was more your tone that was unkind."

"Dead animals… the taxi ones."

Silas let out a loud huffing breath. "Taxidermy!"

"Silas."

"Fine. Sorry, Luca."

"Is dirt dead?" Luca asked.

Cece ruffled his hair. It bounced right back up, reminding Tessa of a cartoon villain. "I mean… it's made from decomposed living matter," she said. "So…"

"So yes! Dirt is dead." Luca threw his head up as he said it, shouting at the top of his lungs. "And I love dirt!"

Silas giggled.

"Why don't you guys go play somewhere else now, hmm? I need to talk to Tessa."

The two hopped off the bed and bounced out of the room, holding hands.

Cece turned to Tessa. "So, are you feeling well enough to get up? I can give you a tour."

Rather than answering, Tessa stood up, stretched, and did a little jump. Then she felt ridiculous and blushed, but Cece was suppressing a laugh, hand over her smiling mouth.

"To your question," Cece said. "It's me, five kiddos, and Jean. Jean-Baptiste de Garmeaux. Make sure you say it Zhhun, not John or god forbid, Jeeen. Don't Americanize it. But Jean, he's not my partner. Well, not in the sense I think you meant. We're a team, raising and protecting these kids. Our coven sent us here—*hid* us here—together. It's been a little over three years now."

"Your coven?" Tessa repeated. She had so many questions, about all of it: the hiding, the timeline of events, but mostly: "What exactly is a coven?"

"A coven is like… a community of Magix."

"It's not just a witch thing?"

"No, no," Cece replied, waving a hand in the air as if to brush the notion away. "That's all Non lore. First things first, you need to take everything you've ever been taught about magic and Magix and get that out of your head. We live; we die. We are human, like you.

Witches haven't sold their souls to Satan; vampires are not undead and they certainly don't bite humans and 'turn them' into vampires. Or at least, that's not typical."

"Not. Typical?"

"Sometimes, the bond between a Familiar and their Magick is so strong the Familiar can become a Magick themselves."

"Wait, what?" Tessa asked. "Like by absorbing their powers? Like osmosis?"

"It doesn't happen very often. I've never personally seen it happen." Cece shrugged. "It's probably a myth. Every Magick I've ever met was born a Magick. Every Magick I've ever read about was born one."

"Ok, but... how?"

"How do we exist?"

"Um... yeah?" Tessa held out her hands, palms up, in such a plaintive and astounded gesture that Cece laughed.

"I'm sorry. It's... you're so..."

"Dumb? Naive?"

"No," Cece shook her head. "Good. You're good, Tessa. I can feel it. Not many Nons are so... good."

Tessa wanted to object, but she'd been working with her therapist on accepting compliments. "Thank you."

Cece smiled, a tired, thin smile that was mostly a grimace. "No one really knows how we came to exist. There are theories, of course." She stood up. "Come on. I'll show you around, take you on a tour of The House, and explain as best I can."

They left the serene white room and entered a hallway that was the aesthetic opposite, walls painted in chevron rainbows with twinkle lights hanging from the high ceiling. It took Tessa a moment to realize that the lights weren't hanging from anything but floating.

"Silas made them," Cece explained. "He decorated this space. My hair." She gestured to the prism beads tucked among her black poofs. "Magix, each clan, be it witches, werewolves, sirens, vampires, we all have our own unique powers—our special skills. Our dear Silas, as you may have guessed, is a fairy. Along with the gift of flight, fairies each have a particular elemental affinity, unlike witches who are adept at controlling all elements. Silas is a fire fairy meaning he has a particular flair for light and color. Fire fairies, ice fairies, and earth fairies, are the most common. There are also air fairies. Very rare, of course. An insanely powerful caste of fairies. Did you know a single air fairy was responsible for the disaster at Chernobyl? I heard they even survived."

Tessa shuddered. She could feel the pinprick sting of radiation against her cheeks, taste the metal in the air like she was scraping her tongue along a rusty nail. She felt that impossible-to-reach-and-scratch itch between her shoulder blades.

"Are you ok?" Cece placed a hand on Tessa's shoulder.

Tessa shook her head, trying to dislodge the thought that continued to grip her with increasing force and frequency: *She* was dying because the planet was dying. "I'm—" She started to speak, but what was the right word? *Insane*, Sanjay would say with a loving smirk and a peck on the cheek. *Sensitive*, her therapist would say. *Aware*, her mother would say. It was impossible to describe Tessa's "episodes," the way the air would seize around her and she would be awash with pain, unable to breathe. Then the feeling would dissipate as quickly as it had come.

"I'm fine," she said. It was true. She was fine again.

Cece hesitated before continuing, "Silas and Luca share this room." She gestured to the open door on the left through which Tessa spotted Luca and Silas building a floating Lego castle. She saw only one bed in the room, hovering near the ceiling. Near the floor was a child-sized black box. *A coffin,* Tessa realized and shivered.

The boys looked up and waved as they passed. "Kiddos," Cece said, holding the door handle. "Less playing, more getting ready for bed. It's late. Past bedtime."

Luca glowered, but Silas gave a thumbs-up.

Cece blew them kisses as she shut the door.

"It's late?" Tessa asked.

"Almost 9:00 p.m."

"Crap. I need to email my boss. Text Sanjay..." She patted her pockets. "Find my phone."

"Astrid has it." Cece put a hand on her Tessa's. "You dropped it in Salem. We're gonna eat a late dinner. Then you can take care of everything."

Tessa took a deep breath. "Ok. Thanks."

Cece smiled, a calm expression that reminded Tessa, in an eye-rolling cliché, of every therapist she'd ever seen. "It's... a lot," Cece added, lowering her head so her eyes were even with Tessa's. "It's ok if you're not ok. You don't have to do this. You don't have to be here."

"I want to be here. I want to do this." She swallowed. "I *can* do this."

As Cece studied Tessa's face, her expression shifted from serene sympathy to something less readable, reminding Tessa of the expression her mother had worn on the day she'd told her she was becoming a foster mom: pride, grief, fear, hope... a kaleidoscopic tapestry of emotions.

Then Cece clapped her hands and her face fixed itself back into a smile.

"So," she continued. "Our little Luca is a vampire."

Tessa nodded. "The whole coffin and death thing..."

"Mmhmm. The Vampiric mutation. Yes, mutation. We're all mutants, see? X-Men style." She grinned. "The origins of magic are built into our genetic code. An extra chromosome here, something out of sequence there, a deletion or two. It's how we came to be. The mutations are, largely, inherited. So a witch will birth witches and a vampire will birth vampires."

"Wait, you said *largely*. Can Magix be born to Nons?"

Cece inclined her head. "Indeed." She gestured to the door across the hallway. "This is Oscar's room—you'll meet him soon." The door boasted an oversized padlock and DO NOT FUCKING DISTURB sign. "He's seventeen, so..." She shrugged. "Magix born to Nons, we call them Waywards. They're quite mystifying, a special kind of Magick in and of themselves." She pressed a hand to Oscar's door before continuing, "Bathroom's on the left plus there's one off your bedroom as well."

"You said Luca's a vampire..."

Cece smiled. "So much information! Luca and Silas get along particularly well because vampires, like fire fairies, have a dash of fire in them. Pyrokinesis and telekinesis are skills that Luca, unfortunately, possesses in excess. Some vampires are necromancers. Vampires also have particular affinity to certain animals: bats, rats, and insects, to be precise. They can communicate with them, command them, sometimes see the world through their eyes. Tropes you're familiar with, yes? So. You can see the churning way that rumors start and grow. The Vampiric mutation originated in the far north, so their skin tends to be more sensitive to light than even the average white person. You can have a vampire as black as me who still needs to lather on the sunscreen or they'll turn a nasty magenta."

"What about witches?" Tessa asked, trying to remember all the witch tropes she'd learned, and thinking mostly of *Hocus Pocus*, and Sarah Jessica Parker flying around on a broomstick or a mop or something while singing about eating kids. Or was it drinking them?

As they stepped out of the hallway, the space opened onto a grand staircase. Tessa gaped up at the vaulted ceiling from which hung all sorts of vegetation: twisty vines with flowers of every color, walls of ivy and rows of string-of-pearls plants hanging just like their name. It was a living ceiling of flowering greens. Through it, bees buzzed and hummingbirds flitted.

"Oh my," Tessa breathed.

"It looks like Astrid's been adding some of her own flare to my greenery," Cece said, gesturing to a string-of-pearls plant. "A lovely touch."

A sharp caw echoed above them. Out of the greenery, a raven swooped down, landing on Cece's shoulder.

"I almost forgot!" Cece exclaimed. "This is Bettie. She's my raven. My *animal Familiar*." She reached up to stroke Bettie's head. "Jean *hates* it when I call her that. He says it's like people who call their pets their children." Cece clicked her tongue at Bettie, who cocked her head to one side, listening.

"She understands you?"

Cece nodded. "And I understand her. One of my *special skills*."

She put a finger to Bettie's head and the bird nuzzled against it. "Like I said before, witches can manipulate elements. Some are bound to the basics: earth, wind, water, and fire. Others—" She snapped her fingers and the stray Legos strewn along the hallway came zooming into her hand. She slipped them into her pocket. "—are adept at manipulating all sorts of materials, including human-made ones. And, of course, some of us can communicate with birds or cats. Go on, sweets," she told Bettie, nudging the bird off her shoulder. The raven took wing and soared overhead in wide circles before perching on a jut of crown molding near the ceiling. "The witch mutation is probably the most widespread. Unlike vampires, our origins cannot be pinpointed to one part of the globe. We are—" She spread her hands in a wide gesture, fingers dancing. "Everywhere."

She turned, leading Tessa down the sloping staircase that seemed to roll like waves beneath them. The motion sent Tessa's stomach turning. It must have shown on her face because Cece held up a hand and the staircase calmed.

"Jean loves the water. Reminds him of home."

Tessa paused, her hand gripping the post at the end of the railing, looking out across the expanse of a haphazard living room with chairs floating near the ceiling, a sofa buried partially in the ground, and a fountain filled with clear, bubbling water. In the fountain floated several chairs and a settee. The majority of the furniture had large bites taken out of it.

"You have a dog?" Tessa asked.

"Twin werewolves, actually. Livy and Lola. They're in bed now; you'll meet them in the morning. They just turned two."

"What's their *special skill*?"

"As of right now, biting. Sometimes, turning into dogs. As they grow older and their skills develop, they should gain the impressive speed, strength, and agility of most werewolves, along with heightened senses and rapid healing abilities, at least for their own bodies. Some werewolves are able to heal others as well. The other bedrooms are down there." She pointed left as they continued to the right. "We call it the east corridor." She hooked a thumb back the way they'd come. "Your room is the west corridor."

"Fancy."

"Mm, very fairy-tale-esque. No forbidden room or anything like that." She raised an eyebrow at Tessa, who reddened.

Cece led Tessa past a dining room, which was similar to the living room in that the furniture hung, stood, floated, or sank to varying degrees and most of it was covered in bite marks.

"Kitchen's on the right." Cece indicated closed double doors through which Tessa could hear a haunting voice singing. She stopped abruptly and Cece had to circle back and grab Tessa's arm to keep her moving, shouting behind her. "Jean, remember we've got a Familiar with us. She's not used to your serenades!"

The singing stopped and a deep voice hollered, "Désolé! My apologies!"

Cece led Tessa into a pristine mudroom, shoes neatly stacked in cubbyholes and coats hung in an ascending rainbow, red to violet, smallest to largest.

"We don't get out much." Cece fingered indigo jacket that was clearly hers, the sleeves cut and flared out. "Unfortunately."

"Would you like to get out?" Tessa asked, then reddened again— why was she blushing so much?—as Cece swung her head around to face Tessa.

"I mean, *I* get out. I have a job. But the kids… I wish they could go out, you know? We do have a backyard. If you go down the east corridor, there's a little inconspicuous door. One of the kids can show you later. They'll have to show you the library too. But this entrance… the kids never use it."

She gestured for Tessa to go ahead, out of the mudroom and back toward the kitchen, but Tessa paused.

"Witches, vampires, fairies, werewolves… what are the other kinds of Magix again?"

"There are shapeshifters."

"Right. They can change forms?" She started walking again.

"Exactly," Cece replied, right behind her, the "x" slithering through her teeth and her breath so close it almost made Tessa shiver. "In many ways, they are a descendant, an evolutionary skip away from vampires, werewolves, and witches. All of us practice some degree of therianthropy. But we cannot take the form of another human. Only a shifter can do that. It's one of the more dangerous magical powers in existence."

Tessa frowned. "Dangerous? How is it more dangerous than, say, pyrokinesis?"

"The power of becoming another human is tremendous. If untethered from rules and morals, it becomes untenable, a force of unspeakable evil."

"Sure, but that could be said of any power. A car is a force of 'unspeakable evil' if you the driver uses it as a weapon."

Cece nodded. "Valid."

"I mean, they—shifters—can't help who they are."

"A tiger can't help what they are either."

Tessa opened her mouth to reply, but a cry from the living room interrupted her.

"Ohé, Cece! Dinner time!"

* * *

**JAN 1978**

## January 9, 1978

*Mr. Engers,*

*Tell you something about myself? Well, I'm a shapeshifter. A shifter. I'm sure our reputation proceeds us and you have all kinds of preconceived notions about what a shifter is. Shifting. By nature, shifty.*

*Try and step into my shoes, to feel what it's like to be constantly suspected of foul play, even by your own people. That's what it means to be a shifter. Shifters, they say, care only about power and money.*

*Me, I care about the future. In that way, aren't you and I the same?*
*Sincerely,*
*Morticia Chernoff*

# CHAPTER
# **FIVE**

**JULY 2023** As Tessa and Cece walked back through The House's bizarre living room, a burly, bearded man came waltzing out of the kitchen carrying an enormous, heavy-looking platter of intricate appetizers as if it were a feather. He bowed to Tessa and Cece, lowering the food to their level, quite a low bend since he was at least six and a half feet tall with the barrel chest and the biceps of someone who could probably lift Tessa with one hand.

"Et voilà!" His was the same deep voice that had boomed from the kitchen earlier. "For hors d'oeuvres, we have a chickpea bruschetta, cucumber slices topped with vegan tzatziki, sweet potato and avocado tartare, and, finally, crostini with cashew cheese spread and pome-granate seeds. Bon appétit!"

Tessa was so hungry she forgot her question and grabbed an appetizer in each hand, not even bothering to introduce herself, before stuffing them into her mouth.

The man stared at her with wide-eyed expectation as she devoured one, two, three appetizers and continued to grab more.

"Delicious," she managed to say after the fifth one.

He bowed his head in acknowledgment.

"Thanks, Jean." Cece picked up her first appetizer. "Tessa, this is Jean. Jean, Tessa."

"Nice to meet you, Tessa," Jean grinned.

"Mmm-hmm!" Tessa mumbled through a full mouth, nodding her head. "So good!" she added, reaching for two more appetizers.

"Should we move into the kitchen?" Jean asked. "The older two children are there. I just went up and put Silas and Luca to bed. They did wonder if you would be in to give them good night bisous, C."

"Yeah, one sec." Cece shoveled in an appetizer before turning to Tessa. "To give more context to my statement: shapeshifters are not inherently dangerous or evil. But shape-*shifting* is the most frequently corrupted power in history."

"How so?" Tessa asked between bites.

"Guy Fawkes, le traître. He was the victim of a shapeshifter, right?"

Cece nodded. "And who do you think was executed for the Gunpowder Plot?"

"Oh shit," Tessa whispered. "The Non?"

"Correct. Some of the most famous traitors and criminals in history were actually shapeshifters who had taken their form: Bonnie Parker, Mata Hari, Judas Iscariot, and Lizzie Borden to name a few."

"Show off," Jean chuckled, then said to Tessa. "Cece is our resident historienne de la magie."

"By day, I teach history to high schoolers." Cece sighed before adding, "*Non* history to *Non* high schoolers."

"She is a brilliant teacher." Jean patted Cece's shoulder.

Cece shrugged. "Someone has to pay the bills."

"Magix have bills?"

"It's a Non's world," Cece replied.

"But couldn't you…" Tessa snapped her fingers. "Bam! Money! Like magic?"

Cece and Jean both burst into laughter. Jean snapped his fingers in a sassy imitation of Tessa.

"You can't 'magic,' as you put it, nothing from nothing," Cece explained. "You have a plant, I make it grow. We have carrots." She gestured to two carrots sitting out on the counter. "Now we have more!"

Tessa blinked. Half a dozen carrots were on the counter.

"Look at this house!" Cece continued. "You think a teacher's salary pays for this?"

Tessa blinked again and massaged her temples. "I—I don't…"

"I make $55,000 a year. And I can make that money stretch much farther than any Non could ever dream."

"So you'll be retiring soon, oui?"

Cece sighed. "I also *like* teaching." She elbowed Jean. "Still, thank god for summer break. Anyway. I'll go kiss the kids good night. Be back in a minute." She started toward the stairs then turned back. "She hasn't met Oscar yet, so introduce her, please?"

"Anything for you."

Cece rolled her eyes before disappearing.

"You love me!" Jean called after her, to which Cece held her hand over her head and gave him the finger. Jean, laughing, turned to Tessa. "Witches, am I right?" He kept laughing, but then quickly sobered. "Oh, your face! I put you in a spot. I apologize. Come with me to la cuisine." He gestured toward the kitchen. "This way, this way."

"You're not a witch?" Tessa asked as they pushed through the double doors and into a kitchen that reminded her of a beach at sunset.

The walls were iridescent teals, seafoam, and whites that sparkled, reflecting the auburn overhead light that bathed the entire kitchen in a coral glow. The floor was sand, but smooth and white and surprisingly firm. Here, too, plants hung from the ceiling, but these plants bore fruit. From oranges and lemons to apples and blueberries, it was an impossible combination and it was perfect. There was a giant kitchen island that seemed to be made entirely of shells. In the corner, a waterfall tumbled into a pool, on which floated a raft—no, a table!—full of more elaborate food: a platter of grilled carrots, zucchini, and peppers, tabbouleh and hummus, falafel, skewers of vegetables, pita, grape leaf wraps, mujaddara, rice pudding, and baklava.

"Wow," Tessa whispered.

"Tonight's cuisine: la méditerranéenne! And no, not a witch. I'm a siren." He laughed. "Again, your face! Did you expect a red-headed mermaid?"

"Kind of, I guess. Sorry."

Jean's smile was full of warmth and genuine affection. "Tessa, this world is all new to you. Do not worry about your assumptions. You will unlearn them with time and care. We will help, fear not." His hand on her shoulder was like a weighted blanket, heavy and calming.

"Thanks," Tessa said, then added, repeating the phrase Cece had used. "What are your *special skills*?"

Jean smiled, a motion that scrunched up his entire face, his blue eyes turning to slits and his golden beard rising almost to his forehead. "Besides cooking?"

"Oh! I didn't realize that was…"

"Magic-assisted? That's *my* special skill. Not siren-related. You meant sirens in general?"

Tessa nodded. "Cece was explaining the different… things? You all… all the types—"

"Clans."

"Clans. Got it. Cece was explaining what the different clans can do."

"Parfait! I will continue. Sirens, we are adept at la hypnose."

"Hypnosis?"

"Yes, and with our songs we can also move objects."

"Like telekinesis?"

Jean wrinkled his nose. "Almost, but instead of thinking movement, we sing it." He laughed again. "You don't have what they call a 'poker face,' hein? Ok, watch." His lips moved, wordless and soundless, as he leaned over a cutting board on which sat a serrated knife and a loaf of bread. As his lips moved, the knife rose and began to slice the bread in a careful, methodic rhythm that seemed to mirror the movement of Jean's lips. "See?" As soon as Jean stopped murmuring, the knife lay back down, lifeless.

Tessa nodded, eyes wonder-wide.

"Also, we can breathe under water. We have a... how did you say?

*Spécial* relationship with water. We can manipulate it. More than this." He waved a dismissive hand at the sliced bread. "Or rather, with less… effort. You know… how it is to speak in the language of your birth as opposed to one you have learned. It is done without thought." He smiled, but the smile was somewhat sad, full of longing and nostalgia. "Oh, and some sirens can speak to sea creatures."

"Like dolphins?" Tessa couldn't keep the eagerness out of her voice. Her childhood dream had involved living with and talking to dolphins. One year, she'd requested a dolphin for Christmas and was disappointed when the dolphin was a stuffy.

"Among others."

There came a derisive snort from across the room. Tessa looked over to see a lanky young Asian man staring at her with arms folded and a smirk on his face. Astrid stood next to him. Tessa smiled broadly at her.

"Astrid! I didn't notice you come in."

Astrid shrugged, then thought-said. *Everything ok?*

Tessa nodded.

"So this is the Familiar, huh?" said the young man, running a hand through his thick black hair which sprung right back up and held in a high plateau. This seemed to be his intended look. His eyes were onyx black, the pupil undifferentiated from the iris. He moved toward Tessa, that crooked smirk staying fixed on his lips. "You thought he was a witch?" he jerked his head toward Jean. "How 'bout me? Do I look like a witch, Familiar?"

Tessa frowned. Though brand new to this world, she was pretty certain of one thing. "Your eyes are black. So… no."

"Wrong, Familiar!" The young man grinned and snapped his fingers. His eyes abruptly changed to that same weird, dancing green as Astrid and Cece, although the color was slightly bluer, more of a jade than a kelly green. "How is an Asian man supposed to blend in with eyes like this? If people like me—like us," he added, gesturing to Astrid, who was watching Oscar with wide-eyed fascination, her lip caught between her teeth. "If we didn't have a spell to hide who we were, we'd be dead."

"Chut, Oscar, please," Jean sighed, walking over to the kid and placing a giant hand on his shoulder.

Oscar wasn't short, but Jean was at least eight inches taller and twice as thick. Oscar went from looking like a menacing warlock man to a boy.

"Her name is Tessa, not Familiar. And she is our guest. And how do we treat guests?"

Oscar took a shoulder-heaving breath and muttered, eyes on his shoes. "We treat our guests with courtesy and respect, Nons and Magix alike."

*What about those Magic Destroyers?* The thought was intrusive, like someone else had dropped it into Tessa's mind. Of course, they wouldn't treat enemies with respect.

Jean was clapping Oscar on the back, booming, "Très bien," and nearly knocking the boy over.

"Not that we've ever *had* a Non as a guest before," Oscar added.

Jean ignored this comment, spreading his arms wide and exclaiming, "Now let's eat! À table, everyone."

He gave a flick of his wrist and the water in the pool began to swell up, raising the table on the crest of a wave that did not break as it flowed toward them and halted between the four of them. Shell-shaped chairs appeared from nowhere and scooped each of them up so that Tessa found herself sitting at the bounteously filled table without having moved her body at all. As quickly as it had come, the water receded back into the pool. Somehow, Tessa hadn't even gotten wet.

"And I suppose we have the Fam—Tessa—to thank for the lack of meat at dinner," Oscar said, pointing his fork toward Tessa's chest.

She glanced down, only now remembering her ratty t-shirt and the phrase on it. She looked over at Jean, who shrugged, before addressing Oscar. "I relish every opportunity to expand my cooking knowledge and expertise. You should be equally thrilled about expanding your palate."

Oscar rolled his eyes and stabbed the falafel with his knife. "Did you make the littles eat this?"

"So Astrid," Jean said. "Has Oscar given you the grand tour?"

"Dude, you can't ignore m—"

"Do you like your room? Is there anything else we can do to make you more comfortable?"

Oscar threw his hands in the air and the falafel went flying, landing in the pool with a small splash. Oscar looked from the pool to Jean. "I'm not getting that."

"Oh yes, you are," said Cece, who had suddenly appeared at the table and was digging into a full plate of food.

To Tessa's surprise, Oscar did not back talk Cece or even roll his eyes. He snapped his fingers and the falafel zoomed over to his plate. Then he tucked his head down and obediently started to eat. Cece and Jean exchanged a look and Tessa was sure this was a typical, though clearly frustrating, exchange. *At least he listens,* she thought.

"So anyway," Cece said. "Astrid, I think you were about to say something?"

Astrid had just taken a large bite of her pita wrap, so they waited for an awkward moment as she chewed. Tessa tried to watch Cece through her eyelashes. She wasn't good at it and almost instantly their eyes met across the table. Tessa made a show of pushing around the food on her plate and scooping up a colorful forkful. She spotted a picture on the refrigerator of Cece, Jean, and the children, including the tiny werewolf twins. She tried to tick off the seven Magick clans in her brain as she studied the photo.

*Vampires.* Luca's fangs were visible as he grinned wide. His red hair almost glowed like it was actually aflame. *Fairies.* Silas hovered beside his brother. He held two fingers behind Luca's head. *Werewolves.* There were the twins, big-eyed with bigger smiles. Dirt on their cheeks. Something wolfish about them, yes. *Sirens.* Jean's eyes sparkled like the surface of the sea. *Witches.* Cece's green eyes, like an answering call.

Bettie flew into the room and perched on Cece's shoulder.

"It's lovely here," Astrid finally said. "Oscar showed me around." She glanced at him with unfiltered and unabashed awe.

Tessa chanced another glance at Cece and found she was looking back at her. Tessa smiled, but then realized that she had parsley in her teeth, and closed her lips, desperately digging at the spot with her tongue.

*Shapeshifters.* Theo. That darks patch of freckles on their cheek. She hadn't thought about Theo in hours. Her heart clenched. Forgetting felt like a betrayal.

"My room's great, too," Astrid added.

"Decorate it however you like," Jean said. "You too, Tessa. The rooms are blank canvases limited only by your imaginations!"

Oscar made a dramatic show of rolling his eyes.

"Dude!" he shrieked, rubbing his nose. His spoon had stood up on end and bopped him.

Tessa smirked, half listening as she tried to remember the seventh clan.

"Not your dude," said Cece. "You know how I feel about the consistent disrespect you display toward Jean, the man who—I will remind you again! Saved. Your. Life."

"Sorry, Jean," Oscar muttered.

"But Cece, violence should never be the answer to conflicts between family," Jean whispered.

Cece sighed. "Sorry, Oscar."

"Ogres!" Tessa exclaimed.

All eyes shifted to her.

"Ogres," she repeated. "You never told me what their special skills are."

Astrid stifled a giggle.

"I believe they have superhuman strength and some amount of pyrokinesis," Cece said. "Anything else, Jean?"

"Affinity with snakes?"

"Right," Cece nodded. "They can talk to them, shift into them. I've even heard some are able to hypnotize, like sirens."

"With eye contact, rather than *la voix*," Jean added, singing the last two words.

"What about the... the AntiMagi?" Tessa asked.

Cece frowned. "The DOMs? What about them?"

"Their mutation? What exactly do they…" She trailed off because the faces in the room had all gone cloudy and unreadable.

Cece cleared her throat. "Let's talk about this another time, ok?"

"I didn't mean any—"

"I know. Another time."

The only sounds were the clink of utensils. Then Astrid set down her knife and fork with a bang that made them all jump.

"So we're just going to sit around here and act like everything's ok? Auntie, my parents are missing. Do you know where they might be? Can you help me find them?"

"Sassy—"

"Don't call me that. I told you! The House is lovely. The food's delicious. Everyone here is…" She glanced at Oscar. "Wonderful. But we don't have time to sit and eat fancy meals or take naps or… whatever! We need to *do* something! Before it's too late."

"I agree," Tessa said, thinking of Theo.

"Yay, the Familiar agrees!" Oscar said.

"Hey!" Astrid shouted. "Leave my Familiar alone, got it?"

Oscar blushed. "I—yeah, ok. Sorry. I-I agree. We should do something. Right, Cece? You guys have a plan?"

Cece looked down at her plate.

"We will!" Jean exclaimed. "In the morning, we will discuss. But first, a good night's sleep."

He snapped his fingers and the dishes and plates zoomed off the table and started cleaning themselves, dumping leftovers into Tupperware, which jumped into neat stacks in the fridge. Then the dishes dove in, one after another like synchronized swimmers. The pool was now filled with soap bubbles and the whole thing vibrated and hummed like a dishwasher, before the dishes suddenly flew into the air, spinning around as a warm breeze filled the room. Next, they all glided into cupboards, stacking themselves in neat piles and rows. The whole thing took less than a minute and Tessa found herself standing again in the middle of a large and empty kitchen. Her mouth was hanging wide open and even Astrid was chuckling at her.

"Ok, so, I guess good night then," Oscar mumbled, pushing past everyone.

"First thing in the morning, Oscar!" Jean hollered.

"We'll meet in the living room at 7:00 a.m. sharp," Cece added.

Oscar groaned. "How about 10:00?"

Cece rolled her eyes. "8:00."

"I'll make breakfast," Jean said.

Oscar's eyes narrowed. "With bacon?"

"Oui."

"Pig bacon?"

Jean glanced at Tessa who shrugged. "It's your house," she said.

"We'll have vegan and meat options, ok?"

"Aight. Pig bacon. 8:00 a.m. Fine," he said, pausing in the doorway. "You coming, Astrid?"

You could have burned down the house with the blaze of Astrid's smile. She practically skipped across the room, before stopping next to Tessa. "Your phone," she said, holding it out. "You dropped it in Salem. That Sanjay guy called a bunch. And someone named Trudy?"

"Shit, my boss," Tessa muttered, then said thanks to Astrid and good night to the others before hurrying upstairs to deal with the tedious details of her real life.

The phone battery was nearly dead and she didn't have a charger. Hurriedly, she typed up an email to her boss, cc'ing the head of HR, requesting FMLA leave for a recent, *emergency* foster placement. She italicized the word, then went back and bolded it as well. She knew she was fudging the timeline, but hopefully an emergency would be enough to explain why she'd gone offline in the middle of a workday without an explanation. She'd probably still get written up for it. Whatever. *A first for everything,* she thought. Her type-A, only-child personality was cringing at the thought, but her rational brain knew that one small demerit was nothing in the face of... of... *magic.* There was a poem about this. Tessa couldn't remember the name, but the words kept scrawling across her brain:

*What's magical, sometimes, has deeper roots than reason.*

Where had she read that? Or maybe it was something her mother had said?

She clicked send, heard the whoosh of the email getting sucked into the ether and past recovery. With the last five percent of her battery, she checked her voicemail.

"He-ey, T." Sanjay's voice sounded distracted. She could hear someone else in the background. "Checking in to see how it's going. I'll stop by tomorrow, k? Give me a call or text when you're done working, yeah?"

Tessa was too exhausted to call and too worried her phone would die mid-conversation, so she typed up a quick text:

*Sorry for delay. Decided to take Astrid out of town for a couple days. Don't come tomorrow since we aren't there. Be back soon.*

She clicked send and then quickly sent another note: *She's ok, I think. Doing better now.*

Sanjay's reply came almost immediately. *U can't just leave n not tell me.* Followed by *where r u?*

*Up north,* Tessa replied and then added, *Sorry,* with a frowning emoji.

*In the Leaf???* And Tessa almost smiled because that was Sanjay, the eternal skeptic and tease. She waited for the follow-up: *how many times did you have to charge it?* or something similar, but nothing came. Did he know she was lying? The Leaf was in her garage, so he wouldn't see it if he'd stopped by. Unless he looked *in* the garage?

Tessa typed. *Mom picked us up. We're in Cedar. With her.*

Three dots appeared then disappeared. She waited for the *omg Kathy!* comment. Sanjay loved Tessa's mom in a way that still baffled Tessa. All of the things that bothered her about her mother endeared her to Sanjay. "Kathy's good people, T," he would always say, which Tessa couldn't deny.

Again, nothing came through.

*Kid was in a bad place. Needed to act quick. Mom's good in a pinch,* Tessa added, hoping that would be enough. She set down her phone, closed her eyes, and was almost asleep when she heard the ding of a text. She groaned and picked up the phone.

*I'm trusting u. Don't make me regret it.*

Tessa frowned at the screen until it went black. Was the text really as menacing as it read? Tessa lay back down and decided to force the words from her mind, but she kept seeing them, black on gray, angry beside her white on blue message with its sheepish sad emoji.

Had she messed up? Was she being wildly irresponsible?

No, she was putting Astrid's needs first. Rule #1. She was trusting her (rule #4!) and following her lead. She was keeping her cool and managing expectations (rules #2 and #3). The situation was bizarre and unbelievable, but she was handling it in the best way she could.

Tessa fell asleep repeating her foster parenting rules over and over in her head, a soothing mantra that conjured memories of Theo's sweet face and, eventually, sleep.

* * *

## JAN 1978

### *January 18, 1978*

*Dear Morticia,*

> *May I use your first name? I've heard Val refer to you as "Tish," but that feels too informal. Or perhaps you are one of those people who detests being called by their full name?*

*Either way, enough with this "Mr. Engers" nonsense. Call me Gunner.*

*I, too, care about the future. Like you, I am a parent. I have two sons, Archer and Anthony. Archer, he's like me. Driven, inventive, and progressive, I dare say. He's also gone into the field of medicine, another hematologist. Anthony, well... he took after his mother, may her memory endure. He is intelligent beyond words, but he tends to focus on near-term problems.*

*Archer and I have been working on a special project for the Department of AntiMagi Health. They call it MAAM PAC: Magix and AntiMagi Projected Amalgamation Confederation. It's a mouthful, I know. But as the name indicates, it is a unifying endeavor. Future-minded.*

*I've been consulting for MAAM PAC for the past couple of years. I'd love to introduce you to the team, Dr. Chernoff. Your research into the DNA differences between Magick Clans was groundbreaking.*

*Your husband casts a wide shadow, but I see more pomp and show than true intellect and grit. For what the opinion of a "DOM" is worth to you.*

*Sincerely,*
*Gunner*

# CHAPTER

## SIX

**JULY 2023**

Someone was in her house. Tessa hovered in the doorway of her bedroom, peering out into the dark hall. She heard a scratching sound like small claws whining against a door. Then, there was a rush of air, not like a breeze, but like a sucking back, as if all the air in the house were being pulled into a giant vacuum. For a moment, there was no oxygen. The scratching turned to footsteps and the air returned. Tessa sucked in a breath, a desperate gasp that was too loud. The intruder would hear! Shit. Shit! She heard a voice then.

"T, you there?" It was Sanjay.

"I thought you said she wasn't home," came a second voice, a woman's, lilting like un-tuned, too-humid piano keys, flat and lazy and wet.

"Just making sure," Sanjay replied. His voice was pinched. He sounded anxious and...

something else. Excited? Afraid? Tessa fought an urge to call out.

"We shouldn't be here," he said.

"Even better," the woman growled.

There was a sound like a tussle, like a fight was happening below. Tessa put her hand over her mouth to keep herself quiet. She could hear their breathing, quick and quickening. And then she recognized the sound for what it was, heard the wet smack of body against body, the crash of her fruit bowl being shoved off the kitchen island, the tumble and roll of apples to the ground, and the moaning, which rose like the slow whine of the city's tornado siren, a low thrum growing louder and louder and louder until Tessa sat up with start, the rush of her pulsing heart like a gong against her eardrums. She was panting.

*Just a dream,* she told herself, looking around, disoriented. Where the hell was she?

It came rushing back to her all at once: the growing plants, Astrid's eyes, the glittery baubles in Cece's hair, the vaulted ceiling of The House, the green and the magic.

Tessa reached for her phone. It was dead. She set it back down and went to the window, drawing back the curtain. Outside, the sky was starting to catch a breath of light and the world was wet with a dousing blue. Her room looked out over someone's backyard. There was a child's ball and half-covered sandbox in the yard. It was so achingly ordinary that she might have been looking out the window of her own house. The thought of her house brought back the chill of the dream and Tessa shivered.

She slid her dead phone into the pocket of her dirty sweatpants as she left the quiet dark of her room, tiptoeing down the dimly lit hallway, above which the magical lights glowed faintly orange. From downstairs, she heard the faint sounds of a waking household: cupboards being opened and the murmur of adult voices. She smelled the deep and smoky scent of a dark-roast coffee and smiled, quickening her step in anticipation.

The sliding doors to the kitchen were wide open. Inside, as she suspected, were Cece and Jean, clad in matching flowery kimono-style bathrobes, cups of steaming coffee clutched between their hands and held close to their faces. Cece had changed her hair, the sparkling puffs traded for a bejeweled pompadour that seemed entirely too fancy for the morning and made Tessa grin.

Jean and Cece breathed in and out, not speaking, not seeing her yet, and the ordinariness of that domestic scene rolled over Tessa. She felt like a voyeur, unwelcome and apart. At the same time, it was hard—nearly impossible—to marry this vision of Cece and Jean, standing inches apart and silent in the intimate way of long-married couples, with the magical, disheveled living room in which she stood. The ordinariness was a farce and it made Tessa more uneasy than the chaos. She cleared her throat. Cece and Jean started at the noise. Their heads turned as one to look at her. Jean's face broke into a grin.

"Ah, bonjour, Tessa!" he exclaimed, arms open wide as he came toward her. Tessa allowed herself to be lifted up in his embrace.

Over his shoulder, Tessa could see Cece, a hint of a smile on her lips as she said, "Jean, for god's sake. You'll scare her off."

Jean set Tessa down, patting her shoulder awkwardly as he did it.

Tessa held up her phone. "Do either of you have an iPhone charger? Or do Magix like… do… technology?"

Cece rolled her eyes before digging into a drawer and hoisting out a lightning cable. "Voilà. We aren't in some tucked-away segregated fantasy world like all your Non writers always seem to imagine. We use tech *and* magic."

"Thanks." Tessa took the cord, plugging it into the wall, then her phone.

"Un café?" Jean asked as Tessa turned around.

"Please!"

Taking the coffee, Tessa held the mug in her hands and lifted it to her nose, inhaling the earthy warmth. She closed her eyes and thought of Theo, sitting at her kitchen island, drinking a mug of hot chocolate, how they'd looked up at Tessa as she entered the room, their nose white with whipped coconut cream, and grinned. They were missing their top incisors. It was the first time she'd seen them grin since they'd come to her.

She opened her eyes and found Cece watching her. Neither looked away, even as the gaze turned awkward.

Finally, Cece said, "Yesterday, I told you we'd talk more."

Tessa let out a breath she didn't realize she'd been holding. She'd been waiting for this, an explanation. She needed it, though she couldn't let Cece know how desperate she was.

"Yeah, sure. Talk about what?" she asked, overcompensating. "I mean... about what? Specifically." Instinct told her it was all part of the same story: what happened to Astrid's parents, the destroyed coven, Morana and Theo. They were connected somehow. She couldn't have verbalized the thought, let alone the rationale behind it. But she *felt* it. These were Theo's people. They would lead her back to them. "There's a lot we need to talk about."

"Oh là," Jean laughed, blowing out a gust of air. "That is... an understatement."

"You think?" Cece said to Jean, before turning to Tessa. "I need to explain... what's going on."

"The war, you mean?"

Cece's eyes narrowed. Even Jean looked taken aback, his mouth slightly open. "How did you—?" Cece began.

"Astrid told me there was a war, between Magix and your opposites, the AntiMagi—"

"The DOMs," Cece cuts in. "The Destroyers of Magic. What else did Astrid tell you?"

Tessa tried to recall everything Astrid had said. She could feel her brow furrowing with the effort. "That it was... worse, than before."

"Again, an understatement. We—Magix—have always been hated by Non society."

"There've been bad times before," Cece piped in. "I'm sure you've heard of some of the greater purges. Salem, of course. The sixteenth and seventeenth centuries were the pinnacle of the DOMs' powers. Their goal then—and now—was to destroy magic."

"They nearly did. We went into even deeper hiding during and ever since."

"Smaller purges have happened since, even a vampire panic in New England in the 1800s. Look it up, if you're skeptical! Nons died of tuberculosis and their families and neighbors dug up their bodies afterwards, mutilating their corpses because they thought they were vampires, rising from their graves to kill off their friends and neighbors. As if a vampire were nothing more than a monster."

Jean swore and muttered, "dégoûtant" with a shudder.

"It's the way of the world," Cece continued. "The DOMs sow their anti-magic propaganda and we're blamed for everything. If you want to understand us—" She wiggled her index finger between Jean and herself, "—and Astrid, you have to understand this. It goes beyond the DOMs hunting us. The fibers holding together the Non world are against us."

"I don't get it," Tessa blurted.

"Don't get what?" Cece folded her arms across her chest. "For the last decade, the DOMs have built up their power. They've made some unlikely alliances that—"

"No, I don't understand why you're afraid of Nons."

"We're not," Cece replied flatly, head cocked to one side.

"Ok, well—the DOMs then. You're afraid of them."

Cece inclined her head in acquiescence. Jean nodded as well.

"The DOMs are…" A shudder convulsed through Cece's body.

"They are different." Jean placed a hand on Cece's arm.

"Different how?"

Cece and Jean exchanged a look. Jean continued, "Their allies include powerful Nons, higher ups in your political system, as high up as—"

"Do either of you actually *know* what the DOMs are?" Tessa interrupted.

Jean's mouth flapped open a few times. Cece shook her head and sighed. "My understanding is that they are also genetic mutants, a human variant."

"So… not really that different from Magix?"

Jean hissed in a breath. It was the sound a devotee makes in the face of heresy.

Cece shook her head. "You have to understand, Tessa. This isn't just about DOMs trying to kill Magix. Their chaos and violence seeps into the Non world, too. The war on Magix affects everyone. Since Magix aren't beholden to the morals of Non society, DOMs exploit that, take advantage of Nons in their—"

"Naïveté?"

Cece sighed. "If Nons are the puppets, DOMs hold the strings."

"This is all a little too conspiracy theory for me," Tessa sighed.

Cece shrugged. "How's this for a conspiracy theory? Right now, a secret government organization within the United States is working to eradicate Magix. Government protection means money and resources beyond any the DOMs have had in centuries."

"If it's secret, then how do you know about it?" Tessa asked.

"Touché," Jean smirked.

"Before our coven was… well, we used to be tapped into a lot of resources."

"Like in the government?"

Cece nodded. "We were gaining power. Maybe a week or two before the… before it happened, a couple of our coven members had discovered evidence that some Magix were working *for* the DOMs."

"Wait, what?"

"Unbelievable, I know, given the DOMs' history and purpose. I don't know much, but I have to think these Magix would be using the DOMs as a means to an end."

"The end being…?"

"The subordination and enslavement of all Nons. In order to do that, they've got to eliminate those of us who dissent, anyone who might, if pushed, fight them."

Tessa realized her mouth was hanging open slightly. She closed it.

"With Magix on their side plus government money and resources," Cece continued, "the DOMs have become far more powerful than they've ever been. Three years ago, amid a global pandemic and a rising tide of violence, they made their first move. It happened all around the country, a series of coordinated attacks. A dozen covens were entirely wiped out."

"How?" Tessa blurted. "You all are *Magix*. How could anyone who doesn't have magic possibly kill you? I mean, I know there's the DOMs, the Destroyers of Magic or whatever. Sorry, but *still*. What is the catch here? You're hiding like you have no power but all I see is power. You can hypnotize people and talk to birds and make plants grow. Couldn't you just choke them out with some aggressive morning glories?" She petered out with a heavy sigh. "I don't get it."

She expected anger and eye rolls, but Jean looked sad, eyes on the ground, and Cece was nodding, her gaze focused, unwavering on Tessa. "We should go for a walk."

"Like outside?" Tessa asked, grimacing when she thought about the air quality.

Cece nodded. "It shouldn't be too bad out there, this early." It was as if she could read Tessa's thoughts. "We'll be back by eight, Jean."

Jean nodded, a smile on his lips, but his eyes were churning and wet. "Take your time, my love."

Bettie swooped down from nowhere to perch on Cece's shoulder as they walked into the mudroom. Cece opened the side door and held it as Tessa stepped outside into an alleyway. As Cece turned to lock the door, Bettie lifted off her shoulder and flew up high into the widening dawn, becoming a black and fading smudge.

"She likes to keep an eye on me," Cece said, locking the door and quickly starting to walk down the alley.

Tessa stood there, looking up at the building they had come out of. It was a tiny, unmarked industrial building with barred windows and a heavy padlocked door.

*Tessa.* Cece's voice was in her ear. She looked up to see that Cece was still walking away from her, head down. *Don't linger. Please.*

Tessa followed after her at a jog, wincing as she filled her lungs with polluted air. But it was better this early in the day. She caught up to Cece once they'd reached the main road. Tessa recognized the area immediately. She'd grown up here.

"Alger Heights," she said. "This is my neighborhood. It's not even a mile from my house. We could've walked."

"I *did* walk yesterday."

It took Tessa a disorienting moment to realize that yes, it had been yesterday that she'd woken up in her own bed. Above her, the edges of the sky were turning orange, like paper catching fire. Even in the brightening light, Cece had her dark sunglasses on. She'd pulled a hood over her head to hide her sparkling poofs. "We hide because of the DOMs and their powers. I can't explain the DOMs' powers. I don't understand them myself. If we have magic in our veins then what runs through them could best be described as anti-magic. I don't know where it came from or how it works. I only know what it looks like." She turned her head toward Tessa and though her eyes were covered, Tessa could tell from the tight set of her jaw and thin line of her lips that she was holding in a tide of grim feelings. "Let's walk a little farther. I'll tell you everything."

* * *

**AUG 1978**                    ***August 18, 1978***

*Internal Memo*

*Re: MAAM PAC's New Direction*

*From: Marcus Brand*

*To: Gunner Engers and Archer Engers*

*Cc: Tish Chernoff, Valerie Hart*

*Objective: to discover if a Magick and an AntiMage can reproduce a living offspring and if said offspring would inherit any or all traits from their parents.*

*Attachments and Prior Research: I have attached the records from your predecessors, a decade's worth of research into what they are calling: in vitro fertilization, or fertilization outside the womb. I am told the Nons have mastered it among their own, but it has been an abysmal failure in meeting our Objective.*

*As such, we will not limit your creativity or scientific methods. Take notes, make hypotheses. We do not particularly care about the "how." We care about results.*

*Due Date: December 31, 1980*

*Result: A live birth or definitive proof that a live birth will not be possible.*

*Our Oversight Committee will be expecting weekly reports on your progress.*

# CHAPTER
## SEVEN

**JULY 2023** Tessa and Cece continued in silence. Their steps on the pavement barely made a sound. They were walking and then Cece was talking, but Tessa couldn't quite remember when she had started. A wave of prose had crashed over Tessa and she was floating about in the churning middle of things.

*We were always strange, as far as covens go. The Grand River Coven was decentralized with a chapter in each quadrant of Grand Rapids: Northeast, Northwest, Southeast, and Southwest. Most covens have one leader; we had seven. Three couples ran three of the chapters and Jean—yes, our Jean—ran the Southwest on his own. If decisions had to be made for the whole of the coven, they voted. Good, old American democracy style. By contrast, most covens are monarchies, with leadership passed down from parent to child. Yes, even in the US, this was the tradition until about a hundred years ago when Grand River was founded.*

*I lived in the Southeast chapter with Astrid. Her parents, Aurora Laveau and Zack Laveau-Miller, were the chapter leaders. I'd known Aura since we were children. I came to the Grand River Coven for her. I'd been coven-less for... well, that's another story.*

*The day of the first attacks started like any other spring day for us. It was mild, such a quintessentially May-in-Michigan morning. Aura and I had gone for a walk. She is my sister, not by blood, but by choice and by magic, which is so much deeper. The Southeast's headquarters were that way, to the north a bit, tucked back in that industrial complex between Eastern and Madison. We liked to walk around it in the earliest parts of the morning, before the asphalt sun-warmed, when you can smell the dew on the grass, feel the light tugging you awake, and hear the birds crying out their greetings and thanks. Mornings like that... I've always felt anything was possible.*

*We lingered on our walk. I was telling Aura some stupid piece of gossip about one of the younger coven members. I remember nothing about the conversation except that it was petty. Then her phone rang.*

*"It's Vasily," she said. He and Aura, leaders of two eastern quadrants, had a meeting scheduled that morning. "He's probably already there," Aura sighed.*

*I rolled my eyes. "He's like fifteen minutes early, then," I said. "Can't he wait?*

*Vasily had been a pain in our asses since he and his wife had taken over the Northeast chapter several years before. They'd come from Denver, previously. The Denver Coven was a bit too... anti-Non for my taste. There are some virulently anti-Non covens, Tessa.*

*Aura ignored the first call. "We should head back." A second call came through. This time, she answered.*

*Her face... I'll never forget the way her jaw dropped after she'd snapped an abrupt "What Vas?" She stopped walking and stood there with the phone against her ear. There were screams on the other end; it took me several seconds to recognize those sounds, high and keening, for what they were. It sounded like a rock concert was happening on the other end, so much loud, undulating sound. After half a minute, Aura started to tremble. The phone almost fell from her grip and I grabbed it and put it to my ear. Then I heard the pop-pop-popping, over and over. To you, it would sound like a machine gun firing. It is the most terrifying sound in the whole of the magical world. It is the sound of the DOMs, the sound of magic—Magix—destroyed. It is anti-*

*magic at work. Literally, it is the sound of a body imploding, the pop of every drop of liquid being sucked from a living, breathing human so that they simply... pop... into ash. I'd heard the sound once before. But this...*

*I looked at Aura. Her lips were moving. Forty-one, forty-two, -three, -four.*

*I realized she was counting the pops, the deaths.*

*How many people were in Northeast coven? And then I realized...*

*"No, no, no! He's... that's our... those are—Vasily!"*

*The line went dead.*

*Aura stood there, her eyes glazed over, her jaw moving without words.*

*"We have to get back," I said, taking her limp hand. I was about to transport us back to headquarters when I heard Bettie's frantic caw coming from above. I knew then, the moment I heard her cry, that it was too late. My Bettie. Oh, in many ways, she is an extension of me, my vision and my heart torn out to soar free. In her call, I heard the breaking of my world, the snaps and pops of my people disappearing.*

*I fell to my knees then. "They're gone?"*

*This must have woken Aura from her shock-trance because she grabbed my hand and pulled me through with her. We arrived to blood and ash. I learned that day that the DOMs have many ways of killing us, of pulling out our magic. There were mummified corpses and fossilized corpses like something out of fucking Pompeii. There was ash.*

*And then there were bodies, bones broken in odd ways, jaws overextended and snapped, eyes missing, organs pulled out and left to rot on the floor. Those bodies, though, weren't the DOMs. That was Magix killing Magix. I didn't realize it, didn't even consider it at the time. I remember looking at the body of the young woman I'd been complaining about mere minutes before. Had she already been like this when I'd spoken those words? Or had her jaw snapped as I was speaking? Had her entrails been ripped from her even before I spoke her name with sour disdain? The look in her dead eyes was so sad. I remember thinking that I would have died with fury on my face, but at that time, I thought DOMs had killed her. I didn't know.*

*It was so goddamn quiet. I could hear a single fly buzz and I hated that stupid-ass creature, alive and eager for its feast.*

*Then the quiet was gone and Aura was shouting for Astrid and Zack. I tried to clap a hand over her mouth, but she kicked me in the gut and kept screaming. No one came. The DOMs had already left, taking the traitor Magix with them. I realized that it was over then; they'd only left the dead in their wake.*

*I let Aura scream then. She screamed and screamed. My phone rang. I heard it as if it was from another world. It was so strange, the sound of it, all morphed and muffled, like it was ringing from under water and fifty feet in the air at the same time.*

*When I finally processed what it was, the call had gone to voice-mail. It rang again. I picked it up without even registering who was calling.*

*"Hello?"*

*"Auntie?"*

*"Astrid?"*

*Aura grabbed the phone from me and between her sobs, manic laughter, and rapid-fire questioning, I gathered that Zack and Astrid were both safe. They'd gone to visit Zack's parents that morning. They'd gotten a warning call, like we had received from Vasily, but from another coven member. They had reached out to the other chapters. No one answered in Northeast or Northwest chapters. But the Southwest had survived. Jean's chapter. I barely knew Jean at the time. I knew he was French and a siren and massive.*

*"We're going to go there," Aura said, taking my hand.*

*I don't remember transporting. I'm sure we took detours, probably several, but it was all a blur.*

*The Southwest's headquarters were beneath an old, abandoned swing bridge, formerly used by trains to cross over the river. Leave it to a siren to erect a water fortress invisible to the Non-eye. The attack left the headquarters in shambles, largely uninhabitable, with water pouring in from half a dozen fissures in the foundation. That kind of damage to magic... it makes me shudder even now. I remember looking at Jean again and again as we worked for hours evacuating the survivors. He was relentless, diving into the rising waters to search for people, hauling them up, half dead, and reviving them. Single-handedly, he must have rescued twenty people.*

*When he pulled up Oscar, I really thought the kid was dead. His eyes were open, unseeing. But Jean wouldn't let him go. Jean put his hands on the kid's chest and the water kept coming up from his mouth. Jean was weeping, crying out, "Aidez-moi, s'il vous plaît, s'il vous plaît!"*

*I knelt beside him and put my hands on Oscar's chest, too. I didn't expect anything to happen; the kid was dead. I had come over to help Jean. But then, oh Tessa, it was the strangest thing I've ever experienced. I'm sure that's hard for you to believe, but in that moment, I must have felt a lot like you've been feeling since yesterday: like everything I thought I knew about the world and myself was wrong.*

*I've never told anyone this. I'm not sure why I'm telling you. Maybe because if you tell anyone, they'll dismiss you as "just a Non." I'm sorry for that. Grateful, too, I suppose.*

*When I put my hands on Oscar, I felt the anti-magic in him. No water in his lungs. He wasn't drowning. A piece of anti-magic was in him, small as a splinter, like shrapnel from a blast. It was lodged in his right lung. I could see it so clearly, this black thing, growing larger on his lung, like a cancer distorting all the magic into something deadly.*

*I didn't think. I didn't contemplate what to do. I just reached for it with my mind and it dislodged for me. I watched it rise from him and come to settle in my hand. As I held it there, it disintegrated.*

*I was so fascinated and appalled by the whole thing I didn't realize Oscar had started to breathe. Jean was holding him to his chest and weeping. If he saw the anti-magic, if he understood what I did, he said nothing. He's never mentioned it since.*

*There, that's my weird secret. I expect you to give me one of your own someday in return, got it?*

*Anyway, later, after we'd rescued the living, we hauled out the bodies of our fallen. There were dead DOMs here too. We left them to waterlog and rot.*

*Aura and Zack led the survivors to a new location, north of the city, a farmstead near Cedar Springs that the coven had purchased decades back but never used much. It doesn't matter anymore. It's gone too, now.*

*Rescue missions were sent to the Northwest and Northeast. At first, we thought the Northwest was obliterated. It had been run by a fairy family. Silas' family. They couldn't find any remains of children. We knew there were children there: a fairy boy and toddler vampire. After much searching, we were able to find the hidden portal that led to a lakeside outpost. Silas and Luca survived out there for the better part of a day before our patrol found them. They were scared, but fine, thank god.*

*As for the Northeast, we found no survivors.*

*And so, the plan was to regroup, move, and consolidate the coven into this rural farm, tucked away and secret. But there were concerns, particularly about a few key survivors: the Laveau-Millers, Jean, Luca and Silas, Oscar, and me.*

*As chapter leaders, Astrid's parents and Jean were obvious follow-up targets. There were many coven members that feared a second attack, particularly if it was learned that Jean, Aura, and Zack were still alive.*

*Astrid, Silas, Luca, and Oscar were the only surviving children. It was imperative to keep the next generation living.*

*And me... well, I'm less famous among my clan than infamous. The Grand River Coven hadn't really wanted me in the first place, but Aura had vouched for me when I joined. Once again, she vouched for me and this time, Jean did as well.*

*Astrid's family left the coven and went into deep hiding among the Nons.*

*Jean and I were tasked with the care and keeping of the children. I was given a new name and identity: Cari Walker, high school history teacher. My real name is Cordelia Connolly, by the way. I don't know if*

*I ever told you that. I don't tell many people that. Another secret for you.*

*Anyway, I own the house, or rather, Cari Walker owns it. As far as any Nons, DOMs, or even most Magix are concerned, I'm the only resident. Jean and the children do not exist.*

*The hope was that, in time, things would settle down and we could rejoin the coven eventually.*

*It goes without saying that things haven't gotten better. There have been small attacks on other covens across the country on and off for the last three years. We believe these attacks are all related, orchestrated by the same group that led the initial, large attack, an alliance of DOMs and Magix. It seems their ranks were severely diminished after the initial attack, so they have slowed their onslaught but not relented. The twins actually were sent to us last year by the Detroit Pack, a coven of werewolves that had lost all of their Magix in a series of small attacks, save the babies and a few elders who had been hiding them.*

*About a year ago, we lost all means of communicating with covens outside of our own. We weren't sure what had happened, but then we heard… rumors at first, then verified reports… that one of our own, the leader of the Northeast chapter, Vasily's wife, who we'd thought was murdered with all the others in the Northeast, was back. She'd been a double agent, the whole time. She was the reason so many had died and she's back to finish the job.*

* * *

# AUG 1979

## August 3, 1979

*Val,*

*My opinion? We're never going to make it. This is an impossible task. My dad is off gallivanting in Haiti looking for ogres to study since all the early studies left them out. He wrote to me about an ogre woman. According to him, when they first met she introduced herself as an ogre and said, "If you are shocked, then I suggest you check your biases. No, we were not obliterated. We are still fucking here, you asshole."*

*She seems impressive and* he *seems quite taken with her. If you ask me, he's distracted. An ogre isn't the solution. Hell, I'm not even sure it is possible, to mix the DNA of a Magick and a DOM. I've reviewed the old studies; they're brutal. Fetuses coming out all sorts of mangled, dead mothers, sometimes even dead would-be fathers. It's... we evolved into very, very different types of humans, Magix and AntiMagi. I sometimes wonder if we can even all be considered the same species: Nons, Magix, AntiMagi. The DNA says we are, but at the same time... if you start mixing Magick with DOM, you get these catastrophic creatures. Un-creatures. And what about Nons? I can't help thinking about how thoroughly unexceptional they are from an evolutionary standpoint. And yet, they endure. Remarkably unremarkable.*

*It's possible we are looking in all the wrong places.*

*Archer*

*P.S. In your last letter, you asked if I preferred AntiMage. I have no preference, but appreciate the concern. Thank you. For me, DOM, AntiMage, it's all the same. Call me Archer. That's all the respect I need. I am me, far more than my upbringing or DNA alone.*

# CHAPTER
# EIGHT



The sun had nearly risen now, but Tessa felt cold as a chill of terror and understanding spread through her.

Cece had stopped walking, pausing in front of a quick-stop convenience store. They were at the heart of the neighborhood, a quiet little city within a city. Across the street was the library. kitty-corner, there was a coffee shop, a restaurant, a grocery store, and a line of other local venues. Around them, traffic was picking up. A man jostled past them. Tessa watched Cece, waiting for her to continue. When she did, the words were so predictable Tessa felt she could have spoken them herself.

"The leader of the Northeast chapter, her name is Morana Aronov. I believe you know her."

Overhead, the rising sun banded the sky with strips of pink and orange. The electric wires cut thick black lines across it, like angry cuts along a tapestry. Tessa watched a raven—Bettie, she realized—tear across the sky and land on a power line. Bettie screeched, a loud and angry sound that called out to the rage simmering through Tessa's body.

"Astrid told me about Theo," Cece started to continue, but Tessa cut her off.

"Why didn't you take them?" Tessa asked. "You took the others, Silas, Luca, and Oscar, but not Theo. They would have been safe with you."

Tessa knew it was irrational, this anger, even as Cece held out her palms in defensive deflection, proclaiming: "We didn't know!"

They hadn't known. Cece had said they thought everyone in the Northeast died.

"Morana didn't want us to know," Cece continued, which made sense.

If Morana was a double agent working with the DOMs, she certainly wouldn't want her kid inundated with anti-DOM rhetoric. *She'd want them somewhere else,* Tessa thought. *Somewhere separate, but safe.* Tessa hated Morana, but a shitty mother was still a mother. Tessa felt her rapid breathing slow, but then Cece went on.

"I don't think Theo wanted to be found either."

"The hell does that mean?" Tessa bristled. "Theo's a *good* kid." She remembered Cece's warning about shapeshifters, how their ability was the most corrupted power in history.

"I didn't say they weren't good. Tessa – listen, Theo, they were safe with you. Safer and probably happier than any Magick could've ever hoped to keep them. Why would they want to be found? They were *out* of it all; all the hate and the violence."

"Now *she* has them," Tessa snarled. "If they'd been hidden, they'd still be safe."

Cece sighed and started walking again, turning a corner onto a side street lined with neat brick and vinyl Cape Cod houses.

Tessa followed after, jogging to keep up. "You never even tried to look for them." Fury pressed against her skull, darkening her peripheral vision.

*Don't let her take me, Mom.* Tessa would never forgive herself for letting Theo go. And if she could never forgive herself, then how could Cece keep walking, back straight, head held high, as if she had nothing to do with any of it, as if she didn't even care?

*If you loved me, you'd fight for me.*

"So why'd nobody want you in their coven, huh?" Tessa's voice was low, a gathering storm.

Ahead of her, Cece stopped walking.

"You say shifters are dangerous and that Theo was trying to stay hidden, which implies—*you* are implying—Theo is dangerous. You don't know them. And I don't know you. Should I trust you? Should I be scared of you?"

Cece turned and Tessa had her answer. Standing before Tessa was a stranger, not the Cece she'd first seen on her doorstep, nor the Cece she'd just been talking to. This was why people—*Nons*—were afraid of witches and magic. Cece was a creature to be feared. Her face had hardened, not metaphorically but literally. It had the chiseled appearance of a sculpture and Tessa knew if she reached out to touch Cece's face, it would feel smooth and cold as granite. Set in her stone face, Cece's green eyes had turned to fire, hot blue and green and white flames dancing within cavernous sockets. She opened her mouth and her voice was the bubbling of potions, the clanging of a caldron, the sickly sweet hum of a temptress, the hiss of a black cat, and the whip and crackle of electricity.

"You should be terrified of me," Cece boomed. "But I'm not the reason Morana has Theo. You are."

Tessa felt her teeth clang firmly against each other as she set her jaw. She clenched her fists, readying for a battle she was doomed to lose.

Cece continued in that roiling cackle. "A Familiar's job is to protect their Magick. You, Tessa, are the reason Theo is no longer safe."

As abruptly as she had transformed into that fearful being, Cece changed back. She shook her head and looked at Tessa with a grimace. "I—I... that was too much."

Only then did Tessa feel the silent tears streaming down her face.

Cece glanced around her, looking for a snooping neighbor dragging out their trash or perhaps a spy in crow or squirrel form. "I shouldn't have..." she murmured as she spun around, preparing for an attack that didn't come. She turned back to Tessa, placed a hand on her arm. "I shouldn't have done that. For several reasons. I'm sorry."

"No," Tessa whispered. "You were right." It was Tessa's fault. It always had been.

Cece gripped Tessa's elbow. "We should get back. But we'll have to transport again. If someone saw, they could follow us on foot."

"Couldn't someone see us leave? If we disappear, wouldn't that freak them out?"

"Nons don't notice those things. If they did, they'd dismiss it as a trick of their eyes or their brains, depending on how highly they think of themselves." She chuckled.

"What about Bettie then?" Tessa's stomach was already churning at the thought of transporting.

"She's probably already back. She's an odd bird. Despises the sun. Now this time, keep your eyes closed and think of kittens or puppies. Something soft and happy."

Tessa closed her eyes, remembering the day she'd brought Theo to a farm, where they'd discovered a litter of tiny kittens hiding under a porch step. Theo had cradled the black cat close and named it Chester and somehow, though she was certain there was no way Theo could have squirreled the cat away, a black kitten had appeared at their front door that same evening. Every night, Chester would come to the door to be fed and curl up with Theo in their bed.

After Theo left, Chester never came looking for them.

* * *

## JAN 1980

### January 3, 1980

*Tish,*

*A strange thing has happened and Tish, I think I've cracked it! Please, don't be angry. You and I—well, I hope you know what you mean to me, what you will always mean to me. I hope you will not let this get in the way of us.*

*I apologize for obfuscating. I'll be direct. I met a woman in my travels this past summer. An ogre woman. I wrote some about her in my notes, but I did not include this: We were intimate on several occasions. Truthfully, I wasn't going to tell you about her. We have never been exclusive, you and I, so I do not know why I hesitated to tell you of her. Perhaps it is because she was more like you, a Magick, than any of my others.*

*I am telling you now because I have received a letter from her informing me she is pregnant and the baby is mine. Can you believe it? She is in her third trimester. It took her some time to track down my information.*

*But Tish—a baby! A baby born of a Magick and an AntiMage. This is everything.*

*Yours, Gunner*

* * *

## January 3, 1980

*Gunner,*

*What incredible news. Incredible! Where is this woman? We must find her and bring her here to deliver in our facilities. Are you free tonight? Come to my house. Andor is out. He'll have the girl, Ana, with him. Val will be here. She can type up notes. I'll invite Archer. We will write to the Committee.*

*Always and forever – Tish*

# CHAPTER
## NINE

**JULY 2023** Back at The House, everyone else was already gathered in the living room with Bettie circling and squawking above. Tessa entered ahead of Cece and at the sight of her, the two toddlers—the twin *werewolves!*—froze, looking up at Tessa with wary gray eyes. If it weren't for the blood on their mouths and chests, they would have looked like little blond cherubs, both dressed only in matching elephant cloth diapers. Not blood, Tessa realized. Ketchup. They had ketchup smeared all over them. There was even ketchup on the tufts of blond hair on their ears and smeared into the thick fur-like hair on the backs of their necks as well. As soon as Cece came into view, they relaxed, faces breaking into wide grins.

"Excuse the mess," Jean chortled, brandishing a wet washcloth at each of the breakfast-dirtied twins. "Come on, children. Clean up time!"

Silas and Luca, sharing none of the twins' reticence, came flying and bounding, respectively, over to Tessa with wild-eyed enthusiasm. Luca was already gabbing on about some book Silas had been reading to him about dragons and asking Tessa if she had ever seen a dragon in real life.

"Dragons aren't real, silly," Silas said. "They're fiction."

"But dragons are reptiles, Silas," Luca countered, his arms spread wide, palms open for emphasis. "And reptiles are real. So dragons are real. Right?"

"Wrong!"

"You know," Tessa said, taking a seat beside Jean on the non-submerged portion of the couch. "Up until yesterday, I didn't think fairies or vampires existed. So maybe dragons are real and we haven't found them yet."

There was a moment of contemplative silence. Then they both shouted, Silas leading and Luca repeating his words moments later, "Mama! Papa! (Mama! Papa!) Can we go dragon searching? (Can we go dragon searching?) Please! (Please!)"

"Not today," Cece sighed, raising her eyebrows at Tessa as she walked over and sat in the chair across from Tessa and Jean, the only open seating that wasn't partially submerged or floating.

She wrinkled her nose and grimaced at Tessa, "Good job there."

"Expertly handled," Jean chuckled.

Tessa mouthed *sorry* to both of them.

Jean waved her off. "Plus de café?"

"More coffee? Yes, please! Black is fine."

Jean was up and back from the kitchen in what Tessa would have previously deemed an impossibly short amount of time. He handed steaming mugs of coffee to Tessa and Cece. Once again, the coffee smelled so normal Tessa nearly swooned from the disorienting whiplash wave. Then Bettie let out a squawk, came down, and landed next to Tessa on the arm of the chair. So much for normal. Tessa took a deep breath and a sip.

"So we're all here now," Astrid said, glaring at Tessa pointedly. "Now let's talk. What is the *plan*?" She sat on one of the floating chairs, pumping her legs back and forth like she was on a swing. The chair rose and fell in response. "We need to find my parents."

"And we should go back to the farmstead, to Grand River Coven's headquarters"

"Jean, you know I already looked," Cece interrupted. "As soon as we lost contact with them, I sent Bettie. There was nothin—"

"—Sending the bird is not the same as going yourself. We must check again to see if anyone else survived and was in hiding when Bettie checked," Jean added.

"Ok, fine," Cece agreed. "We also need to try to reach out to other surviving covens. We have to get stronger if we are going to survive. We may not be able to hide out this round of hunts."

"We've got to fight back," Oscar nodded.

"I never said fight," Cece clarified.

"Hi-yah!" Luca yelled, jumping up and karate chopping a side table.

To Tessa's shock, the thing split neatly in half.

"Bravo!" Jean clapped and Luca beamed, hopping into his lap for snuggles.

"I *said* we may not be able to hide. Not the same as fighting."

Oscar rolled his eyes.

"It's a start," Jean said, leaning forward to squeeze Oscar's shoulder.

Oscar allowed the touch for a second before shrugging him off.

The twins were roasting marshmallows on a pretend fire and throwing blocks into it amicably until one hit the other in the face, causing a shriek, a tussle, and a flurry of fur as both toddlers began to change, growing hairy, their noses elongating into almost-snouts, their ears extending as their fury turned them feral and wolf-like.

"No biting, Lola." Cece lifted her up by the scruff of her furry neck, then shifted her to her hip as Lola quickly morphed back into an adorable human toddler.

Livy, meanwhile, was howling, screaming, "Wowa bited me!" She ran over to Jean who scooped her up as well.

"You're ok, sweetheart," he said, patting her back.

"We need to find my parents first," Astrid continued. "And any other survivors. Before we go to war, we have to have all our people, right?"

Again, Oscar nodded vigorously. "Absolutely."

"Astrid," Cece said. "You know I want to find your parents. But…"

"But you think it's hopeless," Astrid sneered. "You think they're dead."

"No, I don't. I think that Aura and Zack can handle themselves. They'll find a way back to us; I *know* it. I also know they wouldn't want you putting yourself in harm's way to go looking for them. I found you so I could keep you safe and that's what I am going to do."

"I don't need you to keep me safe," Astrid replied, hopping down from the floating chair and coming toward Cece with her chest puffed out, looking so angry and bereft that she seemed decades older than fifteen. "I have my Familiar."

Tessa blanched at the same time as Cece chuckled. It was a derisive, pitying sound and Tessa's face turned even whiter, not from surprise, but from that same cold rage that had filled her earlier.

*A Familiar's job is to protect their Magick.* How could Cece say that and then scoff at Astrid's notion that a Familiar would protect her? *You, Tessa, are the reason that Theo is no longer safe.* It was personal, then. Cece didn't trust *her* to keep Astrid safe.

Tessa's fists clenched. She opened her mouth, but Jean cut in.

"I'll go to the Laveau-Millers' house this morning, d'accord?"

"Jean—" Cece sighed.

"Oh là, Cece, enough of your objections," Jean said, his voice losing its boisterous note and betraying his exhaustion. "We have to try. I'll take Oscar with me. We'll go to the house, then to the farm, see if we can find anything at the coven headquarters, maybe check the nearby houses, too—"

"Bettie checked the houses, too, Jean. She found no signs of life—"

"Cece, please. Once more. That's all I ask.

"Jean, it's dangerous. What if—"

"I won't let anything happen to this oaf, Cece," Oscar cut in.

"Just once more, Cece. Then we can move on, do what you suggest."

Cece shook her head. "Fine. Once more."

"I want to go, too," Astrid said.

"Hell no!" Cece snapped at the same time as Jean blurted, "Oh que non!"

"If there are DOMs or traitor Magix there, they'll be looking for you," Cece said.

"Too risky," Jean agreed.

Astrid looked to Tessa, but Tessa had to shake her head.

"I think they're right, kiddo," she said. "You'll be safer here. There's nothing that you could find that Jean and Oscar can't."

"We are in agreement," Jean said, standing and stretching. "Allons-y," he said to Oscar, who hopped up immediately and saluted Jean.

"It's not a joke," Astrid snapped at him, blushing as soon as she said it.

Oscar's ears reddened as well. "I didn't—I didn't mean to…" He trailed off and kicked at a chair leg. "I'm sorry," he mumbled. "I'll text you if there's anything important you should know. Right away. Promise."

Astrid nodded and gave him a small smile. "Thanks."

"You have eaten?" Jean said to Oscar, who nodded. Jean turned to Cece. "A tout à l'heure. Don't forget to eat breakfast, you two. " He kissed each of Cece's cheeks twice. To the room, he said, "Behave, children! Je vous adore. Au revoir."

"Later gators," Oscar said, giving a half-hearted wave.

And they disappeared. Tessa had never seen transportation magic, only experienced it as the transportee. It was almost stranger to watch than to do. Tessa thought Cece was probably wrong to think that all Nons would simply dismiss seeing people straight up vanish. Then again… Tessa tried to imagine how she would have responded to seeing something like that only a day or two before. She wasn't even sure she would have been able to tell her therapist about it for fear of sounding crazy.

Everyone was quiet, the only sound coming from the twins as they chatted sweetly back and forth, then decided they hated each other and started screaming at the top of their lungs and pulling one another's hair and ears.

"You big meanie, Wowa!" Livy shrieked.

"You biggest meanie evah, Wivy!"

Cece scooped up Lola just before she could sink her teeth into Livy. In blind anger, Livy started to climb Cece's legs, teeth bared and snapping at Lola's leg. "Livy, stop!" Cece cried, then hollered to the room, "A little help, anyone?"

Tessa scooped up Livy who immediately stopped nipping and stilled, eyes wide, staring with stranger-danger terror into Tessa's face before bursting into tears and cries of "Mama!"

With the grace that only a twin-mom could have, Cece took Livy as well and held each twin on a hip. As quickly as they'd begun their fight, they'd forgotten it, both staring warily at Tessa, holding hands across Cece's chest.

Cece shook her head. "The lives of two years olds."

Tessa chuckled.

"I'm hungry," Luca crowed, running through the living room, arms stretched behind him in an imitation of Silas, who flew over his head.

"Me too!" Silas cried.

Cece laughed. "Didn't you already eat?" she asked, letting the twins slide down her legs like firefighters down a pole.

"I'm hungry again!" Luca shouted, zooming past her.

Cece shrugged. "To the kitchen!" she pronounced, following the four littles. At the kitchen door, she called over her shoulder, "Coming, you two?"

Tessa looked over at Astrid, who was still standing in the middle of the living room, arms folded tightly across her chest, watching the spot from which Jean and Oscar had vanished.

"Astrid?" Tessa whispered.

Astrid jumped. She looked at Tessa, then Cece. "Not hungry," she said, turning to go upstairs.

Tessa moved to follow her.

"Let her go," Cece said. "She needs space."

As promised, Jean had provided a "petit" breakfast feast that included pig *and* plant-based bacon, scrambled eggs and scrambled tofu, oatmeal, several stacks of pancakes, a variety of fruits, and a potato and vegetable hash. Tessa filled up a plate with heaping portions, grabbing her phone from where it was charging on the counter.

After a few bites, Tessa felt her phone vibrate. Sanjay. *I'll call him right back,* she thought, silencing it. She took another heavenly bite of that potato hash, wondering if Jean's secret was simply *magic* or maybe—hopefully—something more repeatable. She'd have to ask for the recipe.

Her phone buzzed. A voicemail. Tessa picked it up and saw that she had thirty-five missed calls and fourteen voicemails. All from Sanjay.

"What the—?" Tessa murmured aloud.

"Everything ok?" Cece asked.

Tessa frowned, putting the phone up to her ear. "I don't know," she said. "It's Sanjay." She put the phone to her ear to listen to the first voicemail from Sanjay:

"Hey, Tess, just checking in. Are you all back yet? Call me so I know everything's ok, yeah?"

Normal enough, Tessa supposed. Still—thirty-five phone calls when she'd already told him what she was doing. Either something was seriously wrong or her boy was going to need some clearer boundaries. She played the next message.

"Hey, me again. Sorry, but I wanted to let you know that there might be a woman coming your way, saying she's related to Astrid. She's not. She's got contacts in or something to make her eyes look weird like Astrid's, but we looked her up; no relation. Says her name is Cordelia Connolly: goes by Cece. So just, you know, send her on her way. Or better yet, don't open the door. Don't let her in the house, ok? You know what, she might even be waiting for you when you get back, so don't… don't go right home. Call me first. Call me as soon as you get this."

Tessa felt her lips dip into an ever-deepening frown as she listened. Cece had gone to the agency? Why didn't she mention that? And why would she use her real name? Something wasn't adding up. Tessa started listening to the third message.

"Tess, hey. Just trying again. This is urgent, so call me back."

And then next: "Tessa. Is everything ok? You didn't let her in, did you? She's dangerous. She's a criminal. Call me."

"Tessa," Cece said. "Is everything ok?"

Tessa was frowning so deeply she was giving herself a headache. She looked up at Cece and asked, "How did you know Astrid was with me?"

"Lola and Livy tracked her," Cece answered. "We found some clothing at the house and gave it to the twins. They found her like…" She snapped her fingers. "A werewolf could find anyone within a twenty-mile radius with just a sniff of them."

"You didn't go to the agency?" Tessa pressed.

"Why would I do that?" Cece said, cocking her head to one side. "I'm a Magick."

"So you just walked into a crime scene?" Tessa was trying to picture it: Cece just strolling past the yellow tape, maybe whisking their fingers back and forth to wipe memories of the detectives as she went, like *Men in Black,* but less sci-fi, more fantasy.

"We sent Bettie to the house," Cece replied. "To see if Astrid and her parents were alright. Bettie discovered that Astrid was alive, found the clothing, and brought it to us."

"She never mentioned that."

"It was after they'd taken her to the station. An overheard conversation between some cops, maybe? I don't get all the details from Bettie, but she's useful for reconnaissance work and sending messages."

"You don't email?" Tessa asked. When Cece did not comment or smile, Tessa added, "Joking."

"Birds are more reliable," Cece said, still unsmiling. She offered no follow-up.

"Cool," Tessa said. She went back to the first voicemail and played it for Cece.

"There's fourteen messages from him," Tessa said.

"Play them," Cece said. "All of them."

By the sixth message, Sanjay was at her house. "Tessa, I called Kathy. She hasn't heard from you and your stupid Leaf is still in the garage, so I know you're here and I know you lied to me. Answer the door!"

In the seventh, he was practically crying: "Why would you lie to me? I'm worried about you. Call me. Please."

By the ninth, he didn't sound at all like the mild-mannered man Tessa used to go out with for drinks and karaoke. His voice was hard and angry. "I trusted you. Now I regret it. I told you, Tessa. I told you bad things would happen. This is not going to end well, do you hear me?"

"Tessa, you asshole!" he screamed in the tenth message. "How dare you steal a child! You betrayed me." There was a muffled sound in the background. Another voice?

"Shit," Cece murmured. "Let me try to amplify that," she said, spinning her index finger in a circle, indicating that Tessa should play it again.

Tessa complied and this time, it was as if the sound had been pulled out in a thin string to hang in the air around them. Sanjay's voice was in her ear as he cursed her existence. Then she heard the other voice, clearly:

"They transported from here, so we'll follow th— "

The message cut off.

"That was Mora—" Tessa began, but Cece was waving her hands, saying:

"I know, I know. Next! Play the next one."

Sanjay's voice came blaring out, as if he had the phone pressed right against his lips. "You think this is game, huh? Gallivanting off with a dangerous criminal and jeopardizing the life of a child. For what, T? A chance to get laid?"

The words were venom, trickling into Tessa's ear, sending shivers along her arms.

Again, the second voice came at the very end: "Marie Laveau, how original."

The next message: "You think you've gotten away because of Cordelia's clever little trick. I'll report you to the police; they'll find you."

The second voice laughed, "The DOMs will find them."

Then a third voice shouted: "Mom!"

Tessa dropped the phone. It clattered on the floor before Cece scooped it up, continuing to play the voicemails and looping the voices in a whirring web around them. Tessa wasn't listening anymore. It didn't matter what else Sanjay or Morana said.

Theo was with them.

* * *

## JAN 1980

### *January 3, 1980*

*Meeting Transcript*

*Attendees: Gunner Engers, Tish Chernoff, Archer Engers, and Valerie Hart*

*Transcribed by Valerie Hart*

*Tish: I don't understand.*

*Gunner: I don't expect you to. It's not your child.*

*Tish: If my child had the potential to save the world...*

*Gunner: ...you sure as* hell *wouldn't give her to my people—to DOMs—would you? ... Would you?*

*Tish: ...No.*

*Gunner: So we're in agreement?*

*Tish: Not agreement—*

*Gunner: We won't collect the mother or the child. We'll keep tabs on them, from afar. See what happens. Try the experiment again and see if we can produce another.*

*Tish: What if it's only ogres that can do it? Their particular mutations are less antagonistic toward anti-magic.*

*Gunner: We test that theory. Get a witch or fairy. We've tried multiple in vitro fertilizations with witches and fairies. But not a live insemination.*

*Tish: Just say sex.*

*Archer: *coughs**

*Gunner: There's a fairy right here.*

*Tish: Leave Valerie out of this.*

*Val: I would do it, Tish. If you needed me.*

*Gunner: That's the spirit!*

*Tish: Then I volunteer Archer for it.*

*Archer: T-tish, you're a h-h-hag.*

*Tish: What about that witch girl I've seen you fawn over. What's her name? Mercy?*

*Archer: M-m-m-meredith.*

*Tish: Mmm, Meredith. Lovely.*

# CHAPTER
## TEN

 For the rest of the day, Tessa existed in a fog of nausea. She walked up those rolling stairs to her room and lay on her bed and felt the waves continue to rock her, not soothingly, but with the grim, pestering persistence of an anxious thought.

*Theo. Theo. Theo.*

*What about Theo? What are you going to do about Theo?*

She replayed that last message in her head.

Sanjay's voice like claws digging into an already festering wound. *I'll report you to the police; they'll find you.*

Then Morana, hungry and elated, a predator cornering its prey. *The DOMs will find them.*

And finally, Theo's voice, still a child's but with new adolescent gravity. *Mom!*

*Mom.*

*Don't let her take me, Mom.*

Theo was calling for *her*. Not for Morana, but for Tessa.

*If you loved me, you'd fight for me.*

She touched a hand to that old scar on her right bicep, the Familiar Mark. Theo's claim on her. Theo's mark was tingling and had been for a while, she realized, frowning at the phantom pain. Could a Familiar Mark cause nerve damage? The other, newer mark on her left forearm didn't hurt at all anymore, despite still being swollen and red. *Astrid's mark*, she thought, and the thought was bittersweet as all changes are, a beginning tinged with an ending. This mark would scar as well. Tessa pressed a thumb to it until she felt the pain start up again, a distraction from the dull sting in her left arm.

Tessa was reminded of something Cece had said earlier about *seeing* anti-magic and it being a "weird secret." Anti-magic must be something that most Magix couldn't see. So, what about magic then? Could they see it? Was this mark what magic looked like? Or was it only what it looked like to Tessa, a Non? Because, presumably, Nons couldn't see magic or anti-magic.

Tessa's head started to spin, thinking about whatever invisible-to-her particles might be out there. Her breath started to quicken and catch, the beginnings of a panic attack. Tessa tried to breathe and steady herself.

There was a knock on the door. Tessa hopped up, welcoming any distraction. Cece stood in the hall.

"Hey," she said. "Have you seen Astrid?"

Tessa frowned. "She's not in her room?"

Cece shook her head.

Just then, they heard Jean's boisterous voice holler out, "Bonjour, ma famille! We are back! With Astrid, our little stowaway."

Cece frowned. Tessa shrugged.

"At least she's back!"

Downstairs, everyone had gathered, gravitating to Jean's call. He held a twin in the crook of each arm with Silas and Luca each holding a leg as he growled and moaned like Frankenstein's monster, a towering amalgamation of bodies. His limbs giggled as he walked. Astrid was sitting on the couch in deep conversation with Oscar. She looked up sheepishly when Tessa and Cece entered.

"Well, first things first," Cece said. "Did you find anything?

"We did not, no," Jean said and sighed.

"Indeed," Cece said. "Next question: how did you, Sassy, manage to transport—"

"I came back and got her," Oscar said. "After we went to the house and it seemed, you know, safe."

Cece raised her eyebrows.

"There weren't cops or anything, dude," Oscar added. "It was locked but, well…" He wiggled his fingers, then turned to Jean with a goofy look on his face. "Hey Jean, what kind of key opens a banana?"

"Oscar…" Cece warned. "This is not the tim—"

"*Mon* key," Oscar said in an over-the-top French accent.

Astrid giggled at this, while Silas and Luca burst into hearty laughs. A few seconds later, Livy and Lola began to laugh as well, rolling on the floor along with their older brothers.

"Uhhh là là," Jean sighed.

"How long have you been holding onto that one?" Cece asked.

Oscar shrugged and bumped his shoulder against Astrid's, who smiled again. Tessa smiled at this too, and looked again at Cece. Some of her chill demeanor was gone now, though her lips were still pursed and her jaw tight as she watched Oscar and Astrid.

"Once I saw she was there as well, I didn't have the heart to send her away, Cece," Jean said. "So blame me."

"I do."

"She is fine, is she not?"

"Lucky for you."

Jean threw up his hands. "We searched the house, every room. Astrid, she even conjured a seeking spell, trying to pull the magic from the air, to see if there were any clues, or traces left behind, either from Aura and Zack, or the ones who followed them. There was nothing. After, we went to the farmstead," Jean continued. "We were not able to get close."

Cece frowned. "What do you mean?"

"There were people there," Oscar said.

"DOMs?"

"Perhaps," Jean answered. "Maybe there were some there. I could not say for certain."

"There were Magix," Astrid cut in. "Some witches, a couple vampires, at least one fairy, and a dozen werewolves maybe."

"Did they scent you?"

Jean shook his head. "No, I think not. Besides, we are far enough south now that I do not think they could find us easily. But some of the werewolves…" Jean began, but then trailed off.

Cece came beside him and placed a hand on his shoulder. "What, Jean?"

He shook his head and muttered something in French. Tessa thought she heard the word "Detroit" uttered in the French way—*day twah.*

"Come again?" Cece asked. "You're saying you *recognized* some of the werewolves?"Jean nodded. "From The Detroit Pack."

"Shh," Cece snapped, glancing over at the twins. "No. No, that's not possible, Jean."

Jean shrugged, a gesture of submission rather than nonchalance. "You are probably right. I was far away. I'm sure I was mistaken." He took a deep breath then and smiled, though it did not reach his eyes. "I am happy to be back, in any case. Though, I regret we were unable to do more. I did not think it was safe to approach the people who are now residing in our old coven. Ché pas…" He broke off, rubbing a hand over his face. "I know not why they would be there, and I can think of no reason other than nefarious ones."

"It's fucked up," Oscar added.

Cece shot him a look and opened her mouth, readying to chide him. Tessa could see the internal struggle on her face: to correct or let it go? *A more profound question than any in Shakespeare*, Tessa thought.

"It is," Cece said after a moment. "It is indeed… that."

Jean smirked. He'd clearly seen what almost happened as well. He gave Cece a subtle thumbs-up, hand pressed against his side. She let out a sigh in answer.

"I'm hungry!" Silas exclaimed and then all four of the littles were shouting about how hungry they were, asking when dinner would be and what they would be eating, asking if they could have pizza and french fries or maybe ice cream.

"With chocolate syrup!" Luca exclaimed.

"Please? Please? Pretty please?" Silas added.

"With a cherry on top!" Luca finished.

"Ice cweam! Chewwy on top!" Livy shouted at the top of her lungs.

"Chut-chut, all of you! S'il vous plait!" Jean exclaimed. "I will make pizza. And if behavior is parfait during the meal, then maybe—"

"*Maybe*," Cece reiterated.

"—we can have ice cream—"

"*After* everyone eats their food," Cece emphasized. "Got it?"

A cheer went up as Jean saluted the room and went into the kitchen. Within minutes, the smell of baking pizza filled the air: the crust, warm and yeasty with that slightly alcoholic tang of baking bread; tomato sauce, a punch of acid; caramelized onions, a sweet and buttery scent; mozzarella, a delicate afterthought; and fresh basil, peppery and alive.

"That was fast," Tessa murmured.

"It's called *magic*," Oscar snorted.

Astrid elbowed him in the ribs.

"Sorry," Oscar muttered.

"Tessa," Cece said, inclining her head toward the kitchen. "Will you?"

Tessa followed Cece into the kitchen.

Jean was humming as they walked in. Diced carrots and cucumber tossed themselves into a bowl of greens.

"Jean, there's been a development," Cece said, placing her palms on the counter.

"Development?"

Tessa pulled out her phone and played through the messages from Sanjay again, feeling more and more nauseous as they progressed. By the end, Jean's normally ruddy face was bone pale and Tessa thought hers might be tinted green.

"Bro… was he like playing you this whole time, you think?"

Tessa pivoted at the sound of Oscar's voice. He was standing in the doorway, arms folded across his chest with Astrid standing beside him.

"That's *so* fucked up," Oscar added. His eyes flicked toward Cece, waiting for the chiding comment that didn't come.

Instead, Cece cleared her throat, a choking sound.

"No," Tessa replied. "At least, I don't think so. He was my friend. For years." But how else could you explain Theo's placement in her care?

"It doesn't matter, Oscar," Jean said.

"It matters if she's an idiot who trusts the wrong people."

Astrid placed a hand on his elbow, but Oscar tugged his arm away from her.

"Oscar, that's not fair," Cece chastised. "We've *all* done that before. We all trusted *her*."

"Morana," Oscar spat. "Just say her name."

Cece huffed a sigh. "She doesn't deserve—"

Oscar cut her off. "Why are you so afraid of her?"

Cece shook her head. "I'm not afraid of *her*. Magix don't betray Magix. She is the scum of the earth and—"

"Bullshit you're not afraid of her. You're afraid of her and the traitors and the DOMs. You are all so scared. Why is everyone so goddamn afraid all the time? We hide and moan and cry and do *nothing*."

Cece sighed, an angry sound, like a teakettle nearing a scream. "You don't get it, kid."

"What does that mean?" Oscar snapped.

"If we don't hide, we die," Cece hissed.

"You literally said we wouldn't be able to hide—"

"That's not the same as running into battle!" Cece was practically shouting. "If we don't hold fear in our hearts and heed its warning cry, we will be obliterated. There's history… we have *history*. It's in our blood, the trauma and murder and collective fear, but you couldn't poss—"

"Cece!" Jean warned, stepping forward.

"I couldn't possibly understand the inherited trauma," Oscar finished. "Because I'm a Wayward."

"She did not mean—" Jean began, placing a hand on Oscar's shoulder.

Cece cut him off. "You said it, kid. Not me." She clapped a hand over her mouth. "Shit, Oscar. I—"

Oscar held up a hand, his lip trembling. "I'm not ashamed of who I am. And I'm *not* afraid." He turned and walked out of the room.

"Morana!" Cece shouted at his back. "There, I said her name. Happy?" She lowered her face into her hands, muttering *shit* over and over.

Jean shook his head at Cece and left to follow Oscar.

"I trusted her," Cece said, raising her head back up, her voice choked. "I trusted Morana and she betrayed us." Then she stalked out of the kitchen as well, leaving just Astrid and Tessa in her wake.

A timer went off. Tessa took the oven mitts off the counter and pulled out the pizzas. "Dinner's ready!" she called. The four littles bounded in, but Oscar, Jean, and Cece did not join.

"Bon appétit," Astrid muttered.

Tessa shook her head, sliding steaming slices onto plates. "Bon appétit."

* * *

# 1982

### April 4, 1982

*Mr. Brand,*

*I've attached this week's report on the child. He is developing quite beautifully. Our decision to study him from afar with limited interference and no knowledge of who or what he is, either by him or his family, has been astonishingly successful. We are studying a child's uninhibited growth. We are witnessing the next step of unencumbered evolution.*

*In this file, you will see photos of the child smiling, dressed up for holidays, playing in the dirt. There are also reports from the child's mother on his growth and powers. They are casual and anecdotal in nature. The child has tamed various snakes already, a feat seldom achieved by ogres until they are full grown.*

*Consider if the child were raised in the clinical environment for which the Committee continues to advocate. From where would the snakes come? If we gave the child snakes, and he tamed them, we would still have questions. Would the child be drawn to snakes innately, as many ogres are? Would there be other animals to which they were drawn?*

*Leaving the child to his own devices, we have no such questions.*

*I understand the Committee's ongoing concerns. It is true that we have little control over this subject. But I want to assure you: this child isn't going anywhere. And we are working diligently to develop other children.*

*Sincerely,*
*Gunner Engers*

# CHAPTER
## ELEVEN

**JULY 2023** Eventually, Jean came back, his face masked with a forced smile for the littles. He thanked Tessa for stepping in, helped the kids finish up their meals, and wiped their faces.

"Plates to the sink, children, then to bed! Say good night to Tessa and Astrid."

"Good night!" the four littles hollered in an echoing chorus. Silas ran over to hug Tessa around the waist and Luca followed suit, sniffing at her before letting go.

"You smell like pinecones," Luca said. "And… dragon poop, maybe?"

Silas snorted.

Luca tugged at Tessa's shirt. She lowered herself, her ear near his mouth. "What does dragon poop smell like?" he whispered.

"Not good, I'm sure," Tessa replied.

"Okay," Luca nodded. "Then probably just pinecones." He leaned in and kissed Tessa's cheek. "And cookies, too. I like it."

"I like you," Tessa said.

Luca's eyes went wide and a joyful grin spread across his face.

Tessa remembered something she'd read or seen maybe in a parenting video. *Always delight in your child's presence. A child will see your delight and feel delightful and love themselves with the same joy that you love them.*

"I *love* you," Luca said.

Tessa smiled. "I love you, too, Luca." Luca had delight in his spirit; love had never been withheld from him. Despite the early trauma of losing his parents, Luca showed no signs of being a traumatized kid. "You, too, Silas. I love you both."

And of course, she thought of Theo and the first time she'd told them she loved them. They'd looked at her with such shock, like it was the first time they'd ever heard the words before. What kind of a parent never tells their kid they love them?

"Luca! Silas! Time for bed."

The two boys scampered out of the room, giggling.

Cece must have been right outside the door. Her voice carried as she said good night to the kids and told them she loved them. Tessa heard the smack of multiple kisses followed by the gallop of small steps along the floor and up the stairs. Cece came into the kitchen a moment later. She looked exhausted, almost haggard, Tessa thought. Cece stood quietly, rubbing her temples.

"Everything ok, Auntie?" Astrid asked.

Cece sighed. "No," she said after a moment. "I was out of line. I shouldn't have said what I said. Oscar will need some time to forgive me, I think."

"Is he ok?" Astrid asked.

"I'm sure he's not," Cece replied. "He's in his room."

Astrid left without another word. Tessa noticed Cece's arm spasm toward Astrid as she passed her, like she was going to reach out and grab her, stop her from going to Oscar. But she stopped the motion mid-reach, drawing back her hand with a pained expression on her face.

"Use protection!" Tessa hollered after her.

Astrid was back in the kitchen in a split second. "What?"

"It was a joke?" Tessa replied with a sheepish shrug.

Astrid rolled her eyes. "Tessa—"

"Yep, got it. Familiar, not Mom. My bad!" Tessa exclaimed, holding up her hands in surrender.

Astrid smirked. *He doesn't even like me like* that, she thought-said.

*Don't be so sure,* Tessa thought and was surprised to see Astrid redden slightly before leaving the room again. Had she heard her? Tessa had assumed that only Magix could project their thoughts, but what if… what if Tessa could do it too, at least with Astrid, like some kind of Familiar-Magick bond.

"I'm sorry you had to see that," Cece said. She had scooped up a cold slice of pizza and took a bite out of it, eyes never leaving Tessa. "I… struggle with blaming Oscar for the privileges he has."

"Is it a privilege to be Wayward?" Tessa asked. She thought Waywards would be like "free agents," like Sunny in Nnedi Okorafor's Nsibidi Scripts series, looked down on by others in their magical communities and seen as less-than: less gifted, less magical, less… human, even. Where was the privilege in that?

Cece sighed. Putting her elbows on the kitchen island, she leaned forward and pressed her palms into her eye sockets, pressing against her head like she was struggling through a terrible migraine.

"You have no idea," she said at last. "No idea what it's like to feel the weight of generations of oppression."

"I do not," Tessa agreed. "Just my one generation."

Cece looked up at her with a glare.

"'Cause I'm queer so… I just… sorry," Tessa trailed off. "I wasn't trying to be facetious."

Cece sighed. "Well, I'm queer. And Black. And a Magick in hiding born to Magix in hiding born to Magix in hiding born to Magix in hiding, on and on. It's all in my blood, in *all* of our blood. *The blood is life.*" She put on a grotesque Eastern European accent.

Tessa smirked. "Dracula?"

"Renfield, actually."

"Close enough?"

Cece shrugged. "The point is, a Wayward doesn't have that same generational trauma. They have trauma, sure, but it's not in their bones, you know? It doesn't walk with them."

"Blood isn't everything," Tessa said. "You can inherit trauma in other ways."

Cece nodded. "Absolutely. If you're raised in a family with generational trauma, I think a lot of that will seep into you. Trauma by osmosis, or whatever. And some people are sponges and soak it all in. Others are like little rubber ducks, letting it all slide off. Oscar's like that. So fucking resilient. I don't know why I get so angry about it, despite my best efforts. It's not fair of me."

Tessa couldn't help but nod her agreement. "No, it isn't. He's just a kid."

Cece sighed. "I need to… do better."

"Start with apologizing," Tessa advised. "It's always best to admit when you're wrong."

They were quiet for a moment and then Tessa asked the question that had been clawing at her throat all day.

"What about Theo?"

Cece went to the sink and poured herself a glass of water. When she spoke, she didn't meet Tessa's gaze. "Tessa," she began. "We can't possibly get Theo. Not right now. They're with Morana. It would be suicide."

*Why is everyone so goddamn afraid all the time?* Oscar's words reverberated through Tessa's brain. Cece hadn't answered him. She'd just deflected and lashed out like a cornered animal and Oscar had given up. But Tessa wasn't a kid. She could act like an animal, too. She could meet Cece's wrath head on with one that was equal if not greater.

"What is so special about Morana that you all tremble at the mention of her name?" Tessa's voice was higher and louder than she meant it to be, but she was entering mama bear mode. *Rule #1: Put the kid's needs first.* Theo needed her. Now.

Cece shook her head. "I'm not afraid—"

"No," Tessa said, holding up a silencing finger. "You're not weaseling out of this. Answer me."

"I've *told* you what she did," Cece replied. "She slaughtered our friends, families, all we hold dear. She betrayed us to the DOMs."

"She has my kid," Tessa said. "Theo is *my* kid. I want them safe and I want them back. If it were you, if she had Silas or Luca, what would you do?"

Cece sighed, but said nothing for a time. When she finally spoke, Tessa flinched at the anger in Cece's voice. "I've already told you; if you had wanted Theo safe, you should have kept them safe. Then again, who are you, a Non, to claim parentage of someone like Theo? Forty-eight hours ago, you knew nothing about who and what they truly were. Even now, you've barely scratched the surface of it. How could you possibly understand what it is to *be* Magick? And without that fundamental knowledge, how could you parent a Magick? There's a reason that we take Wayward babes and bring them to our covens to raise them. How could a Non be expected to rear a Magick? How could—?"

"Wait," Tessa interrupted. "You all steal kids from their parents? Is that what happened to Oscar? You stole him?" Her fury was growing to match the pitch and cadence of Cece's and they continued on for a time, shouting at each other, unhearing, until Jean came in.

"Hush!" he snapped. "Both of you. Quiet or you'll wake the enfants."

Cece threw up her hands. "I'm going to bed," she said. "This is too much."

She stalked out of the room, but Tessa's anger didn't vanish with her.

"Did you steal Oscar from his birth family?" Tessa asked Jean, still panting with anger.

Jean's face broke into such a look of shocked hurt that Tessa immediately felt guilty for asking.

"I'm sorry," she blurted. "Cece said…"

Jean held up a hand. "Forget Cece. I do not understand why she is so angry; she won't say. The Waywards, they are sometimes stolen, yes. Not so for our Oscar. There are three ways for a Wayward. The first is to be abandoned or kicked out of Non society. This was Oscar's journey. The second, to be taken by force. This was how it was for many, many Waywards for centuries. And the third, to continue on as a Non in hiding or perhaps even oblivious to the truth of one's nature."

He was watching Tessa intently, eyes narrowed.

Tessa couldn't think of thing to say in response. She glanced at her watch. It was nearly 10:00 p.m. "I should go to bed."

Jean nodded. "Me as well."

"Thank you, Jean. And, I'm sorry."

Jean waved her apology away. "De rien, Tessa. You are learning. It is chaotic. Oh là." He let out a long sigh and patted her on the shoulder. "Tomorrow is another day."

Upstairs, Tessa checked her email. HR was asking for FMLA documentation and there was another voicemail from Sanjay. She deleted both, unread and unheard. She could hear her therapist's voice in her head: *Don't burn bridges.* But sometimes, that was the only way forward.

Her mother had said that once, Tessa was pretty sure. A former friend turned bully or some similar childhood injustice had left Tessa teary-eyed and bereft.

"Chin up, dry your eyes," her mother had said. "And give 'em hell."

* * *

## MAR 1985

### March 3, 1985

*Gunner,*

*I'm enclosing a letter I intercepted from your son to the witch girl. I've said for a long time that he can't be trusted with this task. And now that she is with child... well... here's your proof.*

*-Tish*

*"Dearest Mer,*

*I know why you are afraid and why you doubt me, but know this: I never doubted you for an instant. I promise you; this is me. No spells, no curses, no magic, no tricks. I've been honest with you from the start. You have to believe me. I love you.*

   *Yours forever,*
   *Archer"*

CHAPTER
**TWELVE**

**JULY 2023** Again, the dreams. This time, Tessa and Morana stood shoulder to shoulder on the edge of burning forest.

"Shall we?" Morana asked.

"Shall we what?"

"Enter," Morana said.

"It's on fire," Tessa replied.

Morana shrugged. "Suit yourself." And she began to walk into the fire.

Tessa watched Morana move across the landscape. Piece by burning piece this dreamworld came into clearer focus. They were at the edge of a fog-rimmed lake. Tessa squinted but there was nothing to see of the far shore. Or maybe there was never anything to see. Her feet were pressed into sand, a thin bar that hugged the water before disappearing quickly under flaming dune grass. Beyond the grass, a row of ancient white pines smoldered. The white carcass of a paper birch caught the moonlight that was beginning to filter through the fog. The wind shifted and the acrid stench of smoke filled Tessa's nose and mouth. She gagged.

On went Morana, clothed in nothing but a thin white dress, her hair and skin nearly as pale. She walked into the flames but they did not touch her. She turned to look at Tessa.

"Do you remember?" Morana asked. She was far away now but it was as if her voice were right in Tessa's ear.

"Remember what?" Tessa asked.

Something shifted in her peripheral vision. The moon's light revealed a dock, jutting out into the lapping waves. On the dock stood a lone figure dressed in a bright red poncho. Tessa turned back to the trees, which were no longer burning, but rather the dying reds and oranges of autumn. Morana was gone. The figure on the dock sagged and Tessa realized that they were a child. They turned and looked at Tessa, raising their hands and hollering at her.

"Hey! Help!"

Tessa opened her eyes, but the voice kept screaming at her even in waking, a lingering nightmare. "Help! Please, don't leave!"

*Do you remember?*

Tessa dressed and headed downstairs. It was early still, not even 7:00 a.m., but she could hear the sounds of laughter coming from Silas and Luca's room.

In the living room, Livy and Lola were wrestling, giggles interspersed with shrieks of pain and sudden shouts of anger that caused Jean or Cece to alternately poke a head out of the kitchen or holler, "Everything ok?" every ten seconds or so.

When the twins heard Tessa's footsteps, they paused their play, Lola with an ear to the ground and Livy, sitting on her sister's chest, still as a stone. They followed Tessa with their eyes as she walked into the kitchen. The moment she was out of their sight, Tessa heard them start screaming and giggling again.

"Ah, bonjour, Tessa!" Jean exclaimed, thrusting a cup of steaming coffee into her right hand and plate of pancakes and vegan bacon into her left.

"We were just talking," Cece said, nodding to the kitchen table, where Astrid was already sitting, her plate cleaned.

"Morning," Astrid said.

There was a groan from the doorway and Oscar came in, hair standing up every which way. Jean handed him a cup of coffee and a plate of food as well.

"Pig bacon?" Oscar asked.

"But of course."

Oscar didn't even glance at Cece before walking over to sit next to Astrid. She gave him an exuberant smile, which he returned with equal exuberance, before his face hardened back into his usual wary and somewhat grumpy expression.

Again, Cece had changed her hair dramatically, tying it into a long braid down her back from which flowers were… growing? Yes, there were definitely living blossoms coming from her hair. Cece, catching Tessa staring, shifted the braid so Tessa could get a better look.

Above them, Bettie perched on the top of one of the kitchen cabinets. She squawked at Tessa twice and Tessa nodded back before blowing on her coffee and taking a careful sip.

"Talking about what?" Tessa asked.

"About the prophecy," Astrid replied.

Despite the gravity of Astrid's voice, Tessa snorted. She took a big sip of coffee and then looked from Astrid to Cece to Jean. "Wait, really?" Tessa said. She took another deep drink of coffee. "A prophecy feels a little too 'on trope' here," she added.

Bettie chirruped in what Tessa took to be agreement, but Cece rolled her eyes and Oscar pulled off a sock and flung it at her. Cece opened her mouth as if to chide him, but Oscar shot her an angry look and she closed her mouth.

"That means he likes you," Jean said to Tessa, winking at Oscar, who groaned.

"It's a trope in the Non world, but in our world, I assure you, prophecies are grave and infrequent," Cece said.

Jean shrugged. "I feel like a prophecy crops up every few decades. Ma mère, she told me—"

"Anyway!" Astrid hollered. "Eleven years ago, a Familiar of a powerful Magick was turned, became a seer, made a prophecy, and immediately died."

"Brutal," Oscar muttered.

"They *died!*" came a shriek from just outside the door. Luca burst into the kitchen followed closely by Silas. "They actually *died!*" Luca cried, gesturing with emphatic arms spread wide, palms up in wonder.

Astrid nodded. "Yep."

Oscar snorted. "My morbid little dude," he said with a laugh.

"That was the first piece of the prophecy, actually," Astrid continued. "That the Familiar would die the moment he became a Magick. And that the Magick, in her grief, would start a war that would only end when the one who could unite the seven was found."

"So we're thinking that you all are the seven?" Tessa asked, counting around the room. "But there's six… no, eight of you. Is it like a one plus seven thing?"

"You'll recall there are seven magical clans," Cece said. "And if you would stop interrupting with your sarcasm, you might learn something."

"Ooo, burn!" Oscar laughed.

Again, Cece began to chide him, but Oscar's glare cut her off. She sighed and continued. "So, the logical interpretation of 'the seven' is one member of each magical clan: witches, vampires, werewolves, sirens, fairies, shapeshifters, and—"

"Ogres," Tessa finished. "They're uncommon, right?"

Cece shook her head. "They were nearly wiped out in the late fifteenth and early sixteenth centuries when a particularly nasty DOM made his way to the Caribbean, where most ogres resided, and took it upon himself to slaughter, rape, and murder as many of them as he and his cronies could."

"Christopher Columbus was a DOM?" Tessa gaped.

There were several groans and Luca hissed loudly.

"We don't say his name," Jean said.

"So he's like your Vold—?"

"Ah, we don't say *that* name either?"

"This is a TERF-free house," Oscar added.

Tessa nodded. "Fair enough. But I'm still confused here. What does the prophecy have to do with any of you or Morana? What is so special about all of you that she keeps coming for you?"

"Morana is the Magick who started the war," Cece said.

"How do you know that?" Tessa pressed.

Cece gave her a surprised look. "How do you know that Vladimir Putin started the war in Ukraine? How do you know who won the presidential election of 2020 or 2016? How does anyone know anything?"

"Um, reliable news sources?" Tessa replied.

Cece nodded. "We have reporters and journalists, just like you Nons. And we use most of the same platforms that you do: from print to digital content. It's all enchanted."

"For Magick eyes only," Oscar added.

"And you know, Morana hasn't exactly been quiet about what she is doing," Jean said.

Cece rolled her eyes. "Oh god no. She's all over Magick social media and psycho-enchanted subreddits talking about destroying the Nons."

"More recently though," Jean added. "Only in the last one or two years?"

"No, not two. Barely a year, I would say," Cece replied. "Since, well, since she came back for Theo. The Non reporters ran one story about it. But Morana gave the Magick reporters another version that is, in all likelihood, closer to the truth." Cece started typing on her phone then and a few seconds later turned the screen around for Tessa. "You should be able to see this… I removed the enchantment."

It looked like any other *The New York Times* article. The headline read: *Risen from the Dead: Morana Aronov Tells All.*

"*The New York Times*?" Tessa asked. "This is a Magick newspaper?"

"We have correspondents at all the major newspapers," Cece replied, taking the phone from here. "I'll read it out loud, how's that?"

"This was first published in August of 2022 by Tim Martin."

"Ah, he is my cousin, you know?" Jean exclaimed. "It makes sense that a siren would lure a confessional from Morana." He winked.

"Anyway," Cece said, raising her eyebrows at Jean, who clamped one hand over his mouth and gestured for her to proceed with the other. "Here's what Cousin Tim wrote: '*It has been more than two years since DOMs and traitor Magix led attacks on all the covens of New England and the Midwest, destroying every coven in the state of New York and greater New England, along with many in Michigan, Wisconsin, and Minnesota. Since then, we have learned that the attacks were ordered from one central location, the Grand River Coven, from a woman known as Morana Aronov.*

"'*Little was known about Morana, other than the fact that she was a shapeshifter. Had she been the mastermind behind the attacks, or just a pawn in the DOMs schemes? Until recently, it was believed that Morana was killed in the attacks and the answers to these questions would never be known.*

"'*But now, Morana Aronov has come out of hiding and she is ready for the world to know who she is and what she wants. I was able to secure an exclusive interview with her for* The New York Times, *Magix Edition.*

"'*After a several weeks of remote correspondence via email and phone, Morana and I met at a neutral, undisclosed location to discuss the events of the spring attacks in 2020 and Morana's plans for the future, as well as learn more about who she is.*

"'*Tim Martin: Let's start with the facts. You've alluded to the fact that "Morana Aronov" is not your real name. Will you tell me who you really are?*

"'*Morana Aronov: I suppose there's no harm in it now. I was born Morana—Ana—Chernoff.*

"'*TM: Chernoff? Really? As in—*

"'*MA: As in my father was the late and great Russian author Andor Chernoff and my mother is the brilliant—though, arguably, misguided—scientist Dr. Morticia Chernoff.*

"'*TM: So you're not just a shapeshifter, then?*

"'*MA: I'm a vampire on my father's side and shapeshifter on my mother's. A Magick Mutt, as they say.*

"'*TM: Well, that's a bit of a vulgar way to put it. Mixed Magick is, I believe, the preferred ter—*

"'*MA: Who are you to tell me what is preferred by me?*

"'*TM: Apologies—I...*

"'*MA: Next question.*'"

Oscar snorted. "She is brutal."

"Why would he put all of this in the article?" Astrid asked. "It makes him look—"

"Like a dumbass," Oscar finished.

"It shows Morana for who she is," Cece said. She cleared her throat and continued. "'*TM: Right. People want to know what really happened at Grand River Coven, but more than that, they want to know why. Why did you do it?*

"'*MA: Do what exactly?*

"'*TM: Why did you help the DOMs infiltrate no less than twenty covens and obliterate at least five hundred Magix in a single day?*

"'*MA: Your question implies that I was the only Magick that acted in this manner. You could ask this same question of many other Magix.*

"'*TM: Certainly. But they've all claimed you as their leader. Do you deny that you're the leader?*

"'*MA: No, of course not. Ok, then, Tim Martin, you've got me. Why would I align myself with the DOMs, you want to know? Why would I allow for the deaths of so many of my brethren? To answer this question, I will ask you a question: Do you know much about Ana Chernoff?*

"'*TM: I do not.*

"'*MA: Let me tell you of her then. She was good little Magick and very involved in the Movement for the Unification of Magical Society. You are familiar with MUMS?*

"'*TM: It was a movement in the late 1990s led by Dr. Meredith Connolly—*'"

"Cece's mother," Jean whispered in Tessa's ear. "A woman formidable."

"'*—to create a system of governance among Magix worldwide,* *similar to what is believed to have existed prior to the Great Witch Hunts.'"*

"She sounds brilliant," Tessa whispered back.

"'*MUMS was dissolved upon the murder of Dr. Connolly—*'"

"Murder?" Tessa exclaimed.

"Une tragédie," Jean said, shaking his head.

Cece cleared her throat. "If you're done gossiping?"

"Apologies!" Jean exclaimed. "Continue!"

"Ok then," Cece said. "Morana continued: '*Exactly. You are maybe too young to recall the violence of that time period. Many of those in MUMS went into hiding, including Ana Chernoff. I spent a long time living under another name in another place until I met a Non man by the name of Brian Jenkins... not sure how that's relevant, you can cut that.*

"'*TM: I was hoping to include everything verbatim—*

"'*MA: Do what you will. When I met Brian, something of the old me, of Ana Chernoff, was reborn.*

"'*TM: How do you mean—reborn?*

"'*MA: Ana, she was always fascinated with the Nons and Familiars in particular. The journey of a non-magical being to becoming a Magical one. The union of Non and Magick. I took this man as my lover and made him my Familiar. But when the time came to turn him Magick, things did not go as planned.*'"

Cece went on reading as Morana explained the prophecy and the death of her Familiar, just as Astrid had explained it, but with some added details, "'*MA: Just after the transition, he was murdered in cold blood by his brother, a Non man so bitter and so hateful toward Magix that he could not let even his brother live if he were to be one. A new Magick is weak, as you know. Easy as a baby to kill. When my love was killed, I vowed to exact my revenge. The Nons, they are so stupid, so hideously inferior to us.*'"

"Here," Cece said, looking up at Tessa. "Tim puts a side note stating that '*This does not reflect the views of NYT for Magix.*' But she goes on:

"'*Why should they take the world? They choke the planet with their fossil fuels, with their mountains of trash, their chemicals and oils that poison the fresh water. This world was never meant for them. It is ours. When that virus started killing them, I knew it was a sign that we must start. This is my mission; this is why I do what I do. I tell all Magix: It is us or the Nons. If you will not join in our fight, then you will perish as they soon will.'"*

Tessa was staring at her, open-mouthed. "That's... very messed up."

"Indeed," Cece nodded. "And so based on the timing, we believe that the Familiar was Theo's actual father, not the man who raised them."

"You mean Vasily?" Tessa asked. "He wasn't Theo's bio dad?"

"Read a bit more for her, Cece," Jean said.

Cece continued, "'*MA: And so after it all, I met a man, Vasily Aronov. He was a vampire historian. Very anti-Non.*

"'*TM: So, a lot like your father, then?*

"'*MA: I'll thank you to leave my father out of this. Vasily and I, we joined forces, married, and had our child, Theo Aronov. We were a happy little family for a time. But all things go, as they say. I had to take some time after Vasily's death to recover. But I am back now to set the record straight.*'

"From there, it's just Tim wrapping up," Cece concluded.

"She says right there that Vasily was Theo's dad," Tessa replied.

"When's Theo's birthday?" Cece asked.

"What does that matter? We don't know when she changed the Familiar, when he died, or when she married—"

While Tessa was talking, Cece had been typing quickly on her phone and she turned it around to show Tessa. It was a screenshot of a marriage certificate for Vasily Theodore Aronov and Morana Wilhemina Harker dated July 14, 2012. Theo was born on August first.

"So she was hugely pregnant when they got married," Tessa said, shrugging. "Is this some sort of purity shame?"

Jean snorted and Cece rolled her eyes, saying, "Purity isn't really a concept Magix adhere to. Though it's ironic how most Nons derive their notions of purity from a man who was actually a Magick, but I digres—"

"Jesus Christ?" Tessa practically shouted.

Cece held up a hand. "Another story for another time." She flipped her phone around again. "How about this?"

It was another news article from April of 2012 describing a murder-suicide of two brothers. The article, clearly from a Non source and not a Magick, detailed a neighbor lady's account of gunshots fired and a feud between the brothers over the murdered brother's girlfriend. The article noted that she was pregnant and gave her name as Mina Harker.

"Mina Harker," Tessa repeated. "Harker was the last name Morana gave for the marriage certificate." But the name was more familiar than that. It made Tessa think of dusty libraries and coffee jitters, of sleepless, paper-writing nights that tasted like nineteenth-century sexism and unbrushed teeth. "She's a character in *Dracula*, isn't she?"

Cece nodded, holding her phone close again, scrolling and tapping, before she handed it back to Tessa. This was a screenshot of an Instagram post from @vamp_v_aronov that featured a selfie of a thin, pale, smiling man with crooked teeth and a much younger Morana. The caption read: *Just met the real Mina Harker. And guess what? She's a vampire! #suckitvanhelsing*

The post was dated June 3, 2012.

"They could have met before that," Tessa said. "This doesn't prove any—" But she trailed off, studying the man in the photo who looked nothing like Theo, his hair thin where Theo's curled (*Like Morana's*, Tessa thought), his nose large, where Theo's was small and pointed (*Like Morana's*), his eyes icy-blue, while Theo's were...

"Theo has brown eyes!" Tessa exclaimed with the energy and wonder of *Eureka!*

"Cool story, bro," Oscar snickered.

"Brown eyes are the dominant gene," Tessa continued. "For Magix, too?"

Cece nodded. "And Morana and Vasily both have—had—blue eyes."

"They can't both be Theo's parents," Tessa finished.

"Et voilà," Jean said. "Now you see."

"Theo is the product of the prophecy," Cece said, "and likely the key to its fulfillment. Morana would certainly see it that way. She would see Theo as her key to ending the war."

Tessa's head was spinning with information overload. "Ending the war *she* started?"

"In her mind, she was simply beginning the prophecy," Cece replied. "She is the beginning and Theo is the end."

"But that's not how you all see it?" Tessa said.

Jean shrugged. "Not quite so simple."

"The thing about prophecies is," Cece began, "while they do almost always come true, it almost never unfolds the way you think it will."

"And you have historical data points to back this up, I assume?" Tessa asked with a groan and a smirk.

Cece smiled. "You're getting to know me. An example: There was a prophecy made near the beginning of the Salem trials. It stated that the trials would end when either the last witch was rooted out or the Nons stopped believing. General interpretation of this was that the Nons would need to stop believing in witches in order to stop the trials. What happened, of course, is that Non society stopped believing in the effectiveness of the trials themselves.

"Prophecies," Cece continued, "are vague and meaningless on their own. How we interpret them and choose to act in response to them is what matters."

"So how are we choosing to act?" Astrid asked. "That's the whole point of this, right?"

"We need to unite the clans, of course," Tessa said. "Prophecy or not, the only way to fight fire is with fire, right?"

Cece sighed. "A bit cliché, but—"

"Hiding is great and all," Tessa continued, "but clearly, you guys can't do that forever."

"Yes!" Astrid exclaimed. "That's my Familiar, y'all!"

Tessa smiled at Astrid, but Bettie, with a squawk of displeasure at the outburst, flew over to Cece, landing on her shoulder. Cece looked over at the bird and seemed to speak to her, though it was clear that she was addressing Tessa. "How do you suggest we 'unite the clans,' then? With your extensive knowledge of our world?"

Oscar snorted, but Jean was frowning at Cece.

"Sometimes it takes an outsider to see the full picture," he said softly.

Cece winced at the chastisement. There followed a wide silence, punctuated by some yipping and snarling from the twins and a low hiss from Luca when they got too close to the tower of K'nex that he was building for his cow-dragon.

"In the north, there's a coven of ice fairies and some vampires and werewolves," Cece said. "I hid there for a while in my teens after…" She trailed off, staring pointedly at Jean, but his face was unreadable. "They would let me in. I could talk to them."

"I want to come," Astrid said.

"I don't think—"

"Me too," said Tessa.

"They're not going to let a Non—"

"I'm a Familiar," said Tessa. "I want to help."

Cece sighed, but nodded. "Get dressed. We'll leave in fifteen minutes." Bettie squawked and took off toward the ceiling.

"You're forgetting something," Jean said. He looked up to where Bettie was circling. Silas was floating along the ceiling, upside down, his wings flickering every now and then, nose deep in a thick book. "To get into a fairy coven generally requires a fair amount of flying."

Tessa looked from Silas to Jean and back up to Silas. "He's supposed to carry us?"

Jean shrugged. "I was thinking more for scouting ahead and such. But he probably could, in a pinch. And with some help."

"He's seven," Tessa replied. "And I'm… not small."

"Silas!" Cece hollered. "Put the book down, kiddo, please, and come help me pick up Tessa."

The air around Tessa shifted, picking up like a mini tornado around her. She started to wobble, her feet lifting slightly. Then she felt herself hauled up into the air as Silas pulled her up, while the air continued to buoy her up. Tessa let out a squawk.

"Oh shit! I'm flying!"

"Bravo, Silas!" Jean called up.

Silas raised his hand to give Jean a thumbs-up and Tessa tipped and slipped out of his grip. Thankfully, Cece's wind kept her afloat and lowered her somewhat slowly to the ground. She landed on her bottom with only a wincing amount of pain.

"Sorry!" Silas said, coming to land beside her, breathing hard. "Are you ok?"

"Is she *dead*?" Luca hollered with mild concern, glancing up from his K'nex for long enough to see that Tessa was, in fact, alive.

"I'm ok!" Tessa said.

Silas sighed with relief and across the room, Luca mirrored the sigh, though it sounded more disappointed than anything.

"Good try," Cece said, taking a lock of Silas' hair between her fingers. "Next time, there won't be a distracting Papa around, hmm?"

"Euh!" Jean groaned, smirking. "The four of you should be going. Be safe!"

* * *

**MAR 1985** A thin paved path wound through the rows of flat grave markers. Val sniffed the air. There was so much magic in a northern spring. In the South, spring was an inevitability, a truth the world plummeted toward. Overnight, the trees would overflow with green. Purple azaleas opened the floodgates to waves of blooming white magnolias, yellow oleander, and pink crepe myrtle.

But here in Toronto, there were times when it felt as if spring would dissipate like a broken promise. It danced in and out through March and April and even May, until suddenly it was summer and you couldn't quite recall if spring was ever there at all.

Val felt Archer's approach. His steps made no noise, but the air moved around him, sailing back to her. She could smell his minty aftershave.

Val paused in front of William Lyon Mackenzie's tomb. Archer stopped beside her, as if they both happened to be admiring the same famous grave.

"One of y-yours?" Archer asked.

"No, not that I'm aware," Val replied.

"A Non th-then."

Val nodded. "Indeed. Now, why'd you ask to meet me?"

"Mer's p-p-p—" Archer's voice caught on the word, stress holding his speech hostage.

Val waited. She always had time for Archer, this awkward, loyal friend.

"P-pregnant," he finished, sucking in a deep breath. He was trying not to smile, trying to fight the joy, to temper it with fear and guilt.

"I know, dear." She reached for his hand and squeezed it. Damn whatever Department of AntiMagi Health agents might be watching. "Your father told me."

Archer stiffened and removed his hand from hers. Val looked at him and saw his golden brown eyes were tearing up. She was reminded of difference in their ages, how he was barely thirty and she was pushing forty. Time did so much of its dirty work in your thirties.

Val pushed her glasses up her nose and cleared her throat. "What do you need from me, Archer? I'll help however I can."

"If we d-disap-pear," Archer began, then threw up his hands and slammed a fist against the grave marker. A black crack traveled like lightning down the stone.

Val clicked her tongue and snapped her fingers. The crack sealed itself.

"S-sorry."

"You know you can take your time with me. As much as you need to get it out. I'm listening."

"If w-we d-d-d-disappear, they'll n-need another to rep-p-place her."

Val nodded. "And I'm next on their list."

"You c-could c-c-come away, Val."

Val turned on him, eyes big and blazing behind her spectacles. "I couldn't do that to Tish. She's my—my friend."

"W-why d-doesn't Tish volunteer h-h-her w-w-womb to the c-cause?"

Val wanted to slap him. She clenched her fists. Around them, the air grew humid. The sound of mosquitoes buzzing filled their ears. Archer coughed, tried to suck in a full breath, but his lungs were as damp as the air.

"S-st-top!"

Val unclenched her fists. The air cooled and the screams of insects faded.

"Tish has already found a suitable match for me. An Eastern European AntiMage living in Tallinn. An old friend of your father's, I'm told."

"Y-you d-don't h-have to, Valerie."

Val put a hand on his arm. "I know, Archer. I want to." She smiled up at him.

Against the afternoon sun, his afro formed a reverse halo over his head. Val was struck by how much he resembled his father, those white, white teeth. He looked like a real DOM. She never thought of him as one. He was simply Archer.

"I can buy you and Mer a week, tops. Will that be enough?"

Archer nodded. "I'll n-need a few months to p-prepare. Need to find a p-place and s-such."

"When the time comes, use our signal."

He nodded again, placed a hand on each of her shoulders, and then pulled her close to him. For the first time, she noticed how solid and masculine his chest and arms felt as he squeezed her. She wondered if the body of this other DOM, this friend of Gunner's, would feel like this. For a moment, she wished she could do the horrible thing with Archer or Gunner or someone she trusted instead of a stranger. But no, a stranger was better. Less complicated.

"Good luck, Archer," she said, pulling away from him.

Archer smiled at her and the tears he'd been holding in ran down his cheeks.

"Thank you, Valerie," Archer said, his face contorting with the effort of speech as he tried to get these three words out clearly. He stepped back then gave a small wave, turned, and walked away.

Val remained, rooted in place. A Non man passed her, the musk from his cologne hitting her like the slap of a wave on the shore and fading just as quickly. She suppressed a shudder. It would be like that, she thought, painful but quick. Nothing she couldn't endure.

It was too late to turn back.

## CHAPTER
## **THIRTEEN**

**JULY 2023** This time, they took a detour all the way to France, to the Place du Vieux-Marché in Rouen.

"Where Jeanne d'Arc burned," Cece said.

"Seriously?" Tessa gaped. On her shoulder, Bettie tilted her head to one side, mirroring her skepticism. Tessa had been thrilled when Bettie decided to perch on her shoulder for the journey.

Cece had seemed hurt, but all she had said was, "Bettie doesn't usually like strangers."

Now, standing in the courtyard, surrounded by market vendors selling everything from oranges and raspberries, to cheeses and fish, to oils and vinegars and beers, with people walking in and out, their words a rolling, nonsensical murmur, Tessa couldn't believe that this was the site of such a famous slaughter.

"She was really a Magick?"

Cece nodded. "Leader of a fairy coven, actually," she said, squeezing Silas' hand and grinning down at him. "The distant progeny of which we will be seeing today."

Astrid had walked away from there, arms out and eyes closed, like she was looking for something that her eyes would prevent her from finding.

"Anything?" Cece sniffed the air and closed her eyes.

"No," Astrid said, walking back.

Cece opened her eyes. "Let's make a second detour. Close your eyes, Tessa."

Tessa felt the air around her immediately chill and when she opened her eyes, they were standing on a suspension bridge staring down at a lush green landscape dotted with pagodas, dirt roads cutting thin, winding paths along it. Astrid took off at a run along the bridge while Bettie sailed into the air, circling in a figure eight before coming back down, this time on top of Silas' head. The boy giggled and reached up to scratch her belly.

"Where are we now?" Tessa asked.

"The birthplace of Empress Wu Zetian, the only woman Emperor China has ever had" Cece answered. "Her original birthplace is lost to the Non world. But the magic remains, centuries later."

"Nothing here," Astrid said, walking back to them, shoulders slumped.

Cece sighed. "We'll keep trying on our way back. Now, to the Channels."

Tessa closed her eyes. When she opened them, they were standing at the edge of a lake whose waters were the same blue-green jade of Oscar's eyes. Across the inlet was a rocky shoreline lined with tall pines that stood like sentries on alert. To their right sat a broken and mossy canoe. The purple blooms of fading trillium poked up along the keel and out of various holes in the hull.

"Let's go," Cece said, hopping into the canoe and pulling out two wet, rotting oars. She handed one to Astrid, who hopped in behind her. Bettie was already flying far ahead of them. Silas hovered above them.

"You'll have to push us off," Cece told Tessa, jerking her head toward the stern.

Tessa hesitated. Of course, magic was going to step in here and save the day, but she still had to take several deep breaths before placing her hands on the deck. The wood was spongy, soft, and wet. She closed her eyes as she pushed, releasing the canoe from the muck with slurp and a judder. The bow met the water. She felt it start to float, as her shoes sloshed in the shallows.

"Hop in!" Astrid said, grabbing Tessa's hand and helping hoist her into the middle.

Then they were off, paddling along in a dilapidated, far-from-journey-ready canoe, not only floating, but speeding across the lake, which stayed eerily still beneath them. Silas flew above the bow, guiding them to the little island growing closer and more ominous with each stroke. How were they going so fast? Tessa watched the paddles in the water, how they went in and out without disturbing the water, without even a ripple.

Above the uncanny waters, the sky turned from blue to gray, steadily darkening. A storm was coming in fast. The wind began to pick up, coming from the south, trying to blow them back. The water started to move, small waves capped with white. Their pace slowed. Now, the paddles seemed to stick in the water as if it had turned viscous, syrupy.

Tessa's hair whipped around her face and she clung to the sides of the boat. Then the rain came, thick and solid as sheets of ice crashing down, obscuring everything. Tessa couldn't even see Cece's back in front of her through the deluge. She heard Cece scream for Silas, then she couldn't hear anything over the roar of the rain and the thunder.

A crack of lightning lit the sky and Tessa saw Silas' outline above them, his wings pumping, but sinking under the weight of the water. Then it was dark again.

Tessa reached in front of her, trying to feel for Cece, but her hand met only empty space, then the wooden seat of the canoe. She shouted for Cece, but couldn't even hear her own voice. She reached back for Astrid and felt her knee. A hand grabbed hers and she squeezed it.

*Stay with me*, Astrid thought-said.

Before Tessa could think her reply, the wind lifted her up. Like Dorothy or the Wicked Witch of the East, she was caught up in a whipping tornado, pulled higher and higher, above the storm, so she could see the tops of the trees of the island below. Then she was dropped.

She landed in a large, bouncy net next to Cece. It wasn't raining here. Tessa blinked, shivering in her damp clothes, her hair plastered against her face. Moments later, Astrid was dropped as well. Silas flew down and landed gingerly on a nearby tree branch, spreading his wings wide to try and dry them, just like a heron He shook his wings and a fine dust spread around him like talcum powder. *Some kind of waterproofing*, Tessa thought. She heard Bettie's squawking but couldn't see her.

"The boat was a trap," Silas said, taking flight again and hovering over them.

Astrid groaned, reaching up to squeeze out her hair.

"*This* is a trap," Cece answered. The flowers in her hair lay flat against her braid, drowned in the downpour.

Tessa shivered again, the cold damp on her skin seeping in deeper.

"Can you fly us out?" Astrid asked.

Silas bit his lip. "I don't... you're all awfully... big." He was having trouble keeping himself afloat.

Cece sighed. "Maybe I can—" The moment she lifted her arm to cast a spell, the netting rose up, entwining her arms, legs, and torso. "Shit!" Then it was over her mouth, gagging her.

Silas darted around above them, crying. "Mama! What do I do? What do I do, Mom?"

Astrid raised her arms, shouting, "Get help!" but enchanted netting was already crawling up her, too, holding her down and silent.

At this point, Tessa hardly dared to breathe, let alone speak. Still, she was free. Silas flew close to her and she stared intently into his wet brown eyes, trying to instill him with the strength he'd need. She felt a breeze kick up around them. Silas gave a little nod. She grabbed his arm and he pulled her up before the netting could catch her.

He wobbled as he flew toward the tree holding up the net and dropped her with a heavy sigh and a thud onto a large—but not large enough—branch. The bough sagged, cracked, and Tessa dropped, catching another tree limb and dangling above the net, which was alive and angry as a kraken.

Silas flew down again, trying to pull her up. His brow glistened with sweat and his little wings looked limp as they flitted and flapped.

"Help!" he hollered. "Please, somebody help! We're the good guys, ok?"

A tinkling laugh, like wind chimes or the sound clinking crystal, rang out. Tessa lost her grip—or did the tree push her?—and fell into the still, no-longer-raging net. Cece and Astrid were freed. Silas flew down and into Cece's arms, crying hard.

"It's ok, baby," Cece whispered. "Shh, it's ok."

"I don't want to be in charge anymore," Silas cried. "I'm only seven!"

"Um, Cece!" Astrid's voice sharp and urgent.

Tessa looked up. Half a dozen fairies were descending on them, their wings white and feathery like swans. Their skin ran the gambit of colors, from blue white to onyx black, but their hair was all the same colorless white as their wings. *Ice fairies.* The label was all too fitting.

One by one, the fairies landed on the net and it began to descend like an elevator to the ground, where it lay flat and lifeless. Cece, Astrid, and Tessa stood up to face the six fairies. Cece's hair began to bloom again, only instead of flowers, it was now full of tiny Venus flytraps, their mouths opening and waiting. Silas tucked himself behind Cece, his wings trembling. Bettie was still hidden, though Tessa was certain she remained nearby, ready. She imagined Bettie was the kind of bird that would peck the eyes out of enemies, which made her feel slightly better about the situation.

"Who are you?" the closest fairy asked. Tall and broad with dark skin and white hair piled high in intricate braids, and her lips were tinted blue. She wore a baby-blue pants suit, knife tucked into her belt loop. All the fairies were armed with at least one, if not three or four, weapons, from knives to swords to bows and arrows.

"My name is Cece Connolly, Clan Witch, formerly of the Grand River Coven. This is Astrid Laveau, Clan Witch, formerly of the Grand

River Coven. And Silas Faergas, Clan Fae, formerly of the Grand River Coven."

"You brought a *common*?" spat another fairy, even taller than the first, slender and pale-skinned with wispy white hair and at least five knives sheathed and hanging on her belt plus a sword in one hand, a bow over her shoulder, and a quiver of arrows strapped to her back.

"Tessa Andrews, Clan Familiar, of… The House Coven."

At this, Bettie flew down and landed on Tessa's shoulder.

"Can I be in The House Coven, too, Mom?" Silas asked. "Please?"

Cece pressed her lips together and Astrid put a hand over her mouth to hide her grin.

"Familiar isn't a Clan," the pale-skinned fairy spat back. "And I've never seen a Familiar with a pet raven." She sniffed the air. "You don't smell… quite right."

Tessa wasn't sure how to take that.

The closest fairy held up a silencing hand. "I've never heard of that coven—The House."

"It's new," Cece said, glancing sideways at Tessa and Tessa could tell she was both annoyed and impressed, hopefully mostly the latter. "Grand River Coven..." She trailed off and a hush went through the fairies and even the wood itself seemed to still in reverence to the memory of the fallen. "It's no more," Cece finished. "We have formed a new coven—The House Coven. And the raven," she added, glaring at Bettie, "is mine."

Bettie squawked and hopped to Tessa's other shoulder.

"She might disagree with you on that," the closest fairy in the baby-blue suit smirked, before asking, "How many of you are there in this, um… House Coven?"

Cece frowned. "Enough. We've introduced ourselves. Who are you?"

"You come to our territory and interrogate *us*!" This was the tall, pale fairy again. She pointed her sword toward Cece.

Cece narrowed her eyes. "I remember you. Elsa Murphey, Clan Fae, The Channels Coven."

Elsa took a step back, blinking.

"Your father was Elias, Leader of the Channels. Is he still—?"

"*Cordelia* Connolly?"

Another fairy approached the group. She looked several decades older than the rest, old enough to have white hair. By Non standards, at least, Tessa reminded herself.

"It *is* you," she said, holding her arms out wide in welcome. Besides the quiver on her back, she had no other weapons. She was dressed differently than the others who wore all blues and whites. She wore a wrap dress of deep purple. Her black skin held the same purple undertone and her pearl white wings stood out in glorious contrast.

"Auntie Izotz?" Cece exclaimed, her face alighting with pure joy and the Venus flytraps in her hair closing their mouths, while pink morning glory buds burst forth all around them, the vines twisting around the flytraps, tucking them away.

Both women squealed and ran to one another, hugging and cooing over one another, laughing and talking like old friends, while everyone else stood around them, watching or kicking at the dirt, trying not to make eye contact with anyone else. The tension of an almost fight still bristled in the air and no one quite knew what to say or do, how to greet the other side.

Elsa was watching Cece and Izotz embrace with bewilderment. Tessa imagined her brain working through it, trying to figure out who Cece was and how she knew her. Elsa was probably ten years younger than Cece, so Tessa imagined that she had been just a kid when Cece had lived with the coven.

Elsa's face turned, like a key clicking in a lock, into a sardonic smirk. "You're the half-breed witch girl. The one the coven hid after she murdered her *common* father."

There came an explosion of words from every direction. Tessa watched Cece, trying to gauge the truth of the accusation by how Cece's eyes shifted, how her face turned stoic and blank, how she seemed to stop breathing. The morning glories in her hair closed up. Bettie had come to land on her shoulder and Cece reached up to put a hand on the bird, as if steadying herself with the solidity of Bettie's presence.

"So it's true?" Tessa asked. She hadn't meant to speak it aloud, but suddenly the chattering and hollering around them stopped and all eyes were on Tessa, or Cece, or bouncing between them, overeager for a show.

Cece opened her mouth to speak, but Izotz answered for her. "She was a child. Her father tried to kill her. He *did* kill her mother. Murdered her in cold blood when he found out what she was, then tried to kill his Magick child as well. She had no choice, which was why we covered it up and took her in. Elsa," she snapped at the young woman. "You'd do well to remember the whole story beyond the colorful headline. Your father—may his memory always be of solace—it was his idea, after all." She turned to Cece, taking her by the shoulders and dislodging Bettie, who screeched in dismay. "You had no choice, Cordelia. Never forget this." Then she turned to her people. "This is why we hide. The Nons," and she stared pointedly at Tessa, "they'll always hate us simply for being who we are. We have no choice but to hide from comm—from the Nons, and the DOMs and all who would work to destroy us. It's how we've survived all these centuries, how we will make it through this latest onslaught."

"It's not enough," Cece blurted.

All eyes were on her, including Izotz, who had turned, arms folded across her chest, yielding the floor to Cece with respect and wariness.

"It's never been enough," Cece continued. "We've survived, sure. But at what cost? How many of you grew up on the stories of Salem? How the Boston Coven withdrew its aid to the northern coastal covens, leaving their people to perish at the hands of the DOMs? How many innocent Nons were killed in the slaughter? I'll remind you: half of the people who died weren't even Magix.

"This war was started because a Non killed a Magick. But he was no ordinary Magick. He was a Familiar turned Magick. The Non was his brother.

"As someone who has had her life torn apart by hate, I pity both brothers. I pity the Non for his inability to see his brother was still the beautiful soul he'd always been. I pity the Magick, of course. I pity Morana, his lover, the one who turned him Magick. I pity her rage and her misplaced, warped vendetta. She hates all Nons and sees any Magick who aligns themselves with a Non as an enemy. But never forget: she loved a Non herself. A Familiar. She loved him enough to give him magic and a child. A child like me, born of both worlds, a victim of the hate that killed so many, hidden away for years by people who meant well." She nodded to Izotz. "I've hidden away our children too," she added, gesturing to Silas. "Hiding isn't keeping us safe. The Grand River Coven was hidden. They found us. It's not just DOMs and Nons anymore. Magix have always been able to find other Magix. We have to be ready, in case they come for us next."

Elsa drew a second sword and grunted. "I'd say we're ready."

"Not just ready to defend what is yours. We'll go to other covens, gain allies, unite our forces. Then, if they come for us, we stand a real chance."

"So that's what you're doing, eh?" said the woman with the blue pants suit, head inclined, eyes narrowed. "Recruiting us to join your, um, House Coven?"

"THE House Coven," Silas corrected.

The woman nodded. "I haven't properly introduced myself yet. I'm Regina North, Clan Fae, Leader of The Channels Coven." She held out her hand to Cece. "Formerly of the Coven of Lake Superior."

A collective shiver at this name. Tessa made a mental note to ask about it later, as Cece reached out to take Regina's hand.

"I have spent my life in hiding," Regina said. "I'd like to change that. Tell us how we can help. The Channels Coven is at your service, Cordelia, Leader of The House Coven."

* * *

# NOV 1985

## *November 2, 1985*

*Archer,*

*We haven't heard from you in over a week. How is baby Cordelia? Have you parted ways with the mother yet? Stealing away an infant shouldn't be difficult or this time-consuming.*

*Your father is concerned you're not taking this seriously. In all the history of your kind and mine, since we evolved in concert, a balance to their chaos, we've never comingled. What we are doing—what you are doing—is revolutionary. Don't forget. This is for science, the progress of our people, yours and mine.*

*This is not a matter of the heart. Don't go soft on us now, kid.*

*—Tish*

# CHAPTER
# FOURTEEN

**JULY 2023** They stayed in the Channels until the evening. Cece and Astrid attended a meeting with the Coven leaders. Tessa, Silas, and Bettie were left in the grudging supervision of a teenage fairy named Nas, who wore his white hair in two thick braids and never stopped frowning, and a slightly younger vampire named Marlowe, who was his opposite in every way with loose black hair and an unsettlingly toothy grin.

"My brother's a vampire, too," Silas told Nas.

They'd walked to a clearing in the woods that appeared to be a gathering place for the Coven with ample seating, most of it floated or perched in the towering hemlock trees. Some hammocks stretched between a cluster of white pines along with a few benches, chairs, and tables on the ground. Silas floated just above the bench where Marlowe sat.

"Marlowe is not my brother," Nas called down from a low platform, floating among the leaves of a sugar maple. From where she lounged in a hammock, Tessa had a clear view of him. She'd never made an official Rule #5, but she was thinking she should add one. Maybe, *Trust your Gut*. Nas had a leering way of looking at and talking to others, particularly women, which gave Tessa the creeps. She was glad Astrid wasn't around.

Marlowe was braiding Silas' hair. They'd already painted one another's toes.

"Sister?" Silas asked, looking up at Marlowe, who shrugged.

"Either one, but we're not related," they said.

"Am I related to Luca?" Silas asked Tessa, starting to flit toward Tessa. Marlowe tutted and Silas stopped.

"Related is a funny word," Tessa said. "There's lots of ways to define it and not all are helpful. You and Luca are brothers, not by blood, but by love. That's the most powerful relationship of all."

Silas smiled, rocking his body back and forth a bit. Marlowe, bless them, didn't chide him or try to get him to sit still as they continued to braid his hair. They embraced the movement, ducking and bending with it.

"So if you aren't related, then you don't love each other," Silas concluded.

Tessa could tell from the grin on his face that he knew he was poking the proverbial bear that was Nas' grouchy attitude.

Nas sighed deeply, a full body heave, and dropped to the ground with more force than seemed necessary, given the wings. Not to mention menace.

"He loves me," Marlowe whispered to Silas. "He just finds me very annoying." Then they hollered, "But not as annoying as I find him!"

"That's it!" Nas shrieked, breaking his stoicism and turning, knife high, about to spring on Marlowe, until Bettie, without warning dove down and repeatedly pecked his hand until Nas dropped the knife.

Tessa picked it up with a growl. "Seriously? You're upset because you're not with the grown-ups making plans, but you pull a juvenile stunt like that? Clearly, you're in the right place."

Nas flitted back up into a tree, arms crossed, and a deep lip-puffed-out pout. For the rest of the day, he sat scrolling on his phone. Bettie, for her part, stayed near Nas, berating him with squawks if he so much as shifted his weight.

"I'm surprised you've got reception here," Tessa commented.

"Magic," Marlowe replied in a singsong tone.

Nas groaned.

Around dinner time, Astrid arrived, heaving a platter of food onto the table with a loud clatter and zero words. Tessa debated asking her what was wrong but decided to give her some time and space.

They ate their meal in contemplative silence until Cece came out from wherever she'd been, and then they were on their way, stopping at a wax museum in Hungary to stare into the eyes of Báthory Erzsébet

"Elizabeth Bathory," Tessa read. "A serial killer accused of murdering hundreds of girls. Nickname: 'The Bloody Countess.'"

"A psychopath," Cece said, "who also happens to be Morana's ancestor on her father's side."

"The crazy doesn't fall far from the tree," Astrid muttered. "This isn't somewhere my parents would detour."

"But Morana might have," Cece said.

Astrid sniffed the air. "I don't think so."

Cece nodded. "Worth a try."

"She looks like the Red Queen," Silas murmured. "From *Alice in Wonderland.*"

"The OG Red Queen," Tessa said, laughing at herself. Astrid and Silas stared back and her with blank expressions. Cece patted her shoulder.

"Good effort," she said and Bettie, perched on shoulder, chirped in agreement.

In a blink, they were back home. *Home.* Strange she should think of it that way, but Tessa did. Her mind then drifted toward her actual home, the house she owned, the work she was missing. She *should* email HR back. Her plants would need watering. The food in the fridge would spoil. Did she leave lights on? What about clothing, toiletries? She ran her tongue over her teeth, trying to remember the last time she brushed them.

She turned to Cece with a look of sudden panic and embarrassment, but Cece smiled.

"I asked Jean to move all your things here. Well, as much as he could."

Tessa frowned. "Were you reading my mind? I'd prefer you give me a heads-up!"

Cece's eyes went wide. "No! I would never do that without your knowledge or permission."

She reached out and squeezed Tessa's hand and Tessa wasn't annoyed or angry anymore because Cece's hand was soft and warm. Tessa hoped her hands didn't feel too dry and her breath wasn't rancid and—

"Your face looked… worried," Cece continued. "You should have everything you need now. I'm sorry if you wanted to go back to your house, but for now, you're stuck here." She gestured across the living room, where Silas had joined Luca and one of the twins in a wrestling match while the other twin (Lola, Tessa was *pretty* sure) lay passed out on the couch snoring. "Jean wasn't able to stay long. The house is being surveilled. He had to sweet-talk your little friend into letting him in."

"Sanjay?"

Cece nodded.

Tessa imagined Jean plying Sanjay with a siren song and smiled. Sanjay, the Sanjay she'd known, always preferred the manliest men and womanliest women, oscillating from one to the other, living in binary extremes. Sanjay—her Sanjay; she kept thinking of him as a different creature altogether from the man she'd heard in the voicemails, the man she refused to believe was the real Sanjay—would've been completely enthralled by Jean.

"He won't remember a thing," Cece added. "Memory wiping only works on Nons, however, so Jean had to be quick in case a Magick showed up."

"So he *is* a Non, then?"

Cece tilted her head to the side. "Um... yes?"

"I thought maybe he wasn't, you know? Like he'd tricked me."

"He *did* trick you."

Tessa couldn't explain her complicated feelings. Sanjay had been her friend for years and for some reason, she wanted a grander explanation for his deceit. She wanted a spy thriller, an agent deep undercover, a monster lurking among the unsuspecting, a Magick among Nons. It was probably a prejudice of some kind. She wanted him to be different, for the difference to explain the betrayal and dull the grief. But he was like her: ordinary. And the betrayal, though gilded with magic, was unadorned and artless underneath.

When Tessa said nothing, Cece continued. "It won't be safe for you to go back for a while." She held Tessa's hand in hers, lightly, unthinking. "You'll be safe here, I promise."

"Could Jean try that siren song on my boss?" Tessa asked, then laughed. "Just kidding. I hate my job, so if this whole thing gets me fired, so be it."

"Que sera, sera, huh?" Cece gave Tessa's hand another squeeze before dropping it.

The gentle warmth of the gesture made Tessa smile broadly, despite herself. She closed her mouth, trying to keep the bad breath contained.

"You should get some rest," Cece told her. "And about Sanjay, it probably wasn't all a trick. He can't have been her Familiar for long."

"*Her* Familiar? Morana's?"

Cece nodded. She kept her gaze locked with Tessa's like they were having a staring contest. Tessa found it easy to stare back into the green waves of Cece's eyes, like rocking to sleep on a ship, floating in a wide expanse of calm.

Cece looked away first. "Get some rest," she repeated. "I have to talk to Jean. It's going to be getting crowded around here. At least for the next couple days."

"Crowded? Why?"

"I offered up our house… er… coven as a meeting place."

"For Magix from the Channels?"

"Among others, yes."

"That's vague as hell."

Cece sighed. "Yeah, well, I'm sorry, but you're just a Familiar, so I can't, you know…"

Tessa turned away before she could finish. She wasn't sure how much more of this "just a familiar" spiel she could take. It reminded her of when she'd first gotten licensed to be a foster parent. Social workers were always giving her sympathetic looks and saying things like, "Well, I don't know if you'll be able to handle them all on your own."

Sanjay never did that and Tessa had always loved him for it. She pushed him out of her mind because thinking about him was proving too painful. She couldn't deal with the chaos of her reality and the added grief of losing her best friend to some vindictive vampire shapeshifter, who also had Theo.

"Tessa!" Cece called after her.

Tessa turned. "Did you ever apologize to Oscar?"

Cece frowned. "What does that—?

"I'm *just* a Familiar; he's *just* a Wayward. It's a pattern. You discount people because of what they are, not *who* they are."

Cece gaped. "Damn. I—I—"

Tessa held up a hand. "Don't apologize to me. I'm fine. I'm an adult. Apologize to Oscar. And, like you said, do better."

Cece bowed her head. "Yeah. Ok."

Tess turned to keep walking.

"You're an asshole, by the way," Cece hollered after her, a chuckle in her voice.

"But I'm right!" Tessa called back as she continued up the stairs.

She was relieved to hear Cece come behind, to hear the tentative knock on Oscar's door followed by Cece's hesitant, "Can I come in?"

Tessa went into her room and then into the bathroom to brush her teeth. Her mind drifted to Theo. As she stared at the mirror, Tessa wondered, not for the first time, if Theo's placement with her had been a coincidence. *Sanjay can't have been Morana's Familiar for long.* How could Cece know that? Clearly, Astrid's placement was no coincidence. Was that because Tessa had been "successful" with Theo? They'd been able to stay hidden with her. They'd stayed safe. And when the time had come, Morana had swooped in and easily stole them away.

Tessa came out of the bathroom to find Astrid sitting on the bed, staring down at her feet, head lowered, blonde curls flopping over her face.

"Hey." Tessa paused in the doorway. "You okay?"

Astrid raised her head, curls bouncing to the side to reveal her tear-streaked face.

Tessa sat down on the bed beside her, laying an open palm out on her knee. Astrid took it, squeezed tight.

"How did the talk with Regina, Cece, and the others go?" Tessa asked.

Astrid groaned and flopped backward on the bed.

"That bad, huh?" Tessa flopped back as well.

They both stared up at the blank white ceiling for a few quiet minutes before Astrid lifted a hand, wiggled her fingers, and the ceiling was replaced with a forest canopy. Tessa glanced left and right to see rubber trees taking root along the walls, along with palm, myrtle, and a towering kapok tree. The canopy rose hundreds of feet above them. Tessa could hear the chirps of tanagers and warblers.

"Better," Astrid said. "I've always wanted to go to a rainforest."

"What's stopping you?" Tessa asked.

Astrid laughed, rolling onto her stomach to peer down at Tessa with a chiding smirk. "Though this is probably safer," Tessa added.

"No shit. Also, I can't transport on my own. My parents never finished teaching me." Astrid flopped back down, still on her stomach, her face buried in the soft mattress.

Tessa watched the leaves overhead lilting left and right in an overhead breeze, the glint of sunlight sparkling through them. She was trying to figure out if it was real, or just an illusion. Did it matter? The shadow of a bird passed over. What was that? Something green with yellow and red stripes on its head. Theo used to love bird watching. Maybe they'd know. They probably had a book of tropical birds somewhere, just like the birds of Michigan book they took with them everywhere that first fall they were together. That first fall, when they went walking in the woods together every day after Theo got out of school. Tessa remembered one time, only a few weeks into their time together, when she'd thought she had lost Theo. She'd hollered their name over and over and then a bird, a red cardinal, landed on her shoulder. Absurdly, she stopped hollering and froze. The bird flitted to her finger, cocking its head to the side. It had a brown patch on its neck and weird black markings around its eyes. It looked her straight in the eyes and then flew away. She stood there a moment in the transfixed calm that comes from unexpected communion with nature. The holiness held her in thrall until she felt a tug on her elbow and there was Theo.

"Were you looking for me?" they'd asked her.

Tessa sat up. "The bird was Theo!"

Astrid flipped over. "What?"

"Nothing." Tessa lay back down. "I was… lost in thought."

"They aren't going to look for my parents."

"What?" Tessa turned to her. "Wasn't that the whole point?"

"The point is to stop the slaughter of good Magix." Astrid sighed. "To save our people."

"I mean…"

"I know. I know it's a good thing. The important thing. But…" She shook her head and closed her eyes. "That night, my dad was scouting ahead. He double detoured to the coven and when he got there, it was under attack. When he didn't come back quickly, my mom went, too. They came back too quickly. He was hurt. She forgot to detour. She led them straight back to our house. My dad was bleeding a lot. My mom held him up, tried to tell me what happened, what to do. She looked so scared. I'd never seen her look so terrified. There was a loud bang and I ducked down. Instinct, I guess. I don't know. I hid. I heard voices, shouting. My mom transported again with my dad. She led them away. It was so fast. Later, the DOMs came back and wrecked the place, shot guns to make it look like a murder scene. But they didn't bring bodies. If they were dead, they would've brought them back."

"Where were you?"

"A portal, hidden in the house. Like a panic room, you know? My mom made it in case…" She took a shaky breath.

Tessa reached over to take her hand.

"In case we were discovered. It was where I was supposed to go. They'd gone over it so many times. I thought it was dumb and annoying." She let go of Tessa's hand and sat up, palms flat on her knees as if to brace herself, to hold herself upright and together. "I never even saw their faces. The DOMs. I don't know what they look like. If I knew, then maybe I could—"

"Don't think like that," Tessa said, sitting up and placing a hand on Astrid's shoulder. "You did *exactly* what you were supposed to do. What your parents wanted you to do."

They were quiet, listening to the calls of birds overhead, the whistling screeches of tamarins in the branches, and scuttling of something among the dense ground foliage.

Tessa tucked her feet under her.

"I can put it back after this," Astrid said, doing the same.

A bird swooped low and left some droppings right where Tessa's feet had been. "Maybe just get rid of the animals?"

Astrid winked and snapped her fingers. The room grew quiet and scat free.

"If your parents were hiding, where would they go?"

"I don't know."

"Think about it," Tessa replied, not meaning to press, but feeling her voice rise in both pitch and volume, as her thoughts turned to Theo, wondering where they were, how she could possibly find them.

"You don't think I have been?" Astrid snapped.

Tessa sighed. This was impossible, the whole thing. Not only was magic somehow, *impossibly*, real, but there was a whole new magical world she was expected to be a part of, a war she needed to help fight, and through it all, she had to parent this kid, help her with her loss and trauma, guide her on her journey, literal and emotional. It was an impossible task and she felt the weight of it hit her, like a wave slapping her back and pulling her under.

Maybe none of this was actually happening to her. Tessa closed her eyes. So much of what had happened over the last few days was nonsensical. Maybe this was all a very long and elaborate dream. She'd been embracing this reality. Maybe the key to getting out was to fight it.

*Do you want this to be a dream?* She opened her eyes to take in the ridiculous majesty of the towering kapok tree, its mountainous roots.

She thought about everything she'd experienced in the last couple days, the places she'd been, the people she'd met. She thought about Cece in particular, despite herself.

Her mind settled on Astrid, who was still here, very real, beside her.

*Rule #1: Put the kid's needs first.*

Whether this world was real or not, she was, first and foremost, a foster mom to this kid.

"Maybe they left clues?"

Astrid shook her head. "Like at the house? We can't go back there."

"What about what they said? They must have known this was a possibility, Astrid. They would have prepared you, even if it was subliminally or—"

"What if they didn't?"

"You knew you were supposed to go to the panic room place—"

"The portal."

"Right." Tessa hopped to her feet, thinking she was onto something. "The portal. When they talked about it, what else did they mention?"

Astrid flung her body backward, her bouncing curls reverberating her annoyance. "I wanna go to bed."

Tessa sighed, then nodded. "Fine. We can talk more in the morning."

Astrid groaned, closing her eyes.

"So, this is *my* bed. Your room is... across the hall."

Astrid sat up and looked at Tessa. Filled with tears, her green eyes appeared even more like the surface of the Lake than usual. "Can I stay here?"

Tessa smiled. She'd known this girl for a little over a week, but Tessa was her Familiar now and it felt right to say *yes*, so she nodded. In all her time caring for children, she'd learned each formed attachments at their own pace. Theo, like Astrid, had trusted Tessa quickly and their attachment had been sudden and profound. Now, Tessa understood this was likely due the Familiar bond. Tessa remembered her mother's story of the first time she held Tessa, how she knew with unwavering certainty that Tessa was hers, even though she hadn't carried Tessa in her body.

"Love at first sight," Kathy always called it and while Tessa had grown up scoffing at this, she knew now how true this was.

In Tessa's mind, being a Familiar was a lot like being a parent. Her job was to remain a solid, loving force, open to provide whatever Astrid needed, whenever she needed it. "I can sleep in your room or on the couch?" Tessa offered.

Astrid shook her head. "Can you stay close? I need to know someone's there."

Tessa nodded. "Sure thing."

For a long time, Tessa lay, staring up at the never-ending ceiling, tracing the outlines of tree branches with her eyes. Trying to see the magic.

"Astrid?"

"Mmm?"

"What does magic look like?"

Astrid chuckled, flinging up her arm to indicate the ceiling. "Like this!"

"No, I mean actual magic. While you're doing it."

"Magic doesn't look like anything. It's a feeling. It's everywhere, in everything. I just… grab hold of it and use it."

"It's not like a light?"

"Go to sleep, Tessa."

Closing her eyes, Tessa saw the trees outlined in shifting rainbows against her eyelids, dancing with light and magic.

* * *

## NOV 1985

### *November 12, 1985*

*Internal Memo*
*Re: Hybrids #1 and #2*

*From: Marcus Brand*

*To: Gunner Engers, Tish Chernoff*

*An utter failure. I hope you two realize that. The disappearance of two Hybrids and one of them less than a week old. I've managed to cover that one, calling it a stillbirth. But the ogre child? I can't cover your asses for that.*

*You will be required to attend an inquest from the Committee. If I were the two of you, I'd have something fantastic up my sleeve.*

*Lucky for you, MAAM PAC has fallen down on Leadership's priority list. The inquest will be on April 26, 1986. So you've got time to get your goddamn shit together.*

# CHAPTER
# **FIFTEEN**

**JULY 2023** The next morning, Tessa awoke to the sounds of a house filled with people: loud voices, occasional shrieks, running footsteps, and the clank of utensils against dishware. The smell of eggs and various sautéing meats and vegetables filled the air.

From the top of the stairs, she looked down to find a couple dozen people gathered in the living room. She recognized about half of the adults, picking out Cece, whose hair, freed of all constraints, hung in tight curls all around her head, silver and gold shimmers looping through them and catching the light like a battle helmet glinting in the sun. Tessa then spotted Jean, pacing back and forth from the kitchen with trays of food. She recognized Izotz, Elsa, and Regina from the Channels, but there were another half a dozen adults Tessa didn't know. She saw the teenagers, Astrid, Oscar, Marlowe, and Nas. The little children weaved in and out of the furniture in some elaborate and hilarious game of tag. Tessa watched them and had to count a few times to verify that there were five children, two of whom were Silas.

One of the Silas' glanced up and saw her looking down at the scene in perplexity. A wide grin spread across his face and he sailed up to the second story, stopping in front of Tessa.

"Hi! I'm Silas."

Tessa frowned. The voice was… different? Silas landed on top of the railing, bending so his face was inches from Tessa's. Then he changed. A different dark-haired child stood in front of her. Tessa nearly fell backward down the stairs. The child giggled.

"I'm Evie!" She turned back into Silas. "Boo!"

Thankfully, Tessa did not react this time.

Evie sighed. "It's only ever fun once anyway." She shifted back into her own form.

"I'm Tessa, by the way."

"I know! I'm Evie."

"I heard."

"Are you an ogre? I've never seen one before."

"Um, no. I'm a Familiar."

"A what?"

"A Non."

Evie's brown eyes bugged out. "Seriously!" She jumped up and down. "That's cool. Can I be you?" She shifted into Tessa. "Hi, I'm a Non! My name is Tina."

"Tessa."

"I have no magical powers. I'm soooo boring." She shifted back, and then hugged Tessa tightly around the waist. "That was fun!"

"Evie! Are you behaving?" came a voice from downstairs.

Evie rolled her eyes. "Yes, Papa!"

"Come down and eat some breakfast!"

"Ugh!" Evie sighed, nosediving off the balcony.

Alarmed, Tessa ran to railing, choking out a scream as the child sailed through the air. Above her, Bettie let out an echoing screech and below, all eyes swiveled up. Only then did Evie, inches from the ground, shift into a fairy. She soared to the ceiling, past a disgruntled Bettie, to a round of mild applause, before landing beside a pair of angry looking men, one of whom looked identical to the form into which she'd shifted.

"Hey, Papa! I'm you."

It was strange to hear a child's trying-to-sound-like-an-adult voice coming from an actual adult body. Tessa wondered why the voice didn't shift with the body, too, and added it to a growing list of things to ask Cece.

Evie shifted into the shape of the other adult.

"Hey, Dad," she said in the same gruff voice. "Now I'm you."

"Evie," the man called Papa said, his voice rising testily on the second syllable. A fairy, he was tall and thin, with dark skin and silver-white, almost blue hair. "You know the rules."

"No shifting into Papa or me," the man called Dad finished.

Compared to his partner, who was dazzlingly different, his skin in glorious contrast to his hair, silver-blue wings, and bright blue eyes, this man looked like every other white man in his mid-thirties that Tessa had ever encountered: slightly overweight, thinning brown-ish gray hair, glasses, a button-up shirt tucked into his jeans. As she came down the stairs, Tessa tried to catch a glimpse of his eyes and teeth to see if either would give away his magical power.

"Tessa!" Jean called out. "Come, come! I'll introduce you to everyone." He caught her by the arm and pulled her along. He handed her a plate full of food. "I'll do the talking so you can do the munching."

Tessa nodded, already stuffing a mini tofu quiche into her mouth.

Jean guided her to the two men and their shapeshifting child, who was pouting on the ground, arms and legs crossed.

"She'd cross her ears, if she could," the beautiful fairy man said with a smile. "I'm Dante Martin." He held out his hand to Tessa.

Tessa tried to talk through her mouth full of food. "Mmm… Tedda."

"This is *Tessa*," Jean interpreted. "She's Astrid's Familiar."

"Pleasure." Dante smiled and Tessa could see he meant it.

Here, among the Magix, Tessa felt a little like she was coming out all over again. *Here's Tessa, the Non. Did you know that Tessa's a Non?* Perhaps because she had grown up in a swing county, among hardy progressives and delicate libertarians, stalwart liberals and hippy conservatives, she'd never felt completely safe and secure in her identity. So she watched people, how their faces moved the moment they discovered who she was, what she was. Something always gave them away, especially if the first thought they had on hearing the word "queer" was a negative one.

Magix, Tessa found, responded the same to the word "Non." Dante, to his credit, had smiled without a flinch, or curl of the lip to indicate anything other than acceptance.

"This is Tim," Dante said.

Tim, in contrast to his partner, had stiffened slightly at Jean's introduction. He gave an awkward half wave, half salute. "Howdy. Tim Martin, at your service."

"*The* Tim Martin?" Tessa exclaimed.

"Maybe?" Tim chuckled.

"I read your interview." Tessa lowered her voice to add, "With Morana."

Tim grimaced. "I shouldn't have given her a platform, I know. I still get hate mail full of minor hexes and curses for that."

Tessa frowned. "Sorry… I didn't know."

"It is important to know one's enemy," Jean said. "We are better armed for your troubles, my cousin."

As they were walking away, Tessa couldn't help murmuring, "*He's a siren?*"

Jean clicked his tongue at her. "Oh là, Tessa, do not judge a book by its cover. Contrary to popular Non lore, sirens are almost exclusively male. Do not ask me why. I do not know. Yes, I had a mother. And seven brothers." He shrugged. "Plus, we are not always so pleasing on the eyes. We don't need to be. We have la voix" He winked. "You met the others from the Channels?"

Tessa nodded.

"The one you should watch is Regina North. She's the leader. She'll be calling the shots. Her and those two you just met. They're the co-leaders of the Coven of Washtenaw County. Then there's Deirdre Laguerre." Surreptitiously, he gave a low gesture toward a tall woman who stood alone at the back of the room, arms folded regally across her chest.

She wore an indigo turban that added another six inches to her already imposing six feet. Her skin was the sandy color of dunes at sunset and she'd drawn thick makeup over her eyes so that they stood out, big and yellow against her contoured cheeks. Even from the across the room, Tessa could see the thick black hairs on her lip and chin. She had painted her lips a brilliant magenta.

"She's fantastic," Tessa breathed.

"Formidable. She's from the Second City Coven. They call their leaders Empress or Emperor." He waved his hand. "Something garish. Anyway, she came alone, which is bizarre."

"So it's folks from those three covens?" Tessa couldn't take her eyes off Deirdre.

Silas had flitted over to Deirdre and was hovering near her head, his lips moving fast. Her lips curved into a smile and she held out her hand. A flame danced with it, shifting into the form of a snake. A fiery tongue flicked out. Silas held out his hand and mimicked the gesture, only with his fire, he created a dragon.

"Indeed. From the three remaining covens nearest us to the north, east, and west."

"And to the south?" Tessa asked, keeping her eyes on Deirdre, who was grinning as Silas' fire dragon fought her fire snake.

The dragon won easily, the snake disappearing in a puff of smoke. Then Deirdre must have sensed Tessa's eyes on her. She began to slowly pivot her head, owl-like, as she surveyed the room. Tessa quickly dropped her gaze to her plate of food.

"Cece sent a request to the Bloomington Coven in Indiana. No response." Jean shook his head. "There used to be half a dozen covens between here and there. If Bloomington has fallen…" He sighed, covering his mouth with his large hand. He laughed, a small, sad sound. "I think the next nearest might be Nashville." He uttered a series of French words, none of which Tessa could understand, although from context, she gathered he was cursing out Morana.

Tessa put a hand on Jean's arm. "I'm sorry."

"Merci. Now, listen up."

Tessa was searching the crowd for Deirdre, but she'd disappeared. Was a she a vampire? Tessa knew vampires controlled fire. She hadn't seen wings, so probably not a fairy like Silas.

"Hallo, are you listening?"

Tessa turned back to Jean. "Yes, sorry."

"They will underestimate you because you are a Non. Thus, you can listen."

"What do you mean?"

"Our guests will be here for a couple days. In the east corridor, we have several empty rooms and we can always, temporarily, add more. So, stop looking like a deer in the headlights. Act natural."

Instead of speaking, Tessa ate another tofu mini quiche. She was convinced Jean must be able to imbue his siren magic into the food he prepared. *Magic-infused cuisine.*

"Better. Cece and I will be in the meetings with them."

"Just you?"

"No kids in the meeting."

"Not a kid," Tessa replied.

Jean gave her a look that caused her to scarf down another quiche to remember how much she loved him and his cooking and how she needed to act *naturelle* and not make a scene.

"Outside of the meetings, they will talk to one another, when they think no one, or no one of consequence, is listening."

"So I get to be a spy?"

"Fine, if you prefer. Une espionne."

"*Une espionne*," Tessa repeated. "Maybe I'll be fluent *en français* before this is over."

To which Jean replied in French and cocked his head to wait for her reply.

"But not today."

"So you'll do it?"

Tessa nodded. "I'll lurk and listen." Above her, Bettie squawked and dove, landing gracefully on Tessa's shoulder, her claws digging into her skin enough to give a reassuring sting, but not enough to hurt.

"Bettie can teach you a thing or two about that. Eh, Bettie?" Jean gave the bird's chin a scratch. Then he bent down and kissed Tessa's forehead. "Merci." He started to walk away.

"Jean, wait. How many covens were there? Before?"

Jean blew out some air and looked up at the ceiling. Tessa followed his gaze. The greenery was even denser than it had been a couple days before. More strings of pearls, but also strings of hearts and nickels, trailing jade, October Daphne, and purple-stemmed Ruby Necklace with its yellow blossoms and the sun dancing off its plumage, turning it ruby red.

"Once, maybe five hundred covens in the continental United States. Around the world… it is more difficult to say. Europe, we never quite recovered from the Burnings. Africa is its own space with its own rules. I imagine they are untouched by this. They went undercover during the height of colonization and never looked back. Parts of Asia are similar. South of the United States, there is more unity and openness for Magix, at least in some countries. I digress. Here, more than half were destroyed in the first attack. We are maybe a hundred strong now, maybe less." He sighed. "Probably less. The big-city covens are mostly gone. I was surprised Second City still stands. There are no covens in New York or New England," His voice cracked and he dropped his gaze back to the ground.

Tessa started to reach out to comfort him, but Cece stepped between them and whispered something in Jean's ear.

He nodded. Cece clicked her tongue at Bettie who took flight and sailed ahead of her into the kitchen, into which all adult Magix were walking. Cece and Jean entered last, closing the doors behind them.

* * *

**APRIL 1986**

"So, zaya, Valerie, my little bunny, what do you think?" Andor smiled, not looking at her. He pressed his knife across the gelatinous skin of his kielbasa, sheering through the casing and into the lumpy meat.

Even as she watched Andor, Val appeared to keep her eyes on her borscht, stirring the red broth and limp beets, the pulverized remains for vegetables reminding her of animal flesh.

*You shouldn't have come here,* Tish continued to thought-berate her, never once meeting her gaze.

Val brought her spoon to her mouth and took a dainty sip. "Delicious," she whispered, feeling the slop running down her gullet, smacking against a stomach that still refused to keep anything down. She tried to catch Tish's eyes across the table, tried to convey her desperation in thought-language: *I had nowhere else to go.*

Andor laughed, a sharp boom that caused his bird-like little girl, Ana, to start. Tish placed a steadying hand on her daughter's shoulder. The girl looked up from her untouched food and her blue-gray eyes met Val's across the table. *Tish's eyes.* Eyes like the ocean of their home coven, the ocean that took everything. Tish's eyes on a scraggly tomboy of a nine-year old. Something moved deep inside Val, a new sensation just this past week. Week twenty. Halfway through. *Only* halfway. Christ, she was never going to make it. She recalled a phrase Tish once wrote, *I can hardly bear the love.* In this moment, Val felt the truth of this statement like the dyspeptic raging of her body. To love a thing that was killing you was truly fucked up.

"Not the food," Andor was saying, chewing the meat as he talked. "I meant Pripyat. How do you find my hometown? You are staying at the Polissya, no?"

*Be polite.* Tish thought-warned her, eyes down, a thin smile plastered across her lips. She looked like a doll, eternally beautiful and unmoving.

*You're not listening to me, Morticia.* Val wanted to scream. Instead, she told Andor. "I have a wonderful view of the power plant from my window."

Ana giggled, then slapped both hands across her mouth.

*I told you not to bring that up.* Tish thought-chided.

A muscle in Andor's jaw twitched. He shoveled another forkful of pink-ish meat into his mouth, chewed and chewed and chewed.

The now-familiar wave of nausea began to claw its way up from Val's stomach.

"You are coming to us from where?" Andor continued. "You traveled the Baltics?"

"Estonia," Val managed to gasp out. The sour burn of stomach acid filled her throat, bubbled up into her mouth. *I can't keep—I'm going to be sick.* "Excuse me."

She was up and moving away toward the bathroom before he had a chance to answer.

Tish watched her go, taking in the jut of her shoulder blades and the pallor of her wings. "I'll make sure she's alright," she told Andor. The metal legs of her chair grated against the tile floor. She hated everything in this cursed house, Andor's inherited family home which was now their "vacation home." The maid met her in the hallway and spoke to her in careful English.

"The friend is ill, gospozha," the maid whispered.

She was a Dud, a Non born to a magical family, a type of creature that Tish reviled on instinct. Another inherited thing.

"Your English is shit," she told the girl before pushing past her into the bathroom, where she found Val curled over the toilet.

It was an American toilet, not a hole in the ground. The first of many upgrades Tish had made to this old house. She pressed her back against the door and slid down to the ground. She watched Val retch until she was still. Then she said, "So it worked, then."

Val said nothing.

"Why are you here? You weren't supposed to be here." *You were supposed to go straight back to Gunner.*

*Couldn't travel that far. Too sick. I need your help.* She reached up to flush the toilet and in the rush of sound, she said aloud. "I'm scared."

*Tough shit.* Tish thought-said. *Babies are born every day. You'll make it through.*

Val studied her old friend. Gone was the happy-go-lucky attitude of her youth. In its place sat a prematurely gray-haired woman with deep frown lines around her lips and eyes. "It's too powerful." *It will destroy us all.*

Tish shook her head. *Impossible. The two we already created came from much more powerful stock than you and the nobody DOM you were assigned. Gunner said so himself that the DOM was flaccid and weak. No one wants you hurt, Val. I know a witch doctor who can take care of that nausea. You'll be right as rain.*

"Tish, listen to me," Val whispered. *Please.*

Her voice was a shock wave rattling through Tish's brain. Tish cracked her neck to dislodge the sound. The dish of soap on the counter skittered into the sink.

"Since when can you do *that?*" Tish said aloud.

Val said nothing, stared at Tish with those enlarged brown eyes. She'd lost weight, Tish realized, despite the slight protrusion of her stomach. Her skin had a jaundiced look. Sallow. An intrusive memory of Val's mother kneeling in sand before her dead little girl caused Tish to shudder. Val looked so much like her mother.

"When did we get old?" Tish asked.

Val gave a sad smile and sniffed like she was holding in a sob. *There's more power in me than I can contain. I'm afraid I'll break from it.*

Again, Tish felt a shudder in the air. A crash came from the kitchen followed by a shriek from Ana. "Earthquake!"

"Hush, dochka," Andor whispered, then shouted, "Morticia, Valerie, is everything alright?"

"Fine," Tish shouted back. Her knuckles her white, pressed against the tile floor. "Valerie," she murmured. "What is happening?"

*I think I need to end it.* Val's lips were a thin white line. *If I don't, I think it'll kill me.*

Slowly, Tish moved toward Val, sliding her bottom along the floor until she was less than a foot from Val. Val trembled. Her skin looked almost blue in the fluorescent bathroom light.

*It's not trying to kill me. It's not malicious. It simply is.* Val reached for Tish's long white-blond hair, tucking a strand behind her ear. "We were happy, Tish."

Tish nodded. Tears had come to her eyes. When was the last time she'd cried?

*Will you help me?* Val thought-asked. What was she asking for help with? Even as she thought-said the words, she wasn't sure, didn't know what form the help would take, only that she needed… *something.* An ending. A beginning?

Tish nodded again.

"Not here." Val closed her eyes, imagining the view of the Chernobyl Nuclear Power Plant from her hotel window, recalling the drive into Pripyat, how the air around the sprawling campus felt poised and seemed to pull toward her like she was a magnet. Worse, even. Like she was a prophet, preparing the way for a long-awaited Messiah. *It must be somewhere secluded, uninhabited. It might fight.*

*It's a fetus, Val.* Tish frowned as she watched Val's face, tried to discern the thoughts her friend kept hidden. She came closer to Val, lifted her chin. Val did not open her eyes. Tish pulled off Val's glasses and kissed each of her eyes, then her nose, her mouth. Val stayed still, but Tish, holding Val's hands, could feel the gallop of her pulse. She moved her hands to Val's stomach. Beneath it, she felt nothing, too early for any hiccup-like sensation to make its way to the surface and press against her hand in greeting.

"Have you felt it yet?"

Val nodded.

"I remember that feeling. Little bubbles. I called her Bubbles, you remember? Before she was born."

"I remember you hated Bubbles."

Tish chuckled. "I did. Not enough to end it, though." God, Val looked terrible. More than terrible. She looked like she was starving. Even her hands felt thin. The thing in her womb, Tish probably wanted even more than Val did. She'd pushed her into the pregnancy, hadn't she? And if Val died from it? Tish swallowed, squeezing Val's wrists. She'd never forgive herself. Never.

Val tried to pull away, but Tish tightened her grip on Val's wrist.

"I can do it now," Tish said.

"Not. Here."

But Tish was already using her powers of telekinesis to squeeze Val's uterus, to press against the fetus, to crush it.

Val gasped. "Wait, stop. Not here. Not—I'm not ready!"

Tish shook her head, spoke through gritted teeth. "I won't let it hurt you. I won't lose you."

"I said *no!*" Val screamed.

Tish flew backward and hit the door with a smack. She kept consciousness, but was unable to speak. The air in the room contracted like a uterus preparing for birth. Val was on her feet, hands pressed to her belly.

"No, no, no!" She kept repeating the words. "I said not here!" Her hands flailed around until they landed on her glasses, sitting on the counter. She put them on and pushed past Tish without a word.

Andor's voice boomed out from the kitchen. "Leaving so soon?"

Tish heard the door slam. She heard the explosion. The house shook. She heard the crash of dishes breaking, the screams of Ana and the maid, and Andor's cursing. Then all was, abruptly, still.

Tish moved to the window. There was nothing to see. It was as if the house sat in the eye of a tornado. Around them, there was nothing but thick, gray fog.

CHAPTER
# SIXTEEN

**JULY 2023** The meeting lasted the entire day. At lunch time, Jean brought out sandwiches for the kids, who leaped on them like starving creatures. Tessa was glad she'd eaten too much at breakfast because between four teenagers, two werewolf toddlers, and three more kids, only a few crusts remained.

Besides meal times, Astrid stayed in her room with the door closed. Twice, Tessa went up, knocked, and was told to first "Go away," then, "Are you deaf? Leave me alone! Goddamn."

Tessa put the twins down for their naps. They snuggled up to each other in their toddler bed like a couple of furry cherubs. Sleep seemed to intensify their wolf features. Was staying in human form a conscious effort, falling away with sleep? Or, Tessa wondered, perhaps it was a kind of evolutionary defense mechanism.

Shutting the door behind her, Tessa had to shake her head to clear the endless barrage of questions this newfound magical world raised.

In the living room, she found Marlowe, Oscar, and Nas each sitting in different corners. Each was on their phones. Tessa chuckled. *Some things are universal.*

Around 5:00 p.m., Tessa was finishing up an intense game of

Candyland with Silas, Evie, and Luca while Lola and Livy climbed all over them, trying to snatch the pieces and eat them, when the adults filed out of the kitchen, single-file and bleary-eyed.

Cece took up the rear with Bettie on her shoulder. Unlike the humans, Bettie looked bright-eyed as ever. She called a greeting to the room, before flying up into the plants overhead. Jean and Izotz didn't come out. Presumably, they were making dinner.

Seeing Cece, Livy dove off Tessa's shoulders and Lola rolled out from under the couch to bound over to Cece, jumping into her arms and covering her with slobbery kisses and licks.

Luca looked up from the game at her with a glare. "You were gone a long time."

"I missed you, too, Lukie," Cece laughed.

"Hi, Mama," Silas said, grinning.

Oscar glanced up from his phone and flashed Cece a smile. Cece reached out to ruffle his hair and he ducked her, half-heartedly protesting.

"You apologized?" Tessa whispered.

Cece nodded. "Thank you."

Meanwhile, Evie had shifted into a cat and was hiding under the table from her dads, who were calling her name.

"Evelyn Ximena—"

"She's here." Tessa picked the Evie-cat up by the scruff of its neck. Immediately, Evie shifted and Tessa let go, dropping her half a foot. She flopped and flailed as if she'd fallen several stories. For a moment, Tessa worried Dante and Tim would be angry at her, but they both shook their heads and rolled their eyes at Evie.

"Come on, mija," Dante said.

"Thanks for watching her," Tim said. Smiling, he almost looked handsome. The two men and their daughter left, following the other guests, except for Marlowe and Nas, whose faces remained glued to their phones.

"How'd it go?" Tessa asked Cece.

Cece, who had been squatting to talk to the twins, kissed Lola and Livy and stood.

"Up, Mama," Livy shouted. "I want up!"

"Go see Papa J. All of you," Cece instructed the room. "He might need some help."

The four youngest leaped up and bounded into the kitchen.

"Oscar, looking at you, kid," Cece added, to which Oscar sighed loudly before sliding off the couch like a boneless creature. Cece pursed her lips to hide her smirk. "Do it, or I'll take the phone."

Oscar hopped up and followed the other four House kids into the kitchen.

Cece looked from Marlowe to Nas, neither of whom had even glanced up. "Who do you two belong to?"

They did not respond.

"They're from the Channels," Tessa snitched.

Cece walked over to Nas and took his phone.

"Hey!" he yelped like a hurt puppy, high and whiney. "What gives?"

Saying nothing, Cece waltzed over to Marlowe and took their phone as well.

Marlowe hissed, displaying terrifying white fangs and a blood-red tongue.

"Who's your adult?" Cece asked, holding a phone in each hand. "Auntie Izotz?"

They both nodded.

"Auntie!" Cece hollered.

A couple seconds later, Izotz poked her head out of the kitchen. "Yes?"

Cece gestured to Marlowe and Nas, both sitting sullenly on the couches. She held their phones in the air.

Izotz walked over, hand held out to take the phones. She clicked her tongue at the two teens, who hopped up and, like trained puppies, followed her into the kitchen.

"It went well," Cece said when the door had closed behind them. "Jean talked to you earlier, right?"

Tessa nodded.

"So…" Cece looked from Tessa to the east corridor. "You should probably… be…"

Tessa frowned. "You need to give me more to go on than, 'it went well' if you expect me to be your spy."

"Not a spy," Cece protested, pressing a hand to her forehead.

"Right. I couldn't possibly be trusted with any important information."

"Tessa—" Cece played with a loose thread on her shirt, itched behind her ear, and then tugged at her ear lobe. Her energy was slightly manic. She looked up at the ceiling of plants and Tessa followed Cece's gaze. Bettie flew in effortless figure eights, ducking in and out of branches, swerving among vines.

"How would I know if a piece of information were valuable?" Tessa pressed, sensing the warning signs in Cece's gestures and posture, but ignoring them. "I'm *just a Familiar*."

"Fine," Cece snapped, lowering her gaze, but not looking at Tessa. "Don't help us."

Cece started to walk away, toward the staircase.

Tessa knew she should let her go. She thought about Cece's stone face, how her eyes had turned to fire, twin caldrons bubbling over with green, hissing venom. But she would not be afraid.

She followed her. "I want to help you."

"Could've fooled me." Cece continued to march up the stairs, eyes straight ahead.

Tessa kept her pace, panting slightly. How was she *this* out of shape? "I *do*. I also want to be treated like an equal in this, not some *common* outsider." She spat the slur, though it was still largely meaningless to her. She wanted Cece to feel her rage.

Cece winced, stopped, and opened her mouth. Tessa could almost see the words forming on her lips: *But you are.* Cece closed her mouth, then thought-said. *I'm sorry.*

Tessa waited.

*It's not safe here,* Cece continued.

Tessa frowned. What the hell did that mean? If it's not safe here…

*It's not safe anywhere,* Cece finished, like she'd been reading

Tessa's thoughts, though Tessa didn't think she had been. She wasn't sure mind-reading was something Magix could even do. Thought-talking was more of a projection into a mind than a pulling from it. Bizarrely, Tessa thought of her dreams of Morana: *Can I come in?* She shivered.

Cece continued: *I'm not trying to scare you, though you should be scared. I think someone here is a spy.* She forced her face into a cold smile. "But you are," she said aloud. *We need them to think I don't trust you.* "Common, I mean." In her eyes, Tessa saw green flames, slithering and hissing snakes, fear and betrayal, but she couldn't tell if it was part of the act or true. *But I do trust you. Do you trust me?*

Tessa nodded and then went back down the stairs.

*Thank you,* Cece thought-said.

Tessa glanced back, but Cece was already at the top of the stairs. Tessa stood, immobile, as Cece disappeared down the hall. Bettie swooped in behind her. Tessa heard the sound of Bettie landing, then a firm knock followed by Astrid's muted reply of "Fuck off." Tessa smirked.

"It's Cece!"

"In that case," Astrid's voice reverberated, "Fucking fuck the *fuck* off."

Tessa snorted and continued downstairs, wondering if Astrid could sense her anger at Cece. She paused on the landing and tried to thought-speak a *thank you* to Astrid, closing her eyes in concentration. Nothing seemed to happen. Strange how the only person here over the age of ten (ten, Tessa had decided, was the age people developed a "poker face") who she trusted without reservation was Astrid. Maybe there was something to the whole "Familiar" thing. Maybe she really was bound in a larger-than-life, intangible, soul-binding way to Astrid. Weirdly, magic seemed like the only reasonable explanation for how close she felt to the kid.

Lost in thought, Tessa nearly tripped over Silas, who stood at the bottom of the stairs.

"Ope, didn't see you there!"

Silas giggled. "That's because I was trying to be sneaky."

She studied his face, looking for any signs that he was not actually Silas. There were none. This was Silas.

"Don't worry, it's really me!" He took her by the hand and pulled her down to his level, then whispered in her ear. "Luca's playing hide-and-seek. Will you help me find him?"

"Sure. Where's he hiding?" Tessa whispered back.

Silas pointed down the east corridor. "He went that way."

*Convenient,* Tessa thought, holding Silas' hand and following him down the hallway. She hadn't been to this part of the house yet. The corridor was longer and larger than she'd assumed. Was it always this big or if it had been made temporarily larger to accommodate the additional inhabitants? At least a dozen doors lined the long hallway, which culminated in an open entryway, over which sat a massive stained glass window. Beyond the entryway, Tessa could see little of the room beyond, but even from this end of the hall, she could tell it must be enormous. There was the hardwood flooring covered partially by a ruby and amber-toned carpet runner that seemed to lead on endlessly. Tessa blinked. Maybe the room was poorly lit toward the back. Her vision wasn't what it used to be, but the room appeared to continue on, like the Lake greeting the sky, the other side of it so distant you'd forget it existed.

"That's the library." Silas pointed toward the room. "It's my favorite place. It has every book in the whole, wide world." He tugged at her hand. "Luca's probably definitely in there. Come on!"

With that, they were running down the hallway. Rather, Tessa was running. Silas was fluttering above the ground, holding her hand, pumping his wings in quick spasms so that Tessa had to sprint and slow, sprint and slow, down the long hallway.

A door opened just as Silas had flapped his wings with an extra bit of fervor. Deirdre backed out of the room hurriedly, not looking their way. Silas successfully dodged her, letting go of Tessa's hand and continuing into the library without looking back. Meanwhile, Tessa smashed into Deirdre, knocking her flat on her back and falling on top of her in the process. Tessa sat, straddling Deirdre, panting. Deirdre's turban had loosened in the commotion, revealing something green, shifting, and scaled. Tessa squinted and started to reach out. She wanted to push back the turban, to see what was beneath. A voice from inside called to her, smooth and resonant as the hum of an oboe, reedy and mystical. She thought of deserts, the ripple of mirages over sand, the promise of thirst quenched. She touched the indigo fabric.

"There's something..."

Deirdre reached for her turban, tugging it down with a hiss. "Do you want die today, ti fi?"

Under the turban, something churned, twisted, hissed, then rattled. The spell broken, Tessa jumped up. "Snakes!" Not a vampire, then. Something else. Something *else*? Tessa felt dizzy.

Deirdre was on her feet as well, grabbing Tessa by the wrist, and placing a hand over her mouth. "Hush, little Non. I mean you no harm. Promise you'll be quiet and I'll let you go."

Tessa nodded.

Deirdre took away her hand and then, when Tessa stayed quiet, let go of her wrist as well.

They stood for a moment, staring at each other, Tessa craning her head up and Deirdre peering down.

"What is a Non doing in a Coven?" Deirdre asked at the same moment as Tessa asked her own question:

"Are you a Gorgon?"

Deirdre frowned. "Gorgon?"

"Medusa. Greek mythology? Snakes for hair, turned people to stone."

Deirdre's magenta lips curled up. "What a good little Non you are, too. They've taught you all their clever stories."

"So what's with the snakes for hair?"

Deirdre gave a forced half laugh, a literal *haha*. "Snake. Singular. She's not my hair, but my companion. She is part of my soul, a manifestation of my life force. My people have a special relationship with snakes. Always have. I've heard so many names for us from your people," Deirdre continued. "Nagini, Leviathan, Beithir, Quetzalcoatl, Dragon, Chimera, Oni, and, now, Gorgon, it seems." She smirked. "We call ourselves Ogres."

Tessa had always imagined ogres as fat and green, like Shrek. She almost giggled, her lips twitching. She wondered why Jean hadn't mentioned that Deirdre was an ogre, given how rare ogres were. She recalled Evie, only hours before, asking if Tessa was an ogre, saying she'd never seen one, when all the while, Deirdre had been there, a real ogre, tall as an Amazonian kapok with its exposed roots, a slithering network of possibility.

Deirdre sniffed the air, then turned her nose in Tessa's direction. "Your scent is… interesting."

Tessa tried not to shiver. "Does anyone here know you're an ogre?"

Deirdre narrowed her eyes. "Of course they do, little Non." Her eyes shifted left then right. Tessa heard a rattle, the tsk-tsk sound of a frightened creature preparing to strike.

Tessa forced a smile. "Silly me. I shouldn't have listened to those children."

"Hmm?" Deirdre's expression was nonchalant as a Victorian portrait, everything bubbling below the surface. "What were they saying?"

Tessa shrugged. "They were telling me ogres were a myth. One of them even asked me if *I* was an ogre."

Deirdre chuckled, a hearty, booming thing that lasted several seconds. "Oof!" She wiped her eyes. "That's a good one, little Non. A miniature ogre." She snickered. "Hilarious, really. Run along, little one." She flicked her wrist at Tessa, gesturing away from the library and back down the corridor from which Tessa had come.

Tessa pointed to the library. "I was going that way," she said, stepping forward.

Deirdre stepped in front of her. "Magical libraries are typically reserved for Magix."

A tinkling sound like wind chimes caused both Deirdre and Tessa to pause and listen, though it dissipated before they'd even fully processed it was there.

"Did you—?" Tessa began, taking a sidestep to get around her.

Again, Deirdre stepped in front of her like they were partners in a stilted waltz. "Like I said, that place isn't for people like *you.*"

"You don't live here," Tessa snapped, dodging the other way. "You don't make the rules."

Deirdre jumped in front of her, a grin on her face, wide and menacing.

"Haven't they taught you your place, Non?"

Again, Tessa heard that rattling sound coming from Deirdre's turban. This caused Tessa to step back. The lights flickered, up and down the hallway, strobing as one. She recalled another story about an ogre, older than Shrek, in which knights went to battle, only to be gobbled up whole by the cannibalistic giants. The tsk of the rattle synced with the strobing light. Before Tessa, Deirdre seemed to grow even taller, her legs and arms unfurling and fusing into one long, scaled limb. She looked up to see Deirdre's head above hers, mouth opening wide, wider, jaw unhinging, her teeth lengthening.

She breathed a blast of foul air into Tessa's face as she whispered. "Goodbye, little Non."

Deirdre's tongue, a long, forked thing, kissed Tessa's cheek. Tessa closed her eyes and prayed to the universe, some remnant of her twice-a-year, Christmas-and-Easter-only Christian upbringing screaming through her terrified brain. The tinkling wind chime sound came again, only this time it was deafening. Light flashed so bright that Tessa saw it through her closed eyes.

The universe answered in the form of Astrid's voice screaming down the hall. "Tessa!"

At the same moment, Tessa felt the air around her contract, like a drawstring bag being cinched closed. Deirdre hissed and gagged. The wind chimes and rattling stopped. Tessa opened her eyes. Deirdre was gone. She turned around to find Astrid sprinting toward her only to stop about halfway down the hallway, a perplexed look on her face.

"I thought…" She looked back and then forward at Tessa again, before continuing to walk. "I thought you were in trouble."

Tessa opened her mouth to confirm that she had been in trouble, but then thought better of it. "I'm fine. Thank you. Silas is in the library. He wanted to show it to me."

Astrid put a hand on her shoulder. *Tell me. Like this.*

Tessa pursed her lips. "I don't…"

*You can do it. Just talk to me.*

Tessa closed her eyes. She went back and thought about what had happened. She tried to think it into words, like she was telling a story: her and Silas in the hall, bumping into Deirdre, the snakes, the way Deirdre's mouth unhinged wider and wider.

"Shit," Astrid said.

"Did you—?"

*Yes, I heard you. That's messed up.*

They'd reached the library, a great, yawning space with ceilings so high Tessa had to squint to make them out. The bookshelves stretched up to meet them, jutting out at haphazard angles and curves, some floating in the air, others sinking below the floor. There were ladders and stairways, slides and bridges. Tessa watched as the middle-aged siren, Tim, rode on an enchanted platform that lowered, raised, and moved side to side.

"Should we find Silas?" Astrid asked. A twinge of fear was in her voice. *She wouldn't hurt* him, *would she?*

Tessa shook her head. She was pretty sure Deirdre's whole "I'll gobble you up" bit was Non-specific, possibly an elaborate bluff, a way to scare Tessa. But maybe not. Still, she didn't think Deirdre would eat a Magick. That had to be against the rules. Would Deirdre follow the rules? Eating a Non under the care of Magix was probably also against the rules.

"Yeah, let's grab him."

Astrid nodded and walked into the library, calling for Silas. Tessa stayed close to her.

Cece thought there was a spy in their midst. Tessa should've been convinced Deirdre was the spy. Not only had she tried to eat her, but she was secretly an ogre. Why would she keep that secret if she were truly among her friends and allies? Still, doubt tugged at the corners of Tessa's mind. She'd seen Deirdre interacting with Silas, seen her smiling and him laughing. In Tessa's experience, people who were kind and respectful to children were usually decent people.

They found Silas, nose buried in a copy of *Dragons: A History of the Greatest Reptiles that Never Lived. Or Did They?*

"Silas!" Astrid was having trouble containing the panic in her voice.

Clearly, she was still freaked out about what had happened between Deirdre and Tessa. For her part, Tessa had never been more grateful to be a Familiar, connected to a Magick who had come running to help at the exact right moment.

*Like magic,* Tessa thought and almost laughed aloud at the absurd accuracy. It *was* magic. The thought still caught her off guard at times, like her brain was working triple time to keep up and then, suddenly, stalling. "Did you find Luca?" she asked Silas.

He nodded. "He went outside with Evie and one of her dads."

"Outside?"

"Our backyard." Silas pressed his fingers between the pages of his book as he hopped up to take Tessa's hand, leading her out of the library.

"I thought you said dragons were a myth," Tessa teased him, nodding to the book.

He looked up at her with wide brown eyes and began to gush about the old dragon myths, the speculations that maybe they had been real once.

"So maybe it was like the *Wings of Fire* books only real life. Maybe there really were IceWings and NightWings and SandWings…"

*Why did you have to get him started?* Astrid glared at Tessa over Silas' head.

Tessa smirked. She thought Silas was lovely, but she had lots of practice "listening" to the rantings of precocious chatterboxes. In many ways, Silas reminded Tessa of a little Theo. She liked to think Theo would have been like Silas before she met them, though she knew that was wishful thinking, given how Theo had been for the first few weeks after she got them. She wondered how they were now, back with Morana. Theo had never once spoken fondly their bio mom in the two years they were with Tessa, yet her mark had been left in so many ways: the puckered scar splashed across their thigh, the jagged white lines along their back. The thought was a stone in Tessa's gut, a shot of guilt through her blood, throbbing against her skull.

"...and Nons have always assumed the bones were from *dinosaurs,* but what if..."

*Should we tell Cece?* Astrid pressed. *Or Jean?*

Tessa nodded. She wasn't really listening to either of them. She was thinking about Theo, about something they had once said to her about their bio mom:

"She liked to play games," Theo had said, looking down at their hands

"Like board games?" Tessa had asked. "You like that, too."

Theo shook their head. "Not like that. More like... scavenger hunts. Like she'd set up clues all around the house and I'd have to find them and solve them."

"What kind of clues?" Thinking back, Tessa wished she hadn't asked, hadn't pressed.

"My cat died," Theo said. "She could have told me. She left clues about it everywhere. Blood, fur, a plucked out eyeball. I was supposed to figure out who did it, how it happened. The clues were all there. It should have been an owl. That's what I told her. But it wasn't an owl. It was her." Theo was stiff telling the story, their hands clenched together in their lap, feet flat and firm on the ground. Tessa had reached for them, and they had relaxed into her embrace.

"I'm sorry," Tessa had murmured.

"She said nothing is ever as it seems. She said I should trust no one but myself."

"She was wrong. She was wrong to do that to you."

"I know." Theo had wrapped their arms around Tessa's waist.

Tessa shivered at the memory.

"...so in conclusion, dragons probably *were* real, which means... oh, here's the door to the backyard!" Silas zipped over to the door, whipped it open, and darted outside.

Through a window, Tessa could see Dante, Evie, and Luca playing in a small courtyard containing a tall tree with a tire swing, a free-standing slide, and lots of toys strewn about in various states of filth and disrepair.

*Tessa?* Astrid thought-said. *We're going to tell them, right?*

Tessa didn't answer. The words kept repeating in her mind: *Nothing is ever as it seems.*

* * *

## APRIL 1986

### April 26, 1986

*Brand: Mr. Engers, is it true that the last contact you had with the ogre Hybrid child was on October the 2nd of last year?*

*Engers: Not exactly. I received a letter from the mother of the Hybrid child that day. I—we—our research team had no direct contact with the child.*

*Brand: Can you read the letter supplied by the mother of the Hybrid?*

*Engers: Yes. It says, "Dear Gunner—at my husband's request, I am terminating our correspondence. If you can't fork up child support, you shouldn't get to be involved in Denis' life." The "child support," I should add, is something I have requested funding for on a num—*

*Brand: Denis is the child?*

*Engers: ... Yes.*

*Brand: After you got this letter, what did you do?*

*Engers: I flew down to Haiti, to the family's home. I was hoping to talk to the mother in person.*

*Brand: And what did you discover?*

*Engers: They were gone. They left no forwarding address. I talked to all the neighbors. Some said they went to America, but they didn't know where, had no way to contact them.*

*Brand: So. Your team has effectively lost its only viable Hybrid child?*

*Engers: Well, no. Not quite. We... there is another child. Due at the end of the year. This child, the mother is one of our researchers, so we*

—*we are hopeful that, if the child survives, we will be able to better study them.*

*Brand: In a controlled environment? I thought you were opposed to this?*

*Engers: Yes, in a controlled environment. I am not happy about it, no. But, I acknowledge that, in order to continue our work, we do need to be able to control a bit more of our process, as it were. More money would help, too. The child support for the first Hybrid... if we could have provided that, then perhaps...*

*Brand: We're not interested in excuses, Mr. Engers. Only results. Hey! Excuse me. This is a closed sess—*

*Messenger: Sir, I apologize for the intrusion, but there has been an incident in Ukraine.*

*Brand: Incident?*

*Messenger: A nuclear explosion, the Nons believe, but—*

*Brand: But what? Speak!*

*Messenger: It appears to be the work of a Magick.*

*Engers: Where in the Ukraine? Where?*

*Brand: Christ, cut the transcript.*

*—Department of AntiMagi Health Inquest Transcript Excerpt*

# CHAPTER
# SEVENTEEN

JULY 2023 At dinner, Tessa said nothing, despite Astrid's numerous coughs, thought-nudges (*Tessa, when are you going to* tell *them?)*, kicks under the table, and irritated glances. They ate together in the dining room, the House Coven members and their guests. The room had expanded to fit them all, the smattering of tables and chairs that had been previously setup like a child's half-melted dollhouse were now unified and ordered. They sat on chairs attached to the ground via good old-fashioned gravity in front of a sprawling table overflowing with food and drink.

Candles danced above. Dishes of every color, culture, and cuisine floated back and forth to whomever requested them. Bettie flitted gleefully around them to the mild chagrin of some of the guests who received a black feather or two in their dishes. Lola and Livy both squatted at one end of the table, stripped down to only their diapers, shoveling food into their mouths with violent glee. Beside them, Jean was deep in conversation with Tim. Occasionally, Jean's voice rose above the din with booming exclamations. Across from them, Silas and Luca elbowed each other for no discernible reason, while Evie, who sat beside Tim, built a tower out of her food, lips parted in a grimace of concentration, tongue poking out from between her teeth. Next to Evie was Dante. The vegan dishes floated above him before flitting over to Tessa, back and forth. When he noticed, he leaned forward and raised a glass to her, flashing a dizzying smile that caused even Tessa, queer as she was, to blush and shiver.

"Now *that* is a beautiful man, mm?" Izotz whispered in Tessa's right ear.

Between Izotz and Dante were two ice fairies Tessa had not met. Across from them, sat Cece and Regina, deep in conversation, their heads almost pressed together. Tessa's stomach clenched up.

Across from Tessa, Astrid coughed again.

To her left, Nas grimaced. "The last thing I need right now is to get *sick.*"

On Tessa's left, Oscar grunted. It was unclear whether it was from mirth or annoyance.

"That cough sounds nasty, dear," Izotz chimed in. "Our Regina has a marvelous tincture that'll work wonders. Regina!"

Regina turned her head. "Yes, Auntie?"

Izotz beckoned her over and Tessa let out an audible sigh when Regina rose without protest, leaving Cece. Tessa watched Cece watch Regina move around the table toward them, trying to decipher her expression. Was that admiration? Lust? Love?

Tessa dropped her eyes when Cece gaze turned on her. Her cheeks were hot. She took a bite of her chickpea masala, listening absently as Izotz interrogated Regina about the ingredients in her magical cough medicine.

"Valerian and violet, you say? I've always been partial to licorice root, myself."

Tessa continued to feel Cece's gaze on her, but did not look up. She thought of Cece on that first night, the stone giantess. She'd been as frightened of her in that moment as she had been of Deirdre and her unhinged mouth.

Deirdre. Her eyes were conspicuously *not* on Tessa or Astrid, despite both of them glancing her way every ten to twenty seconds. She sat at the end of the table between Elsa, the only person who seemed unimpressed with the food, and Marlowe. Deirdre's eyes remained on her plate as she slowly brought her fork up and down, up and down, up…

Izotz's voice continued to drone in Tessa's ear, light and tinkling. "I find valerian root tea to be a highly effective sedative. And of course, the buds are lovely as well. Such a pity to uproot such beauty, to tear it from the…"

"Earth to Tessa!" Astrid was snapping her fingers in Tessa' face.

"Do you have a sleeping disorder, dear?" Izotz asked, reaching out to squeeze Tessa's hand. "I certainly wouldn't recommend valerian to you, mm?" She smiled, her taut skin turning to wrinkles in the process, a piece of paper crumpled by an unseen hand.

Tessa said nothing, glancing back toward where Deirdre had been. She was gone.

*Did you see her leave?* Tessa thought-asked Astrid.

Around them, the room continued to buzz with conversation and laughter, the clinking of utensils, the raucous rhythm of hearty masticating and quaffing. Neither Elsa nor Marlowe seemed to have noticed that the woman who'd been sitting beside them was gone.

"Deirdre left?" Tessa tried to sound casual, but her voice sailed a full octave above her normal cadence.

Elsa shrugged. "She was probably tired. It's been a *long* day." She continued to run her fork around her plate, making a teeth-grinding, barely audible, grating clink-creak and not picking anything up.

"Tomorrow will be longer," Cece said.

She'd come around the other side of the table and Tessa, who had been looking toward Deirdre's empty chair, thinking about how it yawned in her absence like wide open mouth, started. At this, Cece placed a hand on Tessa's shoulder. A reassurance, perhaps? Or a warning. Tessa felt adrift on a sea of voices that slipped in and out, in and out of audibility.

"The Sobro Boys will be here in the morning," Cece said.

Izotz replied, but her words sounded muffled in Tessa's ears.

Cece's hand stayed firmly on her shoulder as she replied, seeming to have heard Izotz perfectly, her words also muffled at first, then suddenly clear, "—has fallen, it would seem."

"Nothing closer than Sobro." Izotz clicked her teeth.

Again, the voices faded around Tessa, as if someone had turned down the volume. She looked around and her eyes caught Astrid's, who was watching her with a deep frown.

*Are you ok?*

*No. The sound... I can't... hear well. I—*

The conversation roared back to full volume and Tessa winced, nearly yelping as the sounds of the room, the dishware, the voices, and the laughter, skidded along her eardrums at three times the volume they should have been.

Astrid cut into the conversation. "Cece, can I talk to you?"

She said nothing to Tessa as she took her hand and led her out of the room behind Cece. Bettie followed, soaring lazily above.

Something pulled at Tessa's sleeve. She stopped, causing Astrid to stop as well. Tessa turned. Marlowe had pinched the fabric of Tessa's shirt between their long fingers.

"She didn't go to her room," Marlowe said. "Deirdre." They gestured to the stairway and the west corridor, toward which Cece continued to walk, not noticing she was no longer followed. "She went that way."

"Thanks," Tessa murmured, as she and Astrid started walking again, hurrying to catch up to Cece. Somewhere between standing and talking to Marlowe, the sound in the room had returned to normal.

At the top of the staircase, Tessa paused to look out over the vast expanse of rooms beneath her, the living room in its homey shambles and the dining room, still filled with festive, feeding guests, all buried in their plates or conversations, except one. Izotz was looking up at her. She smiled warmly at Tessa and waved. Tessa smiled back and almost raised her hand to return the gesture, but Bettie took the moment to land on her shoulder and Tessa, startled by the raven's appearance, turned to see Astrid beckoning. She followed her down the hallway to Tessa's bedroom, where Cece had paused, hands on her hips.

"Here?" she asked, swinging a thumb toward Tessa's door.

Tessa nodded. Cece placed a hand on the knob to open it, then paused, frowning and sticking her ear close to the door. Bettie's claws dug uncomfortably into Tessa's shoulder. She felt the bird's feathers bristle against her cheek.

"What the—" Cece whispered, before flinging the door open, arms above her head, electricity crackling along her fingertips as she shouted into the room, "What the hell do you think you're doing?"

A lightning bolt zipped from her index finger and, like something straight out of Star Wars, wrapped around Deirdre's torso, pinning her arms to her sides. In each of Deirdre's hands, she clutched some scraps of tan fabric. Cece's lightning bolt rope squeezed and sizzled and Deirdre shrieked in pain, uttering a string of Creole curses as she dropped the fabric that was, Tessa realized, the soggy remains of her underwear.

"Ew!" Astrid shrieked, coming to the same realization at the same moment but finding her words before Tessa. "What in the name of kink were you doing with those? *Eating* them?"

Still wincing from the pain of being held by magic electrical currents, Deirdre spread her lips into a smile that looked more guilty than evil.

"Answer!" Cece shrieked, her voice high-pitched, beads of perspiration lining her upper lip. Bettie hovered beside her, flapping her wings in wide, rapid movements and screeching at Deirdre, darting close so her beak was nearly touching Deirdre's nose.

"It—it was the n-next best thing!" Deirdre cried, panting for air as Cece squeezed her tighter and tighter and Bettie screamed in her face.

"To what?" Astrid asked.

Deirdre's dark face was getting darker. A bluish tint colored her lips.

"Cece," Tessa said.

Cece flinched at the sound of her voice, but didn't stop squeezing, her hands curled into unnatural balls as if warped by time and arthritis.

The veins in Deirdre's neck bulged. Her eyes bugged out of her skull, pink with burst blood vessels.

"Cece, stop!" Tessa cried, putting a hand on her shoulder.

Cece stopped, dropping her hands with a bitter and tired laugh. The electrical currents vanished, but Tessa could still see a faint glow coming from Cece's hands. *Magic residue,* she thought, then blinked. Cece's hands looked ordinary again.

Deirdre collapsed on the floor, sucking in sweet breaths with the desperate relief of someone who has seen the proverbial light or darkness, depending on theology. She hunched over, clutching at her sides, bringing hands like fluttering wings to her neck. Tessa had a thought, almost a vision, of Deirdre's ancestors, tied up and hanging together like racks of meat hides in a butcher's shop, a fire roaring beneath them while the hairy, sweaty Spaniard Nons, clothed in dirty, sweaty rags and their faces red with angry heat, laughed at the naked, burning flesh. Bettie hovered over Deirdre, like angel of death thwarted, but waiting.

Tessa went to Deirdre and knelt beside her. Again, her turban was dislodged, no hiss or movement lurked beneath it, no slip of yellow-green scales. Tessa reached for turban, tucking it back over Deirdre's black hair.

"You tried to eat me."

"What?" Cece shrieked, but Astrid made a shushing sound and Cece quieted. Bettie drew back, landing on the ground behind where Tessa knelt, ready.

Deirdre nodded. "In a manner of speaking. I've eaten…" Deirdre hesitated, looking Tessa up and down, as if Tessa were an optical illusion she was trying to see clearly. "…Nons. I've eaten Nons before."

"She's a Familiar," Cece shouted. "She has the mark. That's not—"

"Why?" Tessa pressed.

"Why not?" Deirdre met Tessa's gaze with defiance. When Tessa held her stare, Deirdre sighed, a deflated sound. "Would you believe me if I told you they deserved it? Sometimes, if your enemy decides you are a thing, it is simpler to *be* that thing. Being a terrifying, man-eating ogre is surprisingly delightful, though I am also mindful of the adage: you are what you eat. By eating cannibals, I become one as well. How fun and ironic." Her voice was too casual, too playful. Tessa sensed the bitterness running through it all, a flesh-eating poison.

"You're an ogre," Cece stated.

"Vwala!" Deirdre replied, giving a jazz-hands gesture.

"You kept that a secret." Cece's voice was a low growl.

Deirdre put a hand to her chest, as if affronted by the accusation. Her face twitched. The movement was stiff with pain, but she managed to maneuver her mouth into a precise and shocked "O" before replying. "*Secret* implies intention. Malice, even. How was I to know what you and your people did or did not know, Cordelia?"

"So the attempt to eat Tessa was an accident?" Cece snapped. "Free of malice? How about this?" She gestured around the room with sharp hand movements. "Did you stumble in here by accident? Did you accidentally start eating Tessa's underwear?"

Deirdre winced and looked at Tessa as she replied. "Eating, you'll find, can have a few different meanings." She winked at Tessa and gave a coy jerk of her head, then grimaced, the movement clearly causing her more pain than anticipated.

Tessa kept her eyes on Deirdre. In her head, Theo's little voice repeated. *Nothing is ever as it seems.* Behind her, rage radiated off of Cece as she cracked her knuckles.

"Murder probably has 'different meanings' where you come from, too, I suppose," Cece snarled. Bettie crowed and flapped her wings.

"Funny, coming from a notorious Non-murderer," Deirdre chuckled. "Cordelia Connolly, I'm surprised that you of all people would mind me making a little snack of her. Miam!" She licked her lips.

Tessa felt a rush of air and Cece was between her and Deirdre, crouched on the ground, teeth bared like a mongoose ready for attack. Deirdre tried to recoil, tried to draw herself up, but her movement was faltering, a stutter of pain against Cece's smooth prowess. Bettie now hovered above them both, her talons open and waiting.

"Why are you here?" Cece's voice was a gathering roll of thunder. "You're not from the Second City Coven, are you? How did you find us?" Her voice rose and peaked, shaking the room, dislodging twigs and leaves from the forest canopy above. "Speak!"

Tessa heard a holler from below then stampeding footsteps coming up the stairs.

"Cece?" Jean called. "Qu'est-ce que c'est?"

"Nothing to see here, colonizer," Deirdre muttered.

Jean reddened, "Cece, what is going on?"

Deirdre tried to stand, but Cece shoved her back. "Why. Are. You. Here." Each repeated word was a clap of thunder coming from Cece's mouth. Tessa felt the floor beneath her vibrate and shake, heard the little pops and crashes of knickknacks falling in this room and others.

"I could ask her the same thing," Deirdre spoke through clenched teeth, nodding to Tessa.

"I've told you," Cece snarled. "She's a Famil—"

"She is *not* what you think she is!" Deirdre blurted.

Neither Tessa nor anyone else had time to contemplate that statement. A wind started to whip around the room. Others were beginning to crowd the doorway, but Jean held them back with his broad arms. Oscar, ducking under Jean's arms, beckoned for Astrid and Tessa to come out of the room, his fear stirring like potion in his eyes. There came a low moan from high above in the kapok's branches, a protesting sound like the opening of a long-shut coffin or a rusted hinge being roughly shoved open. A corner of Deirdre's turban was loosed and fluttered for moment, an indigo streak licking across her cheek like a smear of angry blush. Then, the whole thing caught on a breeze and flew away, revealing a king cobra, uncoiling itself. It rose, hood flared and hissing, though the sound was lost in the wind of Cece's wrath. Bettie, who had been fighting against the wind to stay close and menacing above Deirdre's head, recoiled at the sight of the serpent, flying back to Cece's shoulder, beak open but no sound escaping.

Deirdre's lips moved. It was impossible to hear her over the thunder, wind, and the creaking of tree limbs above. But the cobra stilled, began to lower itself, coiling into a tight ball on Deirdre's head. As it did so, Cece began to let the wind die down.

"Why are you here?" Cece repeated.

"I had nowhere else to go."

"How did you find us?" Cece's hands were still raised above her head.

"Cece," Jean murmured, stepping into the room, his arms still thrown wide to block entry to anyone else. "We sent word to Second City, remember?"

"She's not from Second City," Cece snapped. The silver and gold in her hair flared red-hot. "Are you?"

Deirdre shook her head. "Not originally, no. I was… there, though… when the message arrived." She nodded toward Bettie, who replied with an indignant squawk and began to preen her feathers, as if to say, *Not my problem.*

"Just you?" Regina pushed her way into the room. She ducked under Jean's outstretched arm. Her arms were down at her sides but her fingers danced across her thighs, as if tapping out an SOS in Morse code. Or battle plans. "Where were the others? Suki? Marshall?"

"I don't know!" The snake on Deirdre's shoulders flashed its scarlet pronged tongue in warning and the onlookers, who had begun to press in, took a collective step back.

Jean raised his arms again, a mother bear collecting her cubs behind her. Even the young children had managed to sneak upstairs by now. Silas flitted near the top of the doorframe and Luca lurked near the bottom, his fangs bared like a cat sniffing something off. Izotz stood near the back, holding each of the twins by the hand. The twins, for their part, seemed to have sensed the danger in the air and looked more wolf-like than ever, their furry ears elongated, the hair on their heads standing on end, their arms stretched nearly as long as their legs, long claws protruding from their fingers and scraping the floor.

Cece noticed the children then. "Izotz, could you please take them downstairs?" Her voice was ragged with frustration.

Izotz clicked her tongue. "This business affects *all* of us—"

"Yes, and I will stay on behalf of the Channels," Regina countered.

Tim stepped forward. "And for Washtenaw." He and Dante

exchanged nods, and Dante drew back, hands on Evie's shoulders, tugging her along.

"Oscar, come," Jean said. "Luca, Silas. Astrid?"

"No," said Astrid. "Tessa and I are staying."

Jean nodded. The crowd withdrew until it was only the six of them, plus Bettie and the cobra, in Tessa's bedroom. The door shut closed with a loud smack.

"Now," Regina said, crossing her arms across her chest. "Where are the actual Second City Coven members?"

"I told you, I don't know," Deirdre said.

"*Bull*shit," Cece spat.

Deirdre sighed. "I came to Second City searching for my brother. He was gone." Her eyes rolled back in her head before she brought her hand over them, drawing the lids down like curtains. "He was dead. There were others there, as well. Bodies, I mean. There were—" She continued to speak with her eyes closed, a hand pressed against each temple. "… so many bodies. I knew it might be like that, after what I'd seen in Santa Fe, in Denver." The snake on her head curled around her shoulders, nuzzling at her cheek like an anxious and empathetic pup. "I had so fervently hoped it would be different. It wasn't, of course. *Fout!*" She uttered several more curses in Creole.

As Deirdre continued to speak, the imprint of evil Deirdre's gaping mouth on Tessa's brain was replaced with an image of frightened Deirdre, pushing open an unlocked door into the foyer of an unguarded house filled with death so fresh the rot hadn't begun to set in yet, despite the heat. A room so thick with corpses Deirdre struggled to get through without stepping on a hand, foot, or torso, without looking into a glassy pair of eyes.

"When I found my brother's body, the heat was still in his cheek, but his eyes had already darkened, begun to turn opaque with death." Deirdre paused. Swallowed. "I vomited in a corner and heaved and retched, wasting several minutes of precious time before I could get myself out of that foyer. All the bodies were there. It was like they'd been waiting. Like they were expecting—"

"That's not possible," Cece blurted.

"No shit," Regina whispered. "If they had known…"

"I can't know what they were thinking!" Deirdre snapped, glancing at each of them. "I wasn't there and I didn't hurt them!"

Regina held up her hands, palms out, as she stepped forward, a hunter trying not to scare their prey. "We never said you did."

Tessa noticed a low humming sound beginning to fill the air, barely audible, like the sound of an old refrigerator that you never notice getting imperceptibly louder until it crosses an undefined threshold and then it's always with you, just below the surface, a thrumming sound you can't ignore.

"They were all in the room?" Regina voice was a long bow against a viola's string, deep and steady. "Like almost waiting for something—"

"Or someone?" Cece offered.

Deirdre's head turned to her. "Yes." Her eyes were wet. "Someone, I think. There were… balloons. It seemed like a… homecoming, perhaps."

"Yours?" Cece asked, her voice still edged with venom.

Deirdre shook her head. "They didn't know I was coming."

"How do you know all the bodies were in the one room?" Regina asked. "Did you explore or…?

"I went looking for survivors," Deirdre grimaced, clenching and unclenching her hands. The snake coiled itself tightly around her neck, squeezed, and relaxed, like she was giant stress ball that it was massaging.

Underneath the conversation, the humming continued. Tessa thought it must be coming from Tim, who stood oddly silent, lips pressed together in a thin, unmoving line. But the sound did not seem to come from him, from anyone in the room, or from any single spot. It was all-encompassing, a surround-sound effect, a wind whistling everywhere.

"You didn't find anyone?" Regina continued.

Deirdre shook her head.

"And you received the invitation. When was that?"

"I'm not exactly sure," Deirdre said. "When I left, the bird was waiting outside the door. That raven." She lip pointed to Bettie.

Cece and Regina exchanged a look. Tessa realized a silent conversation was taking place between them and her stomach clenched up at the thought. Of course, there was nothing particularly special about thought-speech in this world. It was inherently private, but it didn't have to be intimate. Like when Sanjay's mother would join Sanjay, Tessa, and some friends for a game night and she would drop into Hindi whenever she had a criticism of Sanjay, or, occasionally, someone else in the room. The criticism was private by necessity more than intimacy, although the line between the two was thin. Anything shared, even under the most heinous of circumstances, can breed intimacy.

The humming sound had grown louder, but still no one mentioned it.

This time, Cece spoke, "You knew the code."

It was more of a statement, but Deirdre nodded in reply all the same.

"How?" Cece continued.

"I told you," Deirdre spoke through gritted teeth. "I was in Santa Fe and Denver when they both fell. I know the codes, the secrets. I know the spells we whisper to darkness, to our companions and Familiars, in order to shield ourselves and decipher friend from foe."

"And we're supposed to take your word for this?" Cece said. Her voice was rising again and wind was starting up. "You're telling us that you've been at the fall of not one, not two, but three covens, and lived to tell the tale? How convenient." She gave a wry laugh.

The humming had grown to a near deafening peal, high and thin, like the constant reverb of lips too close to a microphone. Suddenly, it stopped.

Tim spoke the next question, his tenor voice as melodic as a French horn. "*You're going to tell us exactly what happened, Deirdre,*" he said. "*Understand?*"

Deirdre's mouth hung slightly open, a line of spittle dripping out between her lips.

*"Deirdre,"* Tim repeated. *"Do you understand?"*

Slowly, Deirdre nodded her head. Her eyes were clouded and Tessa shivered, her pulse quickening, because Deirdre's amber eyes had the same hazy shroud as a dead woman's.

*"Deirdre."* Tim sung the name with the gravity of a cantor leading worship at a funeral, the poised caution of a hypnotist, and the uncanny stillness of a statue. He repeated the name three times. Deirdre's body rocked with each incantation, a cymbal vibrating as it was struck. When Tim stopped singing, she stilled, a shift so sudden, it made Tessa queasy. She thought, not for the first time, that she was seeing into a world she was never meant to see and so, her mind and body were rejecting it.

Tim sang again. *"Tell us the truth, Deirdre."* Again, she convulsed, her neck jerking her head up in a puppet-like motion, dead eyes fixing on Tim. *"Do you work for Morana?"*

"No," came the words from Deirdre's lips, but it was not really her voice. The sound was too mechanical, too robotic to even be human.

*"Do you know Morana?"*

"Yes."

*"How do you know her?"*

"I met her in Santa Fe, my home coven. She tricked me. She used me to kill the others. She spared me because it was a punishment worse than death."

*"Why did you go to Denver?"*

"I've been following her ever since. She left a trail in her wake like the smoke from a fire. I know fire; my people, we were fire-breathers of old. She burns everything she touches."

*"What happened in Denver?"*

"When I got there, her taint, that ashen scent, had already touched the place. The walls appeared blackened to me. No one else seemed to see it. I left the coven, but stayed close."

*"Did you warn them?"*

With this question, Tim's hold on Deirdre's mind seemed to falter. Her humanity surged back in a cry that held all the bitter and guilt-ridden grief of a mourning mother.

"*Deirdre. Deirdre. Deirdre.*" He chanted her name, pulling her back.

The tears stopped flowing and dried on her cheeks. Her eyes glossed over and she replied, a robot once more.

Deirdre's face twisted as she tried to keep her mouth closed, pressing her lips together in a thin pink line, until Tim sung her name again and her mouth flew open. "No, I didn't warn them!"

No one had a reply to this. Tessa watched Deirdre's face as she tried to compose herself, tried to mold herself back into that towering beauty with statuesque serenity. But that Deirdre had never been real; she was a performance. This broken woman before them, red-eyed with grief, hands shaking slightly, her dress crumpled and her cobra twining her neck and pressing reassuring tongue-flicks to her cheek: this was the real Deirdre.

Deirdre spoke without Tim's prompting. "That was five years ago now."

"Five *years*," Cece gaped. "That can't be. The attacks only began three years ago."

"The attacks began in Santa Fe in 2017. Six years ago."

"That's not possible," Regina murmured.

"You're right, Regina North," Deirdre replied. "I'm sorry… it began eleven years ago in Luce County with the Duck Lake Fire and burning of the Coven of Lake Superior."

Regina's nostrils flared and she reached out a hand full of ice to Deirdre, but stopped short of releasing it. "Never. Speak. Of that. Again."

Tessa blinked, looking around the room. She recalled that name: the Coven of Lake Superior, recalled Regina's introduction of herself as *formerly* of that coven, recalled the collective shiver that had run through Magix present. She wanted to ask about it, but clearly, now was not the time.

Deirdre was staring back at Regina, a dare in her eyes.

Cece stepped in. "You're saying Morana destroyed the Coven of Lak—"

"Cece!" Regina shouted, her voice the heavy moan of shifting ice.

"Stop. Leave my people out of this. The past is past. I can't… Please." Her voice wavered on the last word.

Cece turned back to Deidre. "If Santa Fe and Denver had fallen, we would have heard—"

"Would you?" Deirdre asked. "The only evidence to the Nons was a power surge. They destroyed the bodies, but there weren't many. Most of them defected. Santa Fe became their headquarters, then Denver a year after."

"That's not possible," Cece said.

"You've spoken with Denver in the last five years?"

Cece frowned and her brow furrowed. She pressed hands to each of her temples. "It was when we were still with Grand River, maybe only a month before the attack. I spoke—I spoke with Natalie—"

"Natalie Crane," Deirdre interrupted, "was not, and never has been, your ally. I should know." Her eyes flitted from Regina to Tim to Cece to Astrid to Tessa and then landed back on Tim. "Enough with your hypnosis, siren," she said. "I don't need to be bullied into telling you the truth. I want to tell you everything."

"How can we trust you?" Cece asked and Bettie echoed her with a bark.

Deirdre shrugged. "How can you trust anyone these days?"

There was a long quiet in which Tessa studied the faces of the others in the room: Regina, unreadable, watched Deirdre; Tim, frowning, glanced back and forth between Cece and Regina; Cece, eyes on the ground, clenched and unclenched her fists; Astrid, looking side-eyed at Tessa, reached out to take her hand; and Deirdre, head raised, stared straight ahead.

In his mundane speaking voice, Tim asked. "What happened in Denver?"

* * *

**APRIL 1986**

## April 28, 1986

*Archer,*

*Do you know how many times there has almost been a nuclear disaster? It must be in the hundreds. Now, we have this one, this one, across the goddamn globe from us and they're all wringing their hands for change. Is this what it will take to get them to see? We are all hurtling toward the end and no one is paying attention to the almosts, only the actuals.*

*By the way, Tish, Andor, and the girl are safe, but Val's missing. If you care.*

*Always,*
*Dad*

CHAPTER
# EIGHTEEN



"What happened in Denver…" Deirdre repeated the phrase three times aloud. Then, she began to thought-tell her story.

*To say what happened in Denver, shit, I need to go back to Santa Fe. I need to tell you how it fell and how I, like a dumbass, helped it fall, helped it shift from epicenter of Magick power in the Southwest to a war room for Morana, her DOMs and traitor Magix, to their hub for plotting attacks.*

*I am from New Mexico. My first-self was born in Haiti, but my parents, brother, and I emigrated when I was five. On the boat over— we ogres avoid transportation magic whenever possible. Such crass and volatile magic! Nothing should be that easy, as my mother would say. Anyway, on the boat, I shed my first-self, a boy named Denis, and I became Deirdre. We were the only ogres that our new coven had ever seen. It took a long time to build their trust.*

*After nearly fifteen years, my parents left the coven on the eve of the New Millennium. They went back to Haiti and, as far as I dare to hope, they are still there. My brother followed a lover to Chicago. She didn't last, but he remained there. I stayed in Santa Fe because it was my home and I could not imagine another life. For thirty years, I had one life and it was good. It was goddamn good. I knew my place, my people.*

*The leaders of the Grand River Coven's Northeast chapter, Morana and Vasily Aronov, came to visit the Coven of Santa Fe in the spring of 2015. It was an innocuous visit; they even brought their child with them. We showed them around our coven and took them on the standard tour of the city: the art museums and galleries, the caves with the carvings of our ancestors, the forests of ponderosa pines and alligator juniper. The child was exceptionally well-behaved for a three year old, always doing what they were told, never wandering away or asking questions. It was unsettling, actually.*

*When we took them to the meet with the Leaders of the Pueblo de Brujas, the child sat in a corner, kicking their legs back and forth, until Morana shot them this look, not even a word, and the kid sat up straight and didn't move again, other than to breathe and blink.*

*Looking back, I suppose the child was a red flag in and of themselves. The meeting with the Brujas was another, but I was... distracted.*

*The Brujas kept themselves apart. This may surprise your Non, but as the rest of you know, the policies of Non culture since the founding of this nation have infiltrated the Magick world as well. It is typical for Native Covens to have sovereignty. Many do not associate with non-Native Covens at all. But relations between the Brujas and Santa Fe were cordial, strong even. They were our allies.*

*After meeting the Aronovs, La Bruja Jefa contacted Santa Fe to say that the Brujas were revoking our alignment. She gave no reason. I was not involved in local inter-coven politics; I don't recall asking for details. The Aronovs were gone by that time, but I remained distracted.*

*You see, throughout their visit, there had been a growing sexual tension between Morana and myself. At first, I had tried to brush it off as a fiction, a product of my lonely imagination. In the caves, her hand had brushed mine. At the galleries, she stood so close I could smell her perfume, lilacs, balsam, and something almost chemical, like an afterthought of bleach. Among a grove of desert willow, she plucked a flower and tucked it behind my ear. Vasily was deep in conversation with our coven leader, Roberto. During the meeting with the Brujas, Morana asked me to accompany her to the restroom. An innocent question. But she'd taken my hand as we'd walked between the adobe houses. She pulled me into a dark alley, where her lips covered mine.*

*When we returned to the meeting with the Brujas, there was a change in the space, like someone had thrown a bag over the room and was slowly pushing out the air in it. Fucking stifling. Vasily looked pissed and La Jefa kept glancing over at the child like she was trying to figure out a way to smuggle them out. Me, I was dizzy. I wasn't thinking about anything except the feel of Morana's skin, soft and thin, almost papery.*

*From then on, I was hers to do with as she wished. She came back often without Vasily or the child, without telling anyone in the coven but me. She'd show up at my bedroom window and I'd invite her in. I didn't think I was betraying my people. I gave her the keys to kingdom in nods and stories, completely ignorant.*

*The questions she asked were always small.*

*"What do you think of Leader Roberto?" she'd asked, and I'd tell her that Berto was kind, but a bit weak, the type of leader who lacks a backbone, who always takes the path of least resistance. She'd nod while I told her a story of his recent failure to discipline a reckless teenage werewolf who got a Non girl pregnant.*

*"Thankfully, Narcissa took care of the problem," I'd said. She asked me how, and I told her that Narcissa, the coven's second-in-command and a witch with a flair for the old ways, had brewed an abortifacient for the girl.*

*"Had the girl asked for it?"*

*I think I laughed at the question. "She's a Non. We don't ask Nons what they want. We do what we need to do to survive."*

*"And this is Narcissa's opinion?" she'd asked, to which I nodded, before the conversation, like so many of them, faded into passion.*

*Our affair lasted several months. For months, I told stories of my brethren, selling their souls to her, sealing their fates.*

*"Ofelia? Like all earth fairies, she's a bit of a rule-follower, believes we're here to protect the planet and that this includes plants,*

*animals, Nons, and Magix. I'm not sure she's in the right coven, honestly. But it's good to have a dissenting voice sometimes.*

*"Pedro is reckless, but loyal. Tito, his twin, is the opposite: methodical, but utterly lacking loyalty. They keep each other balanced.*

*"The werewolf boy? That's Armand. I think most teen werewolves are like that, don't you? All passion and living in the moment, no regard for consequences."*

*What I didn't know was that, based on my assessments, Morana was targeting and recruiting many of my fellow coven members to her purpose.*

*We were an easy target, as far as covens go. We were new, less than a century, and our origins were steeped in conflict. The first Santa Fe coven, La Aquelarre de Santa Fe, was defeated in the Battle of Santa Fe. The Mexican Nons fled, abandoning the city, but the Magix stayed to face Stephen Watts Kearny, a wretched DOM, and his Army of the West, which was mostly made-up of Nons. The Nons, they called it a battle won with no shots fired, and that's not a lie, but it implies that it was won without violence, which is certainly false. La Aquelarre was an underground coven and its inhabitants were poisoned, killed by toxic smoke, a special brew that Kearny's people concocted, likely with the assistance of a defected Magick, probably an air fairy, although we have no definitive proof or written record.*

*The Coven of Santa Fe was built on the gravesite of La Aquelarre, founded on a hatred of Nons that was more potent, more violent, than most modern covens. For their part, the Nons hated us right back. They didn't know who or what we were. Some thought we were a cartel, la mafia, or un culto. Our interactions with one another were always violent: murder, rape, torture, assault, imprisonment. Once, I caught a particularly belligerent drunken Non who had been flinging trans-phobic slurs at me and burned him alive. Narcissa cooked him for dinner the next evening. I'm not proud of any of it. But it is true. This is why Morana chose us. Many of us were ready and willing to start a war. We'd been waiting for more than 150 years for our revenge.*

*So one by one, she turned the Magix of the Coven of Santa Fe to her cause: the domination of all Nons, the supreme rule of Magix.*

*It was June, six years ago, when Santa Fe fell. Or rather, it was restructured, coopted for a new purpose.*

*Someone knocked on the door of our headquarters, a multi-story apartment complex in downtown Santa Fe where most of the coven members lived. It was disguised as a derelict, uninhabited place, which warded off most Nons, save the occasional runaway teen or particularly aggressive salesperson. Fellow Magix, when they did arrive, avoided the door.*

*All of this is to say that a knock on the door was an event in and of itself.*

*Narcissa answered the door. I remember the way she walked toward it, head high and back straight, her black hair loose and tumbling over her shoulders, straight as the strands of a spider's web shining with dew. She put her hand on the knob and hesitated. It was brief. If I hadn't been watching her, if I hadn't known her, grown up alongside her, hadn't kissed her once when we were teenagers and swore to never do it again, if I hadn't raged with her, rejoiced with her, cried with her, or killed with her, then maybe I wouldn't have seen the hesitation for what it was: a preparation, a firming of her resolve, a steadying breath. She knew what was on the other side. She opened the door.*

*Natalie Crane walked inside. She was short with a solid, almost stocky frame. Young, barely eighteen, if that. She walked—no strutted —like some tough-guy stereotype, a machismo straight out of* Scarface *or* The Godfather *or some other Non-world, white-on-white crime crap. She could've been Italian, I guess. I've heard that at least one of the Mob families in New York are Magix. Anyway, she was some kind of white lady with a big-city attitude. And when she walked in the door, Narcissa did a goddamn curtsy.*

*That's when I knew.*

*There were three of us in the living room: me, Pedro, and Tito, the vampire twins. A couple seconds after Narcissa bowed, there was a ripple, a little breaking of time and space, and the quiet pop of anti-magic. I knew that sound and I had the wherewithal to get my ass out of the way. I ducked behind the armchair I'd been sitting in. That's* when I heard the crash of a body hitting the floor. I pressed my cheek against the cold cement floor and was face-to-face with Pedro and his unseeing eyes. There was a black knot of something between his eyes. As I watched, the blackness grew like a goddamn tumor and as it grew, Pedro shriveled before me. It was like the blackness was sucking the magic out of him. I watched the magic—I have always had the ability to see magic, it's light and vibrancy—drain out of him, until he was nothing but black, dehydrated flesh etched over bone, meat left to char in the oven.

Two feet stood over him. "Levantarse, D," Tito said. "On your feet. Or you're next."

I stood, hands up in that universal sign of surrender. I saw the DOMs then, scattering like a pack of wolves, heeling to the click of Natalie's tongue, charging on her whistle. It didn't make sense, the way they obeyed her. I'd never seen anything like it before. I'd only ever seen DOMs obey other DOMs, but Natalie, well, she wasn't a fucking DOM, was she? I could see her teeth; she was a vampire. There was no doubt in my mind and yet...

Through it all, the hiss and pop of the anti-magic and the screams, I stood there.

I stood while Natalie, Narcissa, and Tito rounded up the others. Some, like Armand, had already converted. I saw him pace by, fully wolfed, with Ofelia's body in his jaws. It seemed Ofelia, like Pedro, had been deemed inconvertible and killed outright, no discussion, no mercy.

Then there were the rest of us, the few remaining holdouts: me, Berto, and three others. I'm not sure what I did or said that convinced Morana that I was anything but loyal to her. Well, she was right, of course. The minute she walked in the door, I tried to kill her. I loosed my cobra on her. Fucking stupid. She killed it without even moving, just a blink of the eye and it exploded in a rain of scaly flesh and sinews and blood. I wiped the gore from my face with a scream and ran at her, but she held up a hand and stopped me. What good is an ogre's strength in the face of that kind of telekinetic power? Honestly, I'd never felt anything like it... and there was Natalie, too, beside her, *smiling and licking her lips. I felt something deep within me shudder under her eyes. Looking back, I couldn't actually tell you which of them was stopping me, Natalie or Morana. At the time, I assumed Morana, daughter of Andor Chernoff, the most powerful vampire in living memory. I didn't know Natalie then the way I do now. It's a wonder she didn't slaughter me. Maybe I can thank stupid Berto for that. He was weeping, begging, and trying to convert like the scum of the earth that I knew him to be.*

*"Sálvame!" he cried. "Spare me! I'll do anything. Anything! Por favor."*

*Natalie made a gesture like a knife slicing across her neck and Berto's neck opened in tandem, a gush of thick merlot. He gurgled on it, red in his mouth, froth on his lips, a final whimper escaping in a rush of air and blood.*

*"You were right about him, Deirdre," Morana said, flashing me that smile of hers that'd weakened me from the beginning.*

*I felt my lips tug up in response, my own free will moving to her pull, her gravity. It would have been so easy to tumble into her orbit.*

*"He was weak. What about you, Deirdre? What will you do?"*

*"I'm not weak," I said.*

*"I know," she replied, her face so close I could smell her damp, cloying breath. She leaned in closer still, her lips soft on my cheek. "So what will you do, my love?"*

*If I tell you that I didn't consider it, not even for a second, would you believe me? I've killed and eaten Nons, but only the ones who deserved it. I do not, never have, and never will condone unwarranted, unprovoked genocide. What ogre, given our history, could possibly advocate for that? Oh, right, you don't know any other ogres. Which means you probably believe all Non-lore about ogres, propagated by Columbus, but with a history that dates back millennia before him, to Magix themselves? If you believe this, then I can never convince you that I am good, in my core, despite the evil things I've done. Because I am an ogre and we are the prodigal sibling, cast away from our magical brethren. There's a whole myth about us: we're the missing star in your constellation.*

*So if I tell you that I, without hesitation, spat in her face, and told her to fuck all the way off, will you believe me? If I tell you that she pinned me to the ground, straddled me and pressed her rose-bud red lips to my skin and opened her mouth and marked me as hers with her teeth, took my blood while the others watched until I was nothing more than a wraith, half dead, will you believe me?*

*"I don't care if you live or die, Deidre." She wiped my blood from her lips with the back of her hand. "You've served your purpose. For that, you have my gratitude. Now, I must go. Until we meet again, darling. I'm sure we will be seeing each other sooner than either of us would like."*

*I passed out from blood loss after that. I woke up in a dirty motel to a cop bending over me, asking me what drugs I was on, saying he was going to have to take me in. I was weak as hell, but still stronger than your average male human, so I took him down quick and got the hell out of there.*

*I was weak, starving, and filthy. And not quite right in the head, not without my cobra. Ogres and their snakes have a deep bond, a bit like witches and their birds, I suppose. That cobra and I had been together for over fifteen years. He was a good old boy, but I didn't have time to grieve him.*

*My own blood in Morana's veins was like a beacon. It called to me, tugged at me, left an oozing trail in its wake, silvery and sticky as the track of a snail. I followed it to Denver. I didn't have money beyond two twenties in my wallet, both of which had red lipstick imprints on them that made me shiver. My credit cards had been canceled and my bank account closed and drained. So I walked or hitchhiked until I got to Taos, which took me a whole five days, limping along and catching a handful of short rides here and there. In Taos, I decided to steal a car and made it to Denver in less than five hours, following that slimy blood trail, my chest hitching with every beat of Morana's heart.*

*Does the Non know that vampires have beating hearts? The Non-world really has the most grotesque stories about our kind. Vampires are dead; witches are ugly; sirens are murders; ogres are cannibals and so on. Then again, the act of dehumanization is probably the most human thing about all of us, isn't it?*

*When I got to Denver, the trail, the pulsing throb of it began to fade. Or no, that's not quite right. It quickened, almost doubling, too fast to be a heartbeat anymore. The tug lessened, too, in the same way that, during a game of tug-of-war, one team might suddenly stop pulling, just for an instant, so that the other team will lose their footing. It was there, hard and firm, and then it was gone. When it came back, it wasn't quite as strong, but it was precise. The shining trail, which had stretched and sparkled as wide as the I-25, became thin as a strand of spiderweb. It led me to a house in fancy ass Cherry Creek, where my short-on-sleep-and-food-and-blood, unwashed-for-a-week, black self stood out like the poor, homeless woman I was.*

*The spider silk trail led to a red brick mansion that was somehow audacious, even for Cherry Creek standards. But before I could go there and confront Morana or whatever lay before me, I had to make a detour. At the Denver Zoo, I coaxed this gal, my Nadja, into becoming my companion. I had to knock her jailor out to do so, but Nadja came willingly and we were in and out within an hour. I left the stolen car at the zoo and made my way back to Cherry Creek and that impudent mansion on foot, Nadja tucked around my neck. You'd be surprised how few people notice a snake in plain view, especially when she is sleeping.*

*When I knocked on the door of the mansion in Cherry Creek, Natalie Crane answered, and the pull in my chest surged, then went limp and didn't return. It was like... maybe they hadn't realized I was following until that moment. Morana, she would have known that there had been a bond forged between us, but maybe she didn't realize that I could feel it, and use it, too. That all changed when I looked into Natalie Crane's onyx eyes, though the bond was not fully severed. There are moments when I lose myself in Morana's reality. Ti fi, little Non, you saw this when I tried to destroy you. Morana's voice in my head surged, told me to eat you up.*

*For a vampire, drinking blood is an intimate act and sacred ritual. Lovers drink one another's blood to bind their souls. Soldiers drink the blood of their leader to pledge fealty. Conquerors drink the blood of their enemies to show dominance.*

*When Morana drank my blood, I was more than her enemy. I had also been her lover. The magic sensed this and responded accordingly. My soul is bound to hers, though my body and heart fight against her.*

*In Denver, when I saw Natalie Crane and the pull that had driven me all those miles, the pull that had kept me going, unwavering, fell away, I lost all resolve. Terror seized me and I ran. I holed up in a nearby motel, paralyzed with fear.*

*Time stretched out until moments pulled with the breadth of infinity. Was I there for weeks, months, years? At the time, I couldn't have said. Now, I know it was only a few days.*

*When Denver fell, I felt it. It... her? Morana. A thrill of ecstasy spread through me, starting in my extremities and ending in a climax so orgasmic that I cried out. I wept tears of joy and then, as I came back to myself, the tears kept flowing. I felt them leaving, one by one, their blood joining mine in Morana's veins until I felt their souls extinguish with a hiss like water dousing the hot coals of a dying fire.*

*If I was a braver woman, maybe I could have done more. Maybe I could have charged in and saved them all, or some of them. But my soul, this core of my being, had been corrupted and I had become a worthless coward. I've been trying to repair myself ever since.*

*After, I went back to Cherry Creek. The place was unchanged. I stood on the sidewalk peering through the iron bars, looking for some sign of the slaughter that I knew had taken place only hours before. But as with Santa Fe, Denver had fallen by coup. The bodies of the dead were surreptitiously removed. Life went on.*

*Against my better judgment, I stayed in Denver. Keep your friends close and your enemies even closer is the old adage, right? They'd expect me to leave, I thought. So I stayed. I found a two hundred square-foot studio in Capitol Hill for less than eight hundred a month and got a job as a barista on the south end of Five Points. I built a new life, hiding among Nons. To my surprise, they weren't as horrid as I'd always presumed. Some were even kind. Most of them knew I was, in their words, "trans," and had zero issues with that. From my outsider's knowledge of Non culture, this was unexpected and pleasing, to have this piece of me accepted. But of course, it wasn't all of me. So I existed in a perpetual state of wariness. Do you know what that is like? I haven't felt truly safe since Santa Fe. Then again, I suppose you, Cece and Regina, probably do know that pain, having lost your covens as well.*

*Long story short, I stayed in Denver and would have stayed forever, cut off from the world of Magix, until a couple of witches wandered into my coffee shop.*

*It wasn't the first time a Magick or two had come along, but it was the first time that they recognized me, almost instantaneously, for what I was. They were young, little white girls in their early twenties at most, and they weren't even trying to hide their magic. Don't look so shocked at that: it is different here. Midwestern Nons don't suffer "strange" in the same way that Southwestern Nons do. Eccentric is a lifestyle. These little witches looked like dirty hippy homeless Nons and if they snapped their fingers to reheat their coffee or moved the table into a patch of sunlight without actually touching it, well... the Nons weren't paying attention to them anyway. None of their business, see?*

*But still. Most Magix, even in Denver, tried to be subtle. So their brazenness was a dead giveaway: these girls were from the Denver Coven.*

*"Holy shit!" the first one, a brunette with chubby cheeks, said when she came up to the counter to order. "You're... an ogre!"*

*"Shit, no way!" the second one, taller, with platinum blonde hair, gaped, jostling the first to get a better look at me. "Omg. You. Are. Gorgeous."*

*"Can I take your order?"*

*They gave their orders and asked my name.*

*I pointed to my nametag, which said Nancy, rang up their order, and started to work on their drinks, while they chattered at me, calling me "Nance," gushing about their coven and how it would be "lit" if they got an ogre. Then, they started talking about their "big ass plans."*

*"Those Midwest assholes won't know what hit 'em," they said.*

*"Who gives a shit about Grand Rapids, Michigan, anyway?" they said.*

*So I asked the obvious question, "What kind of plans you got for Grand Rapids?"*

* * *

## 1987

## February 1, 1987

*Valerie,*

*It's good to hear from you. What's done is done. Dead or alive, I'm sure the child is better off and the fewer people who know the truth, whatever that is, the better.*

*Will you be coming back to ~~me~~ us, dear Valerie? I suppose you don't have much choice. Come back or face the consequences.*

*See, I've been thinking lately about how lucky the fairies are to have the ear of Nons so wholly. In Non culture, fairies are not an evil monolith, the way vampires, werewolves, ogres, sirens, shifters, and even witches, for the most part, are. There are good fairies and there bad fairies. There is a history to this, fairy covens that went out of their way to show kindness to Nons, to help them as brethren. There is a lesson to this, too. History is full of lessons.*

*Are you a good fairy or a bad fairy, Valerie?*

*I suppose History will tell all.*

*Your friend. Always.*

*Tish*

# CHAPTER
## NINETEEN



"Stop!" Cece said, gasping as if she'd surfaced from a deep ocean, nearly drowned, but full of adrenaline. "I can't handle this. No."

Regina put a hand on her shoulder.

"I want her gone," Cece said, her voice crackling with electric rage.

The hairs on the back of Tessa's neck stood on end and Astrid reached out to grab her hand as the energy in the room began to twitch and hiss in time with Cece's fury.

"Cordelia…" Tim whispered.

"No! She knew. You *knew!*" she shrieked in Deirdre's face, spraying specks of froth onto the other woman's cheeks. "And you did *nothing.*"

Deirdre did not close her eyes or flinch against Cece's rage. She stood her ground and took the anger with stoic acceptance. Not defiance, as Tessa would have previously assumed. Now, Tessa could see that for all Deirdre's chipper attitude, weird fetishes, and unsettling vibe, she was trying to do something *good* here. Trying to right a wrong.

"I did nothing," Deirdre repeated. "Nothing to help Grand Rapids. I joined Denver, repenting my former ways. Natalie Crane let me join. The jig was up. It was join or flee or die."

"So you flee or die!" Cece shouted.

"What good am I dead? What good was I if I ran either? I joined because I am a survivor from a long line of survivors and survivors understand that sometimes the right thing is not the best thing to do. Sometimes, you have to do the wrong thing for a while to learn the enemy and survive. Sometimes, you have to sacrifice good people for a bigger cause."

"Fucking tell that to my kids." Cece spoke through clenched teeth, her voice the thin whine of night terrors, sweat-soaked sheets, and bleary-eyed mornings. "They lost their parents, and you're going to talk about sacrifices and greater good shit—"

"Hell yes," Deirdre interrupted. "This is about the greater good. It *has* to be."

"No." Cece shook her head. "Not on my watch." She turned and started to walk toward the door. On her shoulder, Bettie swiveled her head around so that her eyes stayed on Deirdre as Cece continued to speak. "I want you gone."

"Wait, Cece," Regina said. "I have questions—there's more to this story." Regina's voice was low, her mouth pressed close to Cece's ear, but Tessa could still hear the words. "She can *see*, Cece. Not only magic, but *anti-magic*. I've never heard of—"

"This isn't a debate," Cece snapped, jerking away from Regina. "She's leaving."

"And if I refuse?" Deirdre asked, puffing out her chest and seeming to stand up to her full height, towering over all of them.

Bettie squawked at her, snapped her beak, and continued to stare at Deirdre with beady-eyed contempt. Cece did not turn.

"Get out of my house," she said, her voice soft as the padding steps of a tiger stalking its prey. "Get your things and go. Now. I don't think you want to see what'll happen if you don't." With that, she opened the door and left, shutting it with a surprisingly gentle click behind her.

Regina and Tim looked at each other, frowns on their faces. They did not appear to be think-talking. There was a general blankness in the room, as if all of them were collectively thinking, *What now?*

Deirdre stepped forward then, and Regina and Tim moved apart to let her through. As she walked, the snake recoiled itself atop her short black curls and she began to twist her indigo scarf around and around it. She paused to finish tying the turban in a knot at the doorway before opening the door and stepping out of Tessa's room and into the empty hall. The lights above had been dimmed to signify evening. The hallway glowed faintly orange, and in it, Deirdre seemed to glow as well, a shimmering bronze. She had that same statuesque look that Tessa had come to realize most Magix possessed in certain lights.

When she spoke, her voice was hoarse from talking. "If you need me, I'll come back. All you have to do is ask." She looked up then and met each of their gazes with a long stare. When her gaze met Tessa's, she felt that same strange distending of time and muffling of sound that she had experienced at the dinner table.

*Be careful, Tessa, or we'll eat you up.*

Then she was gone.

* * *

That night, after Tim, Regina, and Astrid had gone back to their rooms, Tessa lay on her bed, looking up at the leaves and their echoing shadows and thought over the details of Deirdre's story. There were certain parts of it that caught in her brain, hiccupping against her amygdala: Morana, kneeling over Deirdre, her teeth against her neck, her blood on her lips; the black, magic-devouring anti-magic; and Theo, her sweet Theo, sitting in a corner, kicking their legs back and forth, back and forth.

*Theo.*

Cece wasn't the only one infuriated by Deirdre's inaction. Even now, her cheeks grew hot thinking about little Theo sitting stiff with fear while the adults in their life either abused them or failed to stop their abuser.

Tessa wasn't sure she was any better. Theo was with Morana. She *knew* this, yet she'd failed to do anything about it. She didn't trust Deirdre, and she certainly disagreed with a lot of what she'd done, but at least she'd done, or tried to do, something.

*Sometimes, you have to do the wrong thing for a while to learn the enemy and survive.*

It felt true, but Tessa still shivered at the thought and the memory of Deirdre's last words to her: *We'll eat you up.*

With a sigh, Tessa rolled over onto her stomach and pulled out her phone to do some mindless scrolling through Facebook. Incongruous to her lived experience, she always told herself this would relax her, help her sleep. After watching half a dozen reels about parenting hacks, plant rearing, and odd animal friend pairings, Tessa decided to see if Cece had a Facebook. She typed in Cordelia Connolly. A series of old white ladies, including one rigid-looking, habited nun, popped up. Cece didn't have a Facebook. Or an Instagram. Tessa didn't bother looking on Twitter. Cece was probably one of those anti-social media people anyway.

After contemplating searching for Jean and realizing she couldn't remember his last name, Tessa ended up on Sanjay's page. She'd blocked his number after a particularly foul voicemail that used one-too-many female slurs, but she hadn't unfriended him. She was surprised to see he'd uploaded a new photo. Of him… and Morana. They were smiling, faces pressed close together, cheek to cheek and staring up at the camera in that obnoxious way that new couples always seemed to pose. Morana's pale skin against Sanjay's tawny brown had the same yellow undertones. Both wore shades of purple, her in a mauve dress and him with an orchid bow tie. Maybe they'd been to a wedding together? Had Theo gone with them? No, of course not. Morana wouldn't bring her kid anywhere, if she could avoid it. Tessa's stomach ached like it was being pulled in two directions, rage grabbing it in one fist and anxiety tugging it, weepily, in the opposite direction.

The background of the photo was some kind of art, or maybe a mural. There was only a small portion visible, but Tessa recognized it from somewhere, somewhere close and so innocuous, such a part of her life that her eyes had glazed over it at first because—because that was a mural from her bedroom! Those assholes were in her house, probably copulating—Tessa almost dry heaved at the thought—on her bed and they wanted her to know it.

Why?

Before Tessa could think through an answer, there was a knock on her door.

"It's me," Astrid said. "You up?"

"Yeah, come in," Tessa answered.

Astrid came in, shutting the door behind her and locking it while saying, "Just in case Deirdre, I don't know, comes back," before flopping onto the bed next to Tessa, asking, "What you looking at?"

Tessa showed Astrid her phone.

"Barf," Astrid said, putting her hand over the phone. "Don't even look, fam. That guy is bad news."

"Yeah, well, we were friends for a decade and change, so…" Tessa clicked the phone off. The black screen provided dim reflections of the two of them, cheeks almost as close as Morana and Sanjay's had been, looking like the photograph negatives Tessa had found so creepy as a kid.

"I'm sorry," Astrid said. Her green eyes didn't hold light the way Non eyes did. Their reflection glowed on the phone's blank screen, reminding Tessa of nocturnal predators.

"Me too."

"Fuck him."

"Not interested."

"What about Deirdre?" Astrid asked, trying to hide a smirk.

Tessa nudged her with her shoulder before rolling away and onto her back. "Cece was too harsh on her, but I get it. If I were Cece, I'd probably have done the same thing."

"You can be fighting for the right things and still be an asshole," Astrid finished.

Tessa let out a long sigh. "That *is* the truth, huh."

"Do you believe what she said about the anti-magic?" Astrid asked. "About seeing it?"

"Sure," Tessa said. "Cece can see it."

Astrid sat up. "What? She can?"

Tessa frowned. "I don't think I was supposed to say that."

Now Astrid was frowning, but she lay back down on the bed. "I didn't know that was possible," she said after a while. "Maybe, like, really powerful Magix can do it though."

"I wouldn't know," Tessa replied.

They were quiet for a time. Tessa had already started to drift off to sleep, the black tendrils of a dream gripping the edges of her mind, when Astrid murmured, "I've been thinking about what you asked."

"Mm," Tessa muttered. The black tendrils were taking the shape of a human. The human had green eyes, skin the color of a sunflower's center, smile like its yellow blooms.

"You asked me if my parents left any clues," Astrid said.

The dream-human wore an emerald dress and Tessa looked down to see that she was dressed in a matching peridot one. She reached out her hand to the emerald woman.

"Like when they talked about the portal," Astrid continued. "Remember?"

"Mmhmm." Dream-woman took Tessa's hand.

"So I've been thinking about it, and they would always tell this same story, right?"

"Yesss." Dream-woman's face moved closer to Tessa's her breath smelled like hay, sage, and earth, like growing things, new beginnings, a thrumming, surging petrichor.

"Dude, wake up!" Astrid was shaking her. "I'm trying to tell you something important."

Tessa groaned and sat up. "I was almost—"

"You can have your gross dreams about Cece later," Astrid said.

Tessa frowned and blushed but didn't try to object to the statement.

"So my parents—"

"From the beginning?" Tessa asked, rubbing her eyes.

"When my parents would remind me about the portal, how to use it, they always told the same story. They'd always talk about the first attack, right? How lucky we were because we weren't there when it started?"

"Where were you?"

Astrid grinned. "Exactly." Her green eyes shimmered. "My mom was out with Cece, but my dad and I, we were with my nana and papa."

Tessa was waking up now. "And you think…"

"Maybe it's where my parents are!"

"Where do your nana and papa live?"

"They don't live there anymore. They joined another coven. But!" She flapped her hands in the air, as if trying to move the conversation forward faster. "They used to live at the lake house. I thought they sold it, but maybe not. Because every time, *every* time my parents talked about the portal and what to do if we were attacked, they told the same story. I always thought it was their stupid way of reminding me how I should pay attention. But maybe… Tessa! Do you think they could be there?" Astrid was jumping up and down now and so was Tessa, fully awake like she'd just hit a shot of espresso.

"It's a start! Yes! Let's go talk to Cece about going." She started to leave the room, holding Astrid's hand in hers, but Astrid didn't budge.

"She's not going to let me go."

"What do you mean? Of course she will! She wants you to find your parents. Come on!"

"No, she won't." Astrid stood firm, giving Tessa side-eyed look that said: *Don't be an idiot.* Out loud, she repeated, "You know she won't."

Tessa sighed. "You're probably right, but you never know unless you ask."

Astrid sat back down on the edge of Tessa's bed. "I *know* Auntie. After this shit with Deirdre, she's gonna put the place on lockdown."

Tessa frowned. "Sounds a bit draconian."

"Draconian should be Cece's middle name. Instead of *Archer*… so weird."

Tessa sat next to Astrid. "Someone's coming in the morning," she said. "Sobriety or…"

"The Sobro Boys," Astrid said. "From Nashville. I guess they're still kicking."

"Can we trust them?" Tessa asked.

"Can we trust anybody?" Astrid let out a gush of air that was half laugh, half sob before turning to Tessa and taking both of her hands in her own. "I trust you," she said. "That's it."

"What about Cece?"

"Stop fixating on Cece! When all this is over, you can ask her out or whatever, but right now, I need you here, with me, as my Familiar. I need your help."

There was a sharp pain in Tessa's left arm, the new Familiar mark, and she automatically put her right hand over it. When she removed the hand, the once-red welt seemed to glow with white-hot intensity. Her Magick needed her, and so Tessa made the only response that she could make.

"I have a car at my house," she said, thinking of Sanjay and Morana, their smiling faces staring up at her from out of her bedroom. "We could walk there."

"What about them?" Astrid asked, tilting her head toward Tessa's phone.

Tessa shrugged. "I'm sure they're hoping I'll come back, yeah. But it's the middle of the night, so maybe they'll be asleep?"

"They could have a guard."

Tessa stood and picked up her keys from atop her dresser. "So we should wait until morning, check with Cece and Jean?"

"Are you crazy, fam?" Astrid said, jumping to her feet. "What's the plan?"

"Go to the house and take the car."

"That's it?" Astrid frowned, folding her arms across her chest. "Quickly?"

Astrid bit her lip. "Magic would only attract their notice. And I'm sick of waiting. They're not gonna bother trying to find them. They're trying to fight a war. I have to do this myself. We have to do this." She shrugged. "Maybe it's stupid enough to work."

"Let's go then," Tessa said.

* * *

**JULY 1990**                    *July 9, 1990*

*Dad,*

*This is my last letter. I won't keep risking our safety by continuing contact.*

*I heard you've got yet another Hybrid to add to your arsenal. #4, is it? After Chernobyl, I would've thought you, of all people, would realize the error of your ways. But, if my sources are correct, you clearly have not.*

*I have never seen a child so innately powerful as my daughter— yes, she is my daughter and I will continue to claim her as such and continue to hide her from you and Tish, even Val, and your machinations.*

*I know your intentions in this have always been far purer than those for whom you work, but you must see that they're using you, right? Our so-called superiors want weapons; that is what this is, and has always been, about. At this point, your continued denial can only be chalked up to willful ignorance. These children are ticking time bombs; they are not saviors.*

*I say this as the father of one, a father who loves his child with all his being, who would kill and die for her, who has given up everything so that she could have a chance at a happy life.*

*All the while, I know what she is and Mer knows what she is and we are both in agreement that if, and likely when, the time comes and she, in turn, comes into her full power, we must be prepared to kill her to save the world.*

*Can you imagine what torture this knowledge is for us? As a parent yourself, you must have some inkling. I know you have no contact with any of the Hybrids, but still—could you kill one of them? How about the one you sired?*

*So, here we are. This is the end of the road for you and I. Goodbye, Dad.*

*—Archer*

# CHAPTER
# TWENTY



The house looked deserted. No lights were on. No one moved behind windows. The sun was quickly setting, the streetlights blinking on. Tessa heard the hum of night insects and the electric zap of errant ones. Fireflies, out early this year, lit up her lawn. They waited in the park across the street, Astrid rocking back and forth on the swings, Tessa leaning against a slide and peering through the chain link fence at her house. Was Sanjay in there? Was Morana with him?

Tessa took a deep breath and started to move toward the house.

"You should stay here," she said to Astrid.

*I'm not leaving you,* Astrid thought-told her.

Tessa knew she should argue. Instead, she held the girl's hand. She had to trust the kid.

They approached the house and walked up the driveway, quickly and quietly. Tessa keyed in the code to the garage. It yawned and grunted its way open with deafening conspicuousness. They stood for a moment in the garage's dim orange light. The car was still there: her bug-eyed gray Leaf. Plugged-in, so hopefully fully charged.

"Sweet!" Astrid said, running around to the passenger side as Tessa clicked to unlock it.

As Tessa unplugged the car and hung up the cord, she felt the hairs on the back of her neck stand up. She shivered, heaving open the door, jumping in and slamming it behind her. She started the car and didn't even bother to buckle up, turn on the lights, or look behind her before she gunned the car in reverse, cringing at the warning beeps her otherwise silent car emitted. On either side, she saw dark shadows. She felt them approaching, felt her throat tightening. Sanjay appeared in the garage, alone, in a yellow bathrobe that made his skin look sallow, the rusty bags under his eyes giving him a hollowed-out look like Frankenstein's monster. He lurched, zombie-like toward the car, and then Morana was beside him, pale, hawk-nosed, and smiling, her pronounced canines flashing as Tessa switched on the car's lights and shifted into drive.

"This was a bad idea," Astrid muttered, fastening her seatbelt as Tessa pressed down on the accelerator.

Astrid pivoted to watch Tessa's house fade behind them. Morana's outline was visible under a streetlamp, her arms lifted in the air. Tessa slammed around a corner and then another, trying to get out of the neighborhood, when a howl growled behind them, starting low and rising. It was echoed by another and then another, a roiling chorus.

"Werewolves," Astrid whispered. "They can run!" she said, louder. "You gotta drive faster. Get on the main road!"

Tessa fumbled with her own seat belt as she careened the car through the neighborhood. She turned onto Madison Avenue with a screech. There was a red light straight ahead at the Burton intersection.

"You can't stop!" Astrid squealed.

She could hear their pounding feet. She pressed down on the gas, accelerating into the stop light and praying to the universe that she didn't get them t-boned and killed. There was a loud honk and they were through, swinging left onto Burton and toward the highway. She heard tires squeal and thud, the sound of glass shattering and metal crumpling.

"A car hit one," Astrid shouted, looking back.

There was another squeal and crash.

"Another car collided into that car, blocking the intersection."

"Are any of them following us?"

Astrid turned around, tugging her seatbelt back into position. "Keep driving," she said. "You can get on the highway and head north."

"Then to the Lake?" She heard sirens behind her and it occurred to her that she could be arrested for what she'd done. Cameras had probably caught her plate number. She was surprised by how little she cared. Her heart was pounding and she felt unbearably, beautifully alive as they sped down lamp-lit streets, swerving around slow cars, veering in and out of oncoming traffic, blinded momentarily by head-lights and fear.

"We can't go straight to the lake house," Astrid said. "They'll be looking for the car. We'll have to dump it."

"And walk?"

"Maybe a mile or two, yeah." Astrid turned to look behind them. "There's a few back there. Shit, they're fast! You'll lose them once you get on the highway."

Tessa gunned it through the final light before the highway entrance. "You're sure?"

"They're fast, but not seventy-miles-an-hour fast."

Tessa slowed to take the tight turn, merging onto northbound 131. "This Leaf isn't exactly seventy-miles-an-hour fast." She kept acceler-ating, glancing in the rearview mirror. She saw several figures loping down the on-ramp. "How fast *can* they go?"

The figures running along the shoulder were falling further and further behind them, even with the Leaf hovering around sixty-five miles per hour.

"We're losing them," Astrid confirmed. She turned around again, grinning.

By the time they hit the S curve through downtown Grand Rapids, the wolves were nowhere to be seen. Tessa breathed in and out. That alive feeling, almost like flying, thrummed through her.

"I think we're all clear," Astrid said, reaching for the radio. Kate Bush's pure soprano rang out.

Tessa recalled singing this exact song with Theo, their thin, oboe-like voice rising on the descants while she thrummed along in the alto range.

The heady adrenaline rush was fading and with it, her euphoria. She hadn't seen a werewolf in miles. She felt suddenly queasy. Tessa cut off the radio.

"Hey!" Astrid said. "I love that song. 'Wuthering Heights' is a fucking classic. How can you not love Kate Bush?"

Tessa grimaced. "I like Kate Bush. It's just… Theo loved her, too." Tessa reached over and turned the radio back on. The vocals had finished and they sat listening to the final guitar solo.

"Oh my god, this is such a fucking epic song," Astrid sighed.

Tessa nodded, recalling a lecture Theo once gave her on the under-appreciate genius of Kate Bush. She smiled, thinking how well Theo and Astrid would get along.

They took the left hand exit to merge onto westbound 96. A loud ringing interrupted the final strumming of the guitar.

"Shit," Astrid said. "It's Cece. Should I answer?"

Tessa hesitated. It was past midnight. Had Cece realized they were gone? Why would she be calling, if not? Had she come looking for them?

"Shit," Tessa muttered.

The phone rang again. Cece would be angry. She'd try to find them, which would, at minimum, complicate things and at worst, stop them from completing their mission of finding Astrid's parents. *Mission* had the same energy as *espionne* and Tessa thought it with the same delicious French accent and desire to be part of something larger than herself. She had hoped they would be able to get to the lake house and find Astrid's parents without Cece realizing they were gone, leaving them to return as heroes. She had this bizarre notion that if she could do something amazing and epic, then Cece would *see* her, Tessa, not as a frumpy vegan Familiar, but as someone epic and amazing herself. Someone special, if not magical. She thought about Cece's smooth, dark skin, her self-assured style, and the way she smiled. She recalled the baubles in her hair, the Venus flytraps, such amazing creativity. Cece was also powerful and terrifying, like the statue of a goddess: elevated, stern, stone. *Unreachable*, Tessa thought. It was a silly thing to want.

The phone rang a third time. More important than any of Tessa's stupid fantasies was the fact that Cece was a mama. And Tessa could imagine the panic she was feeling right now, could feel her pulse quickening, the knot rising in her throat, the tightness pulling at her gut.

"Yes, answer it," she said after the fourth ring. She turned off the radio.

"Heeeeey," Astrid said. She put the phone on speaker.

"Where are you?" Cece's voice was calm, not too loud. Tessa heard her take a deep breath and she could hear the effort, the churning behind the mask of patience.

Astrid feigned a yawn. "In bed?"

"Nooo," Cece said, dragging out the word into several syllables. "I'm standing in your bedroom."

"Well, that's an invasion of privacy," Astrid snapped back.

"Luca came into my bedroom and said he saw you leave," Cece continued. "With Tessa."

*Goddamn nightwalker,* Tessa thought, not realizing she'd projected the thought until Astrid rolled her eyes and nodded.

"We're just getting some air," Astrid said, her voice high and falsely chipper.

"Is Tessa there then?" Cece asked.

Astrid looked over at Tessa who mouthed "shit," before hopping in.

"We think we know where Astrid's parents are," she said.

There was no response to that.

"We are driving to find them," Tessa added.

There was a shuffling sound and some cursing in the background, along with Luca's gravelly voice shouting "I told you so!" Then Jean came on the phone.

"Stupide, the both of you. It's the same in English as French so I know you know what I mean." He then followed this up with a string of phrases that were probably curses, but which neither of them could understand. "Cece is very upset. Too upset to talk to either of you, so you need to tell me where you are and I'll come get you. Got it?"

"No," Tessa said. "She's safe with me. We are going to find them. Then we'll be back."

"Ach, non, non, non! That's not acceptable, Tessa!"

"You tell her—" Cece was hollering something indecipherable in the background. Another shuffling and she was back on the line. "Tessa, you don't know what you're doing."

"I'm helping a kid. More than either of you could be bothered with." She hung up.

Astrid's eyes went wide and a huge grin spread across her face. "Badass! I thought you liked her, though?"

"What exit?" Tessa asked. "Soon, I hope? The range on this thing is shit."

Astrid glanced at her phone, before answering, "Nine. Just a couple more miles. Should be good." Then she giggled. "So much for that budding romance."

Tessa sighed. Her cheeks with red from anger and embarrassment. "They were wrong not to help you."

"I know. Thank you, Tessa."

After the exited, they drove down M-104 and through the touristy part of Spring Lake, crossing a bridge and continuing all the way to the lakeshore. They pulled into the parking lot of a beachside park that clearly stated it was closed. Tessa imagined that the place was probably unmonitored and pulled the car into a spot at the edge of the lot, staring out at the dark, unbroken blackness of Lake Michigan.

"It's a mile up the road," Astrid said, gesturing north. "But we should probably go that way a bit." She gestured east. "And then cut back."

"Like, through the woods?"

Astrid nodded. "The less visible we are the better."

They started the trek, Astrid leading the way.

After only about hundred yards, Astrid halted, holding up a firm hand. In the second after their footsteps stopped, Tessa heard it, too: another step, out of cadence with theirs, then silence. Around them, the forest buzzed, swayed, and ticked with life, but Tessa held her breath. In the moonlight, she could see Astrid's outline, her hand held high. Her fingers began to twitch.

*I'm going to take care of this.*

*Are you sure? What if—*

Astrid shook her head. *Duck.*

Tessa dropped to the ground. Astrid's fingers splayed wide as she attacked. Tessa heard two hisses followed by a pop, like lightning hitting a power line. Beside her, Astrid shrieked, shaking her hand. The power surge had been deflected, hitting Astrid. Even in the dim light, Tessa could see the bubbling burn. Above, Tessa heard a piercing squawk. She heard running footsteps coming nearer. Tessa dove to cover Astrid.

"What the hell, Astrid! Are you ok?"

It was Cece. With a chiding mumble, Bettie landed on her shoulder.

"Never attack blind," Cece continued, kneeling beside Astrid and Tessa. "You could have killed me." She took Astrid's hand in hers and kissed the blistering wound. The skin around the angry lesion glowed and stretched, dissolving the burn in a matter of seconds. "I'm sorry I hurt you," she added, closing Astrid's hand into a fist and holding it tightly between her hands. "I didn't mean to deflect it right back at you. Shit."

"I'm sorry I almost killed you," Astrid said, her voice held in a careful monotone, like she was trying to be hard and brave. "Thank you," she added, pulling back her hand and standing. "Come on, Tessa."

Tessa hopped up and started to follow her, but Cece caught her arm.

"We need to go home. This isn't safe."

As if on cue, a low howl rose up from the east.

Tessa turned to Cece, squeezing her hand. "We've come too far to go back now."

Cece sighed. Still perched on her shoulder, Bettie cocked her head to one side and watched Tessa with that uncanny, knowing expression of hers.

"Help us," Tessa pleaded, looking at both Cece and Bettie, too. "Then we'll go."

Astrid continued to forge ahead, so Tessa did not wait for a reply, pulling her hand out of Cece's grasp and running after Astrid. She ducked under a low branch and caught up to Astrid. A second later, Bettie was on her shoulder with a zipping purr. Tessa reached up and gave her chin a quick rub, murmuring, "Thank you."

"She must've put a tracker spell on me back at the House," Astrid muttered.

"We need to hurry," Tessa said, starting to jog along as they came to a long stretch of deer path, largely free of foliage and low branches.

She heard footsteps behind her, and Cece's voice in her ear. "I could take you all back to The House. Right now."

"It's a violation of privacy to put a tracker spell on someone without permission," Astrid retorted.

"It was for your own good. All the kids have them. In case they get… taken."

"Still should've asked."

"I don't need your permission to keep you safe."

Bettie flew into the air with an indignant squawk at this, lifting over a branch and then coming back down to land on Astrid's shoulder and giving Cece a nasty glare.

"I don't need your permission to bring you back, either," Cece added.

"But you want our permission," Astrid replied, hopping over a raised root.

"And you… wouldn't… do that," Tessa added, panting.

"If you were in imminent danger—"

"We're not," Astrid said, holding back a branch for Tessa and dropping it before Cece could duck under.

Bettie clacked her beak, a laughing sound.

Rather than slicing her face with its brittle body, the branch turned flimsy and stroked Cece's face, as she continued, "*When* you are—"

"Then you can bring us back," Tessa said, cutting off Astrid before she could interject.

*Dude, no.* Astrid thought-cried.

"Astrid. Our job… is to protect… you… ok?" Tessa wheezed as they continued to jog down the path, which was narrowing now, close to disappearing into the creeping foliage.

*Only if it's imminent, ok?*

Tessa nodded. *Yes.* It was a lot easier to thought-speak than talk aloud.

*Like, gun to the head imminent, fam.*

*Sure. Not my favorite phr—*

*Gun to the head?*

Tessa nodded.

"Ok," Astrid said aloud.

"Ok," Cece repeated.

"Ok," Tessa added. *Sealing the pact,* she thought. She felt an electric sizzle move between them and wondered if there was something to that thought, a real burst of magic that the triplication of their intent had birthed. She remembered what Astrid had said to her about magic: *I can feel it. It's everywhere, in everything.* Tessa had never *felt* magic before this moment. As they continued on, Tessa made a mental note of "weird." But then the thought fell aside, secondary to the movement through brush, to her jagged breathing, to the sweat lining her brow.

They moved as quickly as they could, occasionally stumbling over a dip in the ground, a stone, or exposed root. Bettie was not visible above them, soaring over the trees. Occasionally, she offered up a light squawk to assure them of her presence.

As they ran, Tessa wondered at the unspoken conversation between her and Astrid. She hadn't tried to think-talk back to Astrid, but she'd done it nonetheless. She'd had to think so hard the first time she'd thought-told Astrid anything. Now, it seemed like Astrid could hear her thoughts without Tessa really *doing* anything.

*I think this is normal,* Astrid thought-interrupted, *for Magix and their Familiars to be able to think-talk without even trying.*

*So I've lost all privacy?*

Astrid shook her head. *If you don't want me to hear, I won't. It's like Bluetooth. You have to sync up.*

They came to a break in the trees, a wide field stretching before them, carved out for telephone wires that stood like petrified giants, looming over the earth. Astrid took off at a run and didn't slow once they returned to the tree cover.

*We're almost there,* she thought-told Tessa.

"Almost there," Tessa panted aloud.

"She told me, too," Cece panted back.

Apparently you could *group* think-talk.

They reached a dirt road and turned west, toward the Lake. A few dozen yards ahead there was a sign: Sunset Villa. Beyond it leaned a row of mailboxes, each labeled with an address.

"1043 is the address," Astrid said, sprinting toward a fork and turning left.

*Wait.* Cece's thought-voice was the snarl of a cornered animal.

Astrid stopped, turning her head to look back at Cece, who pointed toward a thick grove of pine trees hugging the road. The three tiptoed into the tree cover and continued on toward the house in a silence so profound that Tessa was fairly sure Cece had conjured it.

The woods trickled into whistling dune grass. They squatted down among the tall blades, peering out into the darkness. Bettie landed with silent grace on Tessa's shoulder and peered out as well. Ahead of them, the ground took the steep downward slope of a dune. To their right, the house stood atop the dune, a steep drop-off marking the property line.

All the lights were on: the flickering porch, the bright kitchen, the floodlight on the side of the house, and in every bedroom. Even in the basement light shone through the glass block windows.

They waited, watching for movement, listening for voices. The house was lit for a party, but it was empty.

Perhaps someone had heard them coming. Tessa was turning the situation over in her mind, trying to think of an explanation.

Just then, the lights went off. Astrid gasped, then clapped a hand over her mouth. Tessa held her breath. Cece tapped her wrist and her watch lit up: 11:30 p.m. She stood up.

"It's a timer," she said aloud. "It's all on a timer."

"So there's no one here?" Astrid murmured.

"I don't think so. Not anymore. But, I think they may want it to look like someone is here," Cece added, approaching the house.

Tessa squeezed Astrid's hand. *That's a good thing.*

*You don't know that.*

Tessa sighed. *I think it's a good thing. I hope it is.*

They walked up to the door and Cece knocked, before trying the handle, which was locked. She snapped her fingers and there was a click and the door opened. They stepped inside, Bettie taking a soaring lead ahead of them, talons forward and ready, and Tessa felt a surge of affection for the bird and her boldness. She reached for the light switch, but Cece grabbed her hand. There was a howl, again to the east, but farther away than the last time they'd heard it. Tessa wondered if they'd found the car.

"Mom?" Astrid whispered. "Dad?"

There was a faint flapping noise coming from the kitchen that was not raven's wings. They went in. A window had been left open and a breeze blew in, ruffling the curtains. Bettie sat on the kitchen counter, head tilted, watching the room with mild interest.

On the table, there was a vase of fresh cut pink oleander blossoms. Astrid reached a hand out to touch a petal, which curled and wilted at her touch. The flowers and vase turned black and crumbled to dust. Bettie hopped up into the air and landed in the pile of dust, sending up a little spray of it.

"What the—?" Tessa murmured, coughing.

"It's a sign," Cece said.

"Like a burn after reading note?" Tessa asked, to which Cece nodded.

"They're in the South," Astrid said. "Oleander, it doesn't grow way up here."

"That's still a big swath of the country," Tessa said.

Cece shook her head. "They're at Carolina Beach."

Astrid sucked in a breath. "That's where they met, right? North Carolina."

Cece nodded. "And where they got married. On the beach. Aura had a bouquet of pink oleander at her wedding." With each word, the frown on Cece's face deepened.

Oblivious to Cece's distress, Astrid grabbed her hand. "Can we go now? Please?"

Cece said nothing. She stared at the remains of the flowers. "Did you know about the oleander, Astrid?" she asked.

Astrid shrugged. "No."

"There weren't any wedding pictures?" Tessa asked.

Cece shook her head. "It was a small event. No photographer."

"So how would they have expected you to figure that out?" Tessa asked.

Cece raised her eyebrows and opened her mouth, but Astrid cut her off.

"Who cares!" Astrid exclaimed. "Cece figured it out, so let's *gooo*!"

Cece kept staring at the dust, frowning. "No," she finally said. "Tessa's right. Something's… off."

Astrid opened her mouth to protest, but Tessa interrupted, "It's so late, Astrid."

Astrid turned to Tessa, her green eyes wide, catching the moonlight and glowing like a cat's.

"Tomorrow?" Tessa meant to say it, but it came out as a question.

Cece bit her lip, but then nodded. "Yes, tomorrow. You were right, both of you. We should find them. Jean, Regina, and the others can handle the Sobro Boys and battle strategies while we look for your parents—"

Astrid opened her mouth, but Cece cut her off firmly.

"Tomorrow."

Astrid sighed, but lowered her head in acquiescence. Cece took each of them by the hand and they were off. Tessa barely registered the detour. She closed her eyes and when she opened them again, they were back in the House.

She walked upstairs. On the top step, Luca was sprawled out, asleep with his mouth open so that his fangs showed. His red hair was a sweaty mess. One hand clutched a Lego creation.

Tessa picked him up and carried him into the room, tucking him into the empty bed. "Good night," she said to the room. There was no reply. She could hear Silas' deep breathing from above. Tessa closed the door and went into her own room.

She laid down in bed, not even bothering to take her clothes off, heavy with exhaustion. As she drifted off, she couldn't help smiling. The day had been wild. She'd almost been eaten by an ogre and murdered by werewolves but shit! It was amazing to be part of something, surrounded by weird people, fueled by a purpose greater than herself.

Theo would love it here, she thought before she drifted off to sleep.

* * *

**OCT 1994**

## *October 10, 1994*

*Internal Memo*
*Subject: Reorg.*

*From: Marcus Brand*

*To: Gunner Engers, Tish Chernoff, Valerie Hart*

*Effective immediately, the Committee, under the direction of the new AntiMagi Department of Health and Defense has decided to redefine the Magix and AntiMagi Projected Amalgamation Confederation. For the past twenty-five years, MAAM PAC has been a pillar of scientific innovation and discovery and the Committee thanks you for your service. In particular, the Committee has been impressed with the results of Hybrid #4 and your success in monitoring the Hybrid from a safe distance while containing the subject.*

*MAAM PAC and its members have been reassigned to the Defense sector of the Department. You will continue the Hybrid work alongside other assignments. These assignments will be forthcoming within the week.*

# CHAPTER
## TWENTY-ONE

**JULY 2023**

"You keep running away from me," Morana said.

In this dream, they were in a hotel or possibly an upscale apartment building. They stood shoulder to shoulder, waiting for an elevator. The bell dinged. The doors opened. They both went in.

"I'm not running away," Tessa replied.

"Hiding then." Morana pressed the button for the ninety-ninth floor. They were on the ground floor. "So we'll have some time to chat," she said. "Finally."

"I'll stop hiding if—"

"You can't have them," Morana snapped. "Theo is mine. I birthed them."

"Birthing someone doesn't make them yours," Tessa said. They clicked up past the third, fourth, fifth floors.

"Neither does being their Familiar."

"I never said Theo was mine."

The twelfth floor. The fourteenth.

"No, you simply acted as if they were."

Tessa sighed. She could counter that she was theirs as much as they were hers because that was how love worked. But there was no point in arguing. After all, this was a dream. "How *is* Theo?"

"Same old, same old. How's Cece? And Astrid?"

"Same old, same old."

"Where are you all hiding?"

"Why did you try to kill Astrid and her parents?" A wordless song played. Their questions took on the same singsong cadence as the ding-ing, synthetic melody breezing around them.

"Why do you assume it was me?"

"Who else would it be?"

They were rising quickly now, past the fiftieth floor, fifty-eighth floor.

"Well now," Morana said as they soared past the seventy-fourth floor. "That *is* the question."

Tessa woke to find Cece staring down at her, grinning maniacally. Then she noticed the patch of freckles on her check, a unique constellation she recalled from the day before.

"Evie," Tessa moaned and the girl immediately shifted back into her true form.

"You're no fun," Evie shouted, shifting into Tessa's form as she ran out of the room with a bombastic energy and loud wailing that reminded Tessa of a baby goat.

Across the hall came a snort of laughter. As Tessa was getting out of bed with a groan and a stretch, Astrid poked her head in. "Whew, I was hoping that wasn't you screaming down the hall."

"Evie," Tessa replied flatly.

"Figured you wouldn't be begging to play with Silas' Legos."

Tessa shook her head. "Um, I love Legos."

"I smell pancakes," Astrid said, sniffing the air and then giving a small howl.

Tessa winced.

"Too soon?"

Tessa chuckled. "It was a wild night, huh?"

Astrid shook her head and frowned, suddenly stoic.

Tessa sighed. "I've gotta change, then I'll be down for breakfast. Shut the door?"

Astrid nodded but still hesitated in the doorway. They stood there for a moment, facing each other but not making eye contact, Tessa looking up at the branches of the trees overhead and Astrid looking down at her feet, before Astrid finally said, "What if we don't find them?"

Tessa looked at her. Astrid met her gaze.

"Don't say we will," Astrid continued.

"I wasn't—I wouldn't—"

"Because I know we might not find them." The irises of Astrid's eyes were dancing like green flames, like a cauldron's bubbling brew. "I know that they might be…" Her voice broke, expanding into an airy gasp, an automatic, punched-in-the-gut sound, like her thoughts had rammed her body straight into a wall.

"But they might *not* be," Tessa whispered, taking a step toward Astrid, who held up a hand.

"Something isn't *right*," Astrid said. "I can't feel them. Not like I could before. It's gotten… faint."

"Like they're in trouble?"

Astrid shook her head as if she was clearing out water from her ears, a violent shake from side to side. "They're underground. Or enclosed, somehow? We need to get Cece and go. Now."

Tessa nodded. "Yeah, ok. Let me get dressed. I'll meet you down there."

She dressed quickly, splashing cold water on her face and armpits instead of taking a much needed shower. Semi-cleaned up, Tessa hurried out of her room, the smell of pancakes even stronger now. She hoped she'd have time to at least scarf down a pancake or something before they set out.

As she jogged down the hall, Tessa glanced into Luca and Silas' room to find two Silases mirroring one another in somber concentration. When she reached the stairs, a thunderous crash came from the room followed by hysterical laughter. She thought about going back to check on them because the laughter was slightly maniacal and less than reassuring, but then they both came charging out of the room, swooping into the air above her like a synchronized circus act. Watching them, she forgot all about the noise and the urgency of the morning and stared in wonder as they swan-dove, nearly hitting the ground, before rocketing back up. They spun around in the air in wide figure eights before Jean came out of the kitchen, hollering that breakfast was ready, followed by Dante, who gave a loud whistle. One Silas broke form and dove down. The other Silas followed suit, and they both landed on their feet and bowed for their audience. Luca, Livy, and Lola all clapped wildly, while Dante stood with folded arms and a disapproving glower as he ordered his daughter to shift back into her true form. Jean had disappeared back into the kitchen.

Cece, hair in a tight knot that gave off a watery blue-green light, came out collect the littles just as Tessa got to the bottom of the stairs.

"But, Papa!" Evie groaned, still in Silas' form, flopping her Silas-arms at her sides like octopus tentacles.

"You and Silas can play your parroting game in his room or yours *only*," Dante replied. "Shifting is an immense power and you need to learn to use it properly. With consent from all parties involved—"

"I consent!" the real Silas exclaimed.

Dante gave a nod to acknowledge Silas as he continued, eyes on Evie-as-Silas. "And for the right reasons—"

"Fun is a good reason!" Evie-as-Silas retorted.

"In the proper context," Dante finished.

"Which is not here," Cece added, taking Luca and Livy each by a hand. Her hair now gave off a yellow-orange glow, like a desert mirage shimmering over sand. "There are too many adults here that don't really know either of you well. It is confusing and things that are confusing can be dangerous."

"Dangerous?" the real Silas squeaked.

Cece nodded soberly. "We need to know who you are and where you are. At all times. Understood?"

The real Silas nodded vigorously while Evie-as-Silas rolled her eyes.

"I take back my consent!" the real Silas exclaimed. "I un-consent!"

Dante cleared his throat and Evie shifted back to her true form, letting her shoulders droop and arms sag down as she shuffled behind Silas into the kitchen. Lola held her arms up to Tessa, who lifted her up, following Luca, Livy, and Cece, whose hair had gone back to a neutral blue-green. *Like a mood ring,* Tessa thought and smiled.

"Cece," she said as they entered the kitchen, but then stopped in mouth-watering awe.

Like the dining room, the kitchen, which had seemed cramped with just the nine of them the other day, had expanded to accommodate the additional dozen guests, most of whom were already seated with steaming plates.

The kitchen island overflowed with food. There were stacks of pancakes and waffles, several omelet options ("Including a tofu-based one," Jean said with a wink), every kind of berry imaginable, muffins, croissants, bacon, ham, sausage ("Celle-ci, it's vegan!"), with coffee and orange juice by the pitcher. The four teenagers were filling their plates, exchanging wary looks. While the younger children had managed to form an instantaneous bond, the teens appeared to have developed a rapid and festering disdain. Even Astrid was giving Nas and Marlowe a wide berth, following Oscar's lead. He sneered at Nas and Marlowe in turn, who glowered and hissed back, respectively.

"Geez," Tessa murmured. She felt like she'd walked into a performance of *West Side Story.* She was waiting for them to start snap-fighting. The tension was palpable, but too performative, too over-the-top, with too many eye rolls and hair flips to feel legitimate.

"Cece," Tessa said again, as they went through the buffet line and loaded up their plates, Tessa with tongs and spoons and Cece with wrist flicks and a distracted air, glancing at the teens as the forgotten syrup bottle poured a copious helping on top of her omelet.

"Oh, shit," she said when she noticed. Her hair flashed fiery red with surprise. "Did you say something, Tess?"

"Yes." Tessa took the syrup from the air and poured some on her waffle. "Astrid thinks her parents are underground."

Cece nodded, glancing at Astrid. A ketchup bottle lifted up and hovered above her plate.

"And I love your hair."

Cece pressed her lips together in a thin smile, her hair turning pink. "Thanks. And I know exactly where they are," she said. *But Astrid is not coming.*

"What?" Tessa took the airborne ketchup and squeezed some on Cece's plate for her, then her own. *What about me?*

Cece turned her head and gave Tessa a pointed stare. Her hair now had a purple sheen to it reminding Tessa of the Northern Lights, which she'd seen once as a kid on trip to Michigan's Upper Peninsula.

*Also good luck getting Astrid to agree to staying here.* Tessa was having trouble remembering what all the mood ring colors meant. Was purple love or boredom?

Cece glanced over at Astrid, then around the room, taking in the glares between Oscar, Marlowe, and Nas. A croissant took to the air and hovered above her plate. "Just wait. Shit's about to hit the fan."

It seemed a slightly ominous and bizarre statement, until, a few minutes later, Oscar called Nas an idiot and Marlowe replied by pinning Oscar to the wall.

"Marlowe!" Elsa hissed from across the room, but Marlowe ignored her.

Astrid was on her feet. Hands held up in a tightening circle, she squeezed the air and Marlowe began to choke and gag and flail.

At the same time, Luca leaped onto Marlowe's back, hissing and rearing back his head, ready to fight and grinning, his long fangs bared.

Nas, who was sitting next to Astrid, let his white wings spread wide like an angel's, before leaning over and shoving her, breaking her mental hold on Marlowe.

Jean attempted to pull Luca off Marlowe while Dante tried to get Marlowe off Oscar. Tim grabbed Astrid's arm mid-swing, and Elsa wrapped Nas in a bear hug to hold him back. From their high chairs, the twins squealed and flung every bit of food they could grab into the melee. Meanwhile, Evie stuffed grapes into her cheeks and turned into a chipmunk, the grapes popping out of her mouth and spraying around the room as she darted along the table, nibbling on the half-eaten plates. Ever-obedient Silas hovered quietly above, watching the scene below with wide eyes as he shoved blueberries in his mouth like they were popcorn, reminding Tessa of every voyeuristic, just-here-for-the-comments meme she'd ever seen.

Cece took Tessa by the hand and led her out of the rioting room. Tessa grabbed her coffee on the way out and took a long gulp as Cece outlined the plan.

"So, you *do* want me to come, then?" she said, trying to keep the smirk off her lips when Cece's hair flared pink again.

Bettie sailed into the room and landed on Cece's shoulder.

Cece nodded. "*Just* you."

Bettie bit her ear.

"Bettie!" she snapped and the bird opened her beak, cocking her head to one side as if ready to bite again. "I will *happily* bring you as well," Cece said through a fake smile.

With a squawk, Bettie relented. Cece rolled her eyes, keeping her face pointed toward Tessa and out of Bettie's line of sight.

"Astrid will be angry."

"Not if we come back with her parents."

Cece held out her hand and Tessa took it. It was warm and soft. Pressed against Tessa's palm, their fingers locked in perfect alignment.

Tessa closed her eyes.

* * *

## APRIL 1998

### *April 7, 1998*

*My dearest Tish,*

*How are you faring with your new assignment? I imagine weapons building for us DOMs wasn't exactly what you had in mind when you joined. I am sorry it has come to this, but I am eager to hear that you are still continuing our important work. And yes, I want to help.*

*I know you disapprove of my hypothesis, dear one. We have had our differences over the years, you and I, but we have always managed to sort them out.*

*You must admit that the first four successful births have had three common factors:*

*1. Magick mother, DOM father*

*2. A wanted and loved child*

*3. Consent (and pleasure? I know you disagree on this. I'll get to that.) in the conception.*

*I believe the evidence collected from our predecessors ruled out the efficacy of in vitro fertilization. Hence, my previous position that there must be not only consent but* pleasure *in the conception. I admit that I'm not sure if this is wholly accurate. Perhaps, it is simply that the clinical environment is prohibitive or that something essential must happen in the body of the female at conception.*

*So perhaps pleasure is not necessary, as you have always contested. I'll grant you that, Tish.*

*Remember, I've* never *said love between the parents, only love for the child. Let's not reopen old wounds or rehash old arguments.*

*I am willing to concede that the first commonality (Magick mother, DOM father) may not be essential. I think that is as good of a place as any to start. And, as you note, it will likely make for a... hardier... subject.*

*I do worry this could be exactly what our superiors are hoping for. Be cautious, my dear one.*

*—Gunner*

# CHAPTER
# TWENTY-TWO

**JULY 2023** When Tessa opened her eyes, they were standing on a raised path cutting through a marshland area. Tupelo trees grew out of the water. A layer of green algae covered the wetland area.

"Where are we?" she asked Cece. Bettie squawked as if she was asking the same question, before hopping onto Tessa's shoulder.

"Magic is not always recorded as such in your history books," Cece began. "The significance of this place is lost to Non history. It's part of the so-called Trail of Tears. It is the site where humanity was nearly destroyed, where Nons and Magix alike nearly paid the ultimate price for the subjugation of another. It's funny how events that *almost* happen never get the attention they deserve. It's funny how easy it is to forget an almost and never learn a thing."

"What happened?"

"They called it a murder-suicide. One sister murdered another and then took her own life. The Non captors threw the bodies in the marsh here, nameless. The first sister was Leotie and the second was Gola. They were powerful witches. When they were taken from their land, Gola began to develop a spell that would turn the world to winter, ushering a new ice age as punishment for the crimes against her people. When Leotie found out, she begged her to stop. Gola was determined, but Leotie fought her. They both died."

Tessa grimaced. "That's awful."

Cece shook her head. "There was a prophecy then as well. Isn't there always?" She chuckled bitterly. "Basically, the gist was that the world would end if the sisters lived. Leotie sacrificed herself and her sister to save the world."

Tessa blew out a long breath. She could hear the sounds of the marsh, the frogs croaking, the chittering of squirrels, the songs of birds, and something else, almost like a song, humming below it all. "Good thing our prophecy isn't so dire."

"Sure, in the version you were told: The war will end when the one unites the seven. Another interpretation is the world will end when the one unites the seven. Yet another is that the world *as we know it* will end. Maybe 'the one' is actually two, three, or a hundred and the seven is all of humanity, Nons, Magix, and DOMs alike." She sighed, holding her hand out to Tessa. "Don't put a lot of stake in prophecies. Hindsight will always massage the truth out of them."

And they were off again.

This time, when Tessa opened her eyes, they were on the busy boardwalk of a beach town. Bettie immediately soared into the cloudless, cerulean sky, flying in wide circles above their heads. A breeze from the ocean managed to make the heat and sunshine bearable. Around them, humanity of every shape and color pulsed in various levels of disrobement. They wore colorful hats, bikinis, and swim trunks. They smelled of sunscreen and oil and alcohol. They spoke too loudly, walked too closely. The smell of donuts filled the salty air.

"Welcome to Carolina Beach," Cece said. "It's much nicer offseason, if you ask me."

She took Tessa's hand, leading her off the main boardwalk, past a mini golf course, Ferris wheel, and various carnival attractions, past the donut shop, restaurants and bars, crossing the main highway and moving farther away from the ocean, into an area that looked more like a quiet beach town than a hopping tourist destination. Tiny palm trees lined the road. They passed a grocery store, a community center, a senior center, and Bettie's shadow kept pace with them along the asphalt. Finally, they stopped in front of an empty lot. Bettie landed a few feet away.

"There used to be three or four covens in the area, two of which were our allies, back in the day." As she spoke, Cece bent down and drew a series of symbols in the dirt.

Bettie hopped closer but still kept her distance. Cece stood up, hands on her hips, watching the ground. Tessa glanced to the left and right. No one else was around.

There was a tremor, so slight that Tessa first thought her senses had tricked her. Maybe she had some water in her ear affecting her balance momentarily.

"Back in the day being, like, fifteen years ago," Cece continued. "Before all this recent shit, we were a lot better connected."

The ground shook again. This time, it was undeniable. Tessa glanced over at Cece, who was staring with narrowed eyes at the symbols on the ground, arms folded across her chest.

"This is—or maybe used to be—the Pleasure Island Coven. Don't give me that weird look, it's the name of the island. Anyway, I haven't heard from these folks in years. After the attacks, we got selfish, you know? Turned inward."

Another tremor. Well, more like a small earthquake. Tessa nearly lost her balance. She noticed that trees around them did not sway nor did the buildings, even the ones held up on piling foundations.

Cece was unmoved. "I think that's natural. Doesn't make it right, but since when has being human and being right been synonymous?" She chuckled as another earthquake shook the ground beneath them, kicking up dust storms in the dirt and cracking the pavement.

Tessa started to fall, but Cece caught her by the elbow. The quake seemed contained to a small ten-foot diameter around them. The ground encircling them had dropped down nearly a foot lower than the surrounding area. Outside of it, the world appeared untouched by the tremors.

"Underground," Tessa whispered.

Outside the circle, Bettie was squawking and flapping her wings.

"Are you coming or not?" Cece asked the bird.

A man turned onto their side street, walking his dog. He looked in their direction, frowned at the agitated raven, and then glanced away again, seemingly nonplussed.

"He can't see us," Cece said, taking a step toward the edge of the circle. She held up a fist and knocked and to Tessa's surprise, there was a hollow tapping sound.

Tessa reached her hand toward the edge of the circle and found that there was a solid barrier surrounding them.

"You'll need to fly over it," Cece said to Bettie. The bird had knocked her head against the invisible barrier, squawking and flapping her wings without going anywhere.

"How we can we go underground here?" Tessa asked, her voice squeaky high with fear. "It's by the ocean; it has to be on a flood plain. It'll just be water down there."

"Magic, Tessa," Cece replied. "This is a siren-built coven. The water works with them, remember?" She turned back to Bettie. "Last chance!" she said.

There was another shake and Tessa's body was flung against the invisible wall. Bettie hopped back several feet.

Cece shook her head. "Such a coward, that bird."

The shake continued. It did not stop. The ground beneath them began to crumble.

"We're going down now," Cece said, taking Tessa's hand. The cracks in the earth were deafening. "Bettie, go home! Tessa, deep breath on three." She called over cascading rumble of falling rocks and water. "One-two-three!"

Tessa breathed in as the ground beneath her gave way. She fell into the earth, somersaulting through detritus and debris. She landed on her bottom in a pile of mud. Cece crashed into her, flinging her forward and causing her lungs to open up to the wet and dusty air. She coughed and coughed until it turned to hysteric laughter. They were both covered in mud. Cece tried to hit at her clothing and hair, sending dust clouds sparkling around her and causing Tessa to laugh even harder.

"You look like something out of a cartoon," Tessa crowed.

"You look like someone that ought to be banned from a Halloween party." Cece rolled her eyes, pulling a rag out of her pocket. "Fortunately, I came prepared for that atrocity. Wipe your face before you offend me more." But she was smiling and Tessa had never been happier to obey an order.

Once their faces were wiped and their hair and clothes dusted off as best they could, Tessa put a hand on the wall to brace herself as she stood, but her hand disappeared into a cascade of cold water. What had looked to Tessa like nothing but packed dirt, was *water*, flowing straight up. Tessa scrambled to her feet with a squeal.

"It's water," Cece said.

"It's *water*!"

"Remember… sirens?" Cece took Tessa by the shoulders. She turned on the flashlight of her phone to guide them down a dark, unlit passageway.

"Don't you have a spell for that?" Tessa teased. "Like *lumos* or whatever."

Cece chuckled. "Spoken spells. More of your Non-lore. And why would I use magic when it's not necessary? You wouldn't run somewhere if walking would suffice."

"Some people like to run," Tessa pointed out, trying to keep her voice light, trying not to think about the claustrophobic closeness of the water walls.

At a fork in the passage, Cece held up a finger as if testing the air for a breeze. She frowned, then held her hand palm up and blew across it, her breath visible as a momentary green haze. It hung in the air and then drifted down the passage to the left.

Cece gestured that they should follow it. "See, there are plenty of times when magic is the only way to do a thing."

They followed the green haze down the passageway that was slowly, almost imperceptibly, shrinking around them. Tessa felt her heart quicken, her chest clench in mounting panic. She focused on the back of Cece's head. Her hair now gave off an anxious silver sheen that glittered with star-like gems. These twinkled in the dim light, turning her head into a shifting constellation. The walls were definitely getting closer and the ceiling lower.

"Do you use magic for fun?" *Just focus on the conversation*, Tessa told herself. *Take deep breaths.* But she found herself panting. Beads of sweat formed on her forehead and upper lip. The rumbling water walls around them made her think of drowning.

"Of course! Look at my hair!" Cece laughed. They came to another fork and the green dust moved to the right. Cece followed it. "It shouldn't be much farther. They've definitely expanded since I was here last."

She kept talking, kept walking, but her voice seemed to fade, her bobbing constellation dimming in the distance. Tessa's heart felt like it was trying to beat its way out of her chest. She gasped for air, but it was if her lungs were shriveling. She couldn't take in enough oxygen. Her vision tunneled and tipped. She fell to her knees.

Cece's face was in front of hers. She was talking, but Tessa couldn't hear her over the ringing in her ears. Tessa gasped, feeling her throat swelling up. She couldn't breathe. She tried to tell Cece, tried to reach for her, but she was paralyzed. She felt her whole body stiffen, swelling in places, collapsing in others, like someone else had taken control of her internal organs and was pushing them around, squeezing, pulling, and smashing them. She couldn't make her body move. But she knew Cece was still there. Tessa felt her arms around her, felt her breath on her cheek. Then Cece's lips were on her mouth and Cece's breath was filling her lungs. A weight pressed against Tessa's chest, heavy and dense as a body. A heartbeat thrummed next to Tessa's. Tessa felt Cece's hand clasp hers, then go limp.

Then there was nothing.

* * *

"My god, this place hasn't changed a bit," Tish exclaimed, running her finger along the kitchen countertop. "Spick and span, as always." She smiled that too-bright smile of hers.

**MAY 1999**

The apartment had never been clean when Tish lived there, Val knew, but Tish had always seen life through the glow of desire. Time had tinged Tish's teeth to cornsilk, but they still sparkled, as did her eyes, like the morning sun glinting off buildings.

"Rent controlled, I assume?"

"Locked in for life," Val replied flatly.

"Lucky you."

Tish flopped down on the sofa beside Val. Val scooted away. Tish scooted closer and swung her arm behind Val's neck, clutching her shoulder and pulling her close. Their cheeks touched. Val inhaled. Tish still smelled like the ocean, like home.

"They've found Archer," Tish said. "Brand and his team." Under her arm, Tish felt Val stiffen, but she said nothing. "I told you that Brand's been in a rage ever since we lost Hybrid #4."

Still, Val said nothing. She stared blankly ahead and the wall, which was as sparkling white as the day that the two friends had moved into this place, more than thirty years ago. Val had said the white reminded her of the great egret's wings. She'd pulled that feather of hers out of pocket and held it against the wall and declared it perfect. Tish squeezed Val's shoulder again. How could everything look the same and feel so fucking different?

"Brand wants us to extract the child," Tish said.

Val pinched Tish's hand between two fingers and pulled it off her shoulder. She stood up, walking toward the spotlessly clean window, so clear it looked like you could reach out and pluck up the city. "Archer will never allow it. He'll die first."

"He might at that."

"Does Gunner know?"

Tish nodded.

Val turned back around and Tish realized she hadn't seen the nod. She prolonged the moment, noting the hope in Val's big brown eyes. Gunner, beautiful Gunner. He would step in and save his son, wouldn't he?

"Tish?"

Tish tried to swallow, her throat contracting, smacking against itself like two towels stiff from drying in the heat. "They're using the weapon I developed based on our research with the Hybrid #1 and my own abilities. With it, we can control people from afar, without risking the safety of the shifter."

"You're talking about Hypnosis-Induced Possession? But you said it wasn't read—"

"It's close."

"Does it still require eye contact to initiate and maintain? Like ogres do?"

"No, we bypassed that hurdle nearly a year ago. A helpful siren on our team volunteered his abilities up and we were able develop a process wherein a single word or glance is enough to initiate the possession and, when completed, break it."

"And the side effects?" Val remembered the rats. The first one, drowned in its own water dish. The next, refusing to eat until it starved. A third had managed to slice its own neck open on the bars of its cage. Val had transferred to another development team after the third rat.

Tish sighed. "You know they don't care about those." She wouldn't meet Val's eyes.

Val's mouth opened, a protest on her lips. It hung there, the slip of her pink tongue like a bat lurking in a cave. Tish clenched her jaw. Her teeth ground against each other, cogs in a machine that wouldn't stop.

"He really could die," Val whispered.

Tish nodded. "He could." No use in lying about it or trying to mince words. "We'll try to end it before... before the effects take place, but—"

"Does Gunner know?" Val repeated.

Tish nodded. "He knows."

Gunner's exact words had been: "Archer made his choice years ago." When Tish had pressed him, reminded him that this was his son they were talking about, not only that, this was *Archer*, the golden boy, the favored spawn, Gunner had laughed, a hard noise that seemed to come from another person entirely. "Did I ever tell you about my daughter?"

Tish hadn't known Gunner *had* a daughter. How long had they known each other, as friends, lovers, then just friends again? Betrayal curdled in her stomach, but how could she be mad at a man for that kind of tragic omission? Now, she knew everything. Or hoped she did.

"I always thought Archer was his favorite," Tish whispered.

Val sat back down beside her. "His daughter was the favorite."

Tish twisted her head to stare at Val. How long had Val known about the daughter? Tish swallowed a hard remark, tucked in the resentment in the same way she pressed herself into her pants these days, buried under layers of tight-fitting fabric.

"We can't let them get the child, Tish," Val said.

Gunner had said the same thing. The precious little Hybrid #2 must not fall back into the hands of the Brand and the new AntiMagi Department of Health and Defense.

"You're going soft," Tish had told him. She would not tell Val this. Val, who had once been a grubby little girl with perpetually scraped knees and wind-tangled hair. Val, who was now so neat and tidy. This wasn't the Val she grew up with, not the Val that moved to New York City with her, eyes red-raw from weeping over her lost sister. Tish never cried for their coven. Then again, Tish had had no one and nothing to lose, coven-less and orphaned, and taken in by Val's mawmaw and the Hart family. She had cried for the little girl, as quietly as she could, set apart, holding herself so tightly. She'd thought she would fall apart, would tumble right into the water and drown. The fairies kept repeating their stupid phrase: *as the air, so the body*. And she'd risen then, carving herself anew like a goddamn phoenix.

She'd had to be strong for Val.

"What about that cousin of yours in the north?" Tish asked.

Val's face went rigid and blank as the dunes of their youth, cut like cliffs against the bluest sky. A stranger would think she was stone, but Tish could read Val's face, could interpret the pulse of the vein in her temple, the twitch of the muscle below her left eye. Tish knew she was thinking about the others: Hybrid #4, a recent disaster with Val at its bleeding heart, and Hybrid #3, the child she tried to destroy, then birthed in secret, spiriting it away through a network of ghosts. Oh, but Tish had done her research. She'd found the leader of The Channels Coven, the first stop. She'd even spoken with a coven member, one Izotz Marlin. But it seemed that no one, not even Elias, knew what had become of the children after the Channels.

"Elias," Val finally murmured. "What about him?"

Tish smiled. Should she show her hand? No, better not. "He owes you a few favors, yes?"

Val's face softened, her shoulders lowering. Relaxed. Of course, Tish would know about the help she'd offered Elias, introducing him to his wife, helping fund his start-up coven. Yes, this made sense. No need to fear.

"Get the child to Elias. I can help Brand and the others refocus their efforts on new weapons. We can blame Hypnosis-Induced Possession for the failure, get it shelved, once and for all. I know you've always hated that particular weapon."

"I hate *all* weapons," Val clarified. "But, that one is particularly… terrifying," she conceded.

"Maybe we get it traded in for your project. What'd you call it again? WINGS?"

"Weaponized Interface Navigation for Global Security."

"In other words, flying for DOMS?" Tish smirked.

Val nodded, searching Tish's weathering face. Once, Tish had been a book splayed open to her. Once, she had kissed Tish's closed eyelids, the tip of her nose, and thought, *Mine.* What a selfish, stupid thought. That Tish was gone. This Tish, unreadable.

"What about Meredith?" Val asked.

Tish sighed. Gunner had also expressed this concern.

"I worry about Meredith," he had said. "She's become quite the leader among her people. The Movement for the Unification of Magical Society is a powerful force doing a lot of good, not only for your people, but for the planet."

Now, Val repeated him almost verbatim. "She's doing the work we always wanted to do."

Tish said nothing. What was the point? It wasn't that Tish's goal had changed. She still wanted the same thing she'd always wanted: to save the world. No, more than that. To be the one who saved the world. She'd been striving toward this since before Meredith Connolly could walk and if Meredith Connolly became collateral damage in Tish's efforts to save the world, so be it.

The silence settled, an unbreakable, icy presence between them.

Tish tucked her bony hand into Val's, soft and plump. They watched a sliver of sun drop between the buildings, lower and lower. Val leaned her head on Tish's shoulder. Her throat felt taut, like a string of a bow pulled to breaking. If she spoke, she'd lose the arrow. She thought of Archer, his cautious smile and endearing stutter. She thought of Meredith, bright-eyed and snaggle-toothed. She thought of the girl, Cece. All the hope she bore in her strange body.

*Fine, I'll do it,* Val thought-said because she couldn't bear to hear the words aloud. The rest, she kept to herself: the letter she had already sent Gunner stating that, if she did this, she wanted out of MAAM PAC for good and his response, a terse, *So be it.* Not to mention the other letters, Gunner to Val expounding on the changes in Tish, her paranoia and glut for power, Val to Gunner, expressing her concerns about Tish's mental health and possible involvement in the disappearance of Hybrid #4. You could never be too careful. Val had stopped trusting either of them a long time ago.

## CHAPTER
## TWENTY-THREE

**JULY 2023** "Well, I certainly wasn't expecting two." The voice was foreign and far away. It curled like smoke through Tessa's brain but with that resonant, steely insistence that powerful people's voices always have. Tessa thought she ought to be afraid, but she couldn't summon the strength. "Who's this one?" Tessa felt a prodding against her leg.

"N-no one, Tish." Another voice, high-pitched and stuttering. The fear in the voice made Tessa's heart skip.

Tessa was holding something in her hand. Another hand, she realized.

"A Non?" the first voice—Tish—asked. "It's awfully… clingy…"

Tessa felt another hand touch hers and begin to pry her fingers, one by one, off the hand that she was clenching. *Cece's hand*, Tessa remembered. With all her strength, she held onto Cece's hand until the other hand gave up.

"Clingy as hell," Tish repeated and laughed, a caustic sound like the splat of an overripe tomato.

"Maybe it's her Familiar?" the second, scared voice said. "She has the mark."

Tish snorted and then sighed. "The little Familiar lovebird," she sneered. "God, I'm so sick of that trope. You'd think someone like *her*—Christ, she is an exquisite creature, isn't she Valerie? Anyway, you'd think she would know better. Nons are nothing but trouble."

Tessa tried to open her eyes, but couldn't, her lids too heavy. A spell, perhaps? Or remnants of it?

"Did you see that?" Tish exclaimed.

"See what?" Val whispered.

"It's waking! Valerie! Is it waking?"

Tessa felt a hand on her shoulder and a voice—Valerie's voice—think-speaking to her. *Be very still now.* "No, still sleeping," Val said.

"Are you sure?"

"She must have stirred some in her sleep," Val answered casually and then continued to think-speak to Tessa, all the fear still there in her thoughts, *If she knows, she will suspect. Please be very still and there will be time yet.*

Tessa didn't have the energy to answer. Instead, she let herself be carried back into the stillness, let the words of the two strange women (*My captors,* Tessa thought) continue to roll over her in alternating waves of nonsense and clarity. Through it all, she anchored herself to Cece, holding her hand, willing her to wake up.

"Gunner will be pleased," said Val.

"Screw Gunner, Val. I told you. He's out. It's just you and me now. What kind of spell was that anyway? Shit, you air fairies and your toxic chemical compound nonsense."

"It was an airborne opiate."

Slowly, Tessa's senses were returning to her. She could feel Cece's hand, but also the cold ground beneath her, slightly damp and rough like stone. She could hear water, drip drip dripping around her and flowing, too, somewhere farther off, a faint trickling like someone left the tap on.

Tish cackled. She had a voice like glass breaking. "Poppies will put them to sleep, Valerie? Delightful."

Tessa didn't open her eyes, but gradually, she could sense light on the other side of her eyelids, faint and flickering like a candle. The air was almost scentless, though the ground below her had a faint musk to it, not quite like dirt, but like the memory of it.

"I'm not trying to reinvent the wheel here."

Tish let out a snort.

Cece's fingers twitched against Tessa's palm.

*Cece,* Tessa thought-said, squeezing Cece's hand. There was no reply.

The peppy chime of a phone bleated. Tish answered with a rigid, "What do you want?"

*Cece,* Tessa thought-said again. She heard footsteps to her left, approaching. Val was nearby again. She could smell her, the musk of perspiration and the chalky waft of old deodorant. It should have been a foul smell, a sweaty, overworked body kneeling close, but it wasn't.

"Are you kidding me?" Tish said. Her voice was moving farther away. "He went where?" Tessa heard the click of her heels on the stone ground, fading. "What the hell is in Denver?"

Val's hand was pressed lightly against Tessa's back and she was muttering, almost to herself. "You were supposed to be safe."

Tessa felt something fall away from her ankles and her right wrist, the hand that was not holding Cece's. She hadn't realized she'd been shackled, but now she felt the remaining shackle on her left wrist, the one that still bound her to Cece. Tessa opened her eyes. They were in a cave, lit with glowing baubles. *The same way the hallway at The House was lit,* Tessa thought, and the thought was first a pleasure and then a slicing knife of panic.

A face loomed in front of her: a woman with limp and thin brown, but graying hair, one deep-set wrinkle cutting her forehead in half, deep purple bags under her eyes offset by thick-framed glasses. For a moment, Tessa thought she'd fallen down some time-warp rabbit hole. She reached out with her free hand to touch the face, to make sure it was real, someone else, and not the future's reflection. She touched the cheek, taut skin over bony cheekbones. A pair of peridot and olive wings flicked out from behind the woman's back, stretching out several feet in either direction.

"Who are you?" Tessa asked.

"I'm Val. And you're Tessa Andrews."

"How did you—?"

Val shook her head, bending to unlock the final shackle. "You need to get out of here."

Tessa looked at Cece. She was still unconscious, still shackled to a stalagmite. "Where's here?"

"Mountains, outside of Asheville. You won't be able to transport out of here, but once you get to the surface, you will be."

"I can't transport," Tessa said. "I'm a Non."

Val blinked. "Yes. Of course. Silly of me." She giggled, pushed up her glasses, put a hand to her chest. "I'll help you. Get you to the surface. Transport you."

"I'm not leaving without Cece."

Val shook her head. "Just you. If I let her go, Tish'll try to kill me. She might even succeed." Val laughed again, a nervous chitter.

"I'm not leaving without Cece," Tessa repeated.

As if on cue, Cece began to stir. She moaned. She opened her eyes. A loud shout of exasperation echoed from somewhere deep in the cave.

"Oh shit, oh shit, oh shit!" Val whispered, grabbing Tessa by the arm. "You need to come with me. Now. When I get back, I'll tell her I killed you and tossed you in the water." Val gestured toward a deep pool nearby. "It's deeper than it looks," she said. "She'll never know you got away."

"I'm. Not. Leaving. Cece," Tessa hissed through clenched teeth.

"Where am I?" Cece groaned. "Aura? Zack?"

"You tell that little asshole that *I'm* the boss now. Gunner left it all to *me*!" Behind the echoes of Tish's shouts came that same stilettoed click, now approaching quickly.

"This is not a time for heroics," Val whispered, her voice high, her hands shaking as she clawed at Tessa, trying to pull her away from Cece and toward the exit. "This is no time to be brave."

As a child, Tessa had had many fears: spiders, heights, bees, tornados, darkness, monsters… the list went on. Once, at about four years old, she had mustered up the courage to climb to the top of the big playground slide. This was one of her earliest memories, shrouded in all the misty myth of childhood synapses firing, misfiring, and then finding their way through the burgeoning gray dawn of new life. She stood at the top of the slide and she could not move. Eventually, her mother had to climb up and get her. Tessa hadn't asked for it. She had not cried or cried out to her mother for help. She had simply froze and froze for so long that her mother had climbed up the slide, picked her up, and brought her down.

Back on the ground, Tessa's mother had kneeled before her and said. "It's ok, Tessie. You don't need to be brave, sweetie."

She had meant it as a kindness, Tessa thought, but like so many things that parents say to try and fix a problem, it created one. In the back of Tessa's mind, there was always that little voice, her mother's voice, saying, *You're not brave, Tessie.* And then, inevitably, the voice would morph into Tessa's own voice that said, *You're a coward, Tessa.*

"She's coming!" Val was shrieking, pulling Tessa. "We have to get you out of here. Stop trying to be brave! You were never meant to be brave."

Tessa pulled away from her then, like someone jerked from a state of hypnosis by a code word. "Give me the key," she commanded. Val pressed a hand against her pocket, as if to shield the key.

"Give it me!" Tessa growled and Val, too shocked to think past the unearthed fear clawing up through her, handed it over. Tessa knelt beside Cece and hurriedly undid her bonds before helping her to her feet. "Do you trust me?" she asked Cece.

Cece nodded.

The stilettos clicked closer.

Tessa grabbed Val by the base of her wing. Val gasped in pain. "You're getting us *both* out of here." As she spoke, Tessa dug her fingernails into the soft, cartilage part of Val's wing and twisted. "Now." She felt Val wince, heard her give a loan groan.

"Y-yes," Val whispered. "I'll help you. Stop hurting me."

Tessa dropped her hand and Val took it pulling her and Cece into the air.

By the time they heard Tish's howl of rage at the betrayal, they could see the light of the caves' exit. Tessa heard birds calling, closed her eyes, and thought of home.

And then they were there.

* * *

## August 3, 1999

*Val,*

*See enclosed. Don't ask how it came to me. I won't tell you.*

*Tish*

*June 7, 1999*

*To Elias Murphey, Leader of The Channels Coven*

*We have the girl in custody and will bring her to you as quickly as we can. But there are several of us with concerns. This situation is one of the strangest I've ever witnessed and I cannot form a cohesive narrative from it. I've compiled this list of facts in the hope that you will be able to make some sense of this:*

1. *There are DOMs looking for her. I've never seen so many DOMs in one spot, looking for one person, looking for a child.*
2. *I saw Meredith Connolly's body. I know they're saying the Non, her husband, killed her. But I saw the body, Elias. A Non didn't kill Meredith. Only a DOM could have done that.*
3. *The girl does not deny that she killed her father, but at the same time, she keeps saying that it wasn't her father. And I have to tell you, I don't think she killed him either. I saw that body as well and there was something... off... about it. I know what a body destroyed by magic looks like. I know*

*what a body destroyed by anti-magic looks like. This? This body appeared to be destroyed by both.*

*Like I said, I can't make sense of any of it. But we've got the girl and we'll bring her into the fold. I agree with the Alliance's assessment that she is just as much as a victim as the parents. Plus, I couldn't let the DOMs take a Magick, no matter what she'd done.*
*—Excerpt from a letter signed Izotz Marlin*

*August 4, 1999*
*Gunner,*
*Tish has confirmed that The Channels Coven will provide sanctuary for Cordelia. Now, please uphold your end of our agreement. Help me leave.*
*Val*

*August 5, 1999*
*Val,*
*Excellent news. Yes, I will uphold our agreement. You will be free to go, as promised. I'll handle Brand. Please, though, let's keep this information secret, shall we? No one else needs to know what happened to our little #2, just me, you, and Tish. Just the three of us. Like old times.*
*Gunner*

# CHAPTER
## TWENTY-FOUR

**JULY 2023** They were at Tessa's childhood home. It looked the same as when she was a girl, the paint fresh and red on the door, the shutters black, and the tan brick unscathed by time, weather, and Tessa learning to drive.

Morana stood in the doorway. Tessa looked around. Was this real?

"It's a dream," Morana said.

But there was Cece on her left, those glowing lights in her hair real as the stars.

"You brought her with you," Morana said.

And on Tessa's right was Val, her wings folded in, looking hunched, old, and terrified.

"And her, too," Morana added.

"Why?" Tessa asked, but then realized that this answer was obvious. She brought Cece for protection; she brought Val because she couldn't think of anything else to do with her. She brought them. She, Tessa, brought them. "How?"

Morana smiled, revealing those pointy fangs that still gave Tessa goosebumps. "Who can say? Not I. How about you, Tessa? How did you bring them here?"

Cece pinched her arm. "There's no way this is a dream." She pinched her arm again and then shook her head, as if trying to clear her mind. "Fuck it. I don't care about any of that. Where are Aura and Zack? Who the hell is this fairy lady here? Does she work for you? Who was that psycho in the heels?"

"Ah," Morana smiled wryly. "You've met my mother, I see."

Tessa could hear Cece swallow, could hear the saliva in her mouth thicken and scrape like sandpaper down her throat. "*That* was Morticia Chernoff?" she croaked.

"The one and only," Morana replied. "And this is Val. How are you, Auntie?"

Val glared back at her. "Ana…" Her voice was a warning snarl.

"But you already knew that," Morana said to Tessa, her lips curled into a smile that showed a hit of teeth like shark fins hovering in the waves.

"I don't give a shit," Cece said, her body giving an involuntary shiver as she spoke. "Where are Aura and Zack?"

"They're still in Pleasure Island," Val said. "They were bait."

"Bait?"

"For you," Val said, nodding at Cece. "Tish thinks you're 'the one.'" She put the word in air quotes.

"The one?" Tessa pressed.

"The most powerful Hybrid of them all," she said. "Well, the most powerful one to survive, that is. I'm still surprised she gave up on #5 so easily."

"I don't give a shit about Tish or what she thinks," Cece snapped. "Aura and Zack—they're still in the Pleasure Island Coven?"

Val nodded. "We left them there."

Tessa realized she was still holding both Cece's hand and Val's. She dropped Val's hand and turned on her. "Are they alive?"

Val nodded. "They're just sleeping," she said. "The parents of the witch girl, Zack and Aura, I put them to sleep. They'll wake in a month or two, probably."

"A month!?"

"Or two," Val continued. "It's not as precise a spell when you need to sustain the life, you know? Or… well, you wouldn't, would you?" She smiled at Tessa and blinked, her eyes magnified by her glasses and making her look silly and harmless. She was neither. "You've got time to find them," she added. "They're probably safer there than anywhere else on earth right now, asleep in a siren's lair."

"Alone?" Cece asked.

"Under guard," Val replied.

Cece turned to Morana. "Let them go."

"They *are* safe," Val said again.

Morana smirked. "And this has nothing to do with me. Ask Val. Ask my mother. It's them, not me."

"It's you!" Cece shrieked. "It's always been you."

"Mm, and there was your fatal mistake," Morana replied. "All of you."

"Where's Theo?" Tessa asked.

Morana took a step toward her, coming down from the porch like a queen descending from her throne, ready to bestow her wrath or mercy, blessing or curse. Tessa stepped toward her. They walked forward until they stood face-to-face, eye to eye.

"Theo is safe," Morana said.

"They're with you," Tessa replied. "They can't possibly be safe."

Something flickered through Morana's cold blue eyes then. If Tessa hadn't known better, she would say it was hurt. It was there and gone. All that was left in its wake was rage.

"I am their mother," Morana hissed.

"Are you?" Tessa asked. "Would a mother abandon their child?" She heard a hiss behind her. She could feel this dream beginning to slip away. She reached out for Morana and caught her around the neck. "*I am their mother.*"

Morana leaned in close, her coffin-breath on Tessa's cheek. "You served your purpose, sweet Non. And I am grateful. But you can't protect Theo. Look what you did! You led Cordelia Connolly right into my mother's trap." She clicked her tongue, a scolding tsk-tsk. "What if Theo had been with you? Then she would have had them, like she's always wanted. I can't let that happen."

And then she was gone, leaving only the empty porch with the mat that said, "God Bless this Home and All Who Enter!"

Cece grabbed Tessa's shoulder and shook her firmly. "Tessa."

"I'm right here," Tessa replied. "What?"

But Cece just kept shaking her arm and saying, "Tessa! Tessa! Wake up!"

Tessa opened her eyes. The light was fading. Above her there was nothing but wide open indigo sky, stars starting to pop up like lost fireflies. A new constellation appeared before Tessa's eyes: Cece's starry hair. Tessa smiled. "You're like the North Star, guiding me home." Then she winced and closed her eyes again, "That was... stupid," she said, moving her arm to try and sit up. She gasped in pain and fell back. Her back... she'd never felt anything like it. It felt like her spine was about to rip open.

"Are you hurt?" Cece asked.

"I think so," Tessa said. "I don't know... how. How did we get here?"

"I don't know," Cece said. "We were—where were we?"

"A cave," Tessa said. The pain was worsening, making it hard for her to breathe, let alone speak. "My—my dream."

"Ok, ok, no more talking," Cece said, humming to herself like an anxious cat trying to self-soothe.

"V—val," Tessa said, fearing that the strange, bug-eyed woman would be gone, would have gone back to find that Tish woman, who would certainly be hunting them.

"I'm here," Val whispered. "I'm here." Tessa felt a hand slide into hers.

"Am I dying?" she asked.

"No, no," Val said, "nothing like that."

Even in the fading light, Tessa saw the confused and frightened look that Cece shot Val, but all Cece said was, "We need to get you home."

"I wouldn't recommend moving her," said Val. "Not until she's finished the transition."

Again, Cece shot Val the same look. "How do—?"

"I've seen this once before," Val said. "It will be... unpleasant." She squeezed Tessa's hand and leaned in close to Tessa's ear, her voice so low that her breath in Tessa's ear was louder than the words themselves, "Everything is about to change for you, Tessa. I'm so sorry. It wasn't supposed to be like this. Someday, I hope you will forgive me. When this is over, I'll find you. In the meantime, be strong, my girl. Be brave."

The pain was a wave and it bore down on Tessa, crashing over her. Val's hand slipped from her fingers. She heard Cece mutter, "What the fuck!" just before the pain crested in white foam and swallowed her.

* * *

**JUNE 2000** The girl was swinging in the backyard. She was too old to be swinging and the ancient play structure creaked under her weight. *She would be thirteen now*, Val thought. Puberty had come and taken her slender youth. It had been years since Val had taken this detour to see the girl. Too long. The difference between nine and thirteen leaped at Val like a tiger, trying to tug her back with its mighty jaws to the dark pit that had swallowed weeks of memories after the birth. She would not unearth them.

She sat at the bus stop, waving on every bus that stopped, hour after hour. She had a book, which she kept propped open, pages unturning. In the book, she kept three letters, each wrinkled on the edges from handling.

First, she re-read the letter from Elias, his cursive that was somehow both blocky and slender.

*The girl does well here, cousin. Izotz has taken a liking to her. We are not moving her along just yet.*

A mistake. Val had written back multiple times to explain this. She didn't know this Izotz Marlin, other than the passing references from Elias and from the letter that Tish had somehow intercepted.

Another bus came and went. She read the second letter. This one was from Ana:

*Auntie, I don't know what to do. I feel so lost. With MUMS, I had* purpose, *see? Now, I have nothing.*

*You have me,* Val had written. For months now, she had awaited the girl's response. According to Gunner, Morana Chernoff had vanished without a word to her mother or father. And now, Andor was sick. Dying, Gunner said in his latest letter. Val tried to find pity in her heart, but could not.

Still, she clenched the letter from Gunner tightly, more precious than all the others she kept with her as talismans. But it wasn't the news of Andor that had woken Val from her bleary-eyed freedom and sent her, in a rush of panic, to this bus stop, where she kept watch over the girl.

It was this:

*I'm sure Tish told you that we welcomed a fifth Hybrid into our midst this past August.*

Val's nose wrinkled each time she read the first five words: *I'm sure Tish told you...*

In her head, she heard Gunner's voice repeating it, over and over, with every sarcastic inflection imaginable.

*I'm* suuuure *Tish told you...*

*I'm sure Tish told* yoouu…

And so on. He knew they weren't on speaking terms. How could he not know that?

A fifth Hybrid. Christ.

*This one is the spawn of a powerful DOM mother and Andor Chernoff. I call her Natalie. Tish, of course, calls her #5.*

Natalie. Day of birth, it meant. Val shuddered.

*She was born during the total solar eclipse in the mother's home in northern France. The mother died giving birth and so we brought her back here. She has been living with Tish and Andor. Val, she is only ten months old, but already, her power pulls at those around her. It is like a cyclone. Andor wastes away in her presence and Tish, well. She seems unaffected in terms of power, but in other ways, she is a wraith, a fraction of the woman she was.*

*Andor is dying. He will be dead before the months' end and I cannot find the daughter, Morana. Perhaps you can help with that.*

*But Val, I think Andor is the luckier of the two, for dying seems a far better fate than whatever is happening to our Tish. I know it could be unrelated.*

*I do wonder: could this strange new hybrid be affecting the others?*

Here was the crux of it. Here was the reason Val sat on this bench, hour after hour, watching, waiting for the unraveling.

None came.

Once and only once, the curtains parted and Val saw the mother standing in the window. She'd forgotten her name. The mother watched Val, eyes narrowed in a dare, it seemed. She flipped Val the bird, closed the curtains, called the girl inside.

# CHAPTER
# TWENTY-FIVE

**JULY 2023**

"Is she dead now, Silas?"

A small and sweaty palm pressed against Tessa's neck. "She has a pulse," Silas replied.

"So she's dead then, right?" Luca asked.

"No," Silas groaned. "A pulse means alive, Lu-cah!"

"Oh, a pulse means alive. Got it."

"Yo, get out of here, guys!" It was Oscar's voice. "She needs to rest."

"They're so pretty," Silas murmured. Tessa had an odd sensation, like Silas was stroking her arm, but it wasn't her arm. Anyway, he was too far away to even be touching her. She could tell from his voice.

"Dude, don't touch those!" Oscar snapped.

"It won't hurt her," Silas replied. The weird sensation had stopped.

"What are you guys doing?" Cece's voice was a thunder-clapping boom. Tessa felt the children scramble off the bed, heard Cece's footsteps enter the room, and decided she should try and open her eyes.

They were standing in a row, shortest to tallest, Luca, Silas, Cece, and Oscar. They stared at Tessa like she was a marvel, a painting or a statue or a beautiful creature.

Tessa laughed. "Is there something in my teeth?"

No one replied.

"What's wrong with you all?" She tried to sit up, but fell back. Her body was heavy, unbalanced. She laughed, the kind of laugh that bubbles up without thought or reason, exploding at the worst of times. It was the laugh of the grieving at a wake, the laugh of a child after a bully punched him in the gut. It was grief and joy, pain and shock, all in one burst. "What's wrong with me?" Tessa asked.

"Nothing," Cece replied. "You're..."

"You're like me," Silas exclaimed, flapping his wings.

"Shit, she's like me," Oscar added. "Who would have guessed?"

"You're a Magick!" Luca shouted.

Tessa laughed again, trying to sit up. She wobbled, but managed. She looked at Cece, who made a gesture, reaching her left arm over and behind her right shoulder. She gave Tessa an encouraging nod. *See for yourself.*

So she did. She reached around and felt them, first the right and then the left. They were soft, covered in downy feathers, but beneath the feathers, she could feel the sinew and muscle. They were huge, stretching out several inches past her fingertips and reaching up just above her head and down nearly to her knees. They were strong, too. With concentration, she could move them. It was like having a second set of arms, right behind the first. She curled them up in front of her in the same movement as she would have used to hug herself. They were green, similar to Val's, but more vibrant, peridot and olive feathers laced with emerald, shamrock, teal, and turquoise. They glittered in the room's sunlight. They were the most beautiful wings she had ever seen.

But the questions. The goddamn questions. As she moved her wings back and forth, up and down, Tessa's brain surged with questions, blood pounding from heart to wings to brain.

How was this happening? Was she a Wayward? If not a Wayward, then what? "What the hell *am* I?" she whispered. She was so hot. Too hot. What the hell was happening?

"You're a fairy," Cece whispered. Her hair, still charmed to change with her mood, gave off a sheen of affectionate pink, purple wonder.

Tessa blew out air. "No, I'm not. I'm... not."

They were all watching her, Cece, Luca, Silas, and Oscar, open-mouthed, their expressions full of fear and wonder.

"Did you do this to me?" Tessa practically screamed at Cece.

Before Cece could answer, Tessa had an overpowering urge to move, to get away from them. She stood up, moving her shoulders as if she could dislodge the wings.

*Everything is about to change for you, Tessa.*

How had Val known? *I've seen this once before*, she'd said. *This.* What the hell was *this*?

Tessa pushed her way out of the room. Stumbling at first, as she adjusted to the new weight of the wings, she walked then ran down the hall. Ahead of her, the railing grew closer and beyond it, the wide green expanse above the living room. She kicked off with her feet, grabbing the railing and pushing up and over, vaulting herself into the air. At first, she fell. A knot of fear caught in her throat. But then, as if they were more a part of her than even her mind, the wings flapped and lifted Tessa into the air. She hovered there a moment, hanging in the air, fuming. Below her, the room brimmed with Magix, their heads turned up to her, expressions ranging from shock to awe to horror.

*Everything is about to change for you, Tessa.*

Val had *known* and Tessa was pissed. She felt betrayed, lied to. Someone had lied to her. Was it her mother? Or had Kathy been lied to, also?

She pumped her wings. This should have been fucking magical. Above, Bettie circled, squawking at her, calling for Tessa to join her. Tessa could hear the words. *Join me. Fly!*

Instead, Tessa landed in the middle of the living room. Cece, hurrying down the stairs, paused on the bottom step. There was a moment of charged silence, in which no one spoke aloud, but their thoughts buzzed, synapses firing, preparing for battle.

Astrid stepped forward, walking past Tessa without a glance, barreling toward Cece. She slapped her across the face.

"Sassy, what the hell?" Cece exclaimed, clutching a hand to her purpling cheek.

"How could you?" Astrid shrieked. "How could you turn her like that? That wasn't your place. She's—she was—*my* Familiar."

"It was reckless," Izotz said, placing a hand on Astrid's shoulder as she spoke acidly to Cece. "You could have been killed. Turning a Non is dangerous even when there is a secure Familiar-Magick bond. It's miracle you're both alive."

"I didn't turn her," Cece replied.

Tessa let out a breath she hadn't realized she'd been holding, while Izotz let out a snort.

"Didn't turn her? We've all seen this woman, right? Well," She nodded toward three men that stood off to the side. Tessa hadn't even noticed them until now. They were all dark-skinned with sharp smiles and sharper teeth. They wore cowboy boots and ostentatiously wide-brimmed cowboy hats. "The Sobro Boys hadn't. The rest of us," Izotz went on, "can attest to the fact that, two days ago, this woman was wingless and powerless. She was a Non."

"She's a… *Wayward*," Cece said carefully, like she was trying to keep her tone neutral, trying to tamp down her prejudices under layers of willpower like cardboard over weeds in a garden bed. "She… must be. She was under a curse, I think." And she told the story, or most of it, of how they'd gone to find the Laveau-Millers, been captured, and escaped. She left out the weird dream of Morana. She described Val in detail. "That bug-eyed minion seemed to know this was going to happen. She said, *I've seen this before.*"

"I have too," came a low drawling voice. Everyone in the room turned to look at the three Sobro Boys. The eldest of the three men stepped forward.

He looked to be in his late fifties, broad-chested and even broader in the waist and gut. He clasped the shoulder of the scrawniest of the three men, a man of indeterminate age, although he did appear to be somewhere between the eldest and the other man, a boy, really, eighteen at most. The boy was clearly the son of the eldest man, with the same strong, broad chest, but with a young man's figure beneath, slender and taut. The father and son were vampires. The third was not, Tessa realized. He was werewolf. Her initial assessment of the group as a monolith, dark-skinned with sharp white teeth and aquiline noses, was shattered. The scrawny werewolf was darker than the others, with a wide flat nose and teeth of average sharpness. Thick chest hair loomed up where he'd left his shirt's top button undone. Tufts of hair graced his earlobes, the back of his neck.

"When Bash came to us, he was just a pup, isn't that right?" the elder man said, squeezing the werewolf's shoulder affectionately. "No more than eight, maybe nine years old. No memory of any life before us. We thought he was a Non, too. No fur on the ears or neck. No incredible strength. He bled and scabbed and healed. Young, healthy werewolves don't do that, as you know."

"No, I didn't know," Tessa blurted and was immediately taken aback by her audacity. Already, she was acting less like an intruder, like a person who might actually belong in this world. Plus, all eyes in the room were on her anyway. *So what does it matter,* she thought.

The werewolf, Bash, was smiling. "I didn't either," he said. "I'll show you." He drew a long knife from a holster at his side and with a swift, stroke, sliced open his arm.

Tessa's stifled cry came out as a choking gasp. But even as the sound left her body and the blood began to well up along the cut, it was clear the wound wasn't bleeding nearly as much as it should. Already, the blood appeared coagulated. Bash sheathed the knife and then took a rag from his pocket. He wiped the rag along the bloody line on his arm. There wasn't even a mark.

"That," he said, "is how a werewolf bleeds."

"What happened?" Tessa asked. "What changed? How did you, you know, become… you?"

Bash's smiled widened. "Oh, I was always *me*. Haven't you always been you?"

Tessa didn't answer. She wasn't sure *how* to answer. She was suddenly hyperaware of the bodies around her, of their breathing, the air in the room going into them, out of them, into them, out of them, and the stench of it: morning breath and unbrushed teeth, too much whiskey, coffee, cigarettes, mints, apples. Someone was chewing gum. The air was full, buzzing with warmth and scents.

Bash went on, taking Tessa's silence for an affirmative answer. She struggled to follow his words, as his voice stretched and constricted, deepened and diminished. "I don't remember my parents. My first memory was of my foster parents." He nodded at Frank.

"Adopted now," Frank added. "Not long after we took him in, I made him my Familiar."

"I was having trouble fitting in with the family, at school," Bash said. "The Familiar-Magick bond can work both ways, help both parties. It's symbiotic, ya know?"

"As far as we can tell," Frank said. "That started the process. The Familiar Mark. It took…" He whistled, thinking. "Ooh, probably three or four years though. There were little things along the way. Hindsight's twenty-twenty and all that. But when it happened, it was sudden. Just like what you described."

"But how?" Cece cut in. "I've never heard of anything like this before in my life."

"From time to time," Jean said, "there are the Waywards who are oblivious to their powers, right?"

"Yes," Regina piped in, shaking her head. "But usually they're very weak, barely even count as Magix."

"Yes, I knew a Wayward siren who didn't figure out she was a siren until she had a baby," Izotz said. "She was able to hum herself into feeling no pain through the whole labor. But that was the only time she could do more than subdue a stray cat."

"There's more," said Bash. "I'm more than just a Magick."

Cece frowned. "What does that mean?"

Bash looked at Frank, who gave him a little nod. Bash held up his hands, palms a few inches apart and facing each other, and both Frank and his boy stiffened behind him, squaring their shoulders as if they were preparing for a fight. As Bash held up his hands, a black dot appeared between his palms. Slowly, it grew.

"What the hell is he doing?" Elsa snorted.

Tessa looked around the room. Only Cece appeared able to see the black dot growing in Bash's hand. Everyone else was glancing at one another or around the room, unaware.

"Woah!" Astrid shouted, pointing up.

Above them, the green ceiling was dying. The flowers began to wilt and die. Leaves, shriveled brown, fell like raindrops from the ceiling.

There was a shriek.

"That's anti-magic!"

"He's a DOM! He's a DOM!"

Elsa drew two of her swords and Frank's boy did the same in response.

"He's not going to hurt you," Frank shouted, even as he pulled out a weapon as well. "Bash, just put it awa—"

"Wait," said Cece. She held out one hand, palm up. She drew her finger inward toward herself, as if beckoning Bash toward her. Not Bash. The anti-magic. And it came. The little ball of blackness moved through the air and came to rest in Cece's hand.

And then, strangest of all, Tessa realized that she could *hear* the anti-magic.

"It's talking," she said.

No one heard her. They were all staring at Cece, or Bash, or looking from Cece to Bash, or staring up at the still-dying ceiling, eyes wide with fear and wonder.

"It's talking," Tessa said again.

Cece turned. "What?" she asked.

"Can you hear it?" Tessa asked, coming to stand beside Cece. "It says… well, it's not words really. I can't…"

"It wants to be freed," Bash said. He had come over to them as well, and the three of them stood, huddled around the anti-magic that danced above Cece's palm. "It knows you," he said to Tessa.

"It wants to me to... hold it," Tessa said.

Cece nodded. "Yeah, I think it does. Take it."

And Tessa did.

Above them, a tornado began to spin. It sucked the withered leaves off the trees, spiraling them down, down, down into Tessa's palm.

"Shit, shit!" Elsa was shrieking. "The Non is a DOM, too? What the fuck is going on here?"

"She's not a Non," Bash said, grinning at Tessa as she let the anti-magic dance between her fingertips, as the leaves turned to dust and ball of anti-magic grew and grew. "Not a DOM, or a Magick. She's both."

"Both?" Chorused around the room.

"Like a mutt?" Elsa snarled.

Bash winced.

"We call it a *cross*," Frank cut in. "She's a cross between a DOM and a Magick."

"And you're a—a cross, too?" Tessa whispered.

Bash nodded. "You too, Cece."

Cece swallowed. "Holy shit."

The anti-magic landed on Tessa's right index finger. It whispered to her to *please, please* let it go.

She crushed it into dust.

* * *

**APRIL 2006**

*From: Gunner Engers*
*Subject: Mr. Jenkins*
*To: Tish Chernoff*
*Sent: April 7, 2006, 4:21 p.m.*

*Dear Tish,*

*I'm still not convinced I'll ever get used to this goddamned "email." I've always said that typing is an inferior means of communicating. Give me a pen and paper any day.*

*To the point: I've met your "Mr. Jenkins" and reviewed his resume. He seems a stalwart lad, if rather dense. In short, exactly the kind of person your Ana would gravitate toward. He will make her shine even brighter and he can easily pass for a Non.*

*I have sent him forth with our blessing.*
*Gunner*

# CHAPTER
## TWENTY-SIX

**JULY 2023** Outside of The House, Morana Aronov cradled her left hand in her right and cracked her knuckles. Behind her, half a dozen men and women made similar gestures, twisting necks and popping elbows and shaking out their legs. Preparing.

*Time to finish this,* Morana thought.

"Remember," she told her people. "This isn't like other missions. We just want Cordelia Connolly. Alive." There were some murmurs of dissent.

"It's a house of children," Morana hissed back. Visions of the recent massacre at the Second City Coven haunted her. She'd always commanded her people to spare the children, but they had stopped listening to her. "You are not to harm the children, understood?"

There were nods. One of the DOMs, an odious man made entirely of angles and points—elongated nose, square jaw, rectangular frame, knife-like elbows, and sharpened fingernails—replied, "I'll spare the small ones. No one else."

Morana felt her hold slipping. "You're *not* to harm the children," she repeated. "And Cordelia Connolly must be taken alive."

The odious DOM gave a stiff bow. "As you wish, my leader."

*One last mission,* Morana said to herself.

Across the street, Deirdre Laguerre leaned against a telephone pole, stroking her cobra, Nadja. If Morana and her wolves and DOMs saw her, she was confident they didn't care. They didn't know what she was. Deirdre herself had only recently discovered what she was, the truth of her immense powers. But she was powerful and growing more and more powerful by the day. It was The House, she thought. Or someone—some people—*in* The House.

The people in The House might not like Deirdre, but they were *like* her. They were kin. She would protect them.

*Natalie's kin, too,* a voice hissed in Deirdre's ear.

*A bad seed, that one,* Deirdre replied. *The ones here… that little frumpy one especially, they're good.*

*Natalie helped you learn the truth,* the voice hissed back.

Natalie Crane. She'd attacked Deirdre with anti-magic as she tried to leave the Denver Coven. And Deirdre, without a thought, had conjured an equally virulent ball of blackness, which consumed Natalie's anti-magic in one gulp. If Natalie hadn't been so shocked, she might have fought back, might have overpowered and killed Deirdre right then and there. She was powerful, more powerful than Deirdre. Or at least, more powerful than Deirdre had been a week ago. Deirdre was so much more powerful now.

*Don't get cocky,* the voice hissed.

* * *

Across town, Sanjay was in Tessa's house, sitting at her kitchen island across from Theo, who would not look at him.

"What about *Ticket to Ride?*" Sanjay suggested. "You used to love that game. Remember, how we used to all play together?"

Theo looked up at Sanjay, intense rage on their face, and Sanjay winced at his own misstep. *Shit,* he thought to himself. He didn't know what to do. He thought Morana was naive at best and an idiot at worst to think that Theo would ever get over Tessa. He was glad he'd been able to talk some sense into her at least and that they'd figured out where Tessa and the girl were hiding.

"When will she be back?" Theo asked.

"Shouldn't be long," Sanjay replied. "Your mom's gone over to talk to Tessa. And once we work through some things..." Psychiatric help for Tessa, certainly. There had to be some course of action to remedy the harm she'd managed to do. But Sanjay wasn't going to turn her into the police. "Well, then hopefully, she can come back into your life. Your Auntie Tessa."

Theo glared at him. "She'll never agree to that."

Sanjay sighed. "She loves you, kid. She'd do anything to see you again."

"What about the girl? Is Mom gonna hurt her?"

"Of course not!" Sanjay exclaimed. To save face for Tessa, he'd told his supervisor that Astrid had run away. Police were looking for her.

"I saw on the news that she's a suspect in her parents' murder." Theo's tone was flat, but Sanjay still heard the unspoken *because of you.*

Sanjay got up from the chair and opened the fridge, pulling out a lone IPA that he was pretty sure he'd left in T's fridge at Christmas. "She's not a murder suspect," he told Theo. "No bodies, no murders."

He squeezed the beer can tight, reveling in the cold against his palm, the sensation of something different. He popped it open and sighed at the cracking hiss. He pressed it to his lips and drank, long. Hard. Tried to drown out the bad feeling, tried to keep it from creeping up from his gut and into his heart, his brain.

Morana didn't believe the Laveau-Millers were dead. So hopefully, well... hopefully the whole thing would blow over soon and the girl wouldn't be any worse for wear, at least not because of anything Sanjay had said or done.

"You suck," Theo said, stalking out of the room. Sanjay listened to their pounding feet on the stairs, then the slam of a door. He finished the beer in one gulp.

Meanwhile, in a magic-made cavern beneath the North Carolina coast with walls built of water, Aurora Laveau and Zachary Laveau-Miller lay, hands clasped together, eyes closed, gripped by a dreamless sleep. Beside them, crouched a young siren named Jacob. Assigned as their guardian, Jacob talked to the sleeping pair as he watched them.

He told them about his childhood, growing up in the hospital because of his weird ailments. "My mom died giving birth to me and I never knew my dad." He wanted them to know that he knew what their daughter was going through, knew the loss and absence of parents as intimately as he'd come to know the walls of this cavern, a knowledge as smooth and polished as the Petoskey stone he held between his fingers, a gift from one of his foster moms.

Thinking of Tessa Andrews, still made Jacob happy, so he told the sleeping Laveau-Millers about her. "I was fifteen when I got placed with her, only stayed a few months." Those were some of the best months in his memory. After, he'd been shuffled from home to home until he aged out of the system. "I sometimes still dream about her," he told them. "About doing her makeup, and the way she'd laughed..." He'd never felt so at home with anyone ever before. He'd been dreaming about her more and more now, though he hadn't told anyone, not even Val.

"Astrid is safe with her," he assured the parents. "And I'm sorry, about all of this, I really am. If it was up to me, I wouldn't be part of it at all. But..." How to explain the power Morticia Chernoff had over him? How to explain how he heard her voice in his head as loudly as his own? How his first memory was of Tish? How, for years, he'd called her mom until the day Val showed up and told him the truth? And still... he loved Tish more than anyone. Despite her flaws. Because of them?

Jacob hummed a tune, an old coping mechanism to keep himself from spiraling. "Whatever happens, I'll make sure you get back to her. I promise."

Three-hundred-and-fifty miles away, in nature-made cavern near Asheville, Morticia Chernoff sat on the cold, damp ground, her phone cradled limply in her hand. She closed her eyes.

"Tessa," she whispered into the darkness, though, of course, the girl was not there. She was alone, had been alone for some time, she now realized. "I'm sorry." Words she knew could not be heard, not anymore, but that needed to be excised, nonetheless. She needed the words gone and with them, the feeling like drowning. "I'm sorry I couldn't save you, Tessie." Val's little sister. Tish could still feel the sweet girl's hand in her own, could still feel it slipping away. She'd tried to shift, to become a crocodile or falcon, something powerful enough to hold on, to float or fly away with little Tessa Hart. But the water had been stronger. Tish hadn't been a hero. She'd failed.

Every day, she was trying to claw her way back to that moment, trying to fix it.

"As the air, so the body," Tish whispered. "You know, I always hated that fucking fairy bullshit. Oh, right. Excuse my language," she added, remembering that Tessa had only been five, would always be five. "You could just as well say as the earth, so the body. Or as the planet, so the body. Sit back and watch it burn. There's nothing we can do."

She squeezed her phone tightly, waiting for Gunner to call her back, waiting for Val to reach out and explain herself.

"I'll never accept that," Tish whispered. "Never."

She sat there, whispering promises to the ghost of the girl whose loss changed Tish's life, whose loss made Tish the person she was: a failed hero.

She sat there, waiting for a call that would never come.

In Denver, Natalie Crane folded her arms across her chest and leaned back in her chair. Across from her, an old nemesis, Gunner Engers, sat quietly, eyes lowered in deference. His once thick black hair was thin and gray. His dark skin had turned leathery. He was old and worn. He reminded Natalie of a well-read book, cracking at the seams.

"Where is she?" Natalie asked him.

Gunner shook his head. "Tish and I have parted ways."

Natalie hissed. Two men loomed out of the shadows.

"It's the truth," Gunner repeated. "I'm an old man; I wanted out. She's... well, Tish is Tish. She'll never be done until the job is done."

"The job," Natalie snorted. "What a misguided little romp you all went on. How long did you play your little game, pairing up DOMs and Magix, breeding Hybrid children into the world so you could experiment on them?"

Gunner said nothing.

Natalie frowned, leaning back in her chair, arms folded across her chest. "You know I found of another of them? An ogre Hybrid."

"Denis?" Gunner whispered.

Natalie shrugged. "Goes by Deirdre now."

"Is he—is she—alright?"

"She's alive, if that's what you mean. How many more are there?"

Gunner shook his head.

"Answer me!" Natalie growled.

Gunner jumped, wincing with pain. "We were trying to save the world," he whispered.

"How long?" Natalie pressed. "How many?"

Gunner gasped, his shoulders arching back pulled by invisible, agony-inducing strings. "Denis—Deirdre—was born in 1980. For a while— the 1980s, 1990s, even into the early part of the new millennium, there was funding—it was considered—essential, for the DOMs. Top secret. Their way to conquer all. I just—all we ever wanted, Tish, Val, and I, was to unite the powers, magic and anti-magic, to stop the— Nons—the destruction, climate change."

"Spare me the noble spiel," Natalie said, letting her magic press against his skull so that he shrieked. "How many?"

Gunner whimpered. "There were... dozens—hundreds—of attempts. Most died in utero."

Natalie could picture it, those tiny cells trying to multiply, but the dark anti-magic was always hungry, ready to devour the sparks of magic. Or else, the magic burned too brightly, burning everything, all the cells dissolving in a bloody mess. "Most," Natalie said. "Not all."

Gunner managed to nod, wincing. "I know of—six, maybe seven— that were successful."

"I'll need those names."

Gunner was trembling. "I don't—I don't have—"

Natalie leaned forward. "Does Tish have the names?"

Gunner nodded and began to convulse, his eyes rolling back in his head, the sclera of his eyes not white, but black and leaking.

"But you don't know where she is?"

Gunner shook his head. Black tears were streaming down his face.

Natalie leaned in close, her mouth to his ear. "Then. What. Fucking. Good. Are. You."

There was a popping sound and Gunner fell forward, black anti-magic oozing out of his head and pooling on Natalie's desk. Natalie beckoned it to her, gathering it into a whirling ball in her hand. Then she blew on it gently and it was gone.

"Get him out of here," Natalie said to the two men. The men, both DOMs, looked at one another before they compiled. If Natalie noticed their hands trembling as they worked, she said nothing.

Within the hour, one of the men would place a phone call to his direct supervisor expressing some concerns about this assignment to help Morana Aronov and her Magick Corps, particularly regarding a certain Vampiress, who was, in the man's words, "Not a goddamn Magick, not a DOM. She's something else… something evil, something wicked, sir."

* * *

Around this same time, Valerie Hart knocked at a faded red door on a house with chipped black shutters and tan bricks, scarred black in some spots from time and weather. There was a large chip on the side by the driveway, like someone had clipped it with a car. The welcome mat read, "God Bless this Home and All Who Enter!"

A woman with long gray hair and a worried expression opened the door. The worried expression grew frightened when she looked at Val. "You," she said.

"Me," Val replied. "Kathy, we need to talk."

Kathy bit her lip. "Is this about Tessa?"

Val nodded.

"Is she ok? Is she safe?"

Val hesitated.

"Answer me!"

The panic in her voice sent every molecule of air vibrating with unease. Val felt the anxiety fill her own lungs, gulped in a breath. A sudden vision of her own mother sprinting down the beach, wading into the water, screaming for little Tessie. Tessa, her sister's namesake.

Not for the first time, Val wondered if the name had been a curse.

"I-I think so," Val replied. "She's with others, like her."

Kathy frowned. "She knows then?"

Val nodded, glancing up and down the street. "Kathy, let me in, please?"

* * *

Much later, Tessa would learn about all of these things, happening all at once. But for now, all she knew was that there was a knock on the front door of the House. It was firm, three sharp raps. Everyone grew quiet. Even the twins, sensing the fear, creeping like a sudden icy chill through the room, stopped playing and began to whimper. Jean scooped them both up, even as Cece reached for them. He pulled them away from her, pressing them against him.

"Chut, chut," he whispered to them, looking at Cece with rage and horror, like she was a stranger who had just tried to steal his children.

"Jean," she whispered.

He shook his head.

There was another knock, three fast raps, followed by a voice: "Hello, is anybody home? May I please come in?"

Astrid's hand was in Tessa's before she'd realized the girl had come beside her.

"Aren't you afraid?" Tessa asked her.

Around them, most of the Magix had retreated, giving Cece, Tessa, and all three Sobro Boys a wide berth, but Astrid had stepped, trembling, into their inner circle.

"I'm terrified," she whispered. "But not of you, Tessa. I know what you are, all of you. You're the answer to the prophecy. You're our salvation."

Outside, there was loud pop, less like a gunshot and more like the static sizzle of fireworks. The pop was followed by a hiss, a curse, and a shout. Then silence, eerie in its unwavering wholeness, the silence of a laboring woman between contractions, the kind of silence that makes you almost believe an end has come, a trial is done.

If Tessa had been in full possession and knowledge of the powers recently released from their cursed dormancy, she would have been able to see what was happening outside The House, in the dirty alleyway. An air fairy has a unique ability to project their essence through the air, to see far and wide, unburdened by space or distance, just like the air itself. She could have risen above the Magix huddled in the living room and soared up into the foliage above, past Bettie, up and up, through the slightly open skylight and down to hover over the scene below: Morana, her DOMs and Magix, and Deirdre.

The first DOM, that odious, angular man, fell before anyone even realized Deirdre was there. There was the pop, the sizzle of black anti-magic dissipating, and a corpse. The Magick beside the fallen DOM screamed and Morana cursed.

"Show yourself," she hissed. She thought she knew who would emerge and felt fear quicken her pulse. She knew she was no match for Natalie Crane.

Deirdre stepped out.

"You!" Morana exclaimed, her mouth hanging open.

"Not who you were expecting?" Deirdre asked and smiled.

Inside, Bash shifted beside Tessa. Then nodded and started forward, as if he'd settled an internal argument with himself. At first, no one else followed, but then Cece moved to catch up with him. She glanced back over her shoulder at the crowd of Magix, who stood unmoving, not even seeming to breathe, as if they'd been frozen by the strangeness of it all.

Tessa stepped toward Cece and Astrid followed behind her.

"Not you," Tessa said, turning toward Astrid and squeezing her hand.

"Jean," Cece said, her voice trembling as she spoke. His name hung tremulously in the air, a wish and a prayer. Cece didn't have any more words to beg.

"I'll take care of them," Jean said. "Always." He hesitated, then added, "Always, my love." He turned to the gathered crowd. "Hé, attention! There is a secret exit and there is room for all, but we will need to take turns, n'est-ce pas? Follow me! The children will be first."

Tessa kissed Astrid's cheek. "Keep them safe. Keep *you* safe."

Astrid nodded stiffly. "See you soon?"

"Yes," Tessa replied. "Soon."

The three of them, Bash, Cece, and Tessa, gathered in the mudroom. Bash held a finger to his lips. Through the door, they could hear voices.

"Did you miss me?" Deirdre asked.

There was no response.

*There's six of them,* Bash thought-said. *Three DOMs.* He gestured three times to a space through the wall and as he did it, Tessa could picture them, as if the wall had been knocked down in front of her. *Three Magix. One DOM and Magick cross.*

*Deirdre,* Cece thought-answered

*She's on our side,* Tessa replied.

*No shit,* Bash thought-replied. *She's taken down a DOM already.*

*One of the Magix is Morana,* Cece thought-said.

Bash pointed to the door. *That one.*

*Don't kill her,* Tessa thought-said.

Cece raised an eyebrow, but nodded. Her hand hovered over the doorknob.

Bash held up a finger. *On the count of three.*

Despite the wall and space between them, Tessa could hear Morana breathing. She heard her suck in a breath and open her mouth, but no words came out. Tessa could hear the snake hissing, coiling around Deirdre's shoulders.

*One.*

She heard Deirdre click her tongue. "What's the matter, bebe?"

*Two.*

There was another sizzling pop, but this time, it was followed by a grunt and a slap, then the crack of breaking bones.

*Three.*

The doorknob spun under Cece's hand and the door swung wide open.

Morana was crouched on her hands and knees, preparing to run at Deirdre, who was stuck, her arm half crushed beneath a metal dumpster that one of the werewolves had clearly thrown. He still held his arms up. The DOM beside him sucked in desperate breaths, his skin glowing faintly as black lines streamed down his face.

Bash picked up where Deirdre had started. The DOM let out a scream, flying backward as white light punched out of his chest. A moment later, he was nothing but a pile of ash on the ground and dust motes glimmering in the air. The remaining two DOMs looked at each other before they took off then in opposite directions. Tessa reached for one and Cece for the other, pulling them back by the anti-magic that polluted their veins. Cece wrapped a cord of electric magic and then transported them.

"Alaska," she panted to Tessa and winked.

Meanwhile, Bash grabbed Morana up in a chokehold. "Call them off," he said.

Morana laughed, wasting her breath, before she croaked. "What—are you—waiting for?"

The first Magick ran at Cece, whose back was turned and caught her around the throat. Tessa didn't have time to think, only act. Before the werewolf could fully open his massive jaws to bite, there was a pop, like a gunshot, swift and sharp. The Magick fell, exsanguinated and brittle and dead. The other werewolf held up her hands in surrender.

Cece, massaging her throat with one hand, snapped her finger with the other.

"Go," she shouted. "You won't remember this place. Even if you did, you wouldn't be able to talk about it. Go to your home and forget us."

The werewolf turned and ran.

Cece turned back to the others, the body of the werewolf at her feet. The werewolf Tessa had killed to save Cece. Over the body, Tessa and Cece stared into each other's eyes and Tessa knew in this moment, now, she had crossed a bridge over which it would be impossible to return. In Cece's eyes, Tessa saw that she had crossed this bridge many years before. This was why she had been so utterly unreadable to Tessa. No more. Tessa and Cece were the same. They were killers, both of them.

All the old identities: daughter, student, friend, queer, foster mom, Theo's mom, Non, Magick, cross between a Magick and a DOM, everything fell away, eclipsed by this one truth: Tessa was a killer. A murderer.

Cece reached out and took her hand. "Tessa," she said. She repeated her name and it was like the beam of a lighthouse on a dark night, leading Tessa home and back to herself. "Tessa."

She was still herself. She was still Tessa. "Yeah," Tessa whispered. "I'm ok."

A sound rose up from nearby, a laugh spreading from the throat to the chest to belly, deep and broken and sad. Deirdre was laughing, tears in her eyes.

"Didn't I tell you to be careful, Tessa?" she chuckled. She tried to shift the dumpster off of her arm, wincing at each small movement. "You got eaten up," she gasped.

Tessa moved to help her, thrusting her weight against the dumpster. Deirdre shrieked as the weight shifted.

"God, let me," Cece shouted, snapping her fingers and lifting the dumpster up into the air then dropping it a few feet away.

Tessa winced at the sight of Deirdre's arm hanging limp at her side, matted and bloody, the bone peering out, ghost white, splintered, and frayed as Lion's Mane.

"Fuuuuck," she breathed.

"Fuck, fuck, fuck," Deirdre repeated, over and over.

"Bash!" Cece exclaimed, grabbing Morana's arm and pulling her out of Bash's grasp. She nodded toward Deirdre. "Help her."

Bash went to her and knelt beside her, placing a hand on the jagged bone. Deirdre hissed and squealed, jerking in pain.

"Hold her still," Bash commanded, and Tessa tried to, grabbing Deirdre by the shoulders and pressing herself against her, chest to chest. Gradually, Deirdre stopped trying to fight them and her breathing slowed. She was no longer shaking in pain. Tessa looked at the arm and found that the bone was back inside, dried blood and a pink, raised scar the only traces of the injury.

It was then, as the adrenaline began to leave her, that Tessa heard the old, familiar voice in her head. *Tessa, please, help me.*

She turned around to face Morana.

* * *

*From: Morticia Chernoff*
*Subject: The List*
*To: Marcus Brand*
*Sent: March 14, 2007, 11:14 a.m.*

*Dear Mr. Brand,*

*Per your instructions, here is the record. To date, there are six documented cases of successful inseminations, at least five of which we know resulted in live births.*

*I know that you and the Committee have ongoing concerns about the efficacy of MAAM PAC, but I will remind you that it was through our work with Hybrid #1 that we developed the most effective anti-magic weapons in the last 300 years. Our work with #4 led to huge innovations in AntiMagi healthcare. I hope to utilize #6 to develop a Hybrid-locating device. We are currently working on creating a shapeshifter Hybrid.*

*Thank you,*
*Tish Chernoff*

# CHAPTER
# TWENTY-SEVEN

**JULY 2023**

"Where's Theo?"

Morana sighed. "At your house, Tessa. With Sanjay."

Tessa nodded, unfurling her wings, ready to take off.

*Tessa, please don't.* Morana's voice in Tessa's head was almost unrecognizable, ragged and frayed, like a decades-old washcloth, full of holes from cleaning and polishing and scrubbing away grime. *Please. Let me explain…*

"Stop doing that!" Tessa shrieked. "Stop trying to get into my head. Whatever you have to say, you can say it out loud. To everyone."

Cece gripped Morana's arms with such force that the purple outlines of bruises were already appearing, but Morana's face was a mask, like a porcelain doll, half smiling, unblinking. Inside, she wailed with pain. Tessa could hear Morana's whimpers echoing in her own brain.

"Stop it!" Tessa said again. "Cece, you're hurting her."

"Good," Cece replied.

"Cece!"

Cece loosened her grip. Morana allowed a glimmer of relief to cross her face before resetting her mask.

"Ok then," Tessa said to her. "Let's get on with it. Just—speak!"

"Please, Tessa," Morana began. "Please don't go after Theo."

"Why not?"

"They—they don't need to be a part of this. It's not safe."

"Safe?" Tessa's laugh was acid in her throat, burning. "Since when do you give a shit about Theo being safe? They came to me a shell of a child, afraid, neglected, beaten down, and hurting, all because of you, a half-assed mother who couldn't bother to give them the love that they deserve, the basic love that every kid deserves."

"It's not safe for Theo to be with you!" Morana shouted. "It's not safe because you're not safe. None of you are! Don't you get it? You're abominations! You're not supposed to exist. Magix and DOMs are not supposed to coexist let alone procreate."

"Says the person leading a troop of DOMs," Bash laughed.

"A temporary alliance," Morana replied through gritted teeth.

"Why?" Cece asked, squeezing so hard Morana let out a tiny whimper before setting her teeth and growling against the pain.

"Cece!" Tessa hissed.

With a sigh, Cece relented. "Why?" she repeated.

"I wanted it to burn," Morana said. "All of it. Everything my mother worked for. I wanted it destroyed."

"Your mother?" Tessa asked.

"My mother created you," Morana sneered. "Don't you all know? My mother, Morticia Chernoff, fell in love with a DOM. That's your origin story. A simple, stupid love story. From this fated seed, my mother and her DOM boss-mentor-lover, Gunner Engers, came up with a crazy idea that the only way to stop Nons from destroying the planet was to create superhuman Magick/AntiMage Creatures to—to —fuck if I know what they wanted you to do. It's the stuff of zealots and fanatics. Do you know how many people suffered and died for you to exist? Do you know how many of your fellow would-be Hybrids were eradicated in the womb or were born still, with organs outside their deformed bodies or heads caved in from the war inside them? If I'd known what you were before, any of you, I'd have killed you when I had the chance. Tessa, if I'd known, I would've *never* let you take Theo. I thought—I thought—" Her voice caught and through the rage, Tessa heard the keening grief. "I thought you could keep them safe. I thought you were a Non. I thought, well, if they're with a Non then none of it will ever... materialize. They won't become the monster they were born to be. They'd be safe and so would the world. If I'd even dreamed that you—*you*—were one of..."

"Ok, now back the fuck up a second," Deirdre said. "You're saying we're all, what? Lab experiments?"

Morana snorted. "You don't know anything, do you?"

"Enlighten us," Cece hissed, squeezing.

Morana gasped. "Ok... ok." She took a deep breath. "There was an organization. MAAM PAC. The Magix and AntiMagi Projected Amalgamation Confederation. Their goal was to create Hybrids."

"Create how?" Bash asked.

Morana tried to shrug, but Cece's grip on her halted the motion. "I don't know and frankly, I don't care. That's not the point. The point is you didn't just appear naturally. You were bred by my mother and her associates, who thought Hybrids could halt and undo the effects of climate change. But I've *seen* what a Hybrid can do." She stared pointedly at Tessa.

Deirdre snorted. "So you think we're like, what? The harbingers of the end of the world?"

Morana said nothing, staring stonily back at Deirdre.

"I'll take that as a *yes*," Deirdre continued. "And yet, if I'm not mistaken, you were all teamed up with at least one other person like us, another *Hybrid*. Natalie Crane."

"We've... parted ways."

"She's dangerous."

"No shit," Morana laughed.

"She's not like us," Deidre said, gesturing to Bash, Cece, and Tessa.

"Like us?" Cece snorted. "What makes you think that we—" She flapped her index finger back and forth between Deirdre and herself. "—are anything alike?"

"We're Hybrids," Bash said.

"So is Natalie Crane, apparently," Cece replied.

"And Theo," Morana said.

"But Deirdre's acting like 'we' are somehow a unit, the four of us, not Natalie or…" Cece trailed off, as if just realizing the name that Morana had given. Her green eyes met Tessa's.

Around her, Tessa could feel the air, the molecules of it, oxygen's kiss, nitrogen's fond caress, the sting of carbon dioxide, the gentle lapping of water, and through it all, the menace of particulate matter, clawing its way through the air with the indiscriminating indifference of a virus. She'd never thought it was possible to feel so much. And once again—it had been happening a lot recently, Tessa realized—the sounds around her began to stretch and shrink, boom and quiet. Through it all, her pulse throbbed in her ears: *Theo. Theo. Theo.*

"Theo's a Hybrid," Tessa said.

Morana nodded.

"The Non you turned, that died… he wasn't a Non, was he?"

Morana shook her head.

"And you," Tessa turned to Cece. "Your parents… they call you a Non-murderer, but you're not, are you? You killed your dad, but he was a DOM."

"I didn't kill my dad," Cece said. "He wasn't—I don't want to… I don't want to talk about this. This isn't about me."

"Like hell it isn't," Morana snapped. "It's about all of you. You exist, somehow, against all odds."

"But why?" Bash said. "Why did we survive? How are we… alive?"

Morana shrugged. "If I knew the answer, I would have stopped it long before I—"

"You would have aborted Theo," Tessa said.

"I tried to," Morana said. "When I found out what it was inside me. I couldn't. They were un-killable. Whatever brought you all into being, it's made you stronger than any other creature on the planet. So I guess, my mother's thought process was not entirely insane. If anyone could save the world, it would be you all. Likewise, if anyone was going to destroy it… well."

There was a moment of quiet as this thought hit each of them. Bash drew himself inward, hooking his right hand around his left elbow in a gesture that reminded Tessa of a shy kindergartener. Deirdre raised herself up, lifting her right arm so her cobra could twist around it. Cece bit her lip and her face hardened into an unreadable mask. Tessa played back a well-worn memory—*if you loved me, you'd fight for me*—followed by the mantra of her adult life: *Put the kid's needs first. Keep your cool. Never set an expectation you can't meet. Trust the kid.*

"Theo needs us," Tessa said. She gestured to Cece, Bash, and Deirdre. "All of us. You heard her—" She jerked her chin at Morana. "We could save the world."

"Or destroy it," Cece muttered.

"Sure," Tessa said. "But that's a choice. And me, I'm going to choose to save it." She looked at Morana, into her icy eyes and recognized the desperation there. Lurking beneath all the hurt and anger was the desire to change… something? Everything? For the first time since she'd known Morana, since she'd known about her, Tessa felt a desire to not only understand her, but help her. "How about the rest of you?" she asked, her eyes never leaving Morana's.

"You know I'm in," said Bash.

Cece nodded. "Absolutely."

Deirdre shrugged. "I mean, yeah. But what are we gonna do about her?" She lip pointed to Morana.

"I could think of a few things," Cece smirked, tugging Morana toward her and cupping her chin in her hand. Cece's green nails stroked Morana's pale cheek, pressed against her red lips, the green and the red and the white and the brown like some kinky Christmas card mélange, sexy and menacing beneath an innocent surface.

"Jean and Regina and the others can handle her, right?" Tessa said. "I don't—I don't think we should hurt her."

Cece continued to press sharp fingers against Morana's cheek, lips, and neck, leaving pink lines and dots of blood. "Mm, and I don't think that you should get a say in this, Tessa." As she spoke, she punctuated each word with a press of her nail, digging it deeper and deeper into the taut skin of Morana's neck. Tessa could see a blue vein throbbing under the green thumbnail.

"She's falling into this whole leader-savior role quite easily, huh?" Deirdre smirked.

"Pfft," Cece exhaled.

"Typical white lady," Deirdre said.

Cece waved a dismissive hand. "It's not that. Well, it's not *just* that." She turned to Tessa. "What has she taken from you?"

"Theo," Tessa said.

"You'll get them back," Cece continued, her voice as soft as a cat's underbelly. "What she's taken from us." Cece hooked a finger at Deirdre and tipped her chin toward Bash. "We can't get them back. So. Again. I don't think you should get a say in this."

Tessa opened her mouth but Deirdre cut her off with a laugh.

"Always preaching mercy." She smacked her tongue against her teeth.

"I'm not—"

Morana let out the tiniest sound. Cece's fingernail had opened a vein in her neck and a trail of blood was crying out of it.

"Shit!" Bash exclaimed, leaping over to put a hand against Morana's neck, which healed instantly.

"The fuck?" Cece shrieked.

"There's no need to be hasty!" Bash exclaimed.

"She could be useful," Tessa added. "Deirdre," she said, turning to her. "You know that's true. You even said—"

"I know what I've said," Deirdre snapped. She shook her head and nodded to the inconspicuous door of the House. "You all bring her in and I'll clean this shit up."

Tessa thought Cece would protest this change of plans, this shift of sentiment, but she did not. She opened the door for Bash, who shoved Morana ahead, and entered behind, closing the door, leaving Tessa alone with Deirdre and the corpses.

Deirdre snapped her fingers three times. The bodies turned to ash and blew away.

"Mm, now that can't be good for the atmosphere," Deirdre chuckled. "It still smell like smoke to you?"

Tessa nodded and started walking away down the alley. "I'm going to get Theo."

Deirdre fell in step with her. "Been stinking for days now, I swear."

Tessa's vision was blurring a bit. She stumbled and Deirdre grabbed her elbow.

"You ok there?" Deirdre asked.

Tessa nodded, pulling her arm out of Deirdre's grasp. Tessa's head felt foggy, clouded with more than smoke. She was having trouble breathing. The air was so full, so tactile. She could feel it, rubbing against her like a living thing. A dying thing, she realized.

"Do you feel it, too?" Tessa asked.

Deirdre didn't answer.

"The air?" Tessa tried to clarify. "Do you feel… all of it?"

She glanced over at Deirdre, who was still walking beside her, looking down at the ground, her face expressionless.

"I sound crazy," Tessa said, shaking her head.

Deidre shrugged. "You sound like an air fairy. I knew one, back in Santa Fe. This whole—" She gestured to the sky, spinning her finger in a circle. "—climate change shit? She was real sensitive to it. All the changes, the extra ozone in the air and all that. She'd have trouble breathing. Asthmatic, they said."

Tessa frowned. "I had asthma, as a kid."

"Might be coming back, from the sound of you," Deirdre replied. "I'll slow the pace. Deep breaths. Most air fairies have asthma, so I've heard. Most ogres have an excess of body hair," she said, looping a curl of her chin hair around her finger. "Gift and curse, am I right?"

"I didn't know," Tessa said. "How could I have never known?"

"Well, I don't think you were supposed to," Deirdre said and gave a sad chuckle. "You heard Morana, didn't you? She thinks her kid is dangerous. Doesn't want them to know who—*what*—they are. Seems to me like someone had the same fear about you."

"And Bash," Tessa added.

"Mm, him too? Funny."

"But not you. Not Cece."

"Oh, well. I'm not even sure my mother knew what exactly I was. Cece—I can't speak for her or her parents. But Manman, she knew I had a different dad than my brother, of course. We all knew that. I was already around when my papa, the man who raised me, entered the picture, see? But my bio dad? Manman knew next to nothing about him, except a name, and that he had kind eyes and was good to her. Whoever he was, she liked him enough to never speak a word against him. So I have to think she didn't know what he was, or what I am. See?"

Tessa nodded. It was getting a little easier to breathe with each step they took away from the House and, more importantly, toward Theo. Tessa was only half listening to Deirdre and her origin story. She knew she should be listening; she knew she should care about how Deirdre came to be because it was probably the key to how she came to be. And in that thought, there dwelled, like a half-forgotten splinter, an edge of pain, and a vague and unhurried concern for Tessa's mom. What did her mother know, if anything? What was her role in all this? Tessa had always known she was adopted, but it was like knowing she had brown hair. Just a random fact about herself.

No, there was no *way* her mom knew. She wouldn't have kept that from Tessa. Right? She had always been honest with her about her origins: a single mother who couldn't keep her baby.

So where the hell was this woman, Tessa's biological mother?

All this hummed below the surface, in a semi-conscious space that her mind wasn't fully ready to look at, to hold and study and solve. The thoughts that she allowed herself to think, an internal monologue flowing through her like Silas' nonstop dialogue went like this:

*You're gonna see them soon. You're gonna see Theo. Did they miss me? Do they even remember me? Of course they remember you. Do they forgive me? What color is their hair? Have they grown? Of course they have. How much? How many inches? Did Morana help them get their teeth straightened? Did they outgrow that ever-so-slight and ever-*

*so-endearing lisp? Will they be happy to see me? Will they smile? Will they be surprised by the wings? The wings! What will they think of me?*

Outside of her, Deirdre chattered on.

"Can I hide my wings?" Tessa blurted. She thought she'd seen other fairies do it. From a survival standpoint, they needed the ability to conceal themselves, to blend in.

They were almost to Tessa's street. They were less than a quarter mile away.

Deirdre looped her arm in Tessa's. "Calm down, girlie," she said. "Yes, of course you can. But I sure as hell couldn't tell you how. I will say, you are getting a fair number of looks from all these Nons. So if I were you, I'd figure it out soon." She had dropped her voice for the last couple sentences as they walked past a couple on the sidewalk pushing a stroller. "Comic-con convention in town," Deirdre said to them with a smile. "Look at our cute little Tinkerbelle!"

The couple returned the comment with nervous smiles.

"Now or never, Tink," Deirdre said as they turned onto Tessa's street.

As Tessa focused on trying to hide her wings, she had the urge to close her eyes. She closed them and kept stepping carefully, Deirdre's arm locked in hers so that when the sidewalk dipped down and Tessa stumbled, she remained upright.

"Interesting," Deirdre said.

Tessa's wings were no longer visible, although Tessa could still feel them there, behind her arms, poking out of her shoulder blades.

"Weird," Tessa agreed.

Ahead of them, Tessa could see Sanjay's little Prius parked in Tessa's driveway.

"So what's the plan?" Deirdre asked as they passed the next door neighbor's house.

Tessa was running up the driveway. "Plan?" she asked, lifting up the potted plant on the bottom porch step and pulling out her hidden house key. "It's my house. My kid."

Deirdre put a hand on Tessa's shoulder. "Legally speaking: the house is yours. The kid is not."

Tessa shook her off, put the key in the lock, and turned it. The door opened with a sigh like the whole house had been holding its breath and waiting for her to return. Straight ahead was the kitchen and sitting there, with their back to Tessa, hunched over a board game, was Theo. Beside him, Sanjay studied his cards. Neither had heard the door. Neither had seen Tessa and Deirdre standing there.

Theo's hair was green and even from behind, even seated, Tessa could see that they had grown several inches, could see their child's body beginning to lengthen and firm up into an adult. The time they had been apart hit her like a gut punch as her eyes confirmed what her head had known and her heart had denied: she'd missed so much time with them, time she was never going to be able to claw back. And she'd missed *them.* Oh, the ache. It caught in her chest and throbbed there, painful and joyful and real, the most real thing she'd ever felt.

"Theo," she whispered.

Their back straightened, but they didn't turn around. There was a long silence in which Tessa felt the air itself holding her up, keeping her from crumbling to the ground under the weight of all this crushing anticipation.

"Mom," they said, still not turning.

Beside them, Sanjay had gotten to his feet, his hand on his phone, fingers not moving but ready. Tessa didn't care about him. Even as Deirdre had slithered past her to coil a firm hand around Sanjay's wrist, Tessa had forgotten Sanjay. He faded into the background and all she saw was Theo, the back of their head like a beacon.

"Yeah," Tessa replied. "It's—me."

Theo turned. Tears were streaming down their cheeks. "You came," they said.

Then Tessa was running down the hall and Theo was in her arms. She was holding them, kissing their wet cheeks, hers wet now, too, as she marveled at their hair—longer, green, and curling with the whispering changes of puberty—and their new, purple-rimmed glasses and their smell—kiss of honey, the tang of orange peels, the salt of tears, all the same, the same!—and their presence—real, here, now. They were both laughing, crying, trying to talk, but unable to string together any coherent phrases, just mumbling, over and over, *It's you! It's you! I've missed you. So much. I've missed you. Finally. I love you. It's you. It's you. Yes, it's you.*

* * *

*From: Morana Chernoff*
*Subject: Re: Checking in*
*To: Valerie Hart*
*Sent: January 2, 2008, 8:09 a.m.*

*Auntie Val!*

*It's so lovely to hear from you! I am well, really well. If I tell you the reason, you must promise to keep it quiet, yes?*

*I'm in love. He's a Non. Please don't tell my mother! I know she wouldn't approve, but... well, you've always been much more open-minded than either of my parents. I know I can trust you.*

*Love,*

*Ana*

*P.S. I'm going by Mina Harker now... a little "vampire" joke.*

# CHAPTER
# TWENTY-EIGHT

**JULY 2023**

"I'm so sorry, Theo," Tessa breathed into their cheek, their hair, trying to imbue her apology into them.

Theo squeezed her with a shocking strength. "Good," they said, then added. "I knew we'd find each other again. Morana said you weren't coming back, that you'd gone off with your new kid and forgotten me." Theo shook their head, a smirk on their face that looked both sad and amused. "She always said things like that though. She tried to make me feel—"

Theo couldn't bring themselves to finish the sentence, but Tessa heard the unspoken word echoing in their brain—*unloved.*

"I love you," Tessa told them. She said it again and again. She couldn't say it enough.

Meanwhile, Sanjay was repeating his own incantation. "Where's Morana?" he asked, over and over, his voice increasing in volume and raising in pitch with each repetition, each eye roll from Deirdre, every moment in which he was not answered.

It was only when Theo repeated the same question that Tessa heard it. "Where is she, Mom?" Theo asked. "Is she—? You didn't—?"

Sanjay was on his feet, trying to twist out of Deirdre's grasp. "If you hurt her, so help me god, I will fu—"

Deirdre slammed her fist into Sanjay's chin and he toppled back, immediately unconscious, as Deidre managed to catch him almost tenderly and lower him to the ground with only a small thud. Raising herself up, Deidre stretched her arms wide and then leaned to crack her back. "Ah bon, much better" she said. "Oke, come on you two. We should go. I smell wolves."

"Morana is safe," Tessa told Theo and almost added *for now*, but thought better of it. *Keep your cool,* she thought. Theo was kind to their core and Tessa wouldn't want all the anger she had stored up to leak out and poison them.

Theo nodded. "Good," they said, turning to Deirdre. "Who are you?" they asked. Then, as if realizing the question might have been perceived as rude, added, "I'm Theo, by the way. My pronouns are they/them." Theo held out a hand.

Deirdre took it with a wide, if somewhat bemused, smile. "I'm Deirdre. She/her. I love how you young people just put it all out there like that. I think the world is probably worth saving so you can have it and fix it."

Theo nodded politely, but Tessa could see them stiffen with concern at the casual way in which Deirdre had mentioned saving (or potentially not saving) the world.

"Everything's gonna be ok," Tessa told them, hand on their back, not wanting to allow something as thick and alive as the air to separate them. "But Deirdre's right. We have to go."

"Go where?" Theo asked.

"We're bringing the Familiar asshole?" Deirdre asked, lip pointing at Sanjay's unconscious body.

Tessa nodded. "We'll have to transport."

"Have you done it before?" Deirdre asked.

"She's a Non," Theo said to Deirdre at the same time as Tessa replied that no, she hadn't done it on her own before. Theo paled at this reply and repeated themselves, this time to Tessa. "You're a Non. Mom?"

"Apparently not," Tessa replied, allowing her wings to show now, the invisibility spell unfurling away from them like a cloak being tugged away.

Theo gasped. "You—you're a fairy?"

"And so much more!" Deirdre exclaimed. "To be discussed later. Now, we need to go."

Deirdre placed her foot on top of Sanjay's chest before taking Theo and Tessa each by a hand. "Close your eyes and think of England. Or whatever."

The detours were rapid and numerous, too fast to fully process. At one point, Tessa saw the Tower of London flicker in and out of her vision followed by a massive waterfall, where Deirdre paused and said, "Saut-Mathurine, the tallest falls in Haiti."

She breathed in deeply and in her eyes, Tessa saw the reflection of the rushing white water. The reflection lingered even after they had transported twice more and arrived in the center of the living room of the House.

At first, Tessa thought the darkened room was empty. Fear gripped her until she heard voices coming from the kitchen. Looking around, she saw Morana in a corner, bound and gagged with dancing electrical ribbons, like what Cece had used on Deirdre before, but cut off from her body and given an independent, corporeal power, a sizzling force unto themselves that hugged Morana with sadistic orange fingers. Flanking Morana were Nas and Marlowe, faces lit with their phones' blue light. Both had flicked disinterested eyes up when Tessa, Deirdre, Theo, and the unconscious Sanjay arrived, but they'd said nothing and were again engrossed in scrolling.

"Everything ok?" Tessa asked them as Theo walked over to Morana and touched a finger to the cross dangling from her neck.

Nas was unresponsive, but Marlowe looked up and flashed a white smile. "Perfection," they said. "Who's the kid?" they asked, giving a little flick of their wrist at Theo to get them to back up. Theo glared at Marlowe and did not move.

"This is Theo," Tessa said, holding out her hand toward Theo who moved back to take it.

"Pleasure," Marlowe said, making a kissing face at Theo. "And the dead guy?"

"Unconscious," Tessa replied.

"And unimportant," Deirdre added.

"Mm," Marlowe moaned, licking their lips. "And ogre lady's back, too. Fabulous."

Deirdre narrowed her eyes at Marlowe, as if gagging the sincerity of the comment. "Even if you were eighteen, which I'm sure you're not," she said, "I'm completely out of your league."

Marlowe just kept smiling that hungry smile.

Tessa cleared her throat. "Everyone's in the kitchen?"

Marlowe leered. "Some of them," they said. "Others went…" They twirled their wrist in a loose circle. "…elsewhere."

"And they left you fools in charge?" Deirdre snorted.

Marlowe frowned, but Nas chuckled before flicking his wrist and sending a tendril of ice twisting around Morana's neck. She kicked her arms and legs. She bit at the gag, causing sparks to fly. A choking sound came from deep in her throat as she tried to claw oxygen from the solidifying air. Her throat crusted with ice and her lips turned blue.

"Stop it!" Theo shrieked.

Startled, Nas dropped his hand. The ice thawed instantly and Morana inhaled a hungry breath through her nose.

Theo was panting with rage. Tessa placed a hand on their shoulder. To Nas and Marlowe, she said, "You and you, come with me. I don't think you should be… in charge here."

Nas flipped Tessa the bird, but when Deirdre stepped forward, towering above him, he shrunk down. Both he and Marlowe followed Deirdre toward the kitchen.

"I'll be right back," Tessa told Theo.

Theo glanced at Morana, then Sanjay.

"They can't hurt you," Tessa said. "I'll be *right* back." In the kitchen, she found Deirdre explaining to Cece, Bash, Regina, Dante, Frank, and Frank's boy what Nas had done.

"I'm not saying she doesn't deserve that," Deirdre said. "But, I don't think you folks are the sort to abuse and torture your prisoners."

Regina sighed. "No, we're not. Are we Nas?"

Nas said nothing.

"Nas!"

"Ugh, no. I'm sorry."

"Last chance," Regina said. "You hear me? You want to be Leadership someday? I want to see leadership-worthy decisions. Got it?"

Nas gave a thumbs-up.

"I want to hear you say it."

"Got it," Nas said.

"Got it," Marlowe echoed.

They both turned and went back into the living room. Tessa poked her head out to see Theo squatting over Sanjay, talking to him.

"Is he awake?" she said.

Theo jumped and looked up. "No—no."

Deidre pushed past Tessa. "I'll get him," she said.

She picked up Sanjay's limp body, tossed him over her shoulders like a sack of potatoes, and walked back into the kitchen, Theo following on her heels. The other five adults had resumed their prior conversation.

"Without a leader?" Dante asked. "I just don't see how that's possible."

"You keep saying that," Regina said. "What makes you think they don't have a leader?"

"Morana—"

"A *new* leader," Regina interjected.

"Natalie Crane," Deirdre said, her voice low and dark. "She was Morana's second. She's—she's one of us," she said, lip pointing to Bash and Cece and placing a hand on Tessa's shoulder, then Theo's head. "A Hybrid."

"All of you?" Frank said, nodding toward Theo.

Theo shrugged off Deirdre's hand, looking up at Tessa, eyes wide. "What are they talking about, Mom? What's a Hybrid?"

The kitchen doors slammed open. Astrid entered, followed by Jean and Oscar.

"Tessa!" Astrid exclaimed, running into Tessa's arms. The two hugged quickly, before Astrid turned to Theo. "You must be Theo," she said. "I'm so happy you're here, finally. I'm Astrid, by the way. Tessa —your mom—she talked about you all the time."

Theo's face brightened and they smiled shyly at Astrid. "It's nice to meet you," they said. "You're a witch?"

Astrid nodded. "And you're a shifter."

"They're a Hybrid," Deirdre interrupted. "Actually."

"Oh là là, another?" Jean exclaimed. He blew out a loud breath. "This is too much." And he trailed off into a string of French.

Theo opened their mouth to ask what a Hybrid was again, but Tessa placed a hand on their shoulder. "I'll explain everything. Soon," she said. "Don't worry."

Outside the closed kitchen door came the sound of giggling children and Cece's voice carried over the whispering voices to admonish the kids on the other side of the door, "Silas Maxwell and Lucas Leonardo, I want you back in bed this instant or there will be consequences."

There was a brief silence followed by Silas' voice from the other side, "What kind of consequences?"

Cece rolled her eyes and Oscar poked his head out of the door and roared at the boys, who squealed in delight as they ran away. Tessa could hear their feet pounding up the stairs. Whoever came up with the phrase "the pitter-patter of tiny feet" must have been childless, Tessa decided. Children's feet never "pitter-pattered." They rumbled like thunder, an avalanche, like chaos incarnate.

"I'll text Tim to check on them and make sure they actually go to bed," Dante said to Jean and Cece, pulling out his phone. "He's putting Evie to bed now, too."

As soon as the children's footsteps faded, there came an incoming flap of wings. Bettie careened through the kitchen door, which Oscar still held partially open, squawking with frenetic energy, her feathers ruffled, looking uncannily like a cartoon angry bird. She landed on Cece's shoulder.

At the same moment, Sanjay stirred. Deirdre kicked him in the ribs and he moaned.

"Oscar," Jean said. "Will you put him somewhere isolated? And secure? S'il te plaît?

"What about the broom cupboard off the mudroom?" Oscar asked, reaching eagerly for Sanjay's wrists.

"Eh bien," Jean nodded.

"Junior," Frank said to his boy. "Help him, would ya?"

Frank Junior grabbed Sanjay by the ankles and he and Oscar hauled him out of the room, swinging his body with a bit too much enthusiasm.

"Oi!" Jean hollered. "Don't hurt him!"

"Much!" Deirdre hollered. "Don't hurt him *much,* wi?" She winked at Jean who reddened and met Deidre's gaze through slightly lowered lashes.

"Eh, oui," Jean shrugged, smiling back at Deidre.

"Everyone!" Cece said, raising her arms so that the room instantly quieted. "There's been another attack."

It was then that Tessa noticed the red on the Cece's shoulder, on Bettie's talons.

"Cece," she said. "Did she—?"

Tessa reached out to touch Cece, but as her hand moved through the air, Bettie gave a little flap of her wings and the breeze hit Tessa like a foul odor, ripe, raw, and gaping open. In the air (through the air? Tessa wasn't sure. There didn't seem to be adequate language to any of her newfound powers), Tessa relived everything as Bettie had. She was the raven, flying over forests until a wide expanse of field materialized, lines of green and brown, dotted with occasional cows. She soared over the heart of the farm, a silo, a barn, a couple outbuildings, and houses. In the muddy yard, chickens puttered about and the occasional person walked back and forth, followed by a mangy dog. A cat sat nonchalantly on top of a fence post, watching Bettie. Its tail flapped hungrily.

The attack happened so fast that Bettie hadn't realized she was in danger until it was nearly too late. Tessa felt the bird's panic in the rapid flaps of her wings, in the air streaming down past her as she tried to get away, away, away from the slaughter below.

She chanced a pause at the edge of the forest, atop a tall jack pine.

A gaunt face outlined in jet-black hair looked out from across the half mile or so of field right at Bettie. The face was blurred with the distance but Tessa felt a jolt of recognition in her bones: another Hybrid.

"The Grand River Coven—the-the farm, where Morana's people had taken over, they're all gone," Tessa said. "Someone—another Hybrid—did it, I think?" Tessa was panting as if she'd just flown dozens of miles instead of Bettie.

Cece was looking at her with incredulity. "How did—?"

"She's an air fairy," Regina cut in. "They have... unique abilities."

She smiled at Tessa with such kindness that Tessa felt a wave of guilt for having disliked her, even if it was for a very specific, isolated reason.

"Rare," Regina added. "I've known of only two others."

Tessa opened her mouth to tell Regina about how they'd met another air fairy, actually, but Cece cut in. "Bettie says the Hybrid is Natalie Crane."

"Shit," Deirdre hissed. "She must have gone rogue. She was always —difficult—for Morana to handle. With Morana fully out of the picture now, well… it was only a matter of time."

"Morana's been 'out of the picture' for what, six hours?" Cece said, her voice a scoff. "This can't possibly be related to that."

Deirdre shrugged. "I think we should talk to the source."

"Morana?" Jean asked.

Deirdre nodded.

"She's not gonna talk to us," Regina laughed. "Besides, I don't want to hear a word that murderer has to say."

"Then you're even dumber than I thought you were," Deirdre snarled. "Don't you all get it? Morana was never the main threat here; she was never the one calling all the shots. She's a pawn in a scheme that is so much bigger than any of us. All she wanted was to burn it down. She wasn't power-hungry. She was motivated by vengeance and rage, which made her dangerous, but stupid. The ones in charge are not stupid, and they are also dangerous, but for very different reasons. They—"

"You're talking like a crazy person," Cece cut in. *"The ones in charge?* Give me names, organizations, something other than vague conspiracy theories."

"Morticia Chernoff?" Tessa offered.

Deirdre nodded. "For one."

"Morticia Chernoff is a hack," Regina sneered, but others in the room looked less certain.

Dante's posture had gone rigid at the mention of her name. Astrid hugged her elbows. Jean wore a deep frown that seemed to pull his entire face down with it, his hairy upper lip sagging to cover his mouth in ruddy blonde hair. Frank clicked his tongue against his teeth while he and Bash exchanged a long, charged look that Tessa assumed meant they were think-talking.

Through all this, Cece was unmoved by their fear and contempt. "Listen, all of you. So what if Natalie Crane has taken over? She just attacked *our enemies,* the very same people that slaughtered our own."

"But why would—" Deirdre began, but Cece cut her off.

"I don't care why. Sure, this might not be a good thing, long-term. Who can say? But right now, we're safe. We've captured the leader of our enemies and the enemies have turned against themselves. If history has taught us anything, it's that this is precisely what we want. Infighting among DOM factions and rogue Magix allows us the time and space we need to grow stron—"

"To hide." The firm voice cut through the room and they all turned to find Izotz standing in the doorway, Elsa tucked slightly behind her.

"Yo, excuse us," Oscar said, pushing past Elsa and Izotz, along with Frank Junior and Tim, who mumbled ample apologies as he scooted around Izotz's bulk.

In their wake, Nas and Marlowe approached and hovered behind Izotz as well. Now, all the adults and teenagers staying at the House were assembled in the small kitchen, which seemed to breathe out and expand with their bodies. There was a long, pent silence. Even the walls seemed to hold a collective breath.

"We're not hiding," Cece said.

Izotz snorted. "You do what you want. The Magix of the Channels are leaving."

Behind her, Elsa sneered, stroking the blade of a knife between her thumb and index finger. Nas wore a smug expression and Marlowe picked at their fingernails, looking bored.

"You're right, Cece," Izotz continued. "We've been given a gift: a broken and distracted enemy. And history does teach us the significance of such gifts and gives us an easy road map to follow. During the witch hunts, across Europe. Here, too, in New England and—" She licked her lips and spat the word. "Salem—we let the Nons accuse one another, let the DOMs burn them, let them fester in their own hatred, while we went into hiding. Hiding has kept us alive all these many centuries."

"We used to rule the world," Cece said, her voice soft, but filled with a vibrating rage, like a teakettle set unevenly on the stove, dancing with the heat and force within it. "The Kandakes, queens of the Kingdom of Kush, King Solomon, Queen Hatshepsut, Eleanor of Aquitaine, Vlad the Impaler, Empress Wu Zetian, Queen Ælfthryth— should I go on? No? But clearly, you don't care about how great we once were, or even how great we could be. You want to hide. Fine. Leave." She flung her hands toward the door, as if to shoo Izotz and the others out.

Elsa, Marlowe, and Nas took a collective step back, but Izotz was unmoved. She seemed to rise up—no, she *was* rising up—and hovered a couple feet above the ground. Cece had no choice but to lift her chin to look up at her. Tessa was reminded of that first morning she'd spent with Cece, when she first witnessed the true power and thrall of a Magick. Izotz hovered above with the menacing practicality of a falcon about to dive upon its prey.

"How dare you?" Izotz growled, the low rumbling whisper of a portended storm. "After all I've done for you." And she spat in Cece's face.

Cece did not flinch. She did not wipe the spit away. She stood there, eyes closed, as around her, there were cries of dismay from most of the others and a shrill giggle from Elsa. Regina came to Cece's side and put a hand on her shoulder.

"Izotz, if you leave now—"

"Fuck off, Regina," Elsa sneered. "They took a vote last night on the islands. You're out. There's a new leader."

"Izotz!" Regina exclaimed, her ears darkening and her breath quickening as the fury at this betrayal coursed through her.

Izotz shook her head. "Not I," she said. "It was decided that the coven would be better off in the hands of someone with the proper... lineage of leadership."

Regina turned to look at Elsa. "You," she whispered.

"Me," Elsa grinned, her eyes like cut diamonds sparkling with white-hot glee.

Jean, Dante, Tim, and Frank all inhaled swift breaths of reproach, Deirdre hissed, and Bash barred his fanged teeth.

Tessa smelled blood like a gathering storm, saw it on the horizon, a looming black cloud.

"Oh shut up, all of you!" Elsa hissed. "The Murpheys have led the Channels for centuries. You came and stole my throne—"

"You weren't of age yet, Elsa!" Regina exclaimed. "When Elias died, you were sixteen years old. Someone had to lead! We took a vote."

"And we've taken a vote again," Izotz said. "Elsa Murphey is the new leader of The Channels Coven."

Regina crumpled. It was as if whatever spark of vigor that powered her body, lit her face and kept her going, cheerily onward, despite everything, had been snuffed out. She seemed to hang there like wet laundry on an invisible line. She said nothing, as the room around her bubbled and boiled with trouble. Elsa's grin loomed large, Cheshire-cat like, above it all.

Theo grabbed Tessa's hand while Astrid pressed her body closer to Tessa and it was these two, frightened movements that caused Tessa to act.

She took the churning air in the palm of her hand, as if she were carefully holding the body of a tiny, wriggling baby animal, a fox, perhaps, or a wolf. The air was a rabid, wild thing, after all. She cupped it in her hand and commanded it to be still.

And just like that, everyone in the room except for Tessa, Astrid, and Theo froze.

* * *

*From: Gunner Engers*
*Subject: Re: Change of Plans*
*To: Tish Chernoff*
*Sent: September 13, 2010, 5:15 a.m.*

*Tish,*

*I heard about the "change of plans" from Brand himself. They want to see if a DOM can be turned into a Magick. I'm sure you can surmise my assessment, but I'll spell it out.*

*This is a mistake. There will be consequences.*

*Val has told me that your girl is "in love." (Yes, I still correspond with Valerie, on occasion.) If Morana is in love and if he dies, there will be consequences. If he lives and this works, there will be consequences.*

*One of the last things Val said to me before she left was this: "We have spun a web around ourselves and everywhere we turn, we meet sticky threads that cinch tighter and tighter. I can hardly breathe from it."*

*Tish, I thought we were going to save the world, but it's getting worse and worse. The heat waves in Europe and Russia, the flooding in Pakistan, droughts in China and Brazil. The climate is changing faster and faster, and we are no closer to a solution.*

*I know you'll say the only way through it is forward. Perhaps you're right.*

*In any case, I don't see any other doors or windows opening to me. So. Onward.*

*Gunner*

# CHAPTER
# TWENTY-NINE

**JULY 2023**

"Woah," Astrid whispered.

"Double woah," Theo echoed. They reached up toward Deirdre, who was standing nearest to them and touched a lock of her hair that had fallen out of her turban, then immediately withdrew their hand and mumbled an apology.

"I don't think she realized," Astrid said.

While the children stared at the frozen Magix and Hybrids whose faces were contorted in glee or rage, their mouths wide as they shouted, spittle hanging midair in crystalline droplets, their hair and clothing aloft, defying gravity, Tessa stared at her hands. *She* had done this. It was impossible. It was true. And she was terrified.

Theo put a hand on her forearm. "Mom?"

"You ok?" Astrid asked.

*Rule #2,* Tessa thought. *Keep your goddamn cool. Breathe.* "Yeah," she said aloud, lowering her hands to her side. "I'm ok. We're all ok. Right?"

They both nodded.

"Is this because you're a Hybrid?" Theo asked. "What *is* a Hybrid? Can I do this, too?"

Tessa placed a hand on Theo's shoulder and outlined as best she could what a Hybrid was. "You're more than a Magick, Theo. But I don't know if you could do... this. I think this might have been because I'm part air fairy?" She looked to Astrid for affirmation, but Astrid only shrugged.

"Can you fix them?" Theo asked.

Tessa's face must have betrayed her apprehension because panic leaped into Astrid's eyes. "You can unfreeze them, right?"

"Of course I can!" Tessa answered too loudly. "Just—give me a minute. This is all new to me." She frowned in concentration. Nothing happened. What had she done to cause everyone to freeze? Maybe if she did the opposite, she could reverse it. She reached out her palms and made a motion of letting go of the air. Again, nothing. Then a sudden intrusive thought came back to her. Val's words: *I put them to sleep. They'll wake in a month or two...*

Panic was seizing her now. *Keep. Your. Cool.*

"Astrid," Tessa said, taking a deep breath. If she could think of something else, clear her mind, then maybe... "I know where your parents are," she continued, "and they are safe. I promise."

"Where?" Astrid grabbed Tessa's hand. "Let's go. Fix these guys and we'll go. Now!"

Tessa shook her head and explained to Astrid what Val had told her.

"So they're... like this?" Astrid asked, spreading her arm wide to gesture to the rest of the room.

"I—I don't know," Tessa replied. "Maybe? Probably."

"You trust her?" Astrid pressed. "That Val lady?"

Tessa nodded. "I do," she said. "About that, at least. She wasn't lying."

"How do you know?"

Tessa frowned. "I just do," she said and shook her head. "I'm not being facetious. I *know* she wasn't lying. Somehow. The fairy, Val, she said that your parents were bait. That Tish used them as bait to lure Cece to her."

"So they were just… pawns?" Astrid whispered. "That's all?"

"I'm so sorry," Tessa whispered. Her anger renewed as she saw the hurt and disbelief fill Astrid's face. Whenever she found Morticia and Val, she'd make them pay for how they'd treated Astrid. She'd find Astrid's parents and then they'd find the ones responsible and exact their revenge.

With this thought, clarity entered Tessa's mind. She lifted her hands and, like it was something she did every day, released the air in the room, returning everyone back to themselves and the room back to warring chaos.

Almost.

There was a moment before temporality returned to the afflicted Magix and Hybrids, in which their minds all shared one unifying thought: *these are not my enemies.*

And so, to Tessa's satisfaction and Theo and Astrid's surprise, Jean cut off his French insults mid-sentence, Deirdre called off her coiling cobra as Elsa re-sheaved her knives, and Izotz lowered her hands mid-conjure, the electricity between her fingers fading to sparks.

"You're not our enemy," Elsa said. "Regina, I am sorry. But the Channels…" She spread her hands, palms up, and shrugged. "We've been hiding for centuries and we've survived."

"Like the Nons say," Izotz said. "If it ain't broke, don't fix it."

"But it *is* broken, Auntie," Cece cut in. "You know it is."

Izotz mimicked Elsa's shrug. "We must do what's best for our own. Not the world. We're not saviors." Her eyes flicked pointedly to each of the Hybrids, landing, finally, on Theo. She shivered. "The current crisis is over. So. We go home." She turned away.

Nas and Marlowe followed her out of the room, but Elsa lingered for a moment. "You are welcome to return with us, Regina," she said, her gaze lowered. She did not wait for the answer before turning and following the others out of the room.

Tessa heard the tremor in the air as they transported away. How strange. She'd never noticed it before, but now, she could feel the—the aftershocks? Yes, that word felt right. The aftershocks of transportation magic filled her with nausea, like she was at sea on a particularly windy day. She put a hand on Theo's shoulder to steady herself.

A collective sigh ran through the room, then Frank stepped toward the door.

"I'm heading to bed," he said. "Tomorrow, I assume, we'll discuss next steps."

Cece nodded. "Yes."

He stood in the doorway, looking out into the living room toward where Morana was bound. "And what to do with—?" He jerked in her direction.

Cece nodded again.

"I'll keep guard of her," Deirdre offered, as her cobra twisted itself around her arm. "Nadja and I will take shifts."

If Cece and the others had reservations about letting Deirdre into the fold, after everything she'd done, they didn't voice them. Deirdre was many things, but her hatred of Morana was as palpable as the stench of smoke lingering after a fire, bitter and choking.

One by one, the Magix and Hybrids dispersed to their rooms, until only Cece, Tessa, Astrid, and Theo lingered.

"You must be Theo," Cece said, smiling warmly at them. "There should be another room, off yours, Tessa, that Theo can use. We had it... made-up." She smiled again, and Tessa nearly winced at how forced the smile looked, how much Cece was *trying*.

Tessa desperately wanted a moment alone with Cece, to try and process this together, to come up with a plan for how to cope with their new reality. Tessa was afraid that if she didn't figure it out quickly, she'd screw it up even more for Theo. How could she be expected to guide them, to help them figure all of this out when she was groping around in the dark, her mind churning with unanswered questions?

"I want to find my parents," Astrid blurted before Theo or Tessa could reply to Cece.

Cece turned to her and shook her head. "Not a good idea right now."

"We should wait until we have a better idea of how to rescue them. Undetected," Tessa added. "They're bait for Cece, remember?"

Cece frowned. "Have you been thought-talking about me?"

Tessa waved a dismissive hand. "They need to be kept up-to-date, ok?"

"Bait or not, we can't let that stop us," Astrid exclaimed. "Besides, you're all... amazing! You're *Hybrids*. You must be the strongest beings in the entire world!"

Theo's eyes went wide. "I don't—I'm not... I-I—"

"Theo," Tessa said, leaning down so that her face was level with theirs. "Breathe."

"You're still you, kid," Cece added, placing a hand on Theo's shoulder, then sliding it back awkwardly as she rethought the intimate, maternal gesture.

Tessa put her hand on Theo's shoulder instead and smiled at Cece, mouthing her thanks. "We're strong," Cece said to Astrid. "And untrained, completely in the dark about the extent of our powers. Meaning—"

"...you could be dangerous," Astrid finished, hanging her head in defeat.

"Val said your parents were safe," Tessa said.

Astrid shook her head. "I still don't get *why* you'd trust her. You don't even know her."

"She's another air fairy," Cece said.

Astrid blinked. "Another?"

"Wow," Theo said. "Maybe you're related?"

Cece chuckled. "Air fairies aren't *that* rare. But, I think—and, Tessa, forgive me if I'm speaking out of line here—air fairies are not good liars, at least not from one to another of their kind. To know and control the air is to see—" She held up her hands like she was holding an invisible orb.

It was a gesture so much like what Tessa had done moments ago to freeze the room that Astrid and Theo both winced and closed their eyes. But Cece, lost in her imagination, didn't notice. She looked into the liminal space in front of her as if she, too, could see it the way Tessa could. The dust particles spooling out like spiderwebs, pollen blobs like coffee beans and skin cells, like wrinkled up paper balls, cotton microfibers like tiny aliens, hairs like mighty tree trunks, and under it all, the bristling, spike forms of viruses and worming bacteria.

"—*everything,*" Cece finished, the word only a whisper. Her eyes met Tessa's.

Bettie's squawk from out in the living room interrupted them and caused Tessa's breath to catch in her throat. Because it wasn't a squawk. It was words, clear as day.

"Goddamnit, Cece, I'm *hungry.* Lazy, stupid human, always chatting away when some of us need to *eat.*"

Tessa laughed. Cece did too. Then she looked at Tessa, her mouth held open in surprise.

"You heard that?" she asked.

Tessa nodded. "And you can see…?" She gestured to the shimmering air.

Cece nodded, her brows furrowed. She shook her head. "What in the world…"

It didn't make sense. Then again, nothing had made sense in a very long time.

"Astrid," Tessa said. "We'll find them. Soon. I promise." She held out a hand to Astrid, who had crossed her arms across her chest and was glancing angrily between Tessa and Cece.

*How long?* Astrid thought-asked Tessa.

*I don't know. As soon as we can figure it all out. Safely.*

Astrid ran her tongue over her teeth.

"My mom will find them," Theo said, placing their still-so-small palm on Astrid's elbow. "She found me."

This was enough to make Astrid shrug in acquiescence. Reaching for Tessa's hand, she gripped it firmly, tugging Tessa close to whisper in her ear. "I'm trusting *you,* no one else."

Tessa pulled back a bit and cupped Astrid's chin in her hand. "I'll always be here to help you navigate the world," she said, winking at Astrid. "I'll always be your *Familiar.*"

* * *

**APRIL 2012**

"Just do it. Now! Before I lose my nerve."

Still, Morana hesitated. Brian's energy was manic, like a cat in its witching hour. The muscle above his right eye twitched. "Are you sure?"

He grabbed her wrist so hard she winced. "I'm sorry," he said, letting go. "I just—yes, I'm sure." He leaned in and kissed her. "I love you, Mina. I've never been so sure of anything in my life."

Morana nodded and leaned into him, pressing her mouth against that sweet, old scar, the Familiar's mark. She kissed it, felt the electric bite of magic, withdrew.

There was blood. There wasn't supposed to be blood, was there?

"Brian," Morana whispered.

The tiny trickle of blood seeping from the old scar widened, a creek becoming a stream. The veins in Brian's arms rippled and then, like pent-up waters bursting from a dam, cracked open. Morana screamed. There was blood on her face, in her mouth.

Brian fell to his knees. He reached for her hands, whispered, "Ask Val," before the veins in his eyes exploded, popping like overripe tomatoes. He shuddered a final breath and crumpled to the ground, dead.

It was impossible for her to say how long she sat at the foot of the bed beside his broken corpse, her mind empty, feeling the life churn and awaken inside her, even as the fetid stench of the fetus' father filled the room. She must have called Val. She didn't remember calling her, but then Val appeared. She clapped a hand to her nose and pulled Morana out of the room. Did Morana scream? Impossible to say.

Impossible to say, too, where the second body came from. Val kept asking, but Morana couldn't answer. Later, after Val was able to undo some of the rot, after she called the police and the police attempted to interview Morana, receiving only mute stares in return, after Val passed herself off as the neighbor lady and a witness to the murder-suicide, after they'd been banished from the scene, Val took Morana home with her to heal.

After the healing came the questions.

"Why did he die, Val?"

They sat together on the balcony of Val's new house, far away from New York City, in a quaint coastal Carolina town. They sipped tea as the sky blushed and preened with dawn. The fresh air was intoxicating, so much better than the breeze fluttering the floral curtains of Val's spare room. She felt the hiccup of the baby's movement and for a moment, Morana nearly forgot her grief.

"Val?" she repeated when no answer came. Morana's voice was a jagged blade, the tinny reverberation of metal striking glass, a shattering rage.

Val couldn't look at her. The teacup shook in her hand, sloshing over. She steadied it with a second hand and set it down on the small table before speaking. "He was a DOM, Ana."

Morana said nothing. Around and above them, birds chirped and cooed. Morana slammed the teacup onto the table, smashing the cup and splintering the wood top of the table. Val did not flinch. Carefully, she explained about Morticia, Gunner Engers, Marcus Brand and the AntiMagi Department of Health.

"Well, now it's called the AntiMagi Department of Health and Defense. They wanted to see if a DOM could be turned to a Magick. And well... now we know."

"How dare you—"

"To be clear," Val said, holding up a firm hand less than an inch from Morana's face, "I am *not* part of any of it. I left over a decade ago. But I keep tabs on them."

"So you knew about this?"

Val nodded. "I suspected. This is why I talked to Brian, tried to convince him not to throw his life away. I even summoned his brother, Baron, hoping he could stop him, talk some sense into him. Baron's was the other body at the... the site. I'm not sure what happened, but he was dead, too, when I got there."

A spark of memory: a shout, a man's bearded face—Brian! No, not Brian—and a blaze of pain and fury.

"It did appear that a Magick killed him," Val continued, her eyes flicking toward Morana's for an instant, as if to both intimate the knowledge she had and promise not to use it.

The air felt thin, like some had pulled out all the oxygen. Morana's vision swam, then righted. A DOM. A DOM and a Magick. A DOM and a Magick and a… a baby. Impossible.

"He can't have been a DOM," Morana blurted. "I'm pregnant. It's his baby. A DOM and a Magick can't—"

"You're kidding, right?" Val was laughing. What the hell was she laughing for?

"It's not possible," Morana repeated.

Val sobered. "You've never spoken to your mother about this?" There was incredulity in her whisper.

"I don't talk to my mother."

"But—but before you stopped speaking? She must have told you—"

"Told me what?"

So Val had no choice but to explain the Hybrids and when she was done, Morana threw herself off the balcony, headfirst.

Of course, she did not die and neither did the fetus. She flipped midair, caught by a sudden and strong breeze. She landed on her feet, unharmed. From above, Val glared down at her.

"You really think I'd let you die, Ana? Come now. You are so much more than this moment, this tragedy, this pregnancy. I know it's hard. Believe me. I. Know. But you are strong. You are capable and you can survive this." Her knuckles were white on the railing. Her jaw worked up and down. She swallowed. "I can help you, Morana. I will help you, but only if you promise to keep yourself safe."

"And the child?" Morana snarled.

"When it's born, you'll be the mother. That'll be your job, won't it?"

"I didn't ask for this!"

"No. You didn't. But you wanted a child, didn't you?"

Morana's shoulders slumped. "We both did."

"When a child is born, we never know who they could become, what diseases they could carry, how long they'll live. To become a parent, it's a choice and a risk."

"What would you even know about it, Val?"

Val tried to keep her face emotionless, tried to hold in the roiling rage and regret. "Nothing," she lied.

# CHAPTER
## THIRTY



Upstairs, Tessa tucked Theo into bed in the walk-in closet that had suddenly appeared off her own bedroom. Magic continued to jar her, even as she rolled her shoulders and flexed her newly appeared wings. Theo reached out to stroke them once, before Tessa tucked them away, out of sight. She could still feel them, even if they weren't visible and she wondered when it would stop feeling so strange.

"I love you," she whispered into Theo's ear.

"I love you," they replied, eyes already closed and a dreamy half smile on their lips.

Tessa pulled the covers up to their neck, but Theo shrugged them down.

"It's ok, Mom," they murmured. "I know I'm safe, with or without blankets. I've got you." They took a deep breath and exhaled slowly. "I knew you'd find me. Morana said you wouldn't want me. She said you'd forget me, but I knew you wouldn't. I knew you'd figure out a way to fight for me."

Tessa traced the line of Theo's cheek where their constellation of freckles lay, the mark of a shifter. Belatedly, Tessa realized she should have checked for this as soon as she saw Theo because what if…

"That's really her down there, isn't it?"

Theo gave a sleepily grunt.

"Morana, that's her downstairs. Right?"

Theo frowned and opened one eye. "It's her. Her mark is here." They reached up and touched their chest. "She wears the cross to cover it, but I checked her when we came in, remember? It's her."

Tessa leaned in then and put her head on their chest, wrapping her arms around them as best she could from her seated position. "I should have thought of that," Tessa said. "It shouldn't be your job to think of those things. You're just a kid. I—I'll do better." She sat back up, hands still on Theo's slender shoulders. "I promise, sweetheart."

"Or we could work together?" Theo suggested. "Like a team!" They sat bolt upright. "Theo and Tessa, the Double Ts!"

Tessa chuckled. "Oh my god, I've missed you." She kissed their cheek. "Get some sleep, kiddo."

Theo held out their hand toward Tessa, palm facing the ground. "Double Ts?"

Tessa smirked and put her hand on top of theirs. "On three?"

Theo nodded. "One."

"Two."

"Three."

"Gooooo team!" they both exclaimed, raising their hands up.

Theo punched the air, then lay back down with a wide grin. Before Tessa had switched out the light, she could tell they were asleep, their breathing slow and even.

As Tessa was slipping on a tank top and getting ready to lie down herself, there was a knock on her door. Cece stood in the hallway. Her hair was tied up in a golden scarf and she'd changed into an almost sheer nightgown under which she wore a matching set of yellow bra and underwear. Tessa willed her eyes to stay up and hold Cece's gaze. The yellow reminded Tessa of the day they'd met, when Cece had arrived looking like a sunflower and bringing with her a world full of new light.

Had it been only a week that they'd known each other? It seemed far too short a time for all the wild adventures and wilder emotions that Tessa had experienced with Cece.

"I need to tell you something," Cece said. "And no—it can't wait until morning. Or, well, I don't want it to wait." She reached for Tessa's hands and Tessa let her hands be taken up in Cece's warm grip. "My parents never told me what I was, but I think they may have always known. The story that everyone tells about my dad murdering my mom when he found out she was Magick? It's bullshit. He knew she was Magick. The day he killed her, it was like he just... not snapped, but *changed*. He became someone entirely different right in front of us. I killed that person, the person that murdered my mother. But that wasn't my father. My father died, too, but he wasn't the person I was trying to kill. If I could have been more—more *precise*, I could have saved him."

"I'm so sorry," Tessa murmured.

"Shh." Cece squeezed Tessa's hands. "Let me finish. I made a vow to never do what my mother did, to never love a Non because it was dangerous. If my father could be possessed like that, then any Non could be. If my father could turn on us, then anyone could. And I wouldn't be able to protect myself nor anyone else."

Cece stepped in closer to Tessa, pressing their clasped hands between their bodies so that Tessa's fingers brushed against the top of Cece's breasts. Tessa willed herself to breathe. The air was dancing around her, vibrating with the heat of their bodies.

"But my father... he *wasn't* a Non. And, well, you're not a Non either."

Tessa shook her head. "No, I'm not."

Then Cece's lips were on Tessa's and Tessa closed her eyes, returning the kiss as the air twirled and sashayed around and around them.

*Magic,* Tessa thought. *Magic, magic, magic!*

"Mom?"

Cece and Tessa pulled apart. Theo stood at the foot of Tessa's bed, watching them.

"Theo!" Tessa exclaimed, unable to hide the embarrassed irritation in her voice nor the creeping blush from rising up her face.

"Sorry!" Theo replied, also blushing. "I was lonely."

Tessa sighed.

Cece squeezed her hand. "I'll see you tomorrow. Good night, Theo."

"Good night," Tessa and Theo replied in unison.

Tessa closed and locked the door.

"Theeeoo," she said, letting out a heaving sigh.

"I said I was sorry!" Theo exclaimed as Tessa hopped into bed beside them.

"I know," Tessa replied, pulling up the sheets around them and draping an arm over Theo's chest.

"Snuggles," Theo grinned.

Tessa wrapped her arms tightly around them, kissing the top of their head.

"Cece seems nice." Theo yawned. "Does she make you happy?"

"Yeah, I think so."

"Then I like her."

Tessa smiled. As she drifted off, she listened to Theo's breath grow deep and even. She felt the air in the room tickle her face and reveled in the strangeness of it. Strange, but good. Never in her wildest dreams could she have imagined this life. But here it was. Theo was here with her. And for now, they were safe. Home.

Theo's chest was rising and falling. She heard Luca's light snoring through the walls. So much life here and she felt so alive and Cece had kissed her!

She listened to the sounds, the breathing and the snores and tiny thrums and squeaks and sounds of life that filled every house and turned it into a home.

Soon, she was also asleep.

As always, Tessa dreamed of Morana.

In the dream, Tessa stood in the living room of the House. In front of her, Morana slumped in the sizzling electrical ropes. Tessa squinted. The air in the room was cloudy. She stepped closer. Morana's hair hung down like a curtain. Strange. It wasn't white-blonde, but silvery gray and shorter. *Shortening,* Tessa realized. Before her eyes, the figure was morphing into someone else, someone larger, darker and… male.

Sanjay. It was Sanjay.

Behind Tessa, there came a throaty cackle.

"Hello there."

Tessa whirled to see Morana, grinning.

"Tell those sweet boys thank you for the sandwich. C'est délicieux!" She made chef's kiss gesture. "So silly, though. They stuck me in a broom closet with some flimsy ropes, can you believe it?" She cackled again. The cross shifted on her neck and Tessa saw the mark that Theo had mentioned, the constellation of half a dozen freckles. *This* was the real Morana.

"This is a dream."

Morana cocked her head to one side and laughed. "You honestly still believe that, don't you?" She shook her head, her lips sneering with disgust. "You probably also think that *I'm* the one in charge of these 'dreams,' too, hmm? That I'm the one begging you to *let me in*." She gave a snorting laugh. "You've got Theo now, ok? So why are you still coming to me for answers?"

"I'm not—" Tessa began, but Morana held up a silencing hand.

"Don't deny it," she said. "I'm so sick of everyone acting like they're innocent or confused. So you were under a curse for most of your life. So what? Your dreams could have told you everything you needed to know, but you were in denial. You're still in denial, or you'd be shaking your groggy ass awake and coming after me." At this, she grinned again. Her form wobbled, like she was nothing but a projection.

"You're not real. This is a dream."

"Whoever told you that dreams aren't real? Your Non mother, I'm guessing? Sure, I suppose some people's dreams are nothing but fantasies. You and I are not among those people."

"I'm in my bed next to Theo. You're downstairs in the living room, tied up."

"I'd say you're about a quarter right," Morana smiled. "Your body is in your bed, yes. But your mind is… well, with my mind, I suppose. In the ether!" She spoke in an over-the-top accent, like something straight out of Transylvania. Then she smiled and again, her body wobbled and her appearance seemed to fade slightly. "And it seems my body may be about to wake up."

"Downstairs. In the living room. Tied up."

Morana took a step toward Tessa and then another until their noses were nearly touching and Tessa could see every swirling variation of cerulean, steel, stone, sapphire, and sky in her wet and stormy eyes.

"Take care of Theo, Tessa. And don't blame them for this. They were only doing what any child would do for their mother. They were only trying to protect me."

A scream cut through Tessa's dreamscape at the same instant as Morana disappeared from it.

* * *

**MAY 2020**

*From: Morana Chernoff*
*Subject: Theo*
*To: Valerie Hart*
*Sent: May 25, 2020, 5:41 p.m.*

*Auntie,*

*Vasily is dead, but Theo is safe, far away from Magix and DOMs and harm.*

*I know we've had our disagreements over the last eight years, but you must know that I am not one to break a promise. Theo is safe. Safe from me, safe from my mother, safe from you. And you may wash your hands of me now, like you've threatened to so often.*

*You've said you don't want a war. But you must know that you helped start this one, right? You can't fuck with people's lives from the sidelines and not expect it to come back to haunt you.*

*And I know. I know your life was fucked with as much as anyone's. You and I are not so different, except that where you see a common goal, I see a common enemy.*

*You cannot fix my mother, Val. She will never love you like you want her to, like you need her to.*

*You can't fix me either. I'm not broken. This is what I was made for. To start a war. To burn it all down.*

*Raze it to the ground. Whatever survives will be stronger, purer, than what has come before. Only those creatures, the survivors, will be able to set things right, not the Nons, Magix, DOMs, or some laboratory concoctions. Humanity is a lost cause, Val. We deserve this fate.*

# CHAPTER
## THIRTY-ONE

**JULY 2023** Tessa ran downstairs. A couple shouts had joined in after the first scream, but then all went quiet, a dull hum of worried conversation. Since the east wing of the building was closer, a circle of people were already huddled around the chair where Morana was bound: Cece and Jean, each holding a crying twin, and both looking stricken; Bash, Frank, and Frank Junior, their backs to Tessa with the exception of Bash, who was frowning with eyes mostly closed, as if concentrating; Tim and Dante with Evie bouncing between them, immune to the distress of the adults around her. Tessa could hear Regina's voice rising above the others, though she couldn't see her or Deirdre, only Nadja who had risen up atop Deirdre's head, her hood out.

"How could you let this happen?" Regina cried.

"Let this happen?" Deirdre snarled. "Are you fucking serious? I told you, I didn't take my eyes off her. She just—changed."

"No shit, she's a shifter!"

"Do you want me to eat her now, miam miam?" came another, silky smooth voice that Tessa did not immediately recognize as she tried to push past Tim and Dante.

"You need to explain!" Regina said, apparently not hearing the threat.

"I'm trying!" Deirdre snapped.

"Do. Better," Regina hissed. "And don't curse at me."

A tirade of Creole poured out of Deirdre's mouth at that.

Evie wrapped her arms around Tessa's waist, nearly tripping her. "Hi, Non friend!"

Clearly, the girl had missed the previous day's revelation. Tessa let her wings unfurl a few inches so Evie could see them, but she did it too forcefully, and accidentally pushed Evie off her and backward into her papa Dante's arms.

"Sorry, kiddo. Not a Non anymore," Tessa replied, continuing to move past Frank and his boy toward the center of the circle.

"Woah," Evie whispered, too stunned to try to shift into Tessa.

By now, Regina and Deirdre were practically screaming at one another. There were other arguments ensuing, but none as loud as these two. Nadja continued to hiss and hurtle translated curse words at Regina. Bash was studying the snake with narrowed eyes. Tessa assumed that he could also, suddenly, understand Nadja.

"What the hell is going on?" Tessa shouted, but her voice went unheard above the din.

"Everyone quiet!" Jean hollered, his voice a great thunderclap that caused everyone else to go silent.

Tessa shouldered her way past Deirdre. Regina stepped aside to reveal the chair and its captive. Not Morana, but Sanjay, slumped over, barely breathing.

"Jesus Christ," Tessa exclaimed, kneeling before him. She reached for the bands of electrical energy binding him and broke them one by one. He flopped into her arms, limp and heavy. His breathing was so shallow. His pulse was a whisper. "What happened to him? Who did this?"

Oscar had pushed his way to Tessa's side. "I-I don't know," he whispered. He reached for Sanjay, then pulled back. His hands were shaking. "Shit. We locked him in the broom cupboard, right, Frankie J?"

Frank Junior nodded vigorously. He also looked panicked. "We brought him some food before bed because he—" He nodded toward Jean, who had come forward, along with Cece. "He told us to."

"We even helped him eat, since his arms were tied up and all," Oscar continued. His voice was high and cracked on the last word.

Cece put a hand on Oscar's shoulder. "It's ok, Oscar. It's ok."

"He smiled and said thank you," Oscar whispered.

Cece put her arms around him and he let her, leaning down so that his head rested on her shoulder.

The dream was coming back to Tessa now.

*They stuck me in a broom closet with some flimsy ropes.* Morana's voice was a hyena's sharp cackle. *Can you believe it?*

Sanjay's eyes were open, but glazed and unfocused.

"Sanjay," Tessa whispered. "It's *me*, Tessa."

She wiped a hand across his damp forehead. He was burning up. She could feel the magic in him and it was… oh Christ! It was burning him alive from the inside. She pressed fingers to his wrist and could feel his blood roiling beneath the thin layer of skin. His pulse galloped. Suddenly, she could *see* the magic, too: a glowing current of light that rippled through his body. It was everywhere, running through his blood and consuming him. If she could get the magic out… Tessa reached for it. It surged and Sanjay screamed. He began to writhe, a seizure gripping his body. He shook violently in Tessa's arms. His eyes rolled back. Vomit and foam bubbled up in his mouth.

"Flip him over!" Bash shouted, kneeling beside Tessa and helping her move Sanjay to the floor and onto his stomach. He pulled off his belt and managed to shove it into Sanjay's mouth only moments before his teeth clamped down and his jaw locked. "Someone get a pillow or something for his head."

Cece brought a pillow and lifted up Sanjay's head.

Tessa lay beside him, taking his shaking hand in hers. There was blood in the vomit that pooled below Sanjay. He continued to tremble even as the seizure subsided. His eyes were open and they seemed to focus on Tessa.

"I'm here," she said. "It's ok. It's gonna be ok."

The magic was glowing brighter by the minute. Tessa could feel it eating away at Sanjay's organs. She'd had no idea that magic could do this.

"T," Sanjay whispered. He sucked in a wet breath.

"Yes, I'm here, Sanjay. It's me."

"He—elp," Sanjay said, just before another seizure rocked his body.

Tessa rose to her hands and knees, crouching like a feral dog with its hackles raised as she watched the white-hot magic sear Sanjay. Splotchy circles glowed up along his skin leaving charred flesh. It was like several people were taking lit cigarettes and singeing them across his arms and legs. His screams were like nothing Tessa had ever heard before. If she had been able to look behind her, or to think of anyone but Sanjay in that moment, she would have seen Regina curled in a fetal position, rocking on the floor with her hands over her ears, trying to block out the sound of Sanjay's screams, which had opened the floodgates she'd constructed around her past. In Sanjay's screams, Regina heard her mother and father, her siblings, her friends and neighbors, as they burned alive.

Deirdre knelt beside Regina, all anger forgotten. She put a hand on Regina's shoulder, whispering soothing sounds, as she watched Sanjay. The sounds shifted from soothing to conspiring.

But Tessa only had eyes and ears for Sanjay.

Magic was killing Sanjay. There was only one way to stop magic.

She rubbed the fingers of her left hand together and felt the anti-magic gather in them, growing larger as she rubbed and rolled it like dough, until it became a baseball-sized black ball in her hand. With her right hand, she pinched off a piece and a slender black thread danced between her hands. She placed the tiny piece of anti-magic on Sanjay's lips. Breathing in, he sucked the thread of anti-magic into his lungs. The ball in Tessa's hands unspooled and grew smaller as the anti-magic tore through Sanjay. Within seconds, her hand was empty and the brightness that had pulsed through Sanjay had gone dark. He took a shuddering breath and in that moment, Tessa felt a rush of relief. Cece and Bash also sucked in shocked breaths of awe as, in their eyes, Sanjay's body shifted from a battleground to that of an ordinary Non.

But for Oscar, who had felt his own last breath echo in his lungs, Sanjay's shuddering breath sounded exactly like what it was: a death rattle. He felt no shock or surprise when Sanjay released that breath and did not take another, only a profound sadness, well deep and ocean wide. He closed his eyes and braced himself.

At first, Tessa didn't move.

"Sanjay?" she said. She touched his shoulder. His eyes were open, unblinking. "Sanjay!" She shook him lightly, then hard. "No no no no no! No! Fuck you, Sanjay. No! You can't do this." She was hitting him over and over, like she'd hit him on the day Morana took Theo away.

"It's not fair; it's not right!" she had screamed at him. "How could you let this happen?" He had taken it. It wasn't his job and if he'd reported her, she would have lost her foster license. But he'd taken her cries and abuse. Then, he'd held her for hours while she mourned. He'd ordered Thai takeout and they'd watched a stupid rom-com. He'd spent the night on her couch. She'd woken up the next morning to the smell of coffee, pancakes, carrot bacon, and tofu hash.

"Call me if you need me," he'd said as he left, but he hadn't waited for her to call. He'd texted an hour later and he'd brought her dinner that night as well.

He had been there for her every day for the first month after Theo left. He was the only person, besides her mother, that had seemed to give a shit about Theo getting taken, who seemed to *get it*.

Her other so-called friends would say things like. "Well, it's better that they're with their *real* mom, right?"

Or: "If she were actually abusive, they'd never let Theo go back with her."

Or even: "If you were to ask my kids, they'd probably say I was a mean, horrible witch, too, but god forbid someone take them away from me for *that*."

The last comment had been in front of Sanjay, who had countered: "Have you ever actually seen an abused and neglected kid? Have you talked to them? Spent time with them? Loved them? No? Then. Shut. Up."

To Tessa, he'd said: "The system fails kids all the time."

And: "I'll keep an eye on them."

And: "I won't let anything happen to Theo. I promise."

He had kept that promise.

Tessa held his body and sobbed, loud and ugly wails. She thought of his mother, already petite and beginning to hunch with age. How that crotchety woman doted on her only son! Tessa would have to call her. She would have to tell her about Sanjay, that he was… she would have to say the words aloud.

Behind Tessa, Deirdre and Regina slipped away from the gathering of Magix and Hybrids, and, with a quick nod to one another, transported out of the House.

In the moment before she transported, Deirdre saw the child, Theo, appear out of the corner of her eye. They had materialized from the shadows, where they had been blending in, chameleon-like, as Jean, Tim, and Dante had led the five smallest children hurriedly upstairs.

Deirdre had a fleeting thought that this child might know where their bio mom was. But Deirdre had never been inclined to exploit children, even for the greater good. So she and Regina left without a word.

Theo sat on the bottom stair. Quiet tears leaked from their eyes. Sanjay had always been kind to them.

They heard Morana's voice in their head, *Well done, dearest.*

*You promised you wouldn't hurt him.* Theo's fists clenched and unclenched. They thought of the last words they had said to Sanjay, as they undid Morana's bonds: "You'll switch with her, got it? Just for the night, so she can get away?"

*He knew the risks when we switched,* Morana thought-replied.

*He wasn't even aware!* Theo countered, remember how Sanjay, half conscious, had only moaned. "Where are we?" He hadn't said anything more.

Unbound, Morana had gotten up, stretched, and helped Theo haul Sanjay into the chair before redoing the bonds. "Thank you, love," she'd said to Sanjay and kissed him before binding his mouth, too. Then, she'd changed them both to look like one another and fell back on the ground a moment before Nas and Marlowe had come back into the living room.

*We had talked about it before,* Morana continued to thought-speak. *I promise you; Sanjay understood that it would be painful, but he knew it couldn't be helped. He'll recover even—*

*He's dead, Morana.*

There was a long silence. She thought-cursed in Russian a couple times. *He didn't deserve that. I'm sorry, Theo. I know you liked him; I liked him, too, honestly. But I didn't—*

*Tessa… she used the… the black stuff. The stuff you told me never to use. Ever.*

Again, a long silence. *She's an idiot, your so-called mother.*

*Don't call her—*

*Shut up, kid. The Nons, they always suffer the worst of it. It's no goddamn wonder they hate us. She killed him with her meddling. You realize that, don't you?*

Now, it was Theo's turn to stay silent.

Eventually, Morana continued, *If I had known what she was, I would never have agreed to this.*

*But you promised. You promised you wouldn't hurt her. You promised you'd leave us alone if I helped you.*

*Christ, Theo. I know. And I always keep my word.*

*I know, Morana.*

*So, this is goodbye then. I'll sever our connection. I'll disappear, just like you always wanted, Theo, you little shit.*

Theo didn't answer her.

*I do love you, you know. If I didn't, you'd be dead.*

*I know. I love you, too, Mom.*

In another part of the country, Morana Aronov snapped her fingers and felt the magical rope that had tied her mind to her child's for as long as they'd been alive snap. Then, she was finally, completely, alone.

* * *

**JUNE 2023**

*From: Gunner Engers*
*Subject: Goodbye*
*To: Tish Chernoff*
*Sent: June 6, 2023, 6:48 p.m.*

*It is crumbling around us, Tish. You see that, right? There's no more money, no more interest in our work. We had such plans, you and I. But they're all scattered to the wind now. What a waste it's all been...*

*There are fires in Canada. You've seen the news? They're letting them burn. There aren't the resources to stop it. There will be more fires, fires everywhere that will grow and grow and take us all with them.*

*It's like your witch prophet once said: Forgive them, for they know not what they do. The Nons will kill us all with their folly; the DOMs will sit by in their ambivalence; and the Magix—you goddamn Magix —you could stop it all if you just united. Your hubris will kill us.*

*We should have found a way to stop them from killing Meredith Connolly, Tish. MUMS had the potential to be an ally like no other. Imagine a world of unified Magix, what your people could have done for this planet. But what's done is done. We've made so many mistakes, you and I. We watered where we should have weeded and vice versa.*

*I'm so tired, Tish. I've been tired for decades. This is the end of the road for me. I'm out.*

*Don't come looking for me. If you actually ever cared for me, leave me be.*

*Yours always – Gunner*

* * *

*From: Tish Chernoff*
*Subject: A favor*
*To: Valerie Hart*
*Sent: June 21, 2023, 7:44 p.m.*

*Valerie,*

*It's been a while. How are you, my dear?*

*I have a favor to ask of you. Don't worry, you'll want to hear this.*

*There is something—someone—that is calling to me. A Hybrid, I am certain. Somewhere in the north, Michigan or Wisconsin. I say "calling," but I should be clearer. With the help of Hybrid #6 before you stole him away, I was able to develop a Hybrid-honing device. A device that "senses" Hybrids. The Hybrids "call" to it.*

*Unfortunately, it has proven somewhat ineffective as they have to be quite close.*

*But there is someone in the North, growing and coming into their power. I want your help to find them.*

*I want this last thing from you, my oldest friend, who never even bothered with a goodbye when you left MAAM PAC all those years ago.*

*Please, Valerie. I've got no one else. I want to see this through.*

*Do you remember the wren's song? The call of the marsh grass? Do you remember home?*

*Save the world with me, Valerie. Please.*

*Your friend, forever and always - Tish*

* * *

*From: Valerie Hart*
   *Subject: Re: A favor*
   *To: Tish Chernoff*
*CC: Morana Aronov*
*Sent: June 24, 2023, 8:06 p.m.*
*Tish,*

*The one you are looking for is Hybrid #2, Cordelia Connolly. I'll help you. I've spoken with Ana and she will help, too. These are the terms:*

*1. No harm will come to anyone, Magick, Non, DOM, or otherwise.*

*2. Morana's child, Theo, will be left out of everything.*

*3. I have the same request for my own child. Hybrid #3. She is alive and ignorant and I want her to remain that way.*

*4. After the task is completed, we go our separate ways and whatever debts you feel we owe to you or anyone else, are forgiven.*

*—Val*

**JULY 2023** In the House, Bash and Cece whispered to Tessa as they tried to pry Sanjay's stiff body from her hands.

"Tessa, we need to send him back," Cece said. "We'll bring him home, lay him on his bed. To any Non doctor, it'll look like a heart attack."

"I have to call his mother," Tessa repeated for the fifth or sixth time.

Bash let out a frustrated sigh.

"No," Cece said again. "Tessa, she won't understand. We have to… we have to give her a death that she can understand. Otherwise, it could break her."

"It will break her," Tessa whispered. "It will break her."

Cece cupped Tessa's face in her hands and turned it so that Tessa was facing her. "Maybe it will. But if we tell her what really happened, she'll either think you went crazy and killed him, or she'll go crazy. There's no good choice here, but there is a clear better choice."

While Cece spoke, Bash managed to pull Sanjay away from Tessa. "You have his address, Tessa?" he asked.

Tessa shuddered, unlocked her phone, opened her contacts, and handed Bash the phone.

Upstairs in the west corridor, delighted giggles from the five youngest children could be heard as they played hide-and-seek, oblivious to what had happened. Jean, Tim, and Dante stood at the top of the stairs, huddled together in conversation, glancing frequently over their shoulders to make sure that no curious child had strayed onto the balcony to peer over the edge at the scene of death and grief below.

Astrid and Oscar sat on a half-sunken, wolf-bitten couch in the living room. Oscar had both arms around Astrid and she leaned her head on his chest, reveling in the warmth of his body, the smell of his skin and cologne, and feeling a bit guilty about how insanely happy she was, despite everything.

Frank and his boy stood in a corner near the kitchen, casting wary looks at Theo, who still sat on the bottom step of the staircase. Theo's shoulders shook with quiet sobs.

"You really think the kid did it?" Frank Junior asked again.

"Kid had an opportunity is all I'm saying."

"The fairy Hybrid seems to trust him."

"You just wait." Frank shook his head. "There's gon' be a reckoning. Any moment now."

"Hey, Dad," Bash called from across the room. He'd managed to haul Sanjay's corpse over his shoulder but was staggering under the weight of it. "A little help?"

Frank and his boy both moved to take one of Sanjay's legs. Once they had a good grip on him, the three men disappeared.

Tessa watched the space where they had been.

"It'll be ok," Cece whispered.

Tessa snorted, an angry sound that made Cece wince before she looked around the room.

"Regina?" Cece said. "Where did she go? And Deirdre, too?"

Tessa shrugged. "They probably went to find Morana. Maybe they *will* find her," she continued, standing. "And kill her," she added, arching her back and unfurling her wings to their full green glory.

Cece had to hop back to avoid getting smacked. "Tessa," Cece whispered. Tessa didn't sound like herself, not at all. The fury, Cece could feel it radiating off of her.

"Where's Theo?" Tessa asked. Her voice trembled. The air around her wavered with the heat of her rising rage.

Before Cece could stop herself, her eyes darted toward the stairway. Theo had gotten to their feet as well. Their hands were balled into fists at their sides.

Above their heads, Bettie squawked: "Uh oh! Run away!" With a dive and several quick flaps of her wings, she was gone.

Tessa did not turn around as she spoke to Theo. "You did this."

"I—when you were in the kitchen, I helped them switch," Theo replied.

Cece hissed sharply, then clapped her hand over her mouth. What's done was done, and the kid… well, she was their mom, after all. What had they been thinking, leaving them alone together? Careless.

"You lied to me." Tessa tried to keep her tone flat, but she could feel it reverberate through the floorboards beneath her feet.

"I did." Theo's voice did not shake the house, but it was neither small nor timid.

"Did *she* make you do it?" Tessa asked, still not turning. "Did she possess you or something?"

Theo hesitated and then replied, "No."

Tessa turned around then. "No?" Her mantra was spinning through her brain: *Trust the kid, keep your cool, put the kid's needs first, keep your cool, keep your cool, keep your* goddamn *cool.* "No?" she repeated. "Why, Theo?" Tessa felt the anger building inside her, the scalding fury of grief and betrayal. "I *trusted* you." She was shouting now. She had never shouted at Theo before. "And you betrayed me. You let me down! You let Sanjay down! How could you—?"

"She told me she'd leave us alone if I helped her!" Theo screamed back. Their face was red and wet. "And she will; she *is* leaving us alone. She—she cut the tie between us. She's n-not *watching* me anymore."

"Are you kidding me, Theo? You traded Sanjay's *life* so she would leave you alone?" Tessa couldn't stop herself from shouting. She felt the air getting hotter around her as well. Beads of sweat formed on her forehead, on Theo's upper lip, on Cece's, Astrid's, and Oscar's faces. Distantly, she heard Cece tell Astrid and Oscar to leave the room, heard their footsteps as they left, heard the sliding doors of the kitchen shut behind them. All muted, distant sounds. Nothing was as loud or real as the throbbing of her pulse. Her wings were curling up and unfurling in union with her fists and jaw. She clenched and released, clenched and released. She chewed her rage and then spat it at Theo, a thick and oozing pulp. "I expected better of you. Goddammit. You're more like *her* than I thought."

Theo winced.

"Tessa—" Cece said, stepping between her and Theo. "You're upset."

"No shit, Cece!" The energy was building beneath Tessa's skin. The air swirled around her: the beginnings of a cyclone. She tried to breathe, but the air spun faster. *Keep your cool.* "Sanjay was my best frie—" A sob cut off her last word, but she gritted her teeth and shouted, "Sanjay is *dead.*"

"Sanjay betrayed you," Cece said. Her hands were out in front of her, palms facing Tessa as she moved her arms slowly toward her. "*He* joined Morana. He made that choice. He had to have known the risk."

Tessa clenched her fists and felt the air leap and bubble up around her. Cece took another step toward Tessa, her hands up like she was approaching a wild animal and not the woman she'd kissed the night before. The gesture incensed Tessa. Cece was terrifying, not Tessa. Cece was the one who'd turned into a monstrous stone goddess. As she tried to call up memory of Cece's wrath, Tessa saw herself as clearly as if she'd held up a mirror to her own furious face. What the hell was she doing?

"He wasn't supposed to get hurt," Theo whimpered. They were crying and Tessa knew that it was not only because of Sanjay's death. She'd broken every rule of her mantra and she'd hurt Theo. "Mama... I mean, M-morana," Theo continued, "she said it would be temporary. That the magic wouldn't be strong enough to kill him, just hurt him. But then you—you used the black stuff." Theo shook their head and closed their eyes, as if trying to erase the image from their memory. "*You* killed him, Tessa."

Now, Tessa winced. She couldn't remember the last time Theo had called her Tessa. Not only that, she knew they were right. She'd felt it. As she tried to use the anti-magic to heal Sanjay, she'd known that it had been wrong, so wrong. A deadly miscalculation. Her fault. All her fault.

Tessa sagged, her wings drooping and then furling into her shoulders, becoming small, almost disappearing.

Across the room, Theo felt the urge to go to her, to wrap their arms around her, to soothe and fix her. It was an all-too familiar desire. Morana had often required this kind of emotional labor from Theo, pouting her lower lip and telling them about the rigors of her day, sparing no detail, however sexual or violent. She required that they "help Mommy feel better," demanding back massages and their undivided attention to her stories. When Theo was younger, Morana had frightened them into constant submission. She had been an enigma to them, constantly shifting in her whims and affections. Where Vasily was stern but constant, Morana was an amalgam of kisses and smacks, tears and rage.

Over the past year that they'd been reunited, Theo had become Morana's closest confidant. It was this particular brand of abuse, the twisting of the parent-child relationship into a near reversal in which Theo acted at times as parent, at times as partner, to his fragile mother —yes, she was so fragile. Theo had never understood this before spending those years away from her—that had nearly broken Theo's resilient spirit.

"Don't do that," Theo snapped at Tessa. "Don't cry. Don't."

Tessa straightened, flexing her wings before letting them hang limp. She nodded.

"I wish you had told me the truth," she said.

"I wish that, too," Theo replied. "I'm sorry."

"I'm sorry, too. I shouldn't have yelled at you. Sanjay—this—none of this is your fault."

Theo didn't answer. They kept their eyes on the ground.

"And you're nothing like her," Tessa added.

Theo looked up. "Of course I'm like her," they said. "She's my mom, too. I'm a shifter and a vampire, like her. And when I smile, I have her dimples."

"Theo, I—"

"When I was little, I was a towhead blonde, just like her. Might even still be, if I didn't dye my hair every chance I get."

Tessa gave a soft chuckle at this.

"You've always hated her so much. And she's done horrible things, so she deserves some of it, sure. But she did at least one good thing. For me, at any rate. If you love me, I think you have to at least not hate her, Mom. Or just… don't use her against me, ok? Morana, she'd do that all the time! Use my bio dad, this asshole I never even knew, against me. Sure, I looked like him, but I wasn't *him.* She expected me to *be* him, you know? But I'm Theo."

Tessa nodded. "I shouldn't have said what I said. I shouldn't have compared you to her, good or bad."

Theo sighed. "It was easier when you didn't really know her, I guess."

"I'm sorry, Theo. I really am."

"Do you really think Regina and Deirdre are going to try to find her?" Theo asked. "And try to kill her?"

Tessa grimaced. "I shouldn't have said that about her. I shouldn't have wished her dead. I don't wish her dead, not really."

"That's not what I asked, Mom."

"Morana caused both of them a world of hurt." This was Cece, stepping in.

"She hurt you, too," Theo replied. "I remember you, you know."

Cece gave a small smile. "I know. I remember you, kiddo. She hurt you, too."

"Not physically," Theo said. "Not much at least. And not… *not* like she hurt all of you."

"She killed your dad," Cece replied. "Vasily, I mean."

Theo closed their eyes and shuddered. "Yeah," they said, their voice a small squeak, like they were trying to let out the sound and its meaning but nothing more, holding in all of the emotion, the pain, the loss. "But she's my mom. I can't—I can't *not* love her."

Tessa pressed a hand against her mouth to keep herself from sobbing. She wanted to pull Theo to her, to smooth their hair and whisper that everything would be ok. It wouldn't be. Someday, maybe tomorrow even, they would hear news of Morana's death. Most of the world would rejoice. Hell, Tessa would rejoice. Would it be only Theo who mourned?

"Damn," Cece said, shaking her head. "I know adults that are less self-aware than you are, Theo. Hell, I'm probably one of them." She looked from Tessa to Theo. Her arms were still held out warily in front of her, one directed toward Tessa and the other Theo. Slowly, she brought her hands together and down. "We good now?"

Theo and Tessa nodded, each taking several steps toward the other and embracing. Tessa kissed the top of Theo's head. Cece wrapped her arms around both of them and Tessa couldn't help laughing as she squeezed them too tightly before stepping back and smiling at them, arms folded across her chest.

"Mm, I do love a happy ending," Cece said. Her smile was sad.

"I wouldn't call it happy," Tessa answered.

"Getting there, huh?" Cece replied, reaching out to squeeze Tessa's shoulder. "I am so sorry about your friend."

She pulled Tessa into a tight hug and held her for several seconds until Theo whispered, "Sooo... am I gonna get a third mom?"

Tessa gave a mortified squeal and pulled away from Cece who laughed and laughed until they were all laughing.

There was the sound of a door opening behind them and then Astrid hollered, "Can we come out now?"

They were laughing too hard to answer.

"Oh my god, you're so weird!" Oscar said, shaking his head. But he was smiling, too.

"Oi!" Jean hollered down from the top of the stairs. "Tout va bien? Cece?"

"Yeah!" Cece called back. "Everything is ok, Jean."

There was a thunder-clapping sound as five children raced, rolled, and flew down the stairs. They ran past Cece, Tessa, and the others and began jumping on the furniture in the living room. Silas and Evie-as-Silas (despite Dante's vehement reprimand from the top of the stairs) did loop-the-loops in the air (as Tim counted down, "Evie, stop by the time I reach zero!"), while Luca, Livy, and Lola ran an obstacle course around the haphazard furniture (Tim only got to three before Evie landed and shifted back).

Jean came downstairs and Cece whispered something in his ear. His eyebrows shot up.

"You're kidding?"

"I think we should," Cece said. "They'd love it."

Jean chuckled and shook his head. "Cece wants to go on an adventure. Bien. Sounds fun."

"An adventure?" Tessa asked.

"I thought we could take them out," Cece said. "On a walk to a park or something?"

Now, Tessa raised her eyebrows.

"Morana's gone, right?" Cece said, glancing at Theo, who nodded. "And Natalie Crane is… well, she doesn't seem to care much about *our* kind, at least not at the moment. And Morticia is—"

"Somewhere," Tessa said. "She could be anywhere, actually."

"But she is not concerned with the kids," she gestured to Silas, Luca, and the others.

"Except for Theo," Tessa said.

"It's a risk, I know," Cece said. "You and Theo could stay back."

"I wanna go!" Theo exclaimed.

If she thought too hard on it, Tessa knew she'd be overcome by fear. There was so much to be afraid of in this strange new world. So she didn't think about it at all.

"Alright," she said. "Let's go."

* * *

Walking distance from the House was a small, fenced-in playground with a slide, swing set, teeter-totter, and climbing structure. When Luca saw it, he broke into a sprint, his head down, arms bent and fists clenched, his short legs pounding the pavement. Lola began to shout, "Swings! Swide!" and Livy started chattering about "paying on da paygownd, peese?" Silas started to hover over the sidewalk and Jean had to pull him back down.

"No flying," he reminded him. "Keep them hidden, my sweet."

Silas looked only slightly deflated as he ran to catch up to Luca and Evie, who had also run ahead after a third stern talking to in which Tim reminded her (again) that she could not shift into anything ("No, not even a tree. Evie, seriously?").

At the playground's gate, Tessa paused. Cece stood beside her. Everyone else had walked ahead. Oscar and Astrid were trying (and failing) to manipulate the too-small teeter-totter with Theo giggling at them off to the side. Evie, Silas, and Luca raced each other up and down the play structure with Tim below, admonishing them to be careful. Dante and Jean were each pushing one of the twins on a swing. Jean had texted the Sobro Boys to let them know where they'd gone, in case they came back before they returned and Cece had texted Regina to ask if everything was ok. She received a thumbs-up emoji, nothing more.

Overhead, a black shadow sped across the setting sun and Bettie crooned, "Happy day! Happy day! Too-da-loo!"

Cece slid her hand into Tessa's. Astrid gave a snorting laugh and clapped her hand over her mouth, her ears turning purple. Oscar laughed so hard, he fell off the teeter-totter and when Astrid leaned over to help him up, he pulled her in and kissed her. It was a quick peck on the cheek, nothing more. Tessa heard Cece clear her throat, so she squeezed her hand.

"It's fine."

Cece let out a held breath. "I know," she replied, squeezing Tessa's hand.

Now, Theo was helping Luca in the race, lifting him up whenever he had trouble getting his short legs to stretch from one foothold to the next. When Luca won his first race, he and Theo cheered and high-fived. Silas gave them both a thumbs-up, not even whining about Luca's unfair advantage. Evie picked up Luca under his arm pits and carried him around the playground until she collapsed under his weight. Dante was shaking his head and laughing. He looked different with his wings hidden and his white-blonde hair tucked away under a hat. He looked… *Normal* was the word that Tessa thought, but of course, she meant that he looked like a Non.

They all did, she realized. Oscar and Astrid had darkened their eyes and Cece wore sunglasses to cover hers. Her hair hung loose and natural, unadorned. Along with Silas and Dante, Tessa had hidden her wings. Liv and Lola both had baseball caps on to hide their hairy ears. Luca's sharp canines looked like they had been sanded down.

A wave of sadness passed over Tessa, as she observed how each person in their group had hidden themselves in order to do something as simple as play at a playground.

"What's wrong?" Cece asked.

Tessa shook her head and forced a smile. "Nothing. This was a lovely idea. Thank you."

"It'd be lovelier still if we didn't have to hide," Cece said, as if reading Tessa's thoughts. Maybe she had been.

Tessa nodded.

"Someday," Cece said, squeezing Tessa's hand.

There was a loud bang. Tessa flinched. Above them, a red flowering firework lit the darkening sky.

Tessa laughed. "Is it a holiday?"

"The weekend after the fourth," Cece moaned. Another explosion of sound and light. Tessa watched the reflection in Cece's eyes. "Right. Folks sure do love to drag it out."

Theo came over to Tessa and wrapped their arms around her waist. "It's so loud," they said when another firework went off. They covered their ears, but kept their eyes on the sky, which lit up in a dizzying whirl of green spun downward.

Tessa could feel the vibrations and heat pulsing through the air. It reminded her of a dragon: the green and the roar and the fire. The destruction. She could feel the pain that these small blasts were inflicting on the air, already so hurt and saturated with particulates and smoke.

She remembered how Silas had wished to see a dragon. So she gave him one.

She took the spinning green and drew it back, morphing it into the sinewy form of a dragon that reared up as another firework exploded, sending a blast of red fire out of its mouth.

The children squealed and clapped.

"Tessa…" Cece whispered. "I don't…"

"They love it," Tessa replied.

Cece gave a small nod. For another couple minutes, Tessa manipulated the fireworks into dragons and birds, dinosaurs, elephants, and tigers. The children laughed and clapped. No one came to stop them. If the Nons saw, they delighted in the magic as much as the Magix did.

Even more robust than the children's delight was the relief in the air. Tessa could feel it… healing. She couldn't explain it. But when she turned the particulate matter in the air into *magic* matter? Well. There was a noticeable improvement. When it was over, she could almost breathe easily.

They walked back in the dark, hand in hand, a long train of giggling, tired children and smiling, tired adults.

Cece kissed Tessa's cheek in the dark. Theo squeezed their hand tightly against Tessa's. And Tessa promised herself that she would never forget this moment: the feel of Cece's lips, the sound of Astrid's laughter, the smell in the air that reminded her of spring, when everything was fresh and green.

* * *

**AUG 2023**          *August 1, 2023*

*TOP SECRET*

*Here's what we know about the names and whereabouts of the known living Hybrids.*

*1. Deirdre Laguerre, born in Haiti in 1980 - last known location: Michigan*

*2. Cordelia Connolly, born in Ontario in 1985 - last known location: Michigan*

*3. Tessa Andrews, born in 1987 at an unknown location - last known location: Michigan*

*4. Sebastian Michael, born in Tennessee in 1990 - last known location: Michigan*

*5. Natalie Crane, born in France in 1999 - last known location: Denver, Colorado*

*6. Jacob Johnson, born in Indiana in 2002 - current location: Wilmington, North Carolina*

*7. Theodore Aronov, born in Colorado in 2012 - last known location: Michigan.*

# EPILOGUE

Morticia Chernoff handed over the thick file that represented the majority of her life's work. She should have begrudged this requirement, but instead, she felt as if a weight had been lifted from her shoulders.

"I've collected quite a bit, over the years," she said. There were emails, memos, transcripts, notes scribbled in the margins of pages torn out of Andor's books.

Her boss said nothing as he held up one such page, yellowed with age.

Tish shrugged. "There's always method to the madness."

He snorted. His face held no expression.

*Mr. Bland.* A private joke she'd once shared with Val.

"Gunner never did manage to rein you in, did he?" Mr. Brand sighed, setting down the file with a loud thump on his simple, beige desk. No other files were on it. No clutter whatsoever in this beige-walled, beige-carpeted office.

DOMs were such meticulously dull creatures, Tish thought. Well, most of them. Gunner hadn't been like that.

*Gunner would be furious.* The intrusive thought surfaced like it had shot up from a cannon. She could almost hear Gunner's tirade in head: *How could you let all of our hard work fall into* this *man's hands? He's a moron. He's a puppet. He has no* vision. *He will kill them all. You know that, right?*

*Or worse.*

Tish swallowed. *Gunner is dead,* she reminded herself. She'd been reminding herself of the same thought for days, weeks now. She glanced at the page-a-day calendar on Brand's desk: August 8. A month, then. A month as colorless as this goddamn office. She kept thinking back to their last conversation, and then their last correspondence, which was tucked neatly in the back of the file, along with everything else, their life's work. She kept re-reading it all, like it was a puzzle that, if solved, would lead her back to him.

When the DOMs had found her, holed up in a shitty motel somewhere between Asheville and Johnson City, she'd gone with them without a fuss. Now, here she was. Back in Manhattan, back in the DOMs' headquarters, ready to give up every dream she ever had so that she could finally be free. At least, that's what she'd told Val.

"You," Brand spoke to someone else. A young woman with a rat-like face came out of the shadows. "Sort through this. Find whatever is useful and purge what isn't."

The girl smiled and reached eagerly for the stack of papers, but Tish moved faster. She snatched up the file and hugged it to her chest. "I'll sort through it," she said. "I know what you want anyway," she continued, opening the file and leafing quickly through it. She pulled out a single piece of paper that was so thin, you could see the bleeding red stamp clearly on both sides: Top Secret. "It's the list of living Hybrids."

Brand took the list and sneered. His teeth were impossibly white, the most brilliant part of his lumpy, featureless face. "I already have this list."

"Look. Again."

Brand peered at the list through narrowed eyes that gradually widened. "So, you're finally divulging the names." A smile tugged at his sausage lips. "And—are those—?"

"Last known whereabouts," Tish replied. "Or current location, in at least one case."

"Most of them are in… Michigan?" Brand murmured. "What the hell is in Michigan?"

Tish shrugged.

"Michigan's a large state," Brand continued. "You don't have more detail than that?"

Tish kept her face blank as she replied. "Much smaller than the entire country. Sir."

Brand sighed. "Thank you for this, Ms. Chernoff. Sally—" He nodded toward the rat-faced girl. "She'll see you out."

"So that's it?"

Brand set the single page down on his desk and held out his hand for the massive file. Tish handed it over, her breath catching in her throat as she thought about all the privacies contained within those manila walls: love letters, jokes between friends, detailed case notes of failure after failure, transcripts outlining all the many cover-ups and betrayals that Tish, Val, Gunner, and the rest had managed to pull off over the last forty-five years.

Brand tossed the entire file into a box labeled "to shred."

Tish was careful to keep her face neutral as he turned back to her. "This list." He stabbed a meaty finger at the page. "It's all the information we need."

"What will you do to them?"

A smile twitched across the man's face. Tish willed herself not to shiver.

"Thank you for your service," Brand said, turning away from her.

Rat-faced Sally tugged at Tish's sleeve and Tish went along behind her, into the elevator and down, down, out and onto the busy street. The girl left her without a word. Tish stood alone on the pavement, inhaling the putrid, polluted city air: sweaty bodies, sewage, scavenging rodents, dead and decaying rodents, pizza and bagels, and exhaust fumes like the theme pulling the whole, messy fugue together.

They'd let her go. She could hardly believe it was that simple.

They'd taken everything, of course. She'd known they would. As they were stepping out of the elevator, Sally had pressed a wallet into Tish's hands. Tish opened it now. Her face smiled back from a new ID, embossed with a new name: Angelina Fulton. There were a social security card and birth certificate as well as $250 in cash and check for an obscenely large amount of money made out to Angelina Fulton. Tish debated what to do with this. No bank would let her cash it. But if she opened an account under this new, gifted name, they'd be able to track her.

In the end, she decided that any decision she made at that moment would be rash. She pocketed the wallet and moved on.

At a bodega, she used the cash to buy a sandwich, a notebook, pencil, a phone, and a prepaid call card. The man at the counter directed her to the nearest post office for envelopes and stamps. She stood at the post office counter, writing out as much as she could remember. It took a long time. There was a TV playing silent footage of a wildfire in Hawaii of all places. Tish tried not to think about it, but she couldn't help hearing Gunner's voice in her head: *There will be more fires, fires everywhere that will grow and grow and take us all with them.*

Sometimes, she thought he was lucky to be dead. Luckier still it hadn't been her to kill him. Then again, if he'd been killed in the way she thought he'd been killed…

Well. Maybe not.

On the TV, they were showing footage of the fire burning through a city. Two people stood motionless on the street, the fire coming toward them. It was coming. God, why weren't they moving? Then one of them moved, barely noticeable if someone wasn't really watching. With that movement, the fire seemed to move, too. A shift in the wind perhaps? The fire turned away from the two figures, seemed to grow smaller and fade.

Tish let out a long breath.

"Hey lady," said the man at the desk. "We close in like… fifteen minutes, got it?"

Tish held up the envelope and licked it dramatically for him. He gave a dismissive hand wave. She glanced back up at the TV. They'd moved on to another story; a trucking company had declared bankruptcy.

Tish shook her head. The fire growing smaller, that was probably the camera angle anyhow. She knew many Magix that could control fire, but only small ones. A single Magick, even two, would be no match for a wildfire ripping through a city.

On the back of the envelope, Tish wrote down the address Val had forced her to memorize. She addressed the letter to Kathy Andrews.

Could a Hybrid stop a wildfire?

*You better believe it, sweetheart,* Gunner whispered.

She handed the letter to the peeved desk clerk and blew him a kiss on her way out.

A Hybrid in Hawaii. Stranger things had happened. At least Marcus *Bland* and his cronies wouldn't find *that* Hybrid. She wondered who they were. Not for the first time, she wondered if there were Hybrids out there other than "the Seven," as she called them. Hidden children. Children born of chance and love, rather than calculation and perseverance.

On a nearby bench, Tish sat to make a phone call.

Val answered on the first ring. "Done?"

"Yes," Tish replied. "He took the bait and shredded the file. Are you with #6, er… Jacob?"

"Yes, but there's been a… development." In the background, Tish heard shouting, muffled, but persistent.

"They woke up?"

"Mm-hmm."

"Let them go. Send them home. They can warn the others. And get six—I mean, Jacob—out of there before the DOMs come for him."

"Already done. We're on the road now."

"Driving?"

Tish could almost hear Val's shrug. She'd never understood why the fairy enjoyed Non transportation methods so much. *Like those backwater ogres.*

"You wrote, too?"

"I wrote to Kathy."

Val let out a long breath. "Thank you."

"It's the least I could do after everything got so… entangled."

"Well. You *could* have left Tessa out of it. You agreed—"

"I know," Tish interjected, pinching her nose and closing her eyes. "It couldn't be helped. It's not like you or Ana held up your ends of the bargain anyway. Plus, you lied to me. Cordelia Connolly wasn't the one my Hybrid-honing device was seeking. It was Tessa."

"We can't know that for—"

"Val, please. Stop lying to me."

Tish could hear Val breathing, heavy on the other end of the line.

"I still can't believe you managed to hide her from us for all those years. I assumed… well, after the accident, I was convinced you'd managed to destroy her."

"Gunner never thought that. It's how he got me back, you know? He promised to tell the DOMs she was dead if I came back. Otherwise, they might have found her, even with the concealment spell."

"How did you *do* that? I mean, a concealment spell over a Magick is bound to wear off after a decade. Two tops. What you conjured, it kept her hidden for, what? Thirty-six years? Andor couldn't have done that. Val, you might be the most powerful Magick in living memory." Tish thought back to Chernobyl, to that image of Val, wings raised and burning, one hand on her pregnant belly, whispering to the raging creature inside of her. Not for the first time, Tish felt a wave of fear grip her whole body, clutch at her throat. When it passed, she whispered, "You know you could have at least told *me*, Val."

"Bullshit. Less than month after I told you, you gave them her name."

Tish winced at the anger in Val's voice.

"You didn't have to give them the names."

"They wouldn't have let me out if I didn't give them something meaningful. They might have dug deeper into our work. They could've discovered we lied to them almost from day one. You know that. Val, you've been out for more than a decade. You *left* me. And I've been… trapped."

Val sighed.

"You left m-me," Tish repeated, trying to keep her voice hard and even like the edge of a blade, but she heard the wavering softness of it, felt the tears well up. Thank god Val couldn't see her.

"I didn't have a choice, Tish. It was killing me. MAAM PAC was evil, despite all of our good intentions. You must know that."

Tish wiped her eyes and took a deep breath. MAAM PAC was her life's work. *It's not over yet,* she heard Gunner murmur. She smiled. "Kathy will protect the girl. She always has, right? That's what you told me. She loves her like she is her own."

"She *is* her own." Tish was surprised at the bitterness in Val's voice. "In every way that matters."

Tish said nothing to this. "Let the Laveau-Millers go find their daughter and warn her friends. It won't be long before the DOMs come calling. If they're prepared, it shouldn't be… they should be able to survive. And you, well, I can consider our bargain complete, if you'd like."

Val didn't answer. She was quiet, breathing. "What about you?" she finally asked.

"I have one piece of unfinished business."

Val sighed. "You should leave that one alone. She's a powder keg—"

"I didn't call for a lecture. I know all about our prodigal child."

"She killed Gunner."

Tish swallowed. "I know."

"Are you gonna kill her?"

Tish hesitated. "No. I'm going to… befriend her. She's the only one with a DOM mother. Something about the combination seems to have made her… more AntiMage than Magick." *She could be the one, the key.* And Tish could still be the one to solve this problem, unlock the guarded solution, save the goddamn world.

"A euphemism for more dangerous." Val coughed out a bitter laugh. There was a scuffling sound behind her. "I gotta go, Tish. They're getting antsy here. Just—be careful. Whatever scheme you've got in your head… I don't want to hear about your murder from some DOM military asshole, too, got it?"

Tish's throat clenched up. "Yeah," was all she could manage to say.

"And if she has Andor's eyes or some nonsense, don't let her seduce you."

Tish snorted.

"Well. Good luck then. And if I don't—if we don't…" Tish heard Val swallow. "All in all, it's been a privilege, my old friend."

"Likewise, Val. I'll be seeing you." Tish hung up and threw the phone in a nearby trash can. Then she turned down an alley and disappeared.

* * *

On the other side of the Eastern Time zone, Natalie Crane was working in a makeshift office she'd set up at the Grand River Coven's former headquarters.

"Goddamn Midwest hillbilly farmers," Natalie muttered when she couldn't get the window fully open to let in a breeze. Who knew it could get so hot up north? She clenched her fist and the glass of the window shattered. She sighed. A breeze.

There was a knock on her door.

"Come in," she shouted.

The door creaked open. After a moment, hearing no steps or voice, Natalie looked up.

Morticia Chernoff stood in the doorway. "I heard you were looking for me."

Natalie Crane smiled.

*She does have Andor's eyes*, Tish thought and shivered.

# ACKNOWLEDGMENTS

First and foremost, I would like to thank my wife, Clarissa, the first reader of all my writing, good, bad, and ugly. Thank you for always cheering me on and always supporting me in this tumultuous profession.

Thank you to Diane Sorensen for beta reading an early draft of this novel. You were instrumental in getting this book beyond its initial draft.

Huge thank you to Meagan Friedman for giving me this chance and for working with me to make this book the best it could be. I couldn't ask for a better publishing partner on this journey. Thank you to editors Beth Iler and Karen Mann. I'm also grateful to the community of authors publishing with Quills & Cosmos Press. It is an honor to be among such fine company.

Thank you to WolfBell for the gorgeous cover art. Thank you to Alecia Doyley for the amazing character art.

I am especially grateful to both my parents and my in-laws for their progressive values and unconditional support. Thank you to my siblings, both the two I grew up with and all the extra ones I've gained along the way, and my four awesome nephews.

Big thanks to my friends, near and far. Thank you Mary Helen, my "oldest" friend and first writing buddy. Thanks to Ellen and Marie, my local support system, and to Kinscő, Lydia, Alisa, and Reilly for letting me talk on and on about my projects and for all the love and support over all the years.

Thank you to my kids, Xander, Rory, Liam, and Cole, for the inspiration.

Finally, thank you to Philip Gerard, for believing in me and to Jason Bradford, for believing in all of us. I wish you were both here to see this.

# ABOUT THE AUTHOR

Bethany Tap (she/her) grew up as an over-achieving and chronically-anxious oldest daughter in Grand Rapids, Michigan. While she no longer ascribes to the tenets of her religious upbringing, her ethos toward harm-reduction and her progressive values stem from the belief that we should all love our neighbors and be good stewards of our planet.

She received her MFA from the University of North Carolina-Wilmington, during which time she married her wife. Love for family and the Midwest brought them back to raise their four children.

A poet and storyteller, her work has been published in Litmosphere, Fahmidan Journal, *Yellow Arrow Journal*, and *Anodyne Magazine*, among others.

By day, she helps run her family's manufacturing company. In addition to writing, she enjoys cooking vegan meals, singing, and, of course, reading.

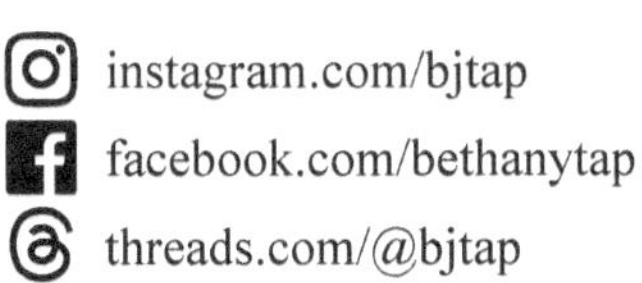

# CONTENT WARNINGS

Violence, murder, and death;
attempted suicide;
attempted abortion